"The banter between these characters was fun to read and I loved the tension that flowed between them . . . a great read to lose yourself in for a few hours."

—*Night Owl Reviews* (Top Pick)

"Readers who enjoy works by Nora Roberts and Luanne Rice will want to give Kramer a try. This reviewer predicts that the beaches this summer will be covered with copies of *Sweet Talk Me*."

—*Library Journal* (starred review)

ALSO BY KIERAN KRAMER

Praise for these other novels of delightful romance by *USA Today* bestselling author
Kieran Kramer

YOU'RE SO FINE

"Kieran Kramer writes a sexy, sassy Southern romance with heart."

—Jill Shalvis, *New York Times* bestselling author

"Kramer dishes up another delightful contemporary romance that is deftly seasoned with sassy Southern wit, snappy dialogue, and plenty of smoldering sexual chemistry. Readers who fell in love with Susan Elizabeth Phillips's *Dream a Little Dream* (1998) or *Ain't She Sweet?* (2004) will definitely want to add Kramer's latest sexy, sparkling, spot-on love story to their reading lists."   —*Booklist*

"Filled with smart, believable characters and fresh, witty storytelling. A sexy, poignant romance wrapped in Southern charm and lightly accented with Hollywood glamour."

—*Kirkus Reviews*

"A superbly written, powerful, and touching book."

—*Fresh Fiction*

SWEET TALK ME

"The   sultry sexual t   his book."

                                        ttle Thing

"A s   romance should bo . . . a knockout."   —*Booklist* (starred review)

A Wedding At Two Love Lane

KIERAN KRAMER

St. Martin's Paperbacks

A WEDDING AT TWO LOVE LANE

Copyright © 2018 by Kieran Kramer.

All rights reserved.

For information address St. Martin's Press, 175 Fifth Avenue, New York, NY 10010.

ISBN: 978-1-250-11106-7

Our books may be purchased in bulk for promotional, educational, or business use. Please contact your local bookseller or the Macmillan Corporate and Premium Sales Department at 1-800-221-7945, ext. 5442, or by e-mail at MacmillanSpecialMarkets@macmillan.com.

Printed in the United States of America

St. Martin's Paperbacks edition / January 2018

St. Martin's Paperbacks are published by St. Martin's Press, 175 Fifth Avenue, New York, NY 10010.

10 9 8 7 6 5 4 3 2 1

To Kathy
My angel who came to my rescue
I'll never forget!
XOXO

ACKNOWLEDGMENTS

To my publishing team at St. Martin's Press, especially my editor Eileen Rothschild, who is so supportive, smart, and fun to hang with; to Tiffany Shelton, a ray of sunshine every time we chat; and to Marissa Sangiacomo and Meghan Harrington: thank you all for helping make my life as a writer such a pleasure!

To Annelise Robey, my lovely agent, thank you for being you. And to everyone at the Jane Rotrosen Agency, I'm so glad you're back home in your gorgeous office! Hurrah!

To Dr. H—you probably never dreamed you'd see your name on the acknowledgments page of a romance novel, so I'll abbreviate it now—thanks for being such a great mentor last year. You kept me on my toes as a writer *and* reader. And to Laura and Katie, my comrades in the *Crazyhorse* office, it was an adventure, wasn't it? Miss seeing you around the table! Best of luck, Laura, at the new Orange Spot coffeehouse (http://theorangespotcoffee house.com), and with your writing. You're so talented! Katie, you're on your way to being chair of an English department somewhere, I just know it!

To my readers, who always make this journey extra special, thank you for your incredible enthusiasm for my stories. I love writing about love, community, laughter, and friendship—we need them more than ever. Come visit me at kierankramer.com anytime!

And as always, thanks to my family, especially to Chuck, who gave up almost fourteen months of my home cooking (which is better than I think, according to him) and my obsession with the *Real Housewives* franchise to serve his country in Afghanistan. Welcome home, honey! And thanks to Steven, Margaret, and Jack for being such troupers while their dad was away. I love you all!

CHAPTER ONE

Greer Jones closed the iron gate with the heart and lovers' initials wrought into it in front of the two-hundred-year-old house at Two Love Lane. "He wasn't the man for me, Mom," she said into her phone. Behind her the house stood tall and proud beneath a canopy of oak and pecan trees. Its windows—three stories of them—sparkled in the sunlight. *Love is everywhere*, it seemed to say. *Come in and we'll help you find it.*

It was Greer's job—and her passion—to help people find love. She was a very successful matchmaker. Every day she was lucky enough to work at Two Love Lane with her best friends and business partners Ella Mancini and Macy Banks, and their office manager and good-luck charm Miss Thing. Greer's specialty was tweaking the secret algorithms they used to make matches to make them as helpful and accurate as possible. She was the brain, the computer whiz, the one with a graduate degree from MIT.

No one knew about her secret hobby—not even her best friends. When she was stressed, she worked on planning her Perfect Wedding. She always thought of it that way: with a capital *P* and a capital *W*. At Two Love Lane she'd sit at her desk and happily cut out photos of her favorite wedding gowns, bridesmaid dresses, and wedding cakes, and glue them in a scrapbook. She also had a secret Perfect Wedding Pinterest page she'd stray to when the number crunching got to be a little much.

Her latest Perfect Wedding endeavor was coming up with a playlist for the reception on Spotify. She wanted a band, for sure, not a DJ. But the band had to be really good. The best, in fact. She was more worried about the music—and whether to have cupcakes or a cake—than she was about finding true love.

Perfect Wedding planning wasn't about *that*. You know, finding a partner. It was about the party stuff! And the girly stuff! The desserts, and the dresses, and the honeymoon location, and the invitations, and the bachelorette parties, and the showers. The list could go on and on.

It was nine in the morning in May, and she'd left the office empty and locked with a sign on the door—BACK AT ELEVEN—to attend a special charity event, an auction for the homeless shelter that Two Love Lane was partially underwriting. So she was anxious to go and support the effort. Ella, Macy, and Miss Thing were in California at a taping of *The Price Is Right*, celebrating Miss Thing's fiftieth birthday. Greer got stressed watching loud, hyper TV contestants who made ridiculous bids without even thinking about them—especially when they *won*—so she told the girls she'd stay behind and run the business and attend the auction. They agreed her idea was probably prudent, especially because the spring wedding season had just ended, and lonely people were calling them off the hook, looking for love.

She was walking down King Street toward Wentworth Street in Charleston, South Carolina, the spring sunshine warm on her face, and the scent of jasmine and garde-

nias filling the air. It was Wednesday, Hump Day. *Yay!*
She was especially glad since she was running the office
alone this week. On Monday, she'd had to ask Pete at
Roastbusters to come down the alley and help her get Oscar, Macy's cat, out of a tree in the backyard. And on
Tuesday, one of Ella's clients had had a huge meltdown
about a terrible date. Greer had also forgotten to mail the
electric bill Miss Thing had left out on her desk.

But she was surviving. And thriving. Who couldn't
when you lived in one of the prettiest, most romantic
cities in the world and you worked in the love business?

So on the phone, she gathered from her mother, Patricia, that it was forty-two degrees in her small hometown of Waterloo, Wisconsin. At first Greer thought that
was why her mom was in a foul mood. But she soon
came to find out it was something else entirely, something that had rocked Greer's world when she'd first
found out on social media. Her ex-boyfriend Wesley—a
guy she'd dated for ten years—was getting married to
someone else.

"He was the one for you, I'm sure of it," her mom said.
"And now it's too late."

Too late for what? To be happy? Greer didn't believe
it. Her Perfect Wedding scrapbooking had completely
stopped by the time she'd finished with Wesley. If that
wasn't a sign to her he was the wrong man, she didn't
know what was.

"What's your reason?" her mom asked. "Your father
and I can't figure you out. Neither can the whole town of
Waterloo."

"You'll just have to get over it, Mom. We broke up four
years ago."

"And he's been pining away for four years! You know
this woman he's marrying is his second-best choice. All

you have to do is snap your fingers and he'll come running."

"I don't want to," said Greer, and peeked at the time on her phone. "We dated up close. We dated long-distance through college, my grad school, and his med school, and we tried to make it work. But it didn't. I have to go. I'm heading to an auction. Two Love Lane is one of the sponsors."

Her mother sighed.

"Isn't my success good enough for you?" Greer asked. "I'm doing really well."

"That's fine," said her mother with all the enthusiasm of a NASCAR driver being told to go under the speed limit.

"It doesn't sound fine. I know you worry—"

"You bet we worry."

"But you and Dad don't have to."

There was a miserable beat of silence.

"You match other people." Her mother sounded on the verge of tears. "Why can't you match yourself? You're thirty years old, Greer. You're logical. Organized. Brilliant, in fact. What's holding you up?"

Her words cut deep. "Mom, we're living in the twenty-first century. I can be perfectly happy without a man. But if a nice one comes along, of course I'll leave my options open." Her Perfect Wedding scrapbooking was in high gear again, after all.

"I hope so." Her mother sniffed. "But Greer . . ."

"What?" She was running out of patience.

"Try harder. Weddings don't just happen by themselves." And with that, Patricia Jones, queen of patience and polite behavior, was gone.

Wow. Her mother had never hung up on her before.

Greer guessed she should have seen it coming. She'd

felt a growing resentment from her parents brewing about Wesley for the last four years, which was a big reason she didn't go home often. Her parents were practical dairy farmers who didn't like conflict. All three of them pretended that everything was fine. Yes, over the dinner table they'd told her they were disappointed she'd broken up with Waterloo's favorite son, but they'd also never acted angry. Now Greer could see that it was because they'd still held out hope she and Wesley would get back together.

But that bridge had now burned, and burned completely.

Greer was long over Wesley, even if her parents and everyone in Waterloo couldn't forgive her for leaving him. It seemed that all her worth—according to them—was tied up in her getting married to him. And now that he was officially out of the picture, her mother had made it clear she wanted Greer to marry someone . . . anyone.

Weddings don't happen by themselves.

At the auction, which took place at the beautiful Alumni Memorial Hall in historic Randolph Hall at the College of Charleston, she sat down and tried to get interested in the items up for bid. There was the Wedgwood blue china plate paired with the simple sterling silver candelabra. A butler to a contemporary British prince visiting Charleston had brought them to remind His Royal Highness of home when he had his morning toast. The prince had left the items behind as a gift to his hostess, a true Southern magnolia with a generous heart and an eye for the perfect donation to a fund-raiser. And then there were vacations and restaurant packages and lots of other home décor items: sofas, chairs, fine lamps, and some gorgeous original artwork. She sat through it all, bidding on nothing, buzzing all over with humiliation.

She was not a loser for being single!

So why did she feel like one?

And then an auction item came up that had just been added to the program. It was a wedding gown that had a name! She never knew dresses could have names. How had she missed that, especially with wedding dresses, which she looked at all the time in magazines and online?

It was called *Royal Bliss*, which instantly made her heart beat faster.

Royal . . . Bliss. Two perfect words, put together!

The auctioneer, an energetic older woman in a purple suit, was Fran Banks, the famous New York talk-show host who'd moved to Charleston. She was the guest celebrity hostess at a lot of charity events in Charleston these days. Greer knew her well, since her nephew Deacon had married Greer's business partner Macy last spring. Fran didn't suffer fools lightly, however well she knew them, and let the world know it.

"There's a bit of extraordinary lore associated with this brand-new gown dubbed *Royal Bliss*," said Fran, "and it's sewn by one of Charleston's own designers who's making a huge splash in New York. She was kind enough to donate her exquisite creation at the last minute. A small heart-shaped patch of this gown's beading, on the center bodice . . ."

And she explained that those beads were taken from a shorter bridal veil worn at the wedding reception of a late, great American icon and actress who became a European princess. The tulle on the veil tore that day, but recently the princess's grown children realized that even in its imperfect condition, it was valuable. The beads attached to it were divided into five groups and sold at auction to benefit the late princess's favorite charity. The provenance of this particular set of royal beads accompanied the gown, making it a one-of-a-kind garment and extremely valuable.

Fran let the crowd stir. Greer's heart pounded. What a story! She wished Ella, Macy, and Miss Thing were with her.

"But the best part of the story," Fran said into the microphone, "is that the beads for the original veil were handmade especially for the American princess by an elderly citizen of the prince's country, a woman who was known to be a good witch. She put a spell of sorts on the beads, a wish from the heart specifically designed to beckon true love to the wearer of the gown. And as you all know, the princess did, indeed, have her happily-ever-after with her prince. She lived to an old age and left behind a large, loving family, as well as her Hollywood acting legacy."

The crowd once again murmured its excitement.

"So," Fran said, "whoever wins this lovely dress tonight is going to be very fortunate. Do we have any brides in the audience?"

Only two women raised their hands.

"I've already got my gown," said one. "My mother's."

Everyone said, "Awwww."

And the other said, "It's so tempting, but my dream gown has always been strapless. Sorry."

Royal Bliss had capped sleeves.

"Perfectly understandable," said Fran, "but where are all the other brides?" She scanned the room. "I'll bet there are a few shy ones right here who didn't speak up."

"The rest are probably at the big bridal show in Charlotte," the bride wearing her mother's gown called out.

Fran shook her head. "My goodness. Bad timing for them . . . no gown at a bridal show in North Carolina can compare to this one, can it, people?"

"No!" several audience members shouted.

Weddings don't happen by themselves.

Greer couldn't get that out of her head! Of course, she didn't believe the beads on that dress would guarantee the wearer true love, but . . .

How could she be sure?

And the dress itself was so gorgeous—and those beads had been worn on the veil of such a famous American actress-turned-princess! Wow! That alone was amazing.

Greer got little tears in her eyes. If she were a bride, *Royal Bliss* was exactly the dress she would want. Part of her felt a twinge of regret that she'd given up her chance to live the fairy tale, at least for now. She'd never felt that way before. Not until her mother's phone call today, and now, this dress—this special, gorgeous gown.

Her wistfulness became discomfort, building and building into a sort of panic. . . .

"Okay, let's start the bidding," said Fran, "at a humble five hundred dollars. Even if you're not a bride, you can bid on this and become a fairy godparent to a bride you know, or if you're extra generous, even a bride you don't know. And remember, every penny from this auction goes to adding beds to the homeless shelter. So think big, people!"

Greer might not have a partner, but she could have a bridal gown. Weddings didn't happen by themselves, right? She was normally so logical and pragmatic, but she was hit with a crazy feeling of utter determination and lust. If she could get this dress, she'd be one step closer to making a wedding come to her.

To heck with having a partner!

She wanted that gown. She wanted it so much, she threw off the voice of reason that usually led her docilely through life and let an impetuous part of her rule the day.

She jumped to her feet. "Five hundred dollars!" she cried.

Fran's eyes nearly bugged out of her head—she had to be wondering how there was even the slightest chance Greer was getting married when she wasn't dating anyone—but she recovered quickly. "That's a fine starting bid. We'll go much higher, I'm sure, but thanks for getting us going."

Greer nodded, aware that she was surrounded by about a hundred people staring at her. She hated being the center of attention, but she often was in Charleston. There was her neutral accent, for one, which had taken her years to cultivate. Now almost no one guessed she'd grown up in Wisconsin (she'd even stopped calling Coke "pop"), but it was clear she was no Southerner, either. She favored monochrome Stella McCartney pant suits and severe yet opulent Chanel briefcases. She didn't have a single monogrammed handbag—Southern women monogrammed everything, including their cars—and she wouldn't be caught dead in a vibrant Lilly sheath.

She smiled at the crowd without really seeing them, which she could do by looking over the top of her signature ivory eyeglass frames. She had four pairs through which she regularly rotated, the same way her mother regularly rotated through vintage farmhouse kitchen aprons she picked up at church jumble sales.

Greer plopped down in her seat. She would have to explain later to Fran that she wasn't engaged. But not now, not in front of all these people.

"Nine hundred," a mild, thin male voice drawled from Greer's left, like a sleepy kitten calling for its mother, and held up his right hand with the fingers spread to clarify the amount because he knew very well no one could hear him.

Greer's insides shrank. That was Pierre Simons—pronounced *Simmons*, which conveniently identified people who weren't local when they said it wrong. He was a Charleston native whose family arrived in the Lowcountry before the Revolutionary War, and the city's leading fashionista. His family's clothing store for women was called La Di Da. The store had been open in the same location on King Street for a hundred fifty years, although until 1949, when Pierre's mother took it over, it had been called nothing more than Simons Fine Apparel. Pierre was a world traveler and frequent visitor to Milan and New York, where he picked up extravagantly priced frocks and accessories to bring home to Charleston.

He was also a snazzy dresser himself, a lover of bow ties, tasseled loafers, fine shirts, and suits. He didn't own a single pair of jeans.

He hated Two Love Lane, the matchmaking agency Greer had started with her two best friends, because they'd never been able to find him his soul mate, and they'd tried three times.

But how do you find a soul mate for a pompous ass, especially one who spoke so softly you had to come close to experience his barbs and braggadocio? Charlestonians weren't pushovers. Even so, Two Love Lane's most spectacular failure of a client managed to have a gaggle of friends—mainly newly arrived social climbers who didn't know any better, and a few gold diggers—but the agency's famous soul-mate-seeking algorithms hadn't been able to locate anyone who was truly compatible with the man.

Oh, and Pierre also hated Two Love Lane because early on, he'd tried to pick up all three owners—at the same time—and failed.

Why would he want the gown? It was outrageous! He

didn't sell wedding gowns at La Di Da, he wasn't getting married, and he was too hard-hearted to be any bride's fairy godparent.

"Nine hundred and fifty dollars!" Greer stood and called out. She held up her index finger, which trembled ever so slightly, and remembered to sit back down. She felt a stab of guilt. She was being rash and irresponsible. It was so unlike her. She didn't need a wedding gown.

She didn't need a man, either, but she wished a handsome lover would show up and sweep her off her feet anyway. Today, especially, after officially disappointing her parents, she was in the mood to be adored, although the world would never know. Her no-nonsense air made sure of that.

A stranger next to her leaned over. The sleeve of his gray plaid blazer was slightly rumpled, and he smelled vaguely of West Indies bay rum cologne. "I always thought I preferred the auctions with little cards you hold up," he said, "until today." And then he chuckled.

She suspected it was at her expense, but she was so agitated, she didn't care. "I don't know what you mean," she said out of the corner of her mouth, her stomach in knots.

She didn't remove her eyes from the gown, which a young man with a bored face held aloft on a hanger. Greer willed him to have a good grip on it.

"You're quite entertaining," the man in the plaid blazer said.

In an English accent. She hadn't noticed it at first. The wedding gown had had her full attention.

She whipped around to face him.

Two amused dark blue eyes looked back. Something shot through her, like a light beam through water. And then it was gone. Before she could process it, she was already cataloging him, Two Love Lane–style, the way she did every new man she met: early thirties, craggy somehow, with a sharp, sunburnt nose and a jutting, square chin covered in fashionable stubble, and too-long golden brown hair.

Professor, hipster, permanent bachelor?

She wasn't sure.

"Are you getting married?" he asked her.

"No," she whispered, and put her finger to her lips.

He spluttered. Or laughed. She couldn't tell.

"One thousand," Pierre said.

This time his social-climbing friend, a young brunette in a high ponytail, held up all the necessary fingers to signify the amount. Her aqua-blue nails were like tiny daggers.

"One thousand one hundred dollars!" Greer called.

Pierre turned and glared at her. So did L.A. Lady.

Greer glared back.

The man in the plaid blazer chuckled again.

"That's how you do it!" Fran said. "But let's get some more bids, people. Whoever wins the gown called *Royal Bliss* will own a little bit of royal history. And have good luck in love besides." She scanned the crowd expectantly.

Royal history! Good luck in love!

Greer uncurled her index finger, prepared to throw it in the air again and bid higher. Funny how things happened. She hadn't even wanted to come to the auction today. It was weird that now *she* was being loud and crazy and was bidding on something—without thinking. She admitted it. She wasn't thinking. She was feeling. She always got into trouble when she did too much of that. Four years ago, she'd genuinely thought she was in love with Wesley, and then suddenly, she'd felt nothing. Not a single loving feeling for him could she conjure, and he hadn't changed. *She* had. And she still didn't know why.

So she'd turned down his proposal, said no to his engagement ring, and broken his heart.

That whole thing had scared her. And it didn't help that everyone back in Waterloo gave her a hard time about it.

"So, one thousand one hundred dollars is our highest bid?" Fran barked, her gavel hovering over the podium. "For this incredible gown?"

Greer held her breath. She might win *Royal Bliss*!

"Two thousand dollars," Pierre said in his soft monotone.

L.A. Lady elbowed him in the side and looked back at Greer.

Greer clenched her jaw. Pierre was so annoying with his fake little voice. He couldn't even get excited enough about winning such a spectacular gown to crank up the volume? The man would probably whisper, "Help," if his house caught on fire.

Wait—*two thousand dollars*?

"Can he do that?" she whispered to the guy in the plaid blazer. "I mean, skip straight up to the next thousand?"

"Of course," he said. "It's for charity, after all."

Everyone shifted in their seats.

"Two thousand dollars," crowed Fran, her face beaming. "What a delightful bid and a shrewd investment decision, but still on the low side. No telling how much this gown will be worth someday. Do I hear more? This is a very exciting day for the shelter!"

What was Greer to do? She didn't have two thousand dollars to spend on a wedding gown! Not now, at any rate. She'd just bought herself a bright red Vespa, a rug and reading chair from Pottery Barn, and an elliptical machine for her apartment. She didn't believe in using credit, either. She chalked it up to growing up on a little farm in

Wisconsin, where she actually churned butter and milked cows.

"How could he?" she whispered to the man in the plaid blazer.

"He's doing you a favor," he replied, his gaze still on Fran.

"No, he's not."

"It's just a dress," the man murmured.

"It's not just a dress. It's *special*."

"The beads?" He mulled it over. "I'll grant you that the story makes the dress a collector's item for some people."

"That's right," Greer said. "At the very least, it's an investment. You heard Ms. Banks. It will only gain in value."

"That's why you want it?" His eyes narrowed. "Because it's an investment?"

"Of course."

"Are you sure?"

"Yes."

"*Really* sure?"

She nodded.

"I think you want this dress for yourself," he said, "and you just don't want to admit it."

Bingo. How did he know she was lying?

"It's purely for investment reasons," she said.

"We all have our little quirks," he said.

"Not me," Greer said. "I'm predictable. And sensible. I told you I'm not even getting married, so why would I want it for myself? Huh?"

"Don't be embarrassed," the Englishman said, and without removing his gaze from hers, added, "Your foot is swinging fairly hard, you know. And your pupils are really large at the moment for such a brightly lit room."

She stopped her foot and felt heat rise up her neck.

"It's an *investment*," she said again, and straightened in her chair. She would ignore this man in the plaid blazer from here on out.

"Whatever you say." He held his hands loosely knitted in his lap. She saw a flat gold signet ring on one of his fingers. "I thought you might have some compelling personal reason, or even a mad, illogical *yen,* to bid on the gown."

He said yen with a lot of emphasis.

"I don't believe in yens," she said.

"Is that so?" he asked.

It was a perfectly innocent question. But somehow it knocked her off her foundations. Maybe because he asked it so clearly. So boldly. With his gaze on hers. As if her answer mattered . . . really mattered.

How silly of her to think that it did, or that he honestly cared. "Hmmph," she said. It was one of those generic answers that covered her bases fairly well when she was flummoxed yet wanted to appear self-assured. He didn't need to know that she had both a yen and a personal reason for bidding. That was *her* business.

He leaned over. "You believe in yens," he whispered.

"No, I don't!"

"Are you sure about that?" And he winked at her.

Of all the nerve! Dear God, people didn't even use the word *yen* anymore.

"Any more bids?" Fran asked.

Greer stood up. "Two thousand . . . and one dollars." That sounded weird to her ears, but that's how they did it on *The Price Is Right*, outbidding the other person by a dollar! She'd seen it happen!

For a moment, nobody said a word.

Then Fran smiled brightly. "Nice try, but the rules of bidding state that bids have to be at least one hundred dollars apart once the amount reaches one thousand dollars."

"Finc," said Greer, remembering too late that she could bid from a seated position. "Two thousand one *hundred* dollars." She was an idiot. But she couldn't stop. She wouldn't. She sat down again and missed. She landed on the left thigh of the man in the plaid blazer.

"Sorry," she said, enjoying the warmth and solidness of his leg very much without wanting to.

"I'm not," he said.

But surely she imagined that. No gentleman would ever say such a thing, and she didn't have time for bad boys. She quickly slid over to her seat and kept her eyes on Fran.

"Five thousand," said Pierre in such a tiny voice everyone leaned toward him.

"There's no way he could have said five thousand," Greer whispered to the man in plaid.

"He said five thousand," he murmured.

There were audible gasps in the room. Charlestonians loved drama. They were also appalled by garish displays of wealth—unless it was at a charity auction, and then they gave themselves permission to act like everyone else.

Greer herself was holding on by a thread to her sense of decorum.

"Halle-frickin'-lujah!" said Fran. "This is turning out to be quite the auction item, and we haven't even gotten to the week in Paris at a five-star hotel or the month at a Hamptons summer cottage for ten. Is there anyone who can top five thousand dollars?"

No one spoke.

"All right, then," said Fran. "Going, going. . . ."

"Wait!" Greer yelled from her seat, then looked at the guy in the plaid blazer.

"*I'm* not going to bid on it," he said.

She was desperate. "I just thought if we went in together, we could outbid him eventually," she said at warp speed.

He lofted a brow. "We'd get joint custody of a wedding gown?"

"Sure." Having it half the year was better than nothing, and way better than seeing Pierre win it.

"I don't live here," the Englishman said. "I'm a visitor from London."

"Oh. That would make sharing hard." She barely hesitated. "How about I'll keep it, and in exchange I'll give you our executive VIP soul-mate search package at Two Love Lane, my matchmaking agency? We work internationally."

"What makes you think I need help in the romance department?" he whispered back. His eyes twinkled merrily. "I'm not James Bond, but—"

"I didn't mean to imply—"

"And why do you assume I've got money to burn on royal relics sewn onto a wedding gown?" He held out his hands, palms up, and looked down at his plaid blazer, which was sporty and cool but, come to think of it, quite worn. His shirt wasn't anything special, just a white oxford that had probably seen better days. He had on jeans, too, and beat-up boat shoes. "I suppose I'm flattered on that account, at least."

Oh, God. What if he was a missionary? Or a poor scholar researching a book no one had paid him for yet? Or was he a crew member on a yacht or a container ship tied up in Charleston harbor, and this was his only day off? He might have to go back and do the captain's bidding, for all she knew, coiling ropes on deck or making up all the bunks.

"I-I'm sorry," she said.

"Gone!" crowed Fran, and pounded her gavel on the podium. "*Royal Bliss* goes to the fine gentleman who bid five thousand dollars!"

There was a squeak of joy from either Pierre or L.A. Lady.

Greer couldn't help stomping her right foot. Just a little. And maybe she bit the inside of her cheek, too.

"Don't be too down," the man in plaid said. "There will always be other investment opportunities, won't there?"

"Right." She was in no mood to be cajoled.

"Good thing you didn't have an honest-to-goodness yen," he said. "Or a personal reason."

"Whatever," she muttered.

"And this is for charity, remember." He stuck his hand in his blazer and pulled out his flip phone. She was right; how rude of her to presume a total stranger would partner with her on an investment of over five thousand dollars, especially a guy who might have bought his entire wardrobe at Goodwill, a man who carried a crummy old flip phone. He started punching in a number. "They just got themselves a cool five thousand bucks, as you Americans say."

She was about to say he had a point, but he abruptly stood and looked down at her.

"By the way," he said with a lazy half smile, "there's another reason I wouldn't go halfsies with you on a wedding gown."

"What is it?"

"Love stinks," he said, and squeezed past all the people to the right of her in the row.

Whoa.

Greer watched his back as he departed. He wasn't the first man to tell her how he felt about love. People vented with her all the time, once they found out what business she was in. But no one had ever spoken so succinctly on the topic.

She couldn't help following him with her eyes as he left the hotel ballroom. It was midday. Why come to an auction unless you planned to bid? Why had he left in the middle? What kind of work was he doing here, if at all? Why had she turned to him and wanted him to bid with her, and how did he know what she was thinking?

He turned around and caught her looking at him. Her heart jerked violently when he gave her a nod but no smile. The gesture was old-fashioned, somehow. She thought of an embattled hero about to disappear forever; she was the movie starlet who would miss him. Something fluttered in her chest, near her heart. And then he was gone, through the tall double doors leading onto the Cistern.

She sighed. It didn't matter. She didn't have time to get hot and bothered over a stranger in a plaid blazer, a stranger who'd obviously had his heart broken at some point. Pierre had won the gown. *Her* gown.

Royal Bliss!

And she was missing out on Miss Thing's birthday. She should have been there at the taping of the show. After her display at the auction, she'd fit right in with those flamboyant *Price Is Right* contestants who had always stressed her out. She'd been too prissy saying no to the trip. Too controlling. And look where it had gotten her: alone at an auction on the day her mother found out Greer's old boyfriend was finally getting married. She didn't regret her decision to break up with Wesley. But her family and friends would be bringing the touchy subject back up again and again, for the rest of her life, no doubt. They'd remind her that no one understood her reasoning.

Well, she didn't, either! It would have been a whole lot easier for her to marry Wesley. But she couldn't. She still didn't know what went wrong. And today especially, she felt lonely. Stupid, somehow. Lacking in her usual confidence.

"Excuse me," she said to the first person to her left in her row. She pulled her briefcase out from under her chair and then scooted past a bunch of knees, refusing to make eye contact with anyone. Was life passing her by? Could a wedding gown take the place of whatever was actually missing?

Because something was definitely missing. Not Wesley . . . but something else. She thought again about wishing a handsome lover would show up in her life, but it was more than just sex that she longed for. More than infatuation.

It was love. *Big* love. The true, everlasting kind. She was selling it every day, wasn't she? Hadn't Macy found true love when she never thought for a minute that she would?

But Greer wasn't Macy. Greer didn't have Cupid somewhere in her ancestry, the way Macy did. Greer had dairy farmers in her family tree, very practical, plain people whose greatest indulgence was icing on a once-a-year birthday cake, white muslin curtains trimmed in scarlet or yellow rickrack, and fresh cream from their own dairy cows on top of their oatmeal.

Greer had thought she'd been in love, and then she'd woken up one day and the feeling had disappeared. She'd hurt Wesley terribly. Not badly enough that he didn't fall in love again—he had. But still. According to her friends and family, he'd been moping for years, thanks to her.

Why hadn't *she* fallen in love again? Was she a robot? What was her problem? Charleston had so many interesting men in it. Sure, a few were man-boys, or had awful personalities like Pierre, but they were the exceptions to the rule.

In the back of the ballroom, she wrote a personal check with a substantial donation to the charity.

Pierre sidled up next to her. "Hard luck," he said in his tiny voice. "Too bad you don't make enough money at your sham of a business to buy whatever you want. You took enough of my money. Where'd it go?"

"Right back in your bank account, as you well know," she told him, and handed the check over to an elderly lady. She was wearing a hearing aid, but there was no way she'd be able to hear Pierre's hummingbird conversation. "We have a hundred-percent refund policy for dissatisfied clients. You're the first and only one to have taken us up on it."

Greer walked away from the table, and Pierre followed her.

"So, you wanted that dress," he said. "Who's the groom?"

"Who's your bride?" she flung back.

He chortled. "You're not getting married. You don't even have an engagement ring on."

"Whether I'm getting married or not, I certainly have no intention of sharing my personal life with *you*."

"What happened? Your momma and daddy said you should be married by now? And you're feeling blue? Gotta daydream instead?"

"Oh, shut up," she said, and strode away. She willed her eyes not to flood with tears. Pierre was perceptive, sadly. And he was also a . . . a punk. She'd never called a grown man a punk before, but he was, and he wasn't worth her tears.

He came running after her. "I bought this dress as a

business investment. You wanted it so you could pine over it in your closet. Believe me, Greer, the whole audience could tell."

"I don't know how you stay in business with your mean attitude."

"*My* business is thriving." He was like a bulldog. "Don't you think it's odd that the co-owner of a matchmaking agency can't even find someone to marry, especially when she says she believes in love all over your marketing materials? What does that say about Two Love Lane's algorithms? And your hypocrisy?"

His words stung, but she wouldn't let him win. "I'm sorry the algorithms didn't work for you. It doesn't mean they haven't worked time and time again for other people. And I do believe in love. I'm not going to marry someone just to get married, though."

She'd learned the best way to deal with small people like Pierre was to treat them like recalcitrant children, with pity and patience.

His little face turned red. "Your algorithms didn't work for me because *y'all* messed up. Don't blame me."

"I'm not," she said. "We told you they're really good but not a hundred-percent perfect, and sometimes we can't make matches, whether we use those or old-fashioned hunches. It doesn't mean something is wrong with you, although if you want the truth, which I've told you before, you refused to listen to any of our coaching advice. I think that stubbornness figured into the outcome. Now please leave me alone." She kept walking.

"I lied, Greer," he called after her in his tiny voice.

She turned around. "About what?"

"About why I bought *Royal Bliss*."

She had to strain to hear his Pekingese-sized voice.

"It's not an investment," he said, his forehead shiny

with sweat. "I bought it so you couldn't have it. I could tell how much you wanted it."

She stood still and took in what he was saying. "You must hate me a lot."

"I don't give a hoot about you." The outrageous L.A. chick came up and put her arm around his waist. She gloated Greer's way. "I'm going to make sure some bride in Charleston gets it," he said.

Greer intentionally loosened her grip on her purse strap. She took time to inhale slowly. "It's been eighteen months since we last tried to help you. You've been stewing on this ever since?"

"Revenge is a dish—"

"Best served cold," she finished saying with him. "Do you watch a lot of bad TV?"

"No." He was so damned literal.

"I'm trying to say I *get* it," she said. "You have the dress. Your revenge is done."

But he didn't hear that last part. When she looked back at him, he was strutting away with his lady friend.

"Whatever, Pierre." Greer's day so far had not gone well. She needed to get home. On Liberty Street, she called the girls in California and told them about her old boyfriend tying the knot.

"Wesley?" Miss Thing said into the phone's speaker.

"Yes," she said back.

There was a long silence.

"Hello? You don't think I should have married him, too, do you? He was the wrong guy for me. Hello?"

"We're still here, and no, we don't think that!" said Macy, the only native Charlestonian among them. She was also a major player on the local social scene. "I'm taking you off speaker, if you don't mind. It's hard to hear. We're in line to get into the studio, and the crowd is stirred up."

"How exciting," Greer said, but she really only felt a pang of guilt for not going.

"Look on the bright side," Macy said, her Lowcountry drawl a little clearer and louder off speaker, "maybe with Wesley finally off the market, they'll be nice to you back home again."

"No, my mom is really upset." Greer was passing college dorms on both sides of Calhoun Street. "But maybe eventually people back home will stop asking me why I dumped the finest man ever to walk the streets of Waterloo."

"I hope so, sweetie," said Macy. "That's so rude and unfair to you."

"His fiancée is so much more compatible with him, too. They're both surgeons."

"Love is crazy," said Macy. "Look at me and Deacon! Who'd have thought I'd ever marry a Yankee from New York City?"

"True." Greer knew Macy had fought her attraction to Deacon tooth and nail. He'd been her client at Two Love Lane, after all, and Macy was supposed to set him up with other women, not herself.

"I'm so glad you followed your gut with Wesley," Macy said. "It freed him up to find his true soul mate. And you, yours. Someday."

That wasn't going to happen. Greer had tried to convince herself she was in love once. Who could say she wouldn't do it again? She couldn't tell her best friends that she'd wondered if there was something inherently wrong with her, like a chip missing in her heart.

But deep inside, she knew that was silly. Her heart was in fine shape. Wesley had simply been the wrong man for her. "It's possible I'll run into them someday, and if I do, I'll be very happy for them. Very, very happy."

"Good," said Macy. "I can tell you're worried that I don't believe you, but I do. I can also tell you think you'll be old and shrunken and alone, but you won't. I promise."

"You really think?" Greer loved how Macy always understood her.

"I *know*," said Macy, and handed the phone off to Ella.

"Stop worrying about what your mother thinks," Ella said in her Bronx accent. She also always seemed to know what Greer was thinking.

"I try not to," she said.

"I know it's hard. My own mother is very involved with all of us Mancini girls. She treats us like we're still twelve. But I just let it roll off my back. Some of my sisters can't."

"What's your secret?"

"I don't know," said Ella. "Once I figure it out, I'll tell you. In the meantime, treat yourself like a princess."

"I'll try."

And then Greer got to talk to Miss Thing, who had an obsession with Queen Elizabeth II and tried to dress like her. She'd grown up in the tiny town of Kettle Knob, North Carolina, up in the mountains near Asheville, before arriving in Charleston in her late twenties. They were only babies when she started cooking and cleaning at the Sottile House, a dormitory on the College of Charleston campus where they would all later meet. She bolstered Greer's spirits with her excitement about being in California and striking their *Price Is Right* adventure off her bucket list. "We're having a wunnerful time," she said. "Just wunnerful."

Oh, dear. That was Miss Thing's tequila voice.

"I hope one of you gets onstage and wins something," Greer said, at the corner of Meeting and Calhoun, one of the busiest intersections in Charleston.

Miss Thing responded with a flurry of talk that Greer didn't comprehend in the slightest because on the other side of the street she saw Wesley—and his fiancée.

She was supposed to run into them back home in Waterloo, a sixteen-hour drive and a thousand miles away. Not here in Charleston.

And they were with the man in the gray plaid blazer.

CHAPTER TWO

On the bustling corner, Greer was riveted to the sidewalk. "I have to go," she said to Miss Thing. "I'm getting another call." She hung up the phone while Miss Thing was talking about winning an RV. It was her dearest hope, she was saying.

But Greer already knew that—Miss Thing said it every time she watched *The Price Is Right*, and she had about ten other dearest hopes, too, including owning a quilted pink Chanel bag and visiting the Great Wall of China. Meanwhile, something big and horrible was happening, and, and . . .

A woman with a camera around her neck glanced over at her. "Are you okay? Your face is really red. Maybe you need some water."

"I'm fine, but thank you for telling me."

"Charleston's almost too much," the woman said. "*Everyone* has window boxes. And dogs that look like they get regular baths. You notice that?"

"Yes." Greer threw her a semblance of a smile. "And sun tea brewed in large mason jars in the garden."

The camera lady gave her a quick once-over. "*You* live here?"

"Yep."

"I'd guess you were from somewhere else." The woman reached over her camera, into her purse, and pulled out her phone.

"Wait—" Greer said. "You mean my accent?"

Her talkative fellow pedestrian turned her back.

"Is it my accent?" Greer had to know.

The woman whipped around, the phone to her ear. "Just your vibe." And she turned back to her phone call.

No, no, no. Not that being from Wisconsin wasn't wonderful, and near and dear to Greer's heart, but she *had to be different since she saw Wesley last.* Since she'd broken up with him, she'd tried her best to change in exciting, good ways just to prove she could to everyone back home. She hadn't spiraled downhill after dumping the greatest guy in Waterloo. She'd blossomed!

Unless she'd been fooling herself. . . .

She decided to look down at her phone. She'd also keep an eye on the other pedestrians' feet and follow them when the stop-n-go light turned green (she hadn't called it that since she'd left Waterloo). She would walk right past her ex and his new woman, and the man in the plaid blazer.

It was time. Feet moved. Instinct made her look up— she was entering a busy intersection, after all. But as soon as she got her bearings—and saw that apparently the trio had not seen *her*—she looked down again. Charleston was one of the most romantic destinations in the world, but it was small enough that a chance meeting with an old love interest was not out of the question. Wesley had to have known that.

Why was he here anyway?

And why was he talking to the man in the plaid blazer? Had that guy known who she was at the auction? Had he *followed* her there?

Nothing made any sense.

"Hello," the man in plaid said.

Greer thought of pub crawls, soccer matches, the Beatles, and a Downton Abbey–style chaise lounge upon which they both were entangled, his fingers pulling slowly at her laced-up bodice. She looked up from the asphalt and white painted crosswalk line.

The Englishman wore a pleasant, curious expression. "Fancy meeting you again," he said, stopping. "So soon."

She paused, too. "In the middle of a busy intersection this time." She widened her eyes in an effort at a comic touch. Wesley and his fiancée were still crossing the street and talking to each other. Cars and trucks hovered mere feet away, engines growling.

"Bye," she said, and took off.

There. She'd been nice enough. On to the rest of her life—which suddenly loomed like a barren desert with a lone tumbleweed skirting across the dunes.

But "Greer!" she heard next. It was Wesley's voice. She had just stepped up onto the sidewalk, too. For a brief second, she shut her eyes. The desert was gone, but nothing came to replace it. Nothing. That was what she felt around Wesley.

She opened her eyes again. Turned slowly. Made eye contact with the lover and friend she'd ultimately rejected as a life partner. He was now walking toward her, his fiancée's hand held firmly in his own. She was all silken black hair, cheekbones, and chic street style.

Greer felt instantly plain and uninteresting, which she never had before. In high school she'd been in a math class with a future Miss Jefferson County, who told Greer she should enter pageants because brainy beauty queens were trending, even if she *was* flat-chested and not great with makeup. And then in college, she'd won an award in Web site design for a Charleston-based fashionista who'd told her she looked just like Scarlett Johansson if Scarlett Johannson had glasses, a slightly different nose, and that squiggle perpetually on Greer's forehead from thinking so much.

No. She'd never felt drab. But now she did.

The man in plaid came with the smiling couple.

"I can't believe it!" Wesley said.

The sea breeze wafting down Calhoun Street from the harbor dwindled to nothing. Greer could feel the heat and humidity curl her hair on her neck. The last thing she wanted was for Wesley to see her sweat.

"Wesley," she said. "*Wow.* What are you doing here?" She backed up a few steps so they could all get away from the corner. Across the street, some hotel dwellers peered down at the crowded sidewalk filled with tourists and locals getting where they had to go. Greer's come-to-Jesus meeting with Wesley wasn't going to be private in the least.

The man in the plaid blazer stuck his hands in his jeans pockets. "You know each other?" he asked, in a perfectly innocent voice.

Wesley smiled the same way he had when he was sixteen and they'd go to the skating rink and skate holding hands. "Serena, Ford, I'd like you to meet an old friend, Greer Jones. Greer, this is my fiancée, Serena. And Ford's a friend."

Greer's hands and feet buzzed with mortification. "Hello," she said, looking back and forth between Serena and the man she could now give a name.

"We've met," Ford said slowly, "in a way."

"Oh?" said Wesley.

"At an auction," Greer said. "A few minutes ago, actually."

"We almost won a dress together," Ford said.

"We didn't stand a chance," said Greer. "Someone else was determined to get it." She wouldn't bother explaining more than that.

"Oh my gosh, what an adventure!" Serena sounded genuinely excited.

Greer hadn't expected her to be so friendly. Or to sound like a Valley Girl from *Clueless*. It wasn't a bad thing. Just took her off guard. She never imagined serious Wesley being with someone like that.

"It's nice to meet you, Serena," she said, and felt a little more herself. "In fact, congratulations. I saw on Facebook—" And then realized she might look like a stalker. She wasn't friends with Wesley. But friends had posted pictures of an engagement party.

"Of course, you'd have seen," Wesley finished for her. "Helen gave us a party." Helen was a mutual friend in Waterloo. They'd all graduated high school together. "Serena and I are getting married this summer."

Serena held out her left hand. A sparkling diamond surrounded by sapphires sat there.

No freaking way.

It was the engagement ring Wesley had picked out for Greer. She would never forget the day he'd offered it to her in its pretty little velvet box. She instantly felt sorry for Serena. And it was the first time she could justifiably criticize Wesley—how selfish of him. How utterly insensitive. She shot him a look. She couldn't help herself.

His pupils widened.

"I know it was originally meant for you, Greer," Serena said, her voice full of concern. "I hope you won't mind."

She *knew*?

"I loved it so much," Serena continued over the sound of cars and trucks streaming by, "I told Wesley not to get a different one. Believe me, he tried. He's not the type of guy to pawn a used ring off on the woman he's going to marry."

"She's into re-purposing." Wesley shrugged. His ears were slightly pink. But he exchanged a loving look with Serena. She was obviously the Girl Who Made Everything Easy. "I just had to get it resized down a notch."

Of course. Serena was model slender.

"Are you okay about it?" Serena asked. "I just love it so much." She got little tears in her eyes.

Wesley hugged her shoulder.

"No, no—please, don't cry—it's fine!" Greer said. And though this encounter was getting weirder by the second, she wasn't lying. "I-I hope you enjoy it." She smiled and nodded a few times. Adjusted her purse.

"Oh, I will," Serena said, and beamed.

Wesley beamed, too.

Let them beam. The truth was, that ring had never been Greer's style.

"It was great to see you, Wesley," said Greer. "And to meet you, Serena." She looked at Ford. "Nice to run into you again."

"Likewise," he said, a gleam in his eye.

She could tell he was reading her BS meter, and yes, it was off the charts. She was doing her best to be civilized, and sometimes you simply had to play a part.

"Ford's an artist," Serena said in her charmingly persuasive manner, which made it impossible for Greer to take off. "We met when he painted my portrait."

"Oh." She should have known Ford was an artist. He was very much alive, humming with awareness. Sensual. She didn't know how she knew that last part. She was mad she hadn't guessed he was a creative type when she'd done her Two Love Lane scope-out at the auction.

"I'd just graduated from a boarding school in London," Serena continued, "and my mother insisted on the portrait. I told her I'd do it if I could choose the painter."

She loved to talk, it seemed. But she was so warm and friendly, who wouldn't listen?

"I honestly thought the whole experience of posing for a portrait would be awful," Serena went on, "but Ford kept me entertained."

"She'd never met a true English curmudgeon," Ford said, "or stood still that long."

"You're *not* a curmudgeon," Serena insisted. "Look how well you've handled yourself lately."

Lately?

"That's her way of saying she's shocked I'm out of bed, dressed, and sober." Ford's dry delivery made Wesley laugh. Greer, too. She couldn't help it.

"Stop it, Wesley and Ford," said Serena. "Greer's going to think we're badly behaved."

"It's fine," Greer murmured. "Charleston has a way of making people want to party until the wee hours and sleep late." There. That was a polite way to skirt the awkwardness.

"Yes, but—" Serena winced like she wanted to say something really badly but knew she shouldn't. "But we have extenuating circumstances."

"We?" Ford asked.

"Well, *you*," Serena said.

"Serena . . ." Wesley chided her.

"I suppose I've no choice now but to mention I was left at the altar by my bride," Ford told Greer.

Thunk. More awkwardness. Greer felt instantly guilty. And horrified.

"Sorry," said Serena, then looked at Greer. "It was awful."

"It happened a month ago," Ford said, ignoring Serena, whose expression registered deep concern for him. "One tends to sleep and drink too much bourbon when that happens. Go to faraway places with lots of humidity and heat. Put shirts on backwards."

Greer wished she could be swallowed up by the sidewalk. The universe was messing with her. Big-time. Wesley was standing right there, stoic and square-headed, like a character on a *Sesame Street* skit. Made of buttons, yarn, and felt. Oblivious. Everything bouncing off him and not getting through. *Hello?* she wanted to say. *You were dumped in a similar manner! Don't you feel awkward hearing this with me here?*

At least she hadn't left Wesley at the altar. He hadn't stood in front of a crowd of friends and family, a preacher at his back, and been abandoned on his wedding day.

But this guy. . . .

"I-I'm so sorry. I truly am." Greer felt Serena's eyes on her. Was Wesley's fiancée putting her in the same category as Ford's ex? And what would that category be? *Vile? Selfish? Immature?*

"Nothing to be sorry about," Ford said.

But he had to be angry still. Or heartbroken. Or both. Greer couldn't tell. She couldn't tell *anything* from his tone or his expression. But he wasn't indifferent. He wasn't an automaton. He'd stuck his hands in the front pockets of his jeans, his thumbs hung over the pocket edges. His back was straight. He had small laugh lines around his eyes. He had the air of being distinctly human. The plaid blazer was maybe a middle finger to the world.

And then there was the auction, where he'd told her "Love stinks," out of the blue. That she'd never forget. And he'd had a very warm, welcoming thigh. He hadn't flinched in the slightest when she'd landed on it. He'd also said something a little delicious or raunchy, depending on how she chose to recall it.

A dose of intuition flooded her being, against her better judgment. Greer sensed he was her cup of tea. It was the exact right phrase: *cup of tea*. Cheery Disney character Mrs. Potts might as well be whispering the phrase in her ear. Greer had never known what her cup of tea was until just now. She'd only known Wesley wasn't it.

And now, this jilted painter whom she didn't know was in fact her cup of tea. What did it mean? She was a coffee drinker. People who drank tea weren't very exciting. She would never in a million years have called anyone her cup of tea until right this very minute.

Maybe she felt drawn to him because of the wedding horror story. Could be a sympathy thing.

"When I heard Ford was here," Serena said, "I told Wesley it's yet another reason Charleston is the perfect place."

Perfect place . . . for what? Greer knew the city was awesome, but what was Serena saying?

Wesley sighed. "Greer, I didn't want to have to tell you like this—"

Her heart started to race. "What?"

He shook his head. "I wanted to call you first, but we ran out of time."

"Wesley, *tell* her." Serena kept smiling. And then she bounced, just once.

"Yes, tell me." Greer braced herself. Something was about to go seriously wrong.

"We're getting married *here*. In Charleston." Wesley had never looked more serious. And scared.

Greer's stomach dropped to her feet. "Oh," she said, and tried to keep breathing. It helped that Ford gave her his calm, steady stare, the one he'd used at the auction. She nodded to give herself time to think. "That's . . . that's nice. A lot of people do that."

Wesley scratched his head. "That's not all."

Good Lord! What could come next?

"We're moving here," Serena said. "We'll be working at the Medical University for a year on a big research project." And she squealed.

It wasn't the worst squeal in the world. She was obviously overjoyed, and Greer couldn't hate her for being excited about moving to a great city.

But out of all the medical jobs in the world, Wesley had to choose one here in Charleston? "That's—that's—" She didn't know what to say. She had to get away from these people. *Now.*

"We're lucky," said Serena, lacing the fingers of her right hand with Wesley's. "It's such a romantic city."

"It's very beautiful," Greer said on autopilot, her brain synapses firing like mad.

"But the cherry on the sundae is having Ford here, at least for a few months," Serena said, never missing a beat in her earnest cheerleader voice that made one want to sit down and listen if you had a heart.

"Why *are* you here?" Greer asked the Englishman.

"I'm working on a particular project I can't seem to

tie down yet," he said. "But I need to. Soon. It's to go to a gallery in Manchester for a big show."

"Wow." Greer was impressed.

"I want Ford to paint my wedding portrait." Serena held up crossed fingers, her eyebrows arched up and outward, the way extra cute comic-strip characters do when they're pleading.

"First I've heard about painting a wedding portrait," Ford said with a shrug. "Sorry, Serena. No time."

There was a shocked silence between Wesley and his future bride.

"You didn't ask him already?" Wesley asked her.

"No," Serena said. "I thought—"

"But you said—" Wesley began.

Serena's lips tightened. Wesley shut his mouth.

Ford rocked back on his heels. "Come by for a cigar later, Wesley, on my studio balcony?"

"Sure," Wesley said. "Got some good scotch?"

"The best," Ford said.

Serena was subdued enough that she adjusted her purse. "Well," she said, "That's men for you. Everything cured by alcohol and cigars."

"Or world war," said Greer. "Very little in between."

She was proud of herself. She sounded perfectly at ease. This Wesley and Serena calamity—because that was what it was—was going to be easier to handle than she thought it would be.

Everything in life could be easy, really. She always forgot that. Since moving from home at age eighteen, she tended to get wrapped up in the minutiae of things and work herself into a lather of nerves. But her farming parents had taught her to carry on, stay polite, and hope that no one noticed that things weren't always fixed or right or acceptable to you. And now here in Charleston, she saw a similar attitude, only dressed up in Southern culture. You persevered. You even brought pie and poured sweet tea until the worst had passed, and then you took a broom, swept up the mess, and went and sat on the porch and waved at your neighbors.

"Now I know your name," Ford said to Greer.

"And I yours," Greer replied. Somehow the words, to her ears, sounded formal and English, like something from an old novel, and she was reminded of how he'd nodded at her at the auction, and vintage-film feelings flooded her body as she thought of heroes and the amazing, colorful women they loved. The heat, too, might have had something to do with it. She was getting dehydrated.

"Charleston's an interesting town," said Ford, and looked over all their heads. "I'd say it rivals London for drama."

Exactly which drama did he mean? The bidding war at the auction? Serena and Wesley's tension over her wedding portrait? The obvious stress Greer was feeling about her ex moving to Charleston and getting married there? Or something to do with Ford himself and Greer? Although why she imagined he might be thinking along those lines, she had no idea. Maybe she was ready for drama. Maybe she was ready for drama with *him*. Sitting on his thigh had been quite the pleasurable experience. She'd rather think about that than Wesley. . . .

"Cheers," Ford concluded, and took off—

Without getting her number, so she'd obviously imagined the drama between them. She was really only dehydrated and desperate.

A horse-and-carriage that had been rolling slowly down the street stopped to turn left at the intersection.

Ford was right. Charleston was full of drama, but on the outside it could be slow and predictable, like any town.

Even more awkwardness descended now that Ford was gone.

"I can't believe he said no," said Serena, looking after him.

"Oh, well," said Wesley. "We'll find another artist. Maybe Greer knows—" he began, and thought better of it.

Greer would take the high road. "I'll be glad to ask around," she said.

"Thanks," said Wesley.

She stuck out her hand—way out—to Serena, who was still watching Ford. He had a cool, understated stride, like an extreme sports skateboarder. Or a guy packing heat. Take your pick. "Good to meet you," she said.

Serena abruptly turned around at the sight of Greer's open palm. "Oh, likewise," she said with a bright smile, and shook it. Her grip was firm, her fingers long and skinny.

Greer thought *surgeon's hands*, and she remembered to like Serena no matter how perfect she was because she saved people's lives. This wasn't the day she expected, but she was better off having seen Wesley finally happy, even if it meant he had to be happy in the same town. At least her guilt about dumping him was gone. Karma was now set to bite at her heels in a big way. Every day she'd be afraid of bumping into him or Serena.

She prayed they wouldn't live downtown or buy groceries at the Harris-Teeter on East Bay Street, the number-one social hot spot on the peninsula.

"I'm glad we ran into each other," Wesley said.

"Me, too," Serena said, and put her arm through his.

"And Greer, thank you for breaking up with him." She laughed.

At least it wasn't a giggle. Greer didn't do well with gigglers. When Macy had been crushing on Deacon, she'd giggled a lot, and it had really gotten on Greer's nerves. Since she'd married, Macy had settled down and was back to her old regular laugh, thank goodness.

"No problem," Greer said. "It had nothing to do with Wesley. He's a prince."

"Serena's not shy," Wesley said, his ears pink, and dragged her away.

Smart of him.

Walking home, Greer realized she'd just been through a living hell that wasn't going to end anytime soon, but it would be endurable if she went to work and *stayed home at night and on the weekends for the next year so she wouldn't run into Wesley and Serena.*

Or maybe she should move.

Her life now officially sucked.

She decided then and there to binge-watch her favorite series, *Breaking Bad,* every day after work without going out until she was done. She would order her groceries online from Harris Teeter and drive to pick them up, already bagged. She would live like a hermit before and after work and on weekends until she figured out what to do.

Things she would not do: (1) make brownies, (2) call her mother, and (3) Google Ford. She didn't even know his last name.

CHAPTER THREE

Ford first saw Greer Jones earlier that day at Roastbusters, his new favorite coffee place on East Bay Street. He'd just picked up his black tea with milk and a teaspoon of sugar—a habit he'd had since he was a child—when she walked in and got a coffee to go. He knew immediately he wanted to paint her. She looked distinctly American with her strong, clean good looks. She also had something else . . . something that made people around her look twice. It might have been her air, which suggested competence and control—and whether she knew it or not, a bold sensuality with her glossy red lips and pin-striped tailored pantsuit.

The artist in him wanted to discover more. So did the man. She was sexy, someone who looked as if she had places to be, a total turn-on. And when his sensitive and primal sides worked in concert, he did his best—and most dangerous—work.

When she left Roastbusters and started walking, he did, too. He flipped open his phone while watching his potential model swing her sleek briefcase at her side and sip at her coffee. Pressed the number he'd carefully programmed to ring in England at Anne's manor house on the Thames.

"Oh, God, Ford, that Hollywood power couple who moved into the neighborhood just came over and borrowed a cup of demerara sugar," Anne told him in that breathy way she had. "They're making chocolate chip biscuits with their twins and ran out."

"Lucky you."

"Not with the paps lurking on the road. He was quite apologetic, but it's not their fault, is it? Guess what—she wanted one of my novels to read by their pool. She said she'd never read a romance, and when I told her my heroines were empowered ballbusters in an era when it was extremely difficult to be one, she was all in."

"Good for you," Ford said dryly, slightly terrified by Anne's historical romance novels, which dropped once a year and made the *New York Times* list every time.

"So how are you, brother dear?"

"I've finally found her," he said. "The woman I want to paint."

"Good. She must be perfect. Is she?"

"I think so."

"Very American looking?"

"She is. Super-independent air."

"In what way is she compelling?"

"I don't know yet, but she is."

"I'm counting on you. The galleries don't think you're in any position to come up with a canvas this fast, but I assured them you don't wait for your muse. You command it to appear at will."

"Tell them I work no matter what, if that's what they're worried about. They don't need to know that if it's no good—which ninety-nine times out of a hundred it's not—I start over."

"No, darling, we won't tell them *that*. We'll hope that you get a lightning bolt of inspiration and get it right the first—or second—time."

"I'll have to."

"How awful for you to be under such pressure. But not really." She sighed. "I know you'd do this whether you got paid or not."

Anne was right. It was who he was, and who *she* was, for that matter. They both accepted that the life of an artist wasn't an easy one. It was filled with angst and doubt. But the compensation was the inherent sense that you knew your purpose. You might be shite at it, but you walked through the world with a map in your head. Many people weren't so fortunate.

"And considering your recent misfortune, this challenge is a good distraction for you," Anne said.

"No painting is ever a distraction." It was always everything. The rest of the world faded away.

"I understand that, but I'm speaking at the moment as your sister, not your manager." An art major at university and avid collector, she'd coveted that role in his career. After his first manager moved to Australia, he'd granted it to her, sure she was making a mistake, considering the time she was required to spend on her own career, but so far, so good.

"Well, don't get too excited," said Ford. "She doesn't even know I exist. I'm following her right now."

"You are?"

The woman who'd come to fascinate him threw her coffee container into a rubbish bin at a corner and turned right.

"She might say no," he told Anne. "How many people can drop everything and pose for a portrait?"

"She won't say no," Anne said. "You know when you know things better than anyone I know."

He tried to wrap his head around that one.

"And if the exhibit—which includes this yet-to-be-painted painting—does well in Manchester, Edinburgh, and Liverpool," she went on, "it may get picked up by the Tate Modern. That's our goal, always. We'll get there."

She rang off before he could speak, and without saying goodbye.

But he wasn't surprised. Anne lived a very busy life apart from being his manager and a full-time novelist. She had four children under age thirteen and a cerebral Oxford professor husband, besides. Not to mention the Hollywood celebrities next door. She could create a business on that fact alone, but she wouldn't dare. She valued privacy too much and could never be anything but a class act.

"The Tate is *your* goal, Anne," he murmured, and put his phone away.

His goal was to paint. And paint. And paint. He hoped the world would like his work, but he wasn't painting to become rich. He was already rich. He wasn't painting to become famous. His family was in Burke's Peerage. The title went back eight generations. And fame was embarrassing. It simply wasn't done. Best to be low-key about one's talents and standing in society.

All he cared about was creating a body of work that represented truth as he knew it. Nothing more. And if other people found his work pleasing, or arresting, or unforgettable—if they remembered him as a painter who captured something elusive and universal about life, then he'd accomplished something worthwhile.

* * *

"Well?" It was Anne again.

He was back in his apartment on Wentworth Street in an old Charleston-style single home. He shared the second floor with two male College of Charleston undergrads, so there were beer cans everywhere and ten-speeds on the balcony. The slight slant to the floor didn't bother him, and neither did the tiny kitchen with its refrigerator empty of everything but beer, a few Cokes, and frozen pizzas. He'd taken the first short-term lease he could find, and he couldn't care less about the state of affairs in the house.

He was in the studio most of the time anyway. That was a space he rented in a co-op on East Bay Street. He had to bike there each morning on narrow roads, with trucks and cars either rushing past inches away or being stuck in traffic jams and spewing exhaust. Occasionally, he'd revert to cracked pavement, which was illegal, and shoot past the lot of them if his hands were itching to grab a brush and paint.

"I never asked her," Ford said. "It just didn't come up."

"So you met her?" asked Anne.

"Yes. And I liked her." *Really* liked her, but he wouldn't tell Anne that.

"*Oh*," she said.

"Stop imagining happy endings for me, will you?"

"Never."

He sighed. "At any rate, she was slightly crazed at this auction I followed her into."

"Crazed? That's good?"

"Refreshing." She hadn't been afraid to be herself. And she was, frankly, mesmerizing. Lovely, sweet, and spirited. He wanted to keep her on his lap when she fell into it. He wished he could have turned her around, put his hands inside her tailored jacket, caressed her back, and made out with her—right there in front of the auction crowd.

It was a mad fantasy. He was English. And he was a baron, besides. He didn't *do* things like that. The only passion he showed publicly was in his paintings. Otherwise, all his lusts and cravings, his rages, his sorrows, his joys . . . they were reserved for display only in the privacy of his homes in Surrey and the Cotswolds, his more primal desires unleashed in his bedroom with women he could trust. Even there, however, he would hold back. He'd been trained since a child to be wary of people who might try to capitalize on his family connections. And sure enough, he'd recently been burned that way, despite his knowing the sting of betrayal could come at any time.

But when it had, he hadn't seen it coming. He thought he'd be able to. That was what kept him up at night. How could he have not seen it coming? For the first time in his life, he felt stupid. And vulnerable.

"So what's your next step?" Anne asked.

"I don't know," he said.

The two lads he lived with were mellow frat boys with summer jobs at the city marina. Their frequent influx of girls who spent the night didn't bother him, either. The young ladies sometimes made breakfast for everyone in the morning, if they stayed that long. Their long, tanned legs and Daisy Dukes shorts weren't a hardship to observe, but when they got too friendly, as they sometimes did when they heard his accent, and assessed him as a potential "older man" boyfriend—he was a ripe thirty—he'd say something about checking in with his parole officer and then leave the apartment, which his roommates appreciated.

From his perch on a stool in the kitchen, he waved at

one of them coming through the front door. It was Gus, who saw him on the phone, waggled his brows, and gave him a thumbs-up. He and the other flatmate, Drake—once they established Ford was not gay, a question they asked him on his third morning there, when he hadn't yet had a girl over—were always hoping Ford would "score with the chicks," as they called it. Gus was carrying a surfboard under his arm, which he placed against the wall in their small living room next to two others. He then plopped down on a shabby sofa and clicked on the television.

"You don't have all the time in the world," Anne said on the phone.

"I realize that." Ford stood and looked out the kitchen window at the street below. Hydrangeas and gardenias rioted in a small front garden bordered by an iron fence, and he had a small stab of homesickness for his mother's garden, much more formal and expansive—overseen by three hired gardeners—but still a labor of love designed by a woman who only cared to bring pleasure to her husband and children. At the curb, a carriage step made of distressed, rounded stone served as a reminder of the city's historic past and was currently occupied by an orange tabby cat soaking up some sun. "I didn't get her number."

"How unlike you," Anne said.

He scratched his head. "It is." And he couldn't explain it. He'd walked abruptly away from her both times they'd met. "I'll come up with something. I know where she works."

"Good," said Anne. "Keep me posted."

"I will." He rang off.

"Ford!" Gus called from the living room. "Grab me a beer, will ya?"

"Sure." He brought out two cans—the boys were on a budget—and tossed one to his blond flatmate. Neither Gus nor Drake had any idea who he really was. They wouldn't care, he was certain—titles meant nothing in the United States, and he loved that fact—but it was easier not to mention it. This way he'd be assured of experiencing Charleston as a regular dude, as Gus was fond of calling him. Gus even called girls *dude*.

Ford sat down on an overstuffed ottoman that immediately tilted sideways. He'd forgotten. But he compensated easily, keeping his beer level, his feet planted a little farther apart, and prepared to *chill*—another word his flatmates were fond of.

"So how's the painting going?" Gus asked him, as he took a swig of his beer from his can.

"Not too great at the moment," Ford replied, downing half of his.

"You don't smoke weed?" Gus squinted at him.

"Nope." Ford shrugged.

A comfortable silence settled between them. Their window AC unit was working, finally, and they both basked in its humming presence.

"So how do you get those creative juices flowing then?" Gus crushed his can and threw it toward the rubbish bin in the corner. He missed.

Ford did the same thing and made it.

"You're an old man," Gus said. "You've had a lot more practice."

Ford gave a short laugh. "Yeah, in the U.K., basketball's a thing."

"It is?" Gus sounded surprised.

"No." Ford laughed. "I've just got better motor skills than you, mate."

"Fuccccck you," Gus said, and laughed.

It was amusing "chilling" with American youth.

"Get back to your inspiration," Gus said. "You don't smoke weed, you're not an alcoholic . . . what do you do?"

"I start," Ford said. "And I hope inspiration will come. Much of the time, it doesn't."

"That sucks." Gus put his fist in front of his mouth and belched.

"You get used to it." Ford stood carefully, putting all his weight out front so he wouldn't fall on his arse, thanks to the missing two wheels on the ottoman's feet. "Actually, I have something now I really want to work on," he said. "I feel loads of inspiration."

"A *shitload* of inspiration," Gus said. "No guy says *loads* over here."

"Right."

Gus picked up the remote and switched channels from ESPN to an HBO movie. Ford had volunteered to enhance their cable options, and Gus and Drake were loving the expanded access.

"Gotta go to the studio." Ford didn't really. He needed to find Greer Jones. But he thought best when he was in his studio, either cleaning up or doing sketches. It was in an old cigar factory on East Bay Street. Some forward-thinking creative had converted the top floor into fifteen spaces, which were rented out at reasonable rates on a sliding scale based on one's income. Ford was paying the top amount, plus making a donation every month, and happy to do it. The light was great, the ventilation top-of-the-line, and it had every modern convenience he needed, including a private bathroom and a shared kitchen down the hall. The open-faced brick walls lent the space old-fashioned charm, and he could play music on his Bluetooth speakers without worrying about disturbing anyone.

"Wait." Gus tossed aside the remote and stood. "You got something in the mail today. From merry old England." He tossed a small, square package to Ford.

"Ta," Ford said, knowing Gus would laugh at his shorthand for *thank you*—which he did.

"You're welcome," Gus said, and laughed again. "God, I love having a foreigner as a roommate. You're like, *weird*."

"Whatever," Ford said, and took the package to his room, a smile tugging at his mouth.

He couldn't tell who the package was from. And then he couldn't open it because there was so much tape around it. So he went to the kitchen and brought back a knife.

"Bloody hell," he said when he finally got the top off a smaller box inside the larger cardboard container. He pulled a lacy ivory negligee from some hot pink tissue paper and held it up. It was tiny. He dropped it on his desk, where it pooled in a slithery, silken heap, and searched for a note.

There wasn't one.

Then he noticed the monogram on the bodice: *TW*, it said, in an elegant, intertwined scroll. And he realized this was Theodora's wedding night attire that she never wore: Teddy's teddy.

CHAPTER FOUR

That afternoon, by the time Greer was done rewatching the very first episode of Season One of *Breaking Bad*, she decided if Walter White and Jesse Pinkman could survive all their dangerous encounters, she could handle running into her ex-boyfriend and his future wife, two harmless doctors out to save the world. What was she worried about? Besides, she had a life to live. If she hid like a hermit that week—and then for a whole year— she'd miss out on the farmer's market, the azaleas blooming on the Battery, the beautiful winter stillness around Colonial Lake, all the great restaurants and rooftop bars, a million fun times with her friends. She wouldn't see Ford, either. Who knew how long he was staying in Charleston?

"I am a coffee drinker," she reminded herself aloud several times as she made herself a cup of Earl Grey tea—in a fancy rose china cup, no less. She took a few sips and stopped. Got a hold of herself. Poured it down the kitchen sink drain. Why was she thinking of Ford at all? It was useless to daydream about an Englishman whose last name she didn't even know and probably never would.

It was why she'd already gotten her friendly neighborhood dry-cleaner delivery service to swing by and pick up her Stella McCartney pantsuit. If it was in her apartment, she'd see it and think about sitting on Ford's thigh. In fact, she decided, maybe she'd leave it at the dry cleaner for a while.

The phone rang, and she immediately thought of the girls at *The Price Is Right*. Had one of them won something? She hoped so! She needed some good news today. Or were they still waiting to tape the show? God forbid not one of them got called up to the stage to bid on something. They had too much personality to be overlooked.

But when she looked at the number, she recognized it as belonging to one of her clients, Jill.

Jill was one of Ella's sisters. There were a lot of Mancini sisters. Jill was the youngest. Everyone doted on her. She was sexy and gorgeous but didn't believe it. That was her problem.

Greer, Macy, and Ella had a special policy when it came to helping close friends and family members find love: let the co-owner of Two Love Lane with the least history with that person take him or her on as a client. Money might not exchange hands, depending upon the family/friend client's financial status and wishes, but the relationship would be handled professionally, just like all the others: advisor-client confidentiality would be upheld, as always. And no one else in the office would be privy to that client's file unless he or she gave written permission.

Since Jill was Ella's sister, and Jill had known Macy a long time because they were yoga friends, Greer became her advisor. So far, Jill hadn't wanted Greer to share any information about her matchmaking status with Ella.

"She already knows everything anyway," Jill said just last week. "Everyone in the family does. And now she thinks she's the worst matchmaker at Two Love Lane because I told her you rocked. Even though I still haven't met anyone. And . . . and I probably never will."

Greer had reassured her that she was highly likely to meet someone compatible. She'd run the numbers using Two Love Lane's highly accurate algorithms, and everything looked really positive. It didn't hurt that Jill turned men's heads right and left, either.

"Please, please meet me at Carmella's," Jill said now. "I *have* to talk to you."

Carmella's was Greer's favorite dessert shop, so that was no hardship. "Is everything okay?"

Jill groaned. "No. I've got a very awkward situation. I can't tell you over the phone, but we'll have to speak really low about it at Carmella's."

"All right." Greer was used to clients wanting to whisper to her. Generally, they were spilling their guts. "Half an hour?"

"I'm already here," said Jill. "If you could get here sooner, I'd appreciate it. I've already eaten one of their mini birthday cakes. They're so good. I'll order you something to drink and a cannoli."

"Great. Black coffee will do. I can be there in fifteen minutes."

"Perfect!" Jill sounded relieved, yet still agitated.

Greer hopped up, stuck a few more bobby pins in her chignon, and left Baker House. She'd take her bike because even if she walked fast, it would take twenty minutes, not fifteen. She saved the red Vespa for times when she needed to get somewhere even faster.

While she cycled down Broad Street, enjoying the breeze on her neck, she remembered she might see Wesley and Serena at any moment. She really didn't feel like running into them. But what could she do? She had a company to run, especially as she was the only one in town at the moment to do so. She couldn't hide out at Two Love Lane and her apartment for a whole year! Being a fraidy-cat wasn't allowed.

And Jill needed her.

Besides, she was over Wesley. She was all about Ford. Yet, try as she might to pedal that feeling away, she felt a sharp stab of lust course through her. She really needed a vacation.

Or maybe she just needed a wild romp between the sheets with a hot guy. Greer didn't shy away from the truth. She hated to admit it, but it had been years, in fact, since she'd slept with someone. She could barely admit Wesley had been her only long-term sex partner. She'd slept with two other guys since their break-up—one time each, hoping she'd feel a spark that never happened. After both those prospects fizzled, she followed the crème brulée rule on dates: she wasn't going to sleep with anyone unless she was willing to knock over a whole tableful of crème brulées to get to that person.

Now she might as well be a nun—a nun with easy access to Charleston's best crème brulées. She had a running list on her phone of where they could be found. Carmella's was one of them.

When she got there, Jill was sitting at a small table and not at the long communal table in the middle of the space—Greer's favorite spot because she always met interesting people there. Jill looked ravishing in a black pencil skirt, a white twin set that showed off her fabulous décolletage, and an emerald green silk scarf wrapped artfully around her head, allowing her curly brown hair to spill out around it. Big gold hoops graced her ears.

Greer pulled out a small wrought iron chair and sat down. Her coffee and cannoli were waiting. She bit into the cannoli and sighed. "Delish," she said. "Thanks."

Not as good as crème brulée but very close.

"You're welcome." Jill wriggled forward, and Greer noticed a couple of guys eyeing her in that casual-cool way guys had in restaurants, which in this case involved pretending to talk to each other while sneaking looks around their pint glasses at the pretty girl in the green scarf.

Greer told Jill about the auction and went into great detail about the wedding gown, but she left out the part about Ford.

"Wow," said Jill. "I love knowing you bid on a wedding gown without even having a boyfriend!"

"That gown was a good investment."

"You make a spectacle of yourself over investments?" asked Jill.

Greer shrugged. "Haven't you ever seen people losing their cool at the stock market exchange?"

"I guess. But this was a charity event in Charleston. People protect their dignity here."

"Sure," said Greer, embarrassed. "But the gown had royal history and a cool story associated with it. Now let's talk about you."

"Okay," said Jill. "I'd tell you to brace yourself, but you're such a rock, I'm not going to bother. That's why I'm confiding in you. And it's not about my love life directly. It's about something else. But I still want client-advisor privilege . . . or just friend privilege, okay? We're friends, aren't we?"

"Of course," said Greer, her curiosity piqued.

"Okay." Jill looked around, then back at Greer. "Do you watch HGTV?"

"Sometimes," Greer said. "I love *Fixer Upper*."

"I do, too," said Jill. "In fact, I want to be a decorator."

"That's awesome," said Greer. But Jill sounded kind of down when she said it. "Isn't it exciting that you're figuring out what you want to do?"

"Oh, yes." Jill frowned. "But in a way, no. Maybe it would have been better if I'd never discovered my passion." She pouted, which only made her look more beautiful.

Greer grabbed her hand. "I know it's scary. Following your passion isn't easy. It's usually hard, in fact. But it's extremely rewarding. You can do it."

"Thanks for the pep talk," Jill said quietly, but at least her voice sounded more hopeful. She leaned closer. "Here's the thing," she whispered. "I don't want to be just any kind of decorator."

"What do you mean?"

Jill hesitated a half-second. "I want to build love nests."

"*L-love* nests?"

"Yes!" Jill's face lit up. "I want to create spaces where you can hide away from the world with your sensual soul mate."

Whoa. The person at the table next door looked over. Greer put her coffee cup down.

Jill's boy brows arched earnestly. "And if you're single, it'll be a place where you can indulge in your wildest fantasies. . . ."

Fantasies. Greer couldn't believe Jill said that word out loud. She was one of the most inhibited sexpots she knew.

"I want my business to be called Erospace Designs," Jill said. "Get it? *Eros*. For the god of love. But it's a play on 'aerospace,' like NASA. On my logo I'm going to have girls in pearls riding on rockets."

"A phallic symbol," Greer said, blinking stupidly.

"For you, I'd do a pink chair studded with fake diamonds," Jill said, and whipped out a folder from her large canvas bag. She spread it open and showed Greer a scene she must have come up with online from one of those decorator sites. "We'd use a matching pink ottoman, fringed lamp, black wrought iron canopy bed with a faux zebra skin comforter, and a dresser decoupaged with Elvis publicity pics."

"My . . . goodness." Greer scanned the page and tried not to act too stunned.

"That's my 'Working Diva Without a Man' theme," Jill said in a cool, professional voice. "You never realized this, Greer, but it's specifically intended to gratify the yearning passions of the sexually frustrated working single woman."

"Yearning passions," Greer murmured, wondering if she'd eaten too much cannoli. She felt kind of bloated. "And . . . and you'll do themes?"

"Yes. We can mix and match. For one room or the whole house. And the company's motto will be, 'We'll make your living space your *loving* space.' Do you like it?"

"I-I love it! But is there a market for what you do here in Charleston?"

Jill laughed. "Is there ever. Have you seen the racy ads in the back of the *City Paper*? Charlestonians just take everything behind closed doors, which is why I think I'll do particularly well here."

"So you've done some research."

"I've even driven to North Carolina to the annual furniture market in High Point and made friends in some fabric companies and furniture lines."

"Wow! That's showing some initiative. And I think this career sounds right up your alley. When will you start?"

"Just today the bank approved my loan request."

"You're on your way. If there's anything I can do to support you, just let me know."

"You can," Jill said, her eyes lighting up. "Please let me do a makeover of your bedroom. Believe me, Greer. It will work."

"Okaaaay." Greer couldn't believe she was agreeing. "Does it have to be pink?"

"Yes," said Jill. "I'll have a moving crew put all of your bedroom stuff—even your mattress—in storage so I can work with a blank canvas. I have a local mattress guy who's giving me great discounts. I can tell already your mattress isn't doing you any favors."

"You can tell?"

Jill nodded. "It's too firm."

"It *is* firm, but—"

"I promise you, you'll love everything." She opened her folder again and pulled out a contract. "I've already put the details in here. There will be no charge. Eventually I might want a testimonial to put in my brochure. You won't mind? I want the marketing materials to be very professional looking, so I'd like to use your full name."

Oh God. Greer's name in a brochure about Erospace Designs? A brochure sporting a woman in pearls riding on a rocket as the logo? What would *her* family think back in Wisconsin?

They'd never know.

And as for everyone in Charleston finding out she had made her living space her loving space . . . Ford's face popped into her head. What would he think? He'd be long gone, probably, by the time Jill finished decorating. As for her clients, Greer could tell them she was only participating in a consumer research project, which was true.

Her "Working Diva Without a Man" bedroom theme wouldn't be seen by anyone but her. No way, no how. She'd either be too busy setting up Charleston's bachelors with other people or choosing crème brulée over canoodling.

"It's fine," Greer said, and gulped down the last of her coffee.

"Great," said Jill. "Sign here." She handed Greer a pink pen.

Which Greer found out a second later used pink ink.

Jill leaned forward. "Just you wait. Merely signing this contract means you're making an inner commitment. Your working-diva mojo is brewing. Don't be surprised if your sex life takes off before I even get your room set up."

"Oh, okay," said Greer with a cheerful smile. Inside, she was, um, skeptical, but she'd gladly indulge Jill, who needed someone on her side.

Jill winked and stood. "Ready to go?"

"Sure," said Greer, then froze.

There were Wesley and Serena. In Carmella's. Leaning over the dessert counter and holding hands.

CHAPTER FIVE

Ford was officially Stanford Elliott Wentworth Smythe, Eighth Baron Wickshire. Had he married Teddy, she would have signed her name Theodora Wickshire and been addressed as Lady Wickshire.

TW.

Was it some kind of sick joke that she'd sent him this package? Ford stuffed the negligee back in the box and pushed it under his bed. What was she thinking? Did she want him to regret their split? It wasn't his fault. In fact, he was the innocent party, the one betrayed. Why would she taunt him?

It seemed too hard to believe, which made him consider that perhaps someone else had sent it as some kind of prank.

He pulled it back out, examined the return address. No, it was from Teddy's office in Notting Hill. She tended to do all her personal correspondence on the job. She worked seventy hours a week, and she felt it was no skin off her employer's teeth to take a few moments here and there to pay bills or mail things, or run out to do a little shopping, especially as she was such a success in the commercial real estate world. She brought the company new clients all the time, high fliers impressed by her sales numbers and social cachet.

Teddy was Theodora Dunhill, daughter of Rosemary Dunhill, the Oscar-winning actress beloved by the British people for her many roles highlighting the best of British culture—she'd played Queen Elizabeth I, Elizabeth Bennett, and Virginia Woolf—and Lawrence Bridgeton, who wrote award-winning spy thrillers often turned into award-winning films. The debut actor Rosemary had met Lawrence on the set of his very first novel-turned-into-film—he'd been called in as a consultant to the director. They'd both been in their late twenties, had a whirlwind romance, produced Theodora *aka* Teddy, and split up before she was two, each going on to madly successful careers.

But Teddy had refused to go into the family business. "The entertainment industry is not for me," she had told Ford the first time she met him. "I'm much more fascinated by concrete, glass, and bricks. Hard things." And then she'd squeezed the top of his thigh, almost at the crease of his groin—they were sitting on a sofa at a loud party—which didn't help him leave, as he'd planned to do.

He should have run.

It would be a million years before he got into a serious relationship again. It would have to be with a woman who offered no surprises. And there would be a polygraph test at some point, no matter what.

No. Even a polygraph wasn't enough to salvage his romantic life. He'd rather buy a fleet of motorcycles and be Uncle Ford to his nieces and nephews than put his heart on the line again. He had better things to do.

Teddy's teddy.

She used to say, "Shall I wear a teddy tonight?" every time she was feeling frisky, and he'd throw back an awful pun, usually something like, "Don't bother. *I'll* be wearing Teddy tonight," and she'd laugh with delight.

After the first time, it was never funny, actually. But he went along with it because she so rarely engaged with him that way. Once he wondered if she actually scheduled sex with him into her calendar. He'd never sneak into her phone to confirm that suspicion. But the fact that he'd wondered had set off warning bells in his head about their relationship, which he'd conveniently ignored. To his detriment.

Obviously. Finding out at the altar that one's fiancée was having an affair with one of your groomsmen wasn't exactly life-enhancing.

He had to call her, of course. He was a guy who liked to let things go, but he wasn't a wimp, and he wasn't simply going to accept this act of aggression through the international post without standing up for himself.

He dialed.

"*You*," Teddy said when she picked up. She had a hopeful lilt to her voice.

Uh-oh. "Why'd you send me a package," Ford said. He refused to call it a teddy, and he didn't want it to sound like a question.

"Because I wanted to," she replied.

"Leave me alone, Teddy."

She sighed. "I made a mistake. It's been a wretched month."

"Not as bad as mine."

"Can I come see you?"

"Absolutely not. We're done."

"I got cold feet. Ford, *please*."

"That wasn't cold feet. That was an outright, premeditated setup, and if you had been a better actor, you'd have got away with it. We'd be married now."

She started to cry.

"I'm done," he said. "Sorry, but it's your problem."

"I was an idiot," she said, and gave a gulping sob. "I'm through pretending life is a game. Love *is* real. I've grown up this past month. I truly have. I know what's important."

"I'm glad. Maybe someday you'll find someone right for you. Alastair's not anymore?"

"He never was."

"You had plans to abandon me, take half my assets, and marry him. He told me. I had his head in the toilet."

"I lied to him. Stupid of me. Forgive me, darling. He means nothing to me."

"If I didn't hate him, I'd think he was a poor bastard. So his heart is broken, too."

"He didn't love me."

"Could've fooled me. He betrayed one of his best friends to win you."

"He's too narcissistic to see the big picture," she said. "He means well, and he'll be fine."

"I don't care anymore, honestly," Ford said. "I only called to say, don't do senseless things like sending me your negligee. You say you're done playing games. So am I. From now on, I'm not going to respond. At all. We're finished, and you need to move on."

"Fooooord," she said, and started crying hard. "I'm *pregnant*."

The blood in Ford's head whooshed to his feet, but he stayed standing. The *tick-tick-tick* of the clock on the kitchen counter seemed louder than ever. "You *are*?"

"Y-yes," she whispered. "I've never been pregnant. I'm scared. *Really* scared."

His chest tightened. "Is Alastair the father?"

"I don't know," she said. "You could be."

"How?" He jetted a quiet breath and vowed to remain calm.

"Don't you remember?"

"What?"

"That night you didn't wear protection. At our wedding shower at the Davises' house. In their bathroom."

"Yes, but you reassured me—"

"I *was* protected. Or so I thought." She paused, and he refused to fill the silence. "But I got pregnant anyway. I think . . . I think I needed a new IUD. I know I did, but I was told I had at least a year left on this one." She laughed bitterly. "It's you or him. I'm not sure. Not yet."

His insides felt cold. "When can you get a paternity test?"

She groaned. "Usually early on. But we have a problem. . . ."

"What kind of problem?" His heart ratcheted about his chest.

"Twins," she said, and started to cry again.

"Good lord," he said. *Twins?* "They can tell already?"

"Yes," she replied. "It's not typical to know this early, but they saw two hearts on the ultrasound three weeks ago."

Two hearts. His eyes stung. What if those babies were his children? And what if they weren't? Either way, it was like being run over by a double-decker bus. He cleared his throat. "Why is it a problem to do the test?"

She sighed. "With twins, they can't determine paternity until after the babies are born. It's a long and complicated medical reason, darling, having to do with whether they're fraternal or identical, and their DNA . . . and actually—"

"What?"

"There's the slightest possibility they could have two dads."

Dear God. "When?" he asked her. "When will they be born?" There was a bit of static. "Teddy?"

"I'm here," she said, sounding more far away. "I'm three and a half months along. So sometime around October."

"You were with Alastair that long ago?" He couldn't believe it.

Another silence. "Yes. I felt . . . ignored."

Ignored? That was such—such utter bollocks! Ford's entire body heated with resentment. "I never ignored you, Teddy," he said. "Ever. I won't discuss this further, however, because you're pregnant, and I don't want to cause you or the babies any upset."

"Too late," she said. "I'm very upset." And she set off crying again. "How can I have twins? I can't take care of babies! But when will I ever have a chance to get pregnant again? Maybe never! My clock's ticking. Mummy thinks this is a blessing in disguise."

"Babies are always a blessing," Ford said gruffly.

"It's easy for you to say," she said. "I'll need a nanny, of course. I can't take care of them alone."

"You *will* take care of them. You're strong. You can do it with a nanny, but you will rise to the occasion."

"An eighteen-year occasion!" She sobbed even more. "I need you, Ford! I need you to help me, even if they're not yours. . . ."

The despair in her voice killed him. The panic, too.

"You're my only friend," she said in the quietest, most serious voice she'd ever used with him. "My only *true* friend. And I threw you away."

He couldn't argue with that. It was a very sad situation. His pride had been dented, but he'd get over that. It was more difficult to get past the sheer banality of it all: She'd cheated on him. She'd gotten pregnant. They weren't together.

How many times was this exact same situation happening around the world at that very moment? He wasn't special. He was, in fact, nothing more than a statistic—a predictable one at that.

He'd always thought his life would add up to something more. . . .

"Listen," he said. "I'm not going to discuss *us*. It's off the table. Permanently. But I can listen if you need an ear. And if either of these children—or both—are mine, I will do right by all of you."

"And-and if they're not? If they're Alastair's?"

"Then you'll make sure he carries his weight as well." He hadn't realized it, but he'd sweated through his shirt.

"Okay," she said in a ragged whisper. "I believe in time. Time heals. I can't give up on us yet."

"Stop," he said. "This is the time to think about your own health, and your babies'. Not us. Try to be at peace, as much as is possible." And with a few more soothing words, he was able to get her to stop crying. By the end of their conversation, she'd even laughed about a joke he made about her mother. Only a little one, about Rosemary's tendency to walk slightly sideways, like a crab, when she had too much to drink—but it was something.

Teddy always liked when he joked about her mother. The world took Rosemary way too seriously, according to her daughter, especially now that she was a madly successful women's wear entrepreneur with high-end shops popping up around the U.K.

When Ford hung up, he was drained. The clock said it was happy hour. He could use that drink and cigar. But he really didn't want to have them with Wesley anymore. He texted him that something had come up.

And then he went to FIG, his favorite restaurant, where you could walk in alone and never feel alone at their long bar. It was situated right next to the front door, the kitchen, and the hostess stand. He'd start there with a scotch, then go to his favorite cigar shop on East Bay Street, Charlestowne Tobacco and Wine, grab a chair on the sidewalk, smoke a cigar with like-minded strangers, maybe get a glass of his new favorite Spanish cabernet recommended by the manager there, and watch Charleston walk by.

It was better than moping at home, wondering if he was a father—

Or not. Twice over, at that. Or once, which meant he'd share Daddy duties with Alastair. *Good God.*

He made the scotch at FIG a double.

CHAPTER SIX

"Nooo," said Greer to Jill. They were still in Carmella's but winding things up.

Jill's eyes widened. "You're not changing your mind, are you?"

"There's a couple behind you I don't want to see," Greer whispered.

"Oh." Jill's forehead smoothed. "Can I turn around?"

Greer gave a slight shake of her head. "It's my ex-boyfriend Wesley and his fiancée, Serena."

Jill's eyes widened. "Oh, my God."

"Yeah, they've moved here."

"Where? Downtown? Or Mount Pleasant? I pray for your sake they live on the other side of the Ravenel Bridge."

"I don't know. They're getting married here, too."

"You're *kidding*."

"No. I was hoping not to see them again today. Or to-morrow. Or for that matter, next week. But they'll be here for a year. I found all this out when I ran into them this morning."

"Was it terrible?"

"It was very weird. But I survived."

"This is the hometown boy Ella says you broke up with a few years ago?"

"Yes." Just the mention of the word *hometown* made Greer feel a little sick with guilt.

"I already got the check," said Jill, "so let's go. I'll try to block them from seeing you."

"Thanks." Greer picked up her purse. "They're still looking in the dessert window. Ready?"

"Sure."

Lots of people. Loud voices. Movement. It was all a blur to Greer as she wended her way through tables. One whole wall to the sidewalk was already folded back, European style, bringing the outdoors into Carmella's. Adrenaline rushed through her. She'd make her escape this time.

"Greer!"

Or not.

Her heart smashed against her ribs. Why did Wesley have to do that twice in one day? Call her from behind like that? She used to love it when they were in high school, and she was walking down the hall, and she'd hear him call her name. She'd turn around and her heart would nearly burst with joy.

She exchanged a rapid-fire glance with Jill. *Sorry*, Jill's expression said.

Greer turned. Once again, Wesley and Serena were coming toward her, hand in hand. They'd changed clothes. She couldn't help wondering if they'd fooled around back at their hotel or wherever they were staying when they'd changed (and probably showered, after the humid, hot day they'd had). It was tacky and rude of her to wonder, but some imp on her shoulder goaded her.

She wasn't at all jealous that Serena and Wesley were

no doubt spending time together between the sheets. Looking at him, it was hard to believe she'd ever been intimate with him, not just in the back of his truck and in his parents' guesthouse but in general. She couldn't imagine leaning on him now, gazing into his eyes, and laughing. Brushing the hair out of his face. Kissing him.

Now that she was older and more confident, Wesley wasn't the type of lover she craved. She wasn't quite sure who her ideal lover would be, but she was ready to find out.

They made some quick small talk. She introduced Jill.

"How about going bar-hopping with us?" Serena asked.

"We could catch up on Waterloo news," Wesley said to Greer.

Greer thought as fast as she could . . . she had to come up with an excuse not to go.

Jill put her arm through hers. "I wish we could go, but we already have a commitment down the street. A trunk show I promised to attend at a little boutique a friend of mine owns. Free champagne. It's actually the annual Spring Stroll shopping tour."

"That's right," Greer said, so relieved. "Sorry."

Wesley's hopeful expression dropped.

"Sounds fun," Serena said. "Maybe afterward you can join us."

"We can always try," Greer said.

"We'll be hanging out pretty late tonight," said Wesley. "We don't have any appointments until noon tomorrow."

"Great," said Jill.

Not great, thought Greer.

That closeness she'd had with Wesley seemed like it had happened in a different lifetime to another person. And that was okay, except that part of her felt sad . . . as if her time with him had been a waste. What had it done for her? Did it mean anything?

Maybe someday she'd figure it out, but these days she was content in Charleston. Sure, she was starting from scratch, and it was exciting and scary, both personally and professionally. Nor was it perfect. But it was so much more *her*.

They said their good-byes once again—it was a very light one on Serena's part because the understanding was that surely they'd run into each other later that evening—and Greer and Jill took off in the opposite direction from the lovebirds.

"Is there really a trunk show?" Greer said low when they were fifty feet away from Carmella's.

"Yes," said Jill. "Let's check it out. It's actually part of a shopping round robin downtown. Five other boutiques are participating. They're all serving wine and snacks until nine tonight."

"Great." She paused. "Maybe. I hope one of them isn't La Di Da."

"It is. The ad was in the paper." Jill named all the shops involved. "Why?"

Greer shrugged. "Oh, nothing. I'm just not crazy about Pierre."

"You *know* him?"

"I do." She wouldn't tell her he'd been a client of Two Love Lane. That was confidential.

"I went in there once," said Jill, "and it was like he was king of Charleston. All these out-of-town customers were fawning over him."

"Yep. He laps it up."

"Well, I'm not planning on going around to all of them. Just this first boutique. They have some new late-season swimwear I want to see."

"Sounds good to me."

They crossed East Bay Street and were preparing to go down Cumberland when a cry of "Greer! Jill!" rang behind them.

For Greer, hearing that voice was like being taken back to her days on the farm, when a particularly naughty goose named Matilda would sneak up behind her and honk, sending her straight up into the air.

"Good God," whispered Jill. "That was loud."

Serena waved and smiled and walked briskly toward them. "Guess who Wesley and I ran into?" she said when she got close.

"Who?" Greer asked, knowing full well. Who else did Serena, Wesley, and Greer have in common apart from Ford?

"Ford," Serena said, and grinned. "He was sitting across the street from Carmella's, about half a block down, smoking a cigar on the sidewalk with some other guys. Wesley wanted to join them, so I said I'd catch up with you, if that's all right, and we can all meet later."

Thunk, went Greer's stomach. She didn't want sweet, kind Serena with them. She didn't want to party with Wesley later, either. But she *did* want to see Ford.

And part of her didn't want to see him—the nervous part that wondered if she should have taken a shower before she came out tonight. And if she had known she was staying out, she definitely would have worn something a little nicer.

"Let's go," Greer said with a smile. She was such a fake.

Serena skipped forward in her cute little silver flats. "We'll have fun," she said, and fell into stride beside Jill.

Greer, in her scuffed white Keds, tried not to believe that she was getting some sort of comeuppance she deserved. But maybe this was what happened when you broke up with someone out of the blue and moved on with your life—or tried to.

"This is going to be great," Jill said, and Greer could tell she was secretly saying that Greer would be okay.

And she would. She could handle being with Serena, and she'd even have a good time. They turned the corner onto State Street and went down to North Market and found the little boutique. The trunk show had already started. They slid into seats in the back row next to a tray of plastic champagne flutes filled with pink bubbly. Serena sat between Jill and Greer.

"This looks fun," Serena said. "I'm looking for outfits for my trousseau. We're going to Paris and then Florence on our honeymoon."

Ack. "What a great trip," said Greer.

"Lovely," murmured Jill, but not in an unfriendly manner. She was focusing on two super-sexy bathing suits the hostess was holding up for everyone to see: little strips of jewel-toned Lycra held together by gold rings.

They were saved from further conversation by a woman coming by. "Here you go," she whispered, then handed them each a Spring Stroll flyer and put her finger to her lips in the universal shushing sign.

Thank God for that. Greer wouldn't have to make more small talk. She drank her entire flute of champagne and signaled to Jill to pass her another one. All three of them took a second glass, touched the edges, and mouthed a silent *cheers.*

Serena was perfectly lovely, drinking and saying nothing, except occasionally oohing and aahing over certain clothes being modeled. It was odd for Greer to see her old engagement ring flash over and over in front of her eyes, but she wasn't bothered by that so much as curious that Serena didn't seem to care. Was it actually that Serena cared very much—and was trying to make Greer feel bad? Highly doubtful. Greer was an excellent judge of character. She could recognize a charlatan from a mile away. It was much more likely that Serena was a genuinely humble person who believed in recycling and wasn't even thinking about the fact that Greer, whom she'd chased down the street to hang out with, was her fiancé's old flame.

If it was the second scenario, then Serena was a way better person than Greer, and Greer should make her her best friend.

"How about another round?" Greer whispered to Jill. "These flutes are tiny."

Jill nodded and tried to pass one to Serena, who declined politely. Jill and Greer kept drinking, until Greer's phone vibrated. She looked down. It was the girls out in L.A.! She made her excuses and crept out the front door to talk out on the sidewalk.

"Hold your horses," said Ella.

"What?" Greer gripped her phone tighter. Her heart was thumping.

"Miss Thing got on TV," Ella went on, her voice strangely quivering.

"And . . . ?"

"And she won. She won the whole thing."

"Wait," said Greer, and started walking in circles. "What are you saying? She won the showcase?"

Ella started laughing. "Yes, but not only that—she's a *double showcase winner.* She guessed ninety dollars lower than the actual value of her showcase! So she won both. She's only the second contestant this year to do that!"

Greer stopped walking. Little tears came to her eyes. "Please, Ella," she said. "Please tell me she won an RV."

There was a short pause. "Her angel husband must be watching over her from Heaven," said Ella. "Greer . . . *she won an RV.*"

Greer shrieked.

"And a trip to Spain," Ella said. "Oh, and some other stuff, like a full set of kitchen appliances. Our Miss Thing hit the jackpot."

Greer laughed and wiped tears at the same time. "You're not kidding me?"

"No." Ella was crying and laughing, too. "Hey, someone's got to win now and then. I'm just glad it was Miss Thing."

"Where is she now?"

"She and Macy are in the bathroom at this gas station we stopped at for gas and some Icees."

"Icees?"

"I don't know what we're doing. We're on a high. Miss Thing got a craving for a Coca-Cola Icee on the way home from the studio. She had to sign a lot of papers before we left. We're all hungry and tired, but no way are we going to go to sleep tonight. Not for a long time. We're heading out to Hollywood to have some fun."

"I'm so glad! I wish I were there!"

"We do, too. That's one reason I'm calling. Miss Thing told me to tell you she's already set up an open bar tab at The Rooftop. She wants you to use it. You and any friends you want to invite out. She wants you to blow it out, Greer. Seriously."

The Rooftop was a popular rooftop bar a few blocks away on the harbor. It had spectacular views of Fort Sumter to the east and the city of Charleston with its church steeples to the west. Sunsets up there were glorious. There was often a stiff breeze since it was a stone's throw from the Atlantic, and cocktail napkins had to be anchored with a heavy drink.

"I will," said Greer, "in her honor. And I can't wait! I'm with your little sister, by the way."

"Oh, good," Ella said. "Tell her hello for me. And take pictures."

"I will. And you do the same. *Lots* of pictures. Talk to you soon."

"Wait a sec," Ella said. "There's something Miss Thing wants to tell you. She's grabbing the phone."

"Hey, darlin'." Miss Thing sounded like she always did, unruffled and warm as honey on a biscuit.

"I can't believe it! I'm so proud of you!" Greer said.

"Thank you," Miss Thing said in her demure way.

"I thought you'd be giddy."

"I am," drawled Miss Thing, "but it's the kind of giddiness that comes when you realize how little we hope for and yet how much is really possible. I feel silly that I've walked through life pulling in the reins instead of galloping."

"Well, you galloped this week in L.A."

"That I did. And I want you girls to start way younger than I have. So you'd better do something crazy before we come home. You need to have a story to tell us. I don't want any of you turning fifty like me and having regrets."

"What did they put in that Icee of yours?" Greer asked.

"Not a damned thing but Coca-Cola," said Miss Thing. "Don't try to change the subject."

"All right." Greer smiled. Miss Thing was always looking out for them. "Love you, you double showcase winner."

"Love you, too, sweetie."

Greer hung up and let herself laugh for a minute. She probably looked like a crazy person, laughing all by herself and not even on the phone. And it had nothing to do with the little buzz she already had from the champagne.

No, she was laughing about life, how strange and wonderful it could be! She was happy that Miss Thing was happy. So off to The Rooftop she would go, with a light heart. Maybe she'd see Ford again. But it could be he wouldn't want to tag along. She could imagine him telling Wesley and Serena he had other commitments, which would be disappointing. She really didn't want to hang out with Wesley and Serena without Ford there acting as a buffer, but she couldn't just make up an excuse and go home. Miss Thing had inspired her to go out and celebrate. How often did friends follow their dreams, crazy as some of those dreams might be? Miss Thing was brave and fun. Greer intended to be the same.

The trifold Spring Stroll flyer from the boutique was stuffed haphazardly in her purse. When she pulled it out to tuck her phone into a side pocket, her eye was caught by a picture on a single leaflet stuffed into it as an afterthought.

And then she gave another little shriek—two in one day!—which was so unlike her. Her arms trembled. She stared and stared at the picture. It was a photo of that morning's wedding gown Pierre had won at the auction, hanging on a mannequin at La Di Da.

"Oh, my God," she murmured.

Attention, all future brides on the Spring Stroll! the leaflet said, *La Di Da is going into the bridalwear business. Our new bridalwear department, La Di Da Bridal, will premiere this fall. Help celebrate our great news by entering our contest to win this magnificent designer*

bridal gown with an illustrious royal history and roman-
tic story attached. Entries capped at twenty. First-come,
first serve. Sign-ups start at the store tonight . . . we're
extending our Spring Stroll hours to 11 P.M.! Contest
details can be found on the store Web site. Some terms
and conditions apply.

Jill poked her head out the door of the boutique. "Are you coming back in?" she said brightly.

Greer tried to pull herself together. "I don't know," she said, and merely stood there, the leaflet in her hand.

Jill's expression changed to concern. "What happened?" She came all the way out and shut the door gently behind her.

Greer wouldn't mention the dress. She didn't think she could discuss it rationally at the moment. Her heart and mind were both racing. "It's great news, actually."

"Really? You look upset."

Greer shook her head. "No, really, I'm okay. It's about Miss Thing."

"Wait." Jill's mouth dropped open. "She got called to 'Come on down'?' "

"Yes. In a big way."

Jill's face drained of color. "What do you mean?"

Greer gave her the details. "It's so unreal, I'm just kind of in shock."

"She's actually a double showcase winner?" Jill's eyes were huge.

"Yes." Greer grinned. "This calls for a major celebration. She says she's opened a tab for me and all my friends at The Rooftop."

"I still can't believe it," Jill said.

"Me, neither."

Jill laughed. "There's no way you can sit still through the rest of a trunk show now. Can you?"

"Absolutely not." Jill didn't need to know she was feeling terribly mixed-up. Happy for Miss Thing, and angry at Pierre. Miserable that such a gorgeous dress was in his hands. Wistful and jealous that another woman would win it, with its charmed beads and beautiful love story.

But happy for Miss Thing. *That* was what she'd focus on.

Jill went back to the door. "I'll get Serena."

"Okay." Greer opened the solitary leaflet again. It must have been printed at the last minute. Pierre's words came back to her about how his revenge would be swift.

Boy, he was right.

He wouldn't expect that she'd know what he'd done. Would he? But wasn't that the whole point? That she'd know and be upset?

She thought about it. There was no way he'd have known she'd go on the Spring Stroll. Something clicked in her head then and gave her a very bad feeling. She looked down at her phone. Sure enough, there was a text from Pierre: *Check our Web site*, was all it said.

The loser.

She'd put her phone on vibrate during the trunk show and had caught Ella's phone call but not his text. Maybe it had come in while she was talking to Ella. She'd been distracted by the news about Miss Thing and never would have noticed.

She had no doubt the La Di Da Web site sported a splashy announcement about the dress giveaway.

Greer had to go look at the gown up close. It would be her only chance. She didn't even care that Pierre would probably be there.

Her throat constricted when she remembered she was with Serena. She didn't want to see the dress with her, or even with Jill. She wanted to go on her own. *Royal Bliss* represented her Perfect Wedding dreams, and those dreams were fragile. Sweet. Her dreams were about romantic love—nothing like the no-nonsense partnership her parents shared. And that was why no one could come with her. Tangled up in her wedding fantasies was a thin wisp of sadness that her parents didn't seem to have the kind of soul-mate relationship she wanted and wouldn't stop believing in.

One time. She had to see *Royal Bliss* one more time, and she didn't care if she had to walk by Pierre to do it. In fact, that would give her tremendous satisfaction. She wouldn't be cowed by a small-minded businessman who sought silly revenge on her.

If she wanted a wedding dress in her closet when she didn't have a partner, that was *her* business. Even if she couldn't have this one, she could stand up for single women everywhere who wanted love in their lives and thumb her nose at Pierre by showing up, unafraid of his scorn.

Or she could just ignore him and his text, of course. He was baiting her. But when she contemplated walking away, she realized the dress had woven its magic on her. She had to go.

Jill came out and said Serena was actually purchasing a couple of skirts and a bathing suit to be shipped to her later, so it would be a few minutes.

"No problem," Greer said. "I'll see you both at The Rooftop when she's done. If you get there first, put whatever you get on Miss Thing's tab. I have to grab my bike. It's still chained near Carmella's. I'm going to ride it home and take a cab back." Which was true. But she was also going to make a secret stop at La Di Da first to look at the dress.

Jill gave her a thumbs-up and went back inside.

Greer took a deep breath. She could do this. She

started walking to Carmella's. Once she got there, she crouched near her bike's front wheel to unlock it, but she felt the back of her neck tingle. She twisted to look up. The setting sun made it hard to see.

"Fancy meeting you here," said a silhouette.

She'd recognize that English voice anywhere. Her heart surged unexpectedly. Not a good sign.

CHAPTER SEVEN

Ford knew Greer Jones was the queen of yens. It was a quirky word, like her. She came across as put together and cool, but beneath her seamless style he saw a goddess of fire and storm. She clearly had guarded passions. It was in her eyes. But he saw past the protectiveness, past the stoicism, to something that made the breath catch in his throat. It was her soul, and it *wanted*.

What did she want?

He wasn't sure, but she moved him. And he wished to paint her. Desperately.

Even had he not been a purveyor of gazes, her body language gave her away. She was controlled in her movements, but he sensed she longed to fling herself at life.

She looked up at him and smiled. "Hi."

When she spoke, he felt the way he did when he climbed the mast of his boat and took in the curvature of the earth. "I see you're leaving," he said. He didn't want her to.

She finished unlocking the bike and stood. "I'm coming back. I have to stop somewhere briefly on my way home, and then I'm meeting my friend Jill and Serena and Wesley at The Rooftop. Serena said they'd try to get you to come, too."

If she wanted him there, too, she was very good at hiding it.

"My bike's right around the corner," he said. "May I ride with you?"

She shifted her stance from one foot to the other. "I do have to stop somewhere," she said again.

"Right, well, if I'll be in the way. . . ." He waved a hand at her. "There was something I wanted to ask you about, that's all. It can wait."

"Oh," she said, committing to nothing.

"See you later." He put his hands in his front pockets and backed away. "At The Rooftop."

"Okay." She tugged on her ear. "Your bike is really close? Go ahead and grab it and come with me," she said. "But I'm going to go fast so I don't keep people waiting. I've been given the gift of an open bar tab at The Rooftop by my friend, Miss Thing, for me to share with my friends. She just won on *The Price Is Right.*"

He laughed. "The game show? We've had a British version of it off and on. I think it's on again, actually."

"Yes. And she won big. Free drinks for you tonight."

"I'm a lucky man." Then he remembered his manners. "To share your company as much as to get a free drink, of course."

"Good catch." She laughed.

He grinned back.

Their bike ride was just as light. For a minute or two, they rode silently while they traveled East Bay Street. But once they hit a side street, they chatted about the heat, the afternoon thunderstorms that came every summer, and the local minor league baseball team. Neither one of them had been to a game. They were talking about Bill Murray,

Charleston's favorite celebrity resident, when they coasted to a stop in front of a store called La Di Da. It had two massive display windows. Through one of them, he could see a small crowd inside sipping wine. They appeared to be listening intently to an older woman holding up a pink satin gown on a hanger and gesturing with her free hand.

"I only wanted to see this," said Greer, standing in front of the other window. It had three dresses displayed on headless mannequins. She was looking at the one in the middle, the only bridal gown. The other two were cocktail dresses.

He recognized it. "Bloody hell, it's the gown from this morning. *That* was fast. Already in a shop window."

"Yes, very fast." It was as if he weren't even there. She had a small, tender smile on her face. She looked. And looked. Suddenly, she seemed to remember his presence. "Sorry. I had to see it. At this trunk show I attended with Serena, there was a photo of it on a leaflet stuffed into a flyer, and it said it was here at Pierre's shop. He's the man from the auction who won the dress."

"He was a strange fellow. I wondered if he had a vocal cord injury."

"No," she said. "Nothing of the sort. He simply likes to speak quietly so he's in control of the conversation. He told me himself." She pulled the leaflet out of her purse and handed it to him.

Ford looked down at the picture and back up. "He's giving it away in a contest?"

She nodded.

" 'To a future bride,' " Ford read from the flyer.

"Correct." She looked over her ivory frames at him and smiled. "And yes, I'm still not getting married. But I wanted to see it again."

He grinned back. "Clearly, this dress is more than an investment to you. I was right this morning, wasn't I?"

She shrugged. "I kind of fell in love with its story."

She was such an American. Bold. Charming.

And he'd be very English and not pry any further. Oh, what the hell—he would. "I understand from Serena and Wesley that you turned down his marriage proposal at one time, and he didn't see it coming."

"That's true. Does it bother you? Particularly as you've been left at the altar?"

"No." He shrugged. "Totally different people, different circumstances. But I'm intrigued that you're so interested in a wedding dress. I can't help wondering why. It must mean . . . you *like* marriage."

"To the right person," she said. "That's the key."

He handed her back the leaflet. "Well, you've still got great taste." It had the look of couture: simple yet elegant. He could see why she was smitten with it. "Shall we go inside and ask about it?"

"No need. I only wanted a look."

"Come on."

"Nah. Pierre texted me that he was doing this. He's hoping I'll show up tonight so he can gloat. I'm actually surprised he didn't put the dress inside so I'd be forced to walk past him to look at it."

"It's too valuable in a historic sense, I'm sure, to display on the floor."

"True." She looked around and then saw the camera on the roof edge. "Hi, Pierre." She waved. Then blew a kiss. "There. That will satisfy him."

"Well done," Ford said.

She looked up at the window again, and he could see her swallow. "Let's head to my place," she said. "I'll

change, and then we'll take a cab back to The Rooftop."
She hesitated.

"Or I can leave you here and meet you at The Rooftop in a little while," he said, to let her off the hook.

She tossed him a sheepish smile. "Maybe that's the best idea." She hopped on her bike again. "Wait. Didn't you say you wanted to ask me about something?"

Yes, he *did* want to ask her something! "It can wait," he said. "I'll see you at the bar."

"Okay." She waved, threw one last glance at the gown in the window, and took off.

He liked the look of her pedaling away from him on the bike. She was toned, sexy, and athletic.

And he might be a father to one or two children, and he didn't want to be with their mother, and his life had spiraled out of control.

He wasn't ready to be a father. He was a bachelor used to a bachelor's ways. Children—well, he wouldn't know what to do with them. Especially Teddy's children . . . he imagined them spoiled. Petulant.

He wished he could talk to someone about Teddy's pregnancy. Anne was the obvious choice of confidantes. But he didn't want to stress her. He would wait for the actual news. And then he would figure out what to do. Anne would advise him.

He lived right around the corner, so he put his bike inside the house. Drake and Gus were out surfing, but they'd left the kitchen a wreck. He pretended he didn't see the open pizza box and empty cartons of chocolate milk (Drake's favorite nonalcoholic beverage), and changed into a black Led Zeppelin T-shirt and khaki shorts.

He loved being the Average Joe in America. In London, he got tired of the pressure to play the role of baron wherever he went. So after he'd made advance arrangements for studio space and bought his plane ticket to Charleston, he'd decided to leave everything but his passport and credit cards behind. When he'd arrived, he'd checked into an airport hotel for a week and rented a car. He'd gone shopping for a few clothes at a local mall, bought toiletries at a drugstore, found his apartment downtown, raided an art store for supplies, and after moving in to his tiny bedroom in the flat, spent most of his time at the studio.

He had ninety days to be there. Then by law he must leave the United States, which was a huge reason he wanted to see Greer at The Rooftop.

The clock was ticking.

The Rooftop was a popular place. Ford had spent the last hour talking to Wesley and Serena, then to Jill and some of her friends, and a few strangers who'd sailed a catamaran up from Miami and were docked at the city marina, but he'd yet to speak to Greer. She was floating around, drinking, laughing, and occasionally taking selfies and videos on her phone to send to California, where a party was also going on with her three friends from Two Love Lane.

When he finally bumped into her, she reminded him to put his drinks on her friend Miss Thing's tab. She was on her way to a good buzz, judging from her flushed cheeks. "Today my mother yelled at me for not being married," she said.

"You're kidding."

"No. She was mad I broke up with Wesley."

"I'm sorry." But he really wasn't sorry. He was glad she was single.

She shrugged. "Now that I've talked too much, tell me about you. I get the impression you're all about art."

"I am."

"I admire that," she said. "A *lot*." She tossed him a pretty smile.

He'd had more than his fair share of one-night stands based on a woman's fantasy of hooking up with a bohemian, Picasso-type. But he actually wanted her to be impressed, didn't he? He wanted to paint her for the Manchester art show. She was the subject he'd been looking for: an American woman of spirit and beauty. But he was looking for more, too, something he couldn't pin down yet. He liked to discover it as he painted. For him, that was where true artistry lay, in overcoming the gap of mystery that existed between the painter and his subject.

"I just hope you're *good*," she went on. "There's nothing worse than seeing someone give up everything for art, and then come to find out, they're not talented." She paused. "Oops. I shouldn't have said that."

He couldn't help but chuckle. "You've separated yourself from my pack of adoring fans already. It's refreshing."

She laughed. "Well, if you need a patron, Charleston is the place to come for one. There are some very well-off art lovers here who might be willing to help you financially if you're struggling at all. Just say the word, and I'll call some people."

The noise level was rising.

"Let's talk over here." He took her by the elbow—she came along with no protest, and he suddenly felt very protective of her—and walked her to a bench. They both sat down. Her skirt rode up to expose a tantalizing bit of thigh, and she tugged it down.

"Your offer is very kind," he said.

"It would be my pleasure," she said back, and then looked away.

"Is something on your mind?" he asked.

Reluctantly, she looked back. "I don't like to gossip."

"Neither do I. Unless it's with someone I trust." He grinned. "Then all bets are off."

She hesitated, then said, "It's a little awkward for me with Wesley and Serena in town." She stole a quick glance to the left. "Oops. Serena's watching us right now."

He did see. "She's like a sweet puppy who becomes a giant and knocks down all the buildings in New York. You can't hate the giant puppy. Or fire missiles at it. Or get helicopters to drop a net on it."

They both grinned.

"She has a vulnerability I can't put my finger on," Greer said. "It allows me to forgive her for being so peppy."

"You're pretty perceptive. She does."

"What is it?"

"She didn't have an easy childhood."

"Really?" She winced. "I feel bad now."

"Don't. We all have our issues, and it's up to us to work through them. For your own sake, you really don't want to get mixed up in their business. They could see it as your showing undue interest in Wesley again."

"I didn't think of that." And then she did. "Oh, gosh, that would be terrible. I'm not at all interested in him."

Ford chuckled. "Why don't we prove it to him? Just in case he thinks you have any lingering regrets."

"How?"

"I could kiss you. Right now."

Her face brightened. "You know what? It may be immature of me to say yes, but okay. Let's do it."

And so he wrapped his arms around her, having no idea he was about to step straight off a proverbial cliff into an abyss of deep, maddening desire, the kind barons of old must have had for their most favored, ballbusting mistresses, at least according to the historical romance novels Anne wrote.

CHAPTER EIGHT

Greer hadn't been kissed in a long time, and now she was kissing someone when her ex-boyfriend was nearby. Tacky. Totally tacky. Except that all day she'd had to endure Wesley and Serena's cute couple-ness, right?

And this kiss was too good to turn down. The heat level was so off the charts, it made no sense. She'd have to find a rational reason for it later. Meanwhile, needs were needs. They trumped logic every time.

She couldn't help little moans escaping her throat. Ford What's-His-Name—what *was* his last name?—knew how to kiss. She put her hands on the back of his neck, beneath his waves of silky hair, and caressed warm skin over taut muscle and tendon with her fingertips. She was glad she'd only recently buffed her nails. His lipwork somehow got even better in response, and he took some liberties with his tongue that were way beyond first-kiss caliber.

She loved every second of it.

A makeout session at The Rooftop. Who ever thought Greer Jones would participate in such a public display of affection? Although she couldn't really say affection . . . she liked Ford a lot, but she didn't know why and didn't want to examine why. True affection had to come from someplace deeper, a place where you were willing to go, and the object of your affection had to prove himself worthy of that feeling.

It would be more accurate to say she lusted after Ford. That was it.

Finally, they both pulled back—it was during a kiss that slid off into nothing, one of those that went from sheer exuberance to sexual frustration because they'd reached the limits of what they could do without getting arrested. They were both sort of panting.

Greer looked up. She couldn't see Serena or Wesley. Jill, on the other hand, shot her a wink from across the rooftop.

"I have a proposition for you," he said.

"I can guess what it might be," she murmured, propping her chin on her hand, her elbow on the tabletop. She was thankful Jill hadn't installed the "Working Diva Without a Man" theme yet in her bedroom.

"It's not *that*," he said. "Although don't get me wrong. I'd love to. You're beautiful. Fun. Sexy."

She grinned. "Wow, thanks."

"Which is why. . . ."

She leaned forward. "What?"

"I'd love to paint you," Ford said.

"*Me?*" She couldn't believe it.

"Yes, you."

Her mind was blown. "But . . . why?"

"All I know is that I get a feeling, and if I can't shake it, I go for it. I paint whoever or whatever inspires me to get to the easel. Usually by the time I'm done, some wrinkle has been smoothed out in my psyche. But I never know what it's going to be."

She was still tongue-tied.

"So, what do you think?" His face was alight with enthusiasm. "It would require a commitment. Painting a portrait is time consuming."

She felt mixed up inside. "I don't know."

"You want to look at my Web site first, and then get back to me?" he asked.

"It sounds amazing," she said, "but I'm busy. I have to stay super-organized to be able to carry off what I do at Two Love Lane. I don't have time to . . . to pose for a portrait. It sounds like something from olden times."

"It's true you have to make time. And you don't move around."

"I don't know if I could handle that."

He lifted his palms and dropped them. "From the first moment I saw you at the coffee shop this morning, I wanted to paint you."

"You saw me there?"

"Yes. And I followed you to the auction."

"Oh, my God," she said, her hand on her heart.

"I'm not a stalker," he said. "I'm a painter. And there was something about you . . ."

She laughed. "I suppose I'm flattered. But then you left me at the auction."

"You weren't exactly tuned into me. You were more into royal artifacts." He paused. "My bad, as you say here in America, for backing down."

"I'll grant you that I wasn't in the mood to talk. But then you saw me again, and didn't ask then, either."

"But we were with Wesley and Serena. I should have got your number, but it was an uncomfortable situation."

"To say the least."

"I knew where you worked—you told me yourself at

the auction—and I decided to go see you there. But I didn't have to. We met up tonight. Sheer luck."

She lofted a brow. "The question is, what kind of luck—good or bad?"

"As yet to be determined," he said, and leaned closer. "I didn't plan that kiss. Honestly. But it worked, didn't it? You looked busy and happy and completely over Wesley."

"True. For a deflection strategy, it worked well. And it happened to be really, really good." She drained her glass. Her heart was beating super-fast.

"I thought so, too," he said.

A beat of silence passed, a thoughtful silence. Greer was thinking about sex. And portraits. She suspected Ford was, too.

"What do you think?" he asked her. "Will you say yes? This painting will go in a show in Manchester, England. An important one."

Pierre's gloating over winning the wedding gown, *The Price Is Right*, Miss Thing's speech about taking risks, the shock of seeing Wesley, Serena's adorableness, Ford's hot-as-hell kiss . . . all of it conspired to give Greer an idea that would qualify as Miss Thing's requirement for her to "do something crazy."

She took out her phone. Fiddled with it.

"What are you doing?" he asked her.

"Turning this into an opportunity."

"How so?"

She looked up. "I have fifteen minutes to get to La Di Da and sign up in the contest to win that dress. I could go without you, but in case Pierre challenges me, I'd like you there, please. As a friend."

"I'm not following your logic. You're not getting married. At the auction you said this dress was only an investment opportunity. But now you want it so badly? Why?"

"Because the heart wants what it wants," she said. "You get that. You want *me*. At least as a painting subject. And you can't explain it, right?"

"True, but I'm still not sure about this contest idea."

"I'm a future bride," she said. "The contest description never said I actually had to have a partner at this point in time to enter."

"Wait a minute . . . give me that leaflet again." He reread it and looked up. "You're right. You should have been a lawyer."

"Being logical is a strong point for me."

"This isn't logical. This is you following a yen. How many women pursue wedding gowns when they have no partner?"

"Just go to Pinterest and see," she said. "Plenty of women have their entire weddings planned out before they find true love. It's a thing."

"That's a thing?"

"Sure! So while I do me—with you as my supportive friend by my side, because this is going to be a little daunting—you can do *you* and paint me. I'll get half an hour of support from you tonight. And who knows how many hours of posing you'll get from me. I'll pose as long as it takes for you to finish, if you can be flexible about my schedule."

"I'm going to need to work fast. So I might be demanding of your time. I'm not sure that I can be entirely flexible."

"Okay, so we'll meet in the middle. Because to tell you the truth, Ford, I'm not sure how much work this contest will entail, either. I'm going to enter as a partnerless bride, but I might need some rabble-rousers cheering me on in the background. Are you in?"

"I'm in," he said.

They shook on it.

CHAPTER NINE

Feeling Greer's palm against his own when they shook hands made Ford think of making mad, hot love to her.

"A cab driver will be waiting outside in one minute," she said. "We could walk to La Di Da, but then I'd only have a few minutes to sign up. I'd rather play it safe."

She said a quick good-bye to her friend Jill, who brazenly eyed him from head to toe and whispered in his ear: "I'll come for you if you hurt her."

"Are you joking?" he whispered back. "She's tough as nails. Haven't you noticed?"

She merely glowered at him.

And then they headed down several flights of stairs.

"Nice girl, Jill," he said. "She just threatened me."

Greer waved a hand. "Oh, her family's from Sicily."

"Right, so that makes it okay," he said dryly.

"She doesn't mean it," Greer said. "She's got a heart of gold."

"As long as she doesn't give me feet of concrete and drop me off the Ravenel Bridge, we should get along."

Greer stopped. "Mafia jokes aren't nice."

"My apologies. Why did the painter cross the road?"

"I don't know."

"To see from the other side."

"That wasn't very funny."

But he'd diffused her pique. Her cheeks were extra pink. At the curb, he said, "What if they ask us how we got engaged? We can say we met in London at one of my shows. You were on a business trip."

"You don't have to pretend to be my fiancé, remember? You're coming as my friend."

"Are you sure? You can wear my signet ring and I'll pretend it's a temporary engagement ring until the one I'm getting designed in London shows up."

"Nope. But thanks." She peeked at the ring. "It's very distinguished looking."

"A classy old gent who took pity on me gifted it to me. Said to look at it and remember honor."

"He sounds nice. What's your last name?"

"Smith."

"A very common name here in the States," she said.

"Fancy that."

"Haven't you ever felt something important was happening, but you weren't sure what or why? Like all the owls gathering outside Harry Potter's house?"

"No." He had, of course. But why share?

"Well, I got that feeling tonight at La Di Da. When I saw the wedding dress. Actually, it happened the first time I saw it this morning, too."

"I'm never one to question a woman's intuition."

"Good," she said.

The car arrived, and they got in. For a moment, the silence was deafening.

She shot him a wry smile. "I do appreciate your coming with me."

"It requires very little effort on my part." And he *was*

glad. Every once in a while, the memory of Teddy's news intruded upon his conscious thoughts, and the stress of it made his chest feel as if it had bands around it, cinching him tight. This situation was a welcome distraction.

"We'll fill out the entry form, stuff it into a box, and that will be that," she said.

"Good."

Her knees were pressed together, and her hands clasped in her lap. "It's a long shot," she said, "but any chance to win this dress is better than none at all."

"If you don't win it, can't you buy another? I know they cost a bomb, but—"

"I have the money to buy one, but no. It has to be this one."

"What if you can order a duplicate?"

"No. It has to be the one in the window. It's the one with the amazing beads with a spell attached to them. I felt something there. It must mean something."

"I'll take your word for it."

She paused. "I admit, this whole thing is crazy. Including agreeing to pose for you."

"Things are rather mad at the moment," he said. "But I'm looking forward to painting you."

"I'm chasing an impulse," she said. "With very little chance of succeeding. That's not like me."

"I'm taking risks, too," he said. "We won't be working under my usual conditions. Time is far too short."

"Did your wedding cancellation break your heart?" she asked out of the blue.

"It rather did," he didn't hesitate to say. "But not because my fiancée and groomsman were disloyal. That was difficult, but there's something else. I'm still trying to figure out why the whole tawdry affair cut me off at the knees. It's why I'm here in Charleston. I need a new perspective."

"Has coming here helped?" She had a genuine look of concern in her eyes.

"So far, no revelations," he said. "But it *has* given me breathing room."

The car rolled up to La Di Da. They both thanked the cab driver. When they got out, the air was warm and humid, but there was a slight breeze coming down the street, rounding the rooftops, from off the harbor. If he craned his neck, Ford could see a half moon above a tall palmetto tree on the corner.

According to Greer, the stores on the Spring Stroll shopping tour were open until nine P.M., but Pierre had extended his store hours until eleven. It was definitely winding down. Only two shoppers were browsing inside.

At the door, she held out her right hand. "Thanks for being here," she said.

"Glad to be of service," he replied, and clasped it. He was once again surprised how good it felt to hold her fingers in his. He tugged her toward the door, then let go of her to open it.

That didn't last long enough, he thought. She ducked under his arm, and a whiff of her citrus scent activated a more primitive part of his brain. *More, more, more.* He could feel it thrumming in his temples, his limbs, his groin, making him crazy with the need to get close to her, to kiss her again, to have her beneath him.

But he was a civilized male, for God's sake. He needed to keep his lusty thoughts in check. He crossed the plush carpet of the distinctly feminine shop behind Greer.

An older woman in a lilac dress and expensive-looking sage green paisley scarf greeted them. Her name was

Henny, and she wore glasses on a beaded chain. "You're here to enter the contest?" She looked at Greer.

"Yes." A faint pink tinged Greer's cheeks.

"You made it just in time." Henny had a melodious Lowcountry accent.

Greer picked up a pen and started writing. She looked as innocent as a kitten held by a nun in church. Ford knew better. "I'm so glad we made it," she said. "Is Mr. Simons here?"

"He left for the evening," Henny said. "I'm holding down the fort."

"Lucky you," Ford said.

"I don't mind." Henny smiled. "I've gotten to meet some lovely brides-to-be. We're nearly at our cap, and we're sure to reach it tomorrow, probably as soon as we open. So good thing you made it."

"How many spaces are left?" Greer asked.

Henny held up two fingers.

Greer sucked in a breath. "Only one left after I sign up?"

"That's right. We got a bride from as far away as Greenville, four hours away by car. Her mother was on the Spring Stroll, the young lady drove down, and came in to sign up. You just missed her. We also had one from Columbia. That's only two hours, but it's exciting that word spread so far and fast."

"My," Greer exclaimed. "I almost missed my chance."

"Don't think of it that way," Henny said. "Just be happy you made it."

Ford wasn't sure what to think, other than that Pierre Simons was a master marketer. He had the whole state buzzing. Ford himself certainly couldn't get excited over a few beads with an interesting story. He hoped he and Greer would be out of there in five minutes tops.

"Oh, I see they want a partner's name, too," Greer said.

"Just for our information. Only you're in the actual contest."

"I don't have a groom yet," Greer said.

Henny's eyebrows flew up, and she looked at Ford. "Well, who's this?"

"A good friend," he said. "Greer is a *future* bride."

"A future bride?" Henny asked doubtfully.

"Sure," he said. "She's a planner. Very organized. She's not averse to getting the wedding gown before she finds a soul mate."

Henny's brow furrowed. "I'm sorry, but . . . but you need a *partner* to enter this contest."

Greer smiled. "That's not what the leaflet says. It only says I need to be a *future* bride. I plan to be. Someday."

"Good Lord," said Henny. "We've registered brides with partners and wedding dates already lined up. It's not fair to them to let you in."

"Most women dream about their wedding day," Greer said. "I'm one of them. Don't I have just as much right to look forward to and plan my wedding as any woman with a partner already in place? I certainly have the financial resources to plan. The only thing separating me from the other brides in the contest is a matter of timing. My true love will arrive eventually. And I'll be ready to go."

Henny stood frozen, her lips slightly parted.

"You ever see that film *Field of Dreams*, Henny?" Ford asked.

"Well, yes," Henny said, "but—"

"If Greer gets the dress, the guy will show up," Ford said. "Kind of like 'If you build it, he will come.' Kevin Costner listened to that voice, didn't he? He built that field, and they came."

Henny's brow furrowed.

"Weddings don't just happen," said Greer.

"That's right," said Ford. "You have to chase after them. Be proactive."

"I suppose I see what you mean." Henny hesitated. "I don't know what to do. I need to call Mr. Simons."

She looked so rattled, Ford took pity on her. "We'll be happy to wait," he said.

"It's been a crazy day setting this up so fast," she murmured as she picked up the phone at the register and dialed. "We only got the gown this morning."

Ford looked at Greer. She smiled back as if she hadn't a care in the world, the minx. She was stirring up trouble, and she knew it.

"We already had Spring Stroll activities planned," Henny said, her palm over the phone receiver, "but Mr. Simons rightfully decided *Royal Bliss* deserved the spotlight."

"It does," said Greer.

They waited some more.

"He's not answering," Henny said, sounding worried.

"Maybe he's asleep," said Greer. "At any rate, here's my entry form." And she thrust it at Henny.

Henny put the phone back on its receiver then, with a bit of hesitation, took the piece of paper. "I can't guarantee you'll actually be in the contest, young lady," she said, not unkindly. "So don't be too disappointed if you get a phone call telling you you're disqualified."

"Mr. Simons knows where to find me if he'd like to talk," Greer said.

"I'm a hundred percent behind Greer's effort," Ford told Henny. "Do you realize how many women on Pinterest are planning their future weddings without having a partner in place yet?" He'd never actually opened Pinterest himself, but she didn't need to know that.

Henny drew in her chin. "No. I wasn't aware."

"It's a thing," he said.

"A thing?" Henny replied.

"It most certainly is," he said.

There. He'd done his duty.

Henny led the way to the shop's front door. "You're a very bold young woman," she said to Greer, then turned back to Ford. "You're a good friend. I can see that."

Which was her proper way of saying his lady friend was different, and he was a saint to put up with her neuroses. He got it. His mother and all her friends did the same thing: spoke in code.

"Thank you for coming in to La Di Da," Henny said to Greer. "And assume you're entered into the contest if you don't hear from Mr. Simons. Which means you'll need to go to the cocktail party tomorrow night."

Greer's eyes widened. "What cocktail party?"

Henny chuckled. "Did you think he'd merely draw a name out of a hat?"

"Yes," said Greer, and looked at Ford.

He raised and lowered his palms.

Henny leaned closer to them both. "This contest," she said, as if it were a great secret, "is a marketing tool. Mr. Simons intends to squeeze every drop of publicity out of it that he possibly can."

There was a beat of silence.

"What does that marketing entail exactly?" Ford asked.

"There's a La Di Da Bridal announcement party," Henny said in firm tones, "tomorrow night at the Dewberry Charleston Hotel on Marion Square. All contestants are required to attend, and the public is invited as well. Cash bar and lots of fun. And that's not all. A few more events are scheduled before the winner is chosen."

"Wow," said Greer, looking a bit scared and excited all at once. They said their good-byes, and when they got to the corner, she stopped and looked at Ford as if she hadn't just turned the small world of La Di Da ladies' apparel store upside-down. "I think . . ." she said.

"You think what?"

"That we did it." She smiled.

"There's an actual possibility that we did," he said back, and had a sinking feeling.

CHAPTER TEN

Leaving La Di Da, Greer was elated. Wait until she told Miss Thing and the girls that she *had* done something crazy while they were gone! She whirled to face Ford. "Can you believe Pierre decided to start an entire bridal department so he'd have an excuse for this gown contest, all so he could punish me for not finding him a soul mate?"

"He's diabolical. Bright, too. He'll make a great deal of money, eventually, from this revenge he seeks." Ford put his hands in his pockets and jingled some coins. "I'd like to hire him as my villain-on-call if I ever need one."

"Me, too." Greer stopped. "Thank you so much for going to bat for me in there with Henny."

"I was using a metaphorical *cricket* bat, I'll have you know." He smiled.

"Whatever it was, I appreciate it."

"You're very welcome. You'll have to show me some of these wedding boards on Pinterest."

"I'd love to. It's nice of you to be interested."

They started walking again. The moon was high in the sky.

"*You* interest me," he said, and grabbed her hand.

A jolt of adrenaline surged through her. "You interest me, too."

"Tell me about where you live." His thumb stroked the back of her hand.

That sent shivers up her spine. "It's called the Baker House. It's on Colonial Lake."

"I love Colonial Lake."

"Isn't it pretty? Anyway, the Baker House is the dignified, red-bricked building on the corner of Ashley and Beaufain."

"Oh, yes. It's very different looking."

"It's rare in Charleston to see such a mix of architectural styles. It's eclectic, with mission *and* craftsman influences."

"It's apparent you've given tours."

"I have. To all my friends and family when they come over. It used to be a hospital, mainly for women delivering their babies."

"Interesting."

"Every morning at seven A.M., I leave my apartment on the top floor, cross the street, and walk around the lake ten times. Then I eat breakfast and get ready for work."

"Sounds like a nice routine."

He was a good listener.

"I like knowing I live in a place that used to cater to women before women had a lot of clout in society," she said. "And these mothers didn't have the comforts of modern anesthesia or the authority to create their own destinies whatsoever. . . ."

"You sound quite inspired right now—"

She let go of his hand, saw an expanse of blank sidewalk coming up, and took advantage of it. She skipped ahead a few paces, faced him, and walked backward while she spoke: "Yet they showed up and persevered, and they literally created the next several generations . . . before the hospital expanded and moved somewhere else. After that, Baker House was turned into apartments." She stopped, and he walked right up to her, mere inches away. He cradled her elbows with his hands, and she felt a kiss hovering between them.

"Sometimes," she said, her nose almost touching his, "I feel the hope of those women in the floors and walls. And sometimes, late at night, their suffering. Their worry."

"You do?"

"Yes. My living room used to be a recovery area. I have a large, arched window there, and the sun pours in. I like to think of exhausted mothers lying there with their babies and dreaming about their futures. . . ."

"You're got quite the romantic soul," he said.

"But I'm logical. And practical. Like my own mother."

"Why can't you be everything at once?"

She shrugged. "I suppose I could. It's not very logical of me to want to kiss you, that's for sure."

"It's absolutely disastrous for me to kiss *you*," he said. "I'm supposed to be shattered by my abandonment at the altar, after all. I'm on the rebound, the gossips would say. You should beware."

"You should beware, too."

"Why is that?"

"For years, I thought I was happy with Wesley. Then I rejected the engagement ring he offered me, to mine and his utter shock."

"Hmmm. Are you sure he was as shocked as you seem to think he was?"

She'd never considered that. "I think so. I mean, he acted like it at the time."

"Have you never actually spoken to him about the break-up? After the fact, that is?"

She sighed. "No. And I want to. I want to tell him I'm sorry. I did when it happened, but you know how people always say they're sorry when they're afraid to get in trouble for being awful. And I looked very much like an awful person. I mean, I *was* one."

"That's not fair to say. Were you supposed to continue on and get married when you didn't love him? That would have been far worse."

"Yes, but I didn't have a good *reason*. Nothing about him had changed. *I'd* changed."

"You can't always make sense of things. Your gut was following a logic your brain had no access to—or was ignoring. Trust your gut."

"Mine is saying to trust *you*."

He winced. "I've got issues," he said. "Really big issues, beyond being abandoned by my bride-to-be and still having to pay for the wedding and the honeymoon."

"She didn't help?"

He shook his head. "And hell if I was going to ask her mother—who happens to be a well-known actress—to cover her daughter's expenses."

"Who is she?"

"Rosemary Dunhill."

"*Rosemary Dunhill?*"

"Uh-huh."

"That was nice of you. Rosemary Dunhill must have millions of British pounds." Greer couldn't help feeling curious. "She also has a chain of high-end women's clothing stores in the U.K., I've heard, with trunk shows in New York and L.A. I have a friend who's been to one in New York."

"Yes, she does. In Vail and Dallas, too."

"You run in elite circles, it sounds like."

"That's a kind way to say decadent, depressed, and fickle circles."

"Yikes."

"As an artist looking for exposure," he said, "the price of admission to the show is a thick skin. One minute, you're 'in' with the critics and the public. The next, you're out. There's no mercy."

"That must be rough."

"It's not easy, but it's also not the worst thing in the world. You tend to meet very interesting people. Risktakers. And I paint what I want. I don't look for ways to tap into the market. Chasing it can make you mad as a hatter. But when something I do makes waves, I ride it, like one of the surfers at your Folly Beach. Because you never know when the next good wave will come along."

She didn't answer. She felt like skipping ahead again, looking back at him. Neither one of them spoke. But they were having some kind of silent fun—just being together, she supposed.

They were approaching Colonial Lake, walking up Beaufain, when she got a text notification. It was quiet out, except for some laughter coming from the upper piazzas of one of the old houses. College kids. They tended to be up until the wee hours, and sometimes the neighbors would write letters to the editor about them. But she liked them. They kept the city young and vibrant. And once she was inside her apartment at the Baker House, a veritable fortress, she never heard them anyway.

Her apartment was her retreat, her cozy space, with its worn hardwood floors, floor-to-ceiling bookcases, and secondhand furniture she'd picked up at antique stores in the North Carolina mountains and either painted or reupholstered herself. She liked to play Martha Stewart in Macy's garden shed behind her house on the Battery, with Oscar, Macy's orange tabby cat, watching her every move, and Macy bringing her cups of coffee and fat slices of her homemade pound cake.

"It's pretty late for a text," she said, and then remembered the girls were in L.A. and three whole hours behind. It was only nine o'clock Pacific time.

Sure enough, it was a photo from Macy. All three of them were lined up on barstools and holding massive drinks. Miss Thing was grinning from ear to ear. Macy was laughing hard about something. Ella was looking directly into the camera, her smile serene.

"I love them so much," Greer said with a hitch in her voice. "I can't believe I'm not there." She held the phone out so he could see the picture up close.

He grinned. "They're a good-looking group. The older one—"

"Miss Thing."

He laughed. "Miss Thing reminds me of someone from the 1940s. It's her hair."

"She'd love hearing that. She's obsessed with the Queen."

The houses they passed were big, shadowy, and filled with stories. Greer wished she could go into each and every one of them.

"What really big issues do you have?" she asked.

"We're getting deep tonight, aren't we?"

"Something is bothering you a lot," she said.

"You talk about Baker House and the mothers who had dreams for their children," he said.

"Yes?"

He ran a hand through his hair, and then he looked at her a certain way.

And she knew.

"You have a child," she said.

"I'm not sure," he admitted. "My ex is pregnant with twins. I might or might not be the father. I'll know after she has them. Something about paternity testing being too difficult before then."

Greer gulped. "Wow."

"I told you," he said, and kicked at an invisible stone with his sneaker. When he looked back up, his eyes were stormy. "She was sleeping with one of my best friends. He could be the father. Either one of us. Or both of us, oddly enough. It's been known to happen that twins can have different fathers."

"I-I don't know what to say," she said. "I mean, you're right. It's really big news."

"I only found out this afternoon. It was why I was at the wine and cigar place on East Bay. I didn't want to stay in my flat and think about it. And I was in no mood to meet Wesley at the studio for a drink." He gave a little laugh. "He and Serena found me anyway."

"I'm sorry." Greer exhaled a breath. "Not about your being a father. That's for you to decide how you feel about it. I'm just sorry you couldn't think about all this in peace." She gave a little shudder. "And then I pulled you into *my* situation. Ugh. I feel bad getting you involved when you had far weightier matters on your mind."

"I didn't mind." He pulled her by the hand and up the stairs of the Baker House. "I liked it."

"You did?" She thought about him jingling coins in his pockets and telling Henny that he supported her one hundred percent in her quest to win that dress without a partner in tow. How nice of him, when he'd only just heard his whole world might be turned even more completely upside-down.

He nodded. "To tell you the truth, being with you has been the saving grace of the day."

Her heart warmed. *Saving grace.* She'd never been called that before. "That's very sweet of you to say."

He looked over her shoulder. Colonial Lake in the moonlight was a sight to behold. "I'm not being sweet." He hesitated, then looked back at her. "I'm taking advantage of you. I wasn't lying when I said to beware. So many things have happened to me lately. I'm in no place to get involved with someone. And I'm afraid that's exactly what I've done. Pulled you in."

She felt the weight of his worry. She was worried, too. "I could just as easily say I pulled *you* in."

He laughed. "Just this morning, you were a stranger in a coffee house."

"And you were a man in a plaid jacket who was highly distracting at an auction."

"What are we going to be to each other now?" he asked her softly.

And they both knew: *lovers.*

CHAPTER ELEVEN

He kissed her on the steps of the Baker House, with almost all the world sleeping around them. The college kids had finally quieted down the street. Far away, the sound of cars crossing the drawbridge over the Ashley River—*clack, clack, clack*—made a soothing background noise. His lips were warm and perfect on hers—hard, manly, his finesse wreaking havoc with her libido. She was in good hands. Very, very good hands. But the best part was being cocooned in his embrace. She loved the togetherness, the feeling of wanting someone so much.

She hadn't realized how much she'd missed that, how much was inside her that she was holding on to, things she wanted to share, both good and bad. She'd been working so hard, and she craved being held and made love to so that everything she didn't quite understand about life could float away.

She wanted the comfort and certainty of knowing all she needed to know . . . at least for a little while.

When he dropped down a step and looked at his watch, her heart sank. "It's killing me to leave." He shot her a handsome grin, but it was tired, too. "It's half past eleven, and at four in the morning, I have to be awake to Face-Time a gallery in Manchester. They have a buyer coming in who's interested in a series I painted last year."

She released a breath. "We both lead complicated lives. It's best that we just . . . stay friends."

"It's true I can't see myself sleeping with anyone—even someone as beautiful and desirable as you," he said, "the same day I find out I might be a father. I want to be respectful of the news and of her, even though we're no longer together."

"That makes total sense," Greer said. "In fact, I admire that. Are you"—should she ask?—"are you still in love with her?"

"No. Which makes this all the more complicated if I'm the dad."

She sighed. "This is heavy stuff."

"But life goes on." He grinned. "What are your plans tomorrow? Can we get started on sketches?"

"I'm running the office alone tomorrow, but the girls will be back from L.A. tomorrow night. And I might be busy fighting Pierre to stay in the contest. If he doesn't throw me out and I can bring someone to the cocktail party tomorrow night, are you in?"

"I'm in for as long as you need backup. It's only fair. But we need to start sketches by at least the day after tomorrow."

"Fine. We'll make it work."

"Cheers."

"See you."

She watched him cross the street. He looked back at her from the opposite corner and waved. She smiled, feeling wan inside—lovesick, almost, which was impossible this soon—and waved back.

She took the elevator up to her apartment. Her stomach dropped as it ascended. But she knew it was more than just the elevator. She had a crush. Already. On a stranger. And she'd been willing to sleep with him on the first day she'd met him.

What had happened to cool, logical Greer Jones?

When she got to her apartment, she threw her purse on her bed and let out a massive sigh. What an incredibly long, strange day it had been. Maybe that accounted for her falling for Ford . . . she'd entered a contest to win a wedding dress when she didn't have a groom. And Miss Thing had won a veritable fortune! She'd also seen Wesley—which was a huge shock—and was more glad than ever that they'd broken up.

But the most interesting thing was that she'd met this really awesome guy who was unavailable.

Unavailable.

She could see the word in big letters across a picture of Ford in her mind. Or should she say, *she* was unavailable? Because, of course, she didn't want to get involved with a man with such complex personal issues. Becoming a father was a big deal, and who knew how parenthood would change his relationship with his ex. Greer wasn't going to touch that situation with a ten-foot pole.

At the most, they could have fun, provide each other some temporary stress relief, and help each other reach a special goal. But that was all.

"Let's hope tomorrow is much more calm," she said to Fern when she snuggled under her covers.

Fern was her twelve-year-old Boston fern who sat on a table beneath her bedroom window. She was the best listener Greer had ever known.

But the next day was just as hectic. Greer worked all through the morning and afternoon, putting out fires at work, mainly two clients who were unsure how to handle their fourth date with each other. Should they or should they not sleep together? Both of them really wanted to, but would it jinx them? Things had been going so well!

"I'm afraid she'll start expecting a ring any day," the guy told Greer. "I like her a lot, but I'm not sure how far I want to take this. I'll never know until I sleep with her, though. What's a guy to do?"

"I'm worried he'll get bored with me once we make love," the woman said, "and I don't want him to. I really like him."

Greer talked them both through it separately on the phone.

The woman cried a little. "I-I'd love to have sex with him. I have needs, too! But whenever I go that route too soon, my dates never call me back afterward!"

"She's hot, and sex between consenting adults is never a bad thing, is it?" he asked.

The guy got defensive when Greer reminded him that Two Love Lane was all about connecting people with their soul mates, not hook-ups. "A nice guy like you is going to miss out on fantastic women if you push too hard to have sex too soon," she told him.

"But—"

"No buts. Are you looking for true love or a fling? Be honest. Because you need to get off the Two Love Lane bus if our long-term mission here doesn't suit you."

And the woman didn't like it when Greer said, "Maybe it's time to be more assertive and honest with your dates. Tell them you've been hurt before, and if they can't hang on a while before having sex with you, then you might as well call it a day."

"But what if they walk?"

"Then they walk," Greer said. "And you're better off. It's a good measuring stick of a guy's intentions."

"You sound like my mother."

"I'm only reflecting back things you've expressed to me but are afraid to say to your dates. Time to saddle up and take the reins."

She couldn't wait to hear what happened. It was such a waiting game. It was hard to have patience. She was always so concerned about her clients and had to work hard not to get too personally involved. But it was true, when one of their hearts broke, hers did, too. And when they fell in love, well, she was walking on air right along with them.

The internet was down at Two Love Lane, too, that day—some sort of wi-fi issue. Then at four P.M. she raced to the airport to pick up Macy, Ella, and Miss Thing. She still hadn't heard from Pierre, so she assumed she was welcome to go to the cocktail party.

Macy, Ella, and Miss Thing shrieked when they saw her—they were in one of their three sets of *Price Is Right* T-shirts—and they all fell into a big huddle. It took them a good five minutes to remember to walk to the baggage claim area. Greer told them on the way over about the contest.

They all stopped again so they could laugh. Miss Thing couldn't stop repeating, "I *told* you to do something crazy. I *told* you."

"Well, I did," said Greer.

"I think this whole 'no partner' strategy is an unusual but possibly effective way to get things moving for you romantically," said Macy.

"You sound like me," Greer said.

"Macy's right," Ella said. "Especially now that Wesley's

going to be here for a whole year. You need some major distractions."

"Dang tootin'," said Miss Thing.

"What will you wear tonight? Will any press be there?" Ella asked.

"I'm not sure," Greer said. "Not that—"

"How many people off the streets do you think will come?" Macy interrupted her. "Was it advertised in the paper?"

"I have no—"

"Did Pierre *really* get twenty future brides to participate?" Miss Thing asked.

"I—"

"Are you sure it's not a prank?" Ella asked.

"Part of me wondered." Greer basked in the sudden silence. "I mean, Pierre himself told me he bought the dress to keep it from me. He sure is going to great lengths to give it away, don't you think?"

"His resentments tend to run deep," said Macy. "His family's always been that way."

"I don't trust him," said Ella.

"Neither do I," said Miss Thing. "But you'll go to the cocktail party tonight. You won't let him intimidate you."

"No, I won't," said Greer. "Will you guys come with?"

"Of *course*," her best friends said together.

"Sometimes it feels like we're the Mouseketeers," Greer said.

"I never saw that show," said Ella.

"Me, neither," said Macy.

"Neither did I," said Greer.

Miss Thing rolled her eyes. "You all are *lame*. That was a great show. Ask Britney Spears and Justin Timberlake. And a generation before them, Annette Funicello."

They turned around and saw they were the only people

left at the baggage claim. All their suitcases were spinning around it. Greer's life had felt like that for a while, and she hadn't even noticed. But she wasn't going in circles anymore. She'd found some direction beyond her goals as a matchmaker. She was going to start working on herself again and not let guilt about Wesley hold her back.

"Ready, ladies?" she asked, and grabbed Miss Thing's large royal purple suitcase.

"The question is, is Pierre Simons ready for the ladies of Two Love Lane?" Macy chuckled.

"Oh, and there's this guy who might be coming with me tonight, too," said Greer. "So I might have to meet you at the Dewberry."

Miss Thing perked up even more than usual. "*Guy?*"

And until Greer dropped off all three of her friends at their respective homes downtown, she wasn't allowed to stop talking about Ford Smith, English painter. She told her friends almost everything that had happened between them.

"You're posing for him?" Miss Thing put her hand on her heart. "Lord, I've always wanted to do that."

"Me, too," said Ella. "It's so romantic."

"You're such a boss, Greer," Macy said. "Look at all you did while we were gone. I'm so proud of you."

"Thank you." Greer was proud of herself. She'd surprised her friends. That was a good thing. But there was one thing she'd left out. "Ford might be the father of twins. He won't know until they're born. His ex is pregnant. So please don't go getting absurd daydreams about us getting together."

They were suitably surprised and, she could tell, disappointed.

"Well, that's all right," Miss Thing said. "Maybe he's not the father."

Greer shrugged. "We won't know for a long time. Meanwhile, he plans on staying a part of his ex's life while she navigates this pregnancy. I'm not really interested in getting involved. That's a serious situation, and who knows if they still have feelings for each other. It was an ugly break-up, but you never know."

"It's smart to stay a little removed," said Macy.

After Greer dropped them off, she could focus on the fact she had to surprise Pierre by actually showing up that night at the Dewberry Hotel. She bet he thought she'd back down.

And then she had another bad feeling. She pulled her phone out of her purse and saw she had a message. Of course, from Pierre: *Hello, Miss Future Bride*, he wrote. *Looking forward to seeing you tonight—if you're brave enough. . . .*

We can always try to find you a match again, she wrote him back. *Wouldn't that be easier than going through all this revenge stuff? It must have cost a fortune to rent the Dewberry ballroom.*

Hah, he wrote. *And lose my momentum? Don't think I came up with La Di Da Bridal because of you and your obsession with Royal Bliss! We've needed something fresh at the store for a long time.*

He always wanted the last word.

Charleston was full of eccentric people. Friends who didn't live there simply didn't believe her. All they saw were glossy magazines depicting the sophistication of the city. Well, it turned out that some of the most cultured residents were also the strangest, but they prized their quirks, the way most people prize their good reputations. Or gold.

Their eccentric habits made these people who they were. Pierre was a Simons, and Macy had told her Simons folk took revenge and didn't give a hoot how they came across to anyone. They were rich and well-established and God help anyone who challenged them. They had the resources at their beck-and-call to run a small international war, if they wanted to.

Oh, well. Greer was their latest enemy. Nothing to do about it but put up her dukes and fight back.

CHAPTER TWELVE

So Ford was totally on board with going with Greer to the Dewberry and asked what the attire was. "Business casual," she said.

"Then let's dress up," he said. "Drake and I are the same size, and he's got a white tuxedo jacket. He goes to a lot of fraternity and sorority formals. I'll wear that, and you dress to the nines, too."

"Are you sure?"

"Why not stand out?"

"In a way, standing out is bad, don't you think?"

"Don't ever say that again, Greer."

"Well, you know, like on the National Geographic channel. The zebra who's standing away from the crowd is the one the lion attacks then eats."

"But you're a human. You have many more resources at your disposal to fight against bullies than a zebra does. All it has is its legs, to run. You can outwit Pierre at his own game."

"Well, I do have a couple of long gowns."

"Wear the flashiest one," he said.

"Okay."

When they arrived at the door of the ballroom at the Dewberry, Greer was in awe of how beautifully decorated the room was: white lights wrapped around palm trees, low-burning candles on white linen-clad tabletops, amazing flower arrangements on all the tables. It was as if Pierre had hired a complete wedding planning company. The bars scattered across the room were well stocked. The appetizers on the buffet tables were elegant and plentiful, the smell of roast beef and puff pastry so delicious, her stomach growled. There was a champagne fountain. There was even a local musical act, a College of Charleston band called the Stone Tigers, composed of kids who looked excited to get their big break. She could just see their dreams on their faces. That warmed her heart. And on the main stage, a huge banner proclaimed LA DI DA BRIDAL, COMING THIS FALL. There was also a podium and at least forty chairs onstage.

But the biggest eye-catching sight was *Royal Bliss*. It was on stage inside a giant Plexiglas box. It was stunning. She wanted it *so* badly.

But she was also completely caught off guard by the large size of the crowd. "Do you think Pierre hired a bunch of College of Charleston students to come fill the room?" she asked Ford, who was resplendent in Drake's tuxedo. "Or is the band that popular?"

"Drake and Gus would have told me if he'd tried to fill the ballroom," he said, "so no. As for the band's following, you can see them there." With one hand he pointed to a clutch of long-haired girls clustered around the portable stage, and he put his other arm around her waist. She shivered from the pleasure of it. "There's no way this ballroom is filled with band groupies. These people want to be here to see the contestants, and they want to see the gown."

"Okay." She was unable to say more than that because he made her crazy with longing.

"You look amazing," he said in her ear.

She was in heaven being with him. He was the most handsome man in the room. His white tuxedo jacket made him look like James Bond. He had a natural presence that made women and men look twice. And she really liked him. *Him*. His personality. His honesty. His humor. The way his eyes lit up when he smiled.

"What a shame that jacket belongs to Drake," she told him. "I hope you get rich someday and can buy your own custom-made tuxedo and wear it to all the best parties."

He laughed. "I'm not interested in any 'best parties.' I'm only interested in gazing at you." He paused. "I'm obsessed with painting you, of course. Don't let it go to your head."

He'd already told her she was beautiful when he came to pick her up in a cab. The driver had kept sneaking looks back at her in the mirror—her gown had a plunging neckline and lots of silver sequins—but his polite ogling hadn't moved her a bit.

Ford's admiring looks, on the other hand. . . .

They were surrounded by a ridiculous amount of people. Nineteen other future brides and all their friends and family, plus random romantics, including several book clubs, bunco clubs, and office groups who wanted to see how the contest would go. Everyone stared at them dressed in their fancy duds as they walked by, and started whispering.

"Don't look now," Ford said, "but Wesley and Serena are here."

"Really?" Greer craned her neck and saw the two of them talking to a few people she didn't know.

"I didn't tell them about it," Ford said. "Did you?"

"No, but Serena saw the flyer when we were on the Spring Stroll together," said Greer. "And I see Jill!"

Jill made a beeline for them. "So I heard the cool news from Ella," she said. "You're entering the contest with no groom."

"I am," said Greer.

Jill chuckled. "I think it's fantastic. I know so many women who are already planning their weddings on Pinterest with no partner in sight."

"It's a thing," Ford and Greer said at the same time.

"It is," said Jill. "You have fun, Greer, and remember I'm rooting for you. *Royal Bliss* is beautiful!" Then she leaned in and whispered, "I'll be decorating your room tomorrow while you're at work."

"Oh," said Greer. She had a sinking feeling. But Jill looked so excited. "But I'm worried about Fern. My fern. She lives in my bedroom. I don't want her to leave."

Jill's brow furrowed. "She'll mess with my vibe. She'll be too green and natural. Can't she stay in the kitchen or living room?"

Greer shook her head. "I talk to her at night."

"I'll figure something out," Jill said. "I'll come by later to get the key. You don't mind a few cute college boys coming with me, right? They'll do all the heavy lifting."

"Uh, sure," Greer said.

"Awesome." Jill said.

It was time to get the contest ball rolling. Greer turned to Ford. "What happened to Wesley and Serena?" It was surprising they hadn't shown up yet to chat.

"I don't know." His face registered surprise, too. "Maybe they haven't seen us yet."

"It would be pretty hard not to," Greer said. Her sequins sparkled under the beautiful white lights. And Ford's jacket almost glowed white. For the first time, she felt some nerves. She literally jumped when she heard a drumroll.

"Ladies and gentlemen, it's time to start our evening," said Pierre from the stage.

For some reason, Greer was shocked to see Pierre himself at the microphone. Hearing that whisper of his through the loudspeakers on the walls wasn't pleasant. Next to him stood L.A. Lady from the auction, in a faux fur white shrug and leopard print capris. She was apparently the "Golden Globe" girl who would walk around the stage doing nothing but look like Pierre's mistress.

Greer stood closer to Ford and listened while Pierre explained again about the store's new idea, La Di Da Bridal, and that to kick off the celebration, they'd be giving away *Royal Bliss*, which Pierre dubbed the most beautiful and interesting gown in the world, to one lucky bride.

L.A. Lady's name turned out to be Kiki. What a surprise! Kiki walked over to *Royal Bliss*, stuck out her arm to point at it, and stood there staring at the crowd.

"Tonight's a big night," Pierre said in his raspy voice. He ogled Kiki, who winked at him. "Out of twenty future brides, only five will remain, all based on your text votes. Those five brides will then have to win points through a couple challenges, and whoever gets the most wins the dress."

It was a rambunctious younger crowd with lots of shouting and whistling.

Henny took over after that and called all twenty candidates and their partners up to the stage. Kiki began to escort them to their seats, but she got confused, gave up, and went back to stand by Pierre.

"I want to go onstage with you," Ford told Greer.

"Thanks, but I don't want to misrepresent myself," she said. "I need to go alone."

"I get it." He squeezed her hand.

And in that moment, she wished there were a bridge between them that made it possible for them to explore a real relationship. But she knew it was out of the question. He lived in England. She lived here. If he had children, he'd want to stay in England to be near them. And she wanted to stay in Charleston. Plus, she really didn't know a thing about him. She was being silly, and romantic. The logical side of her was appalled.

She told herself to put Ford firmly out of her head and went up onstage alone. She did feel a little forlorn when she took her seat with all the couples. She was definitely a fish out of water. She looked around, mainly from nerves, but also from a curiosity to see if she knew any-one—

And saw Serena and Wesley two rows behind her.

No. Just no.

Serena was going after *Royal Bliss*, too?

Wesley's future bride grinned at her and waved. Wesley himself looked a bit sick to his stomach.

Like a robot, Greer smiled and waved back, but inside she was thinking how she couldn't shake them and, as a consequence, an awkward, painful part of her past. And now Serena might win *Royal Bliss!* She'd look fantastic in it. She was the quintessential beautiful bride-to-be.

Greer's stomach felt sick. She wanted to go home.

But she couldn't do that.

She wasn't sure if she was imagining it, but it did seem like the crowd was staring particularly at her. And then she remembered it was probably because she was in a sequined gown. Everyone else—except Kiki, of course—had stuck to business casual. Funny, but she didn't feel embarrassed. Maybe it was because she could look out into the crowd and see the glow of Ford's white tuxedo jacket.

It was never bad to be different, he'd told her.

She would cling to that if anyone gave her any trouble tonight.

"Everyone out there," Henny said, "please eat, drink, and be merry while our future brides introduce themselves and their partners at the microphone."

Kiki sauntered to center stage and stood there with the mike, which she jutted under everyone's chins when they walked up.

When it was Serena and Wesley's turn, they said they were both doctors who specialized in operating on children. The whole crowd cheered. And then Serena kissed Wesley—the first of the couples to do so—and everyone went crazy again.

After that, all the couples kissed, trying to outdo each other.

Three of the other twenty candidates, when they introduced themselves, presented the men with them as stand-ins for their partners. Two of the absentee true loves were stationed overseas in the military, and one was on call at the fire station that night. The audience had no problem with any of those absences and clapped and whistled accordingly.

It was Greer's turn. She was dead last, probably not by accident. "Hi," she said at the microphone, in a surprisingly steady voice. "I'm Greer Jones, and I don't have a soul mate—yet." There was a moment of silence, and then there were murmurs from the crowd. "Let me explain. My mother told me recently that weddings don't just *happen*." The buzz got a little louder, and Kiki made a moue of utter disdain, but Greer forged on. "I didn't like hearing that, but then I realized, I already knew that. I'm a matchmaker by trade, and I tell my clients all the time that they have to be open to meeting that special someone. You have to say to the world, 'I'm here and I'm ready.'" She paused a second. "But on that journey, you also have to say, 'I'm enough, and I deserve this.' My winning *Royal Bliss* would be a major affirmation for single women everywhere who hope to find love—women who love themselves enough to reach for their dreams instead of waiting for them to show up."

There were a few catcalls. And then a chorus of voices yelled, "Go, Greer!" She was sure that contingent was led by her Two Love Lane colleagues. She blushed and blew kisses.

"Ultimately, all I'm asking is for you to please not discriminate against the partnerless," she said. "We're future brides, too. Plenty of women like me will want to explore La Di Da's new bridal department along with brides who already have their soon-to-be spouses in place. Whether we're engaged right now or not, every woman I know wants to celebrate the power of love. Ask a single woman next to you. She might be like me. I have a Perfect Wedding Pinterest page I've been working on for a couple years. I also have Perfect Wedding scrapbooks. I cut pictures out of *Bride* magazine and *Southern Living* and any magazine that does wedding features. I've never told anyone that, but why not now?"

She laughed. Then stopped. And stood there. Okay, so maybe she'd just outed herself for having a weird hobby and should be embarrassed. But she wasn't. At least she was being herself. No one could fault her for that.

"Thanks for listening," she said, and left Kiki at the mike.

You could hear a pin drop in the room, but then there were a few whistles and some cheering and clapping. She figured she probably wouldn't final. But she'd done her best. She waved at everyone, smiled, and hoped Miss Thing was proud of her for doing something different.

Henny came to the podium. "Freshen up those drinks, everyone, and exactly an hour from now we'll vote for our top five brides and get instant results. Meanwhile, the Stone Tigers will get the dancing started, so stick around for a great party!"

"How did it feel to bare your soul?" Ford asked Greer when she came off the stage. He was waiting at the steps. She was happy to see him.

"Pretty good," she said, and wanted to kiss him in celebration, or consolation—she wasn't sure which. She'd done her best, but she was likely out of the contest.

Then she remembered: *Off limits. Potential daddy. Lives in England.* So kissing him was a bad idea.

"Oh, my gosh!" Serena came running up and threw her arms around Greer. Wesley trailed behind her. "You're so brave."

"You and Wesley were bold yourselves," Greer told Serena.

Greer locked eyes with Wesley for a moment. It might have been hard for him to hear her say she hoped to find true love. Maybe he considered it a diss to their past relationship. But it also wasn't her fault that he was there, and she needed to continue living her life, didn't she?

"And Greer made some thought-provoking points," Ford said.

She loved Ford's English accent. Even the way he said *thought-provoking* made her want to kiss him. Add that to the fact that he seriously had her back, and she was falling hard already. Which her logical mind knew was impossible. You couldn't fall in love that fast. But since yesterday, when she'd seen that dress, everything had felt different.

"I really, *really* want to win this dress," Serena said. "What would you do with it?" she asked Greer.

"Until I get to wear it myself," she said, "maybe loan it out to friends getting married. Spread the good luck around. You're into re-purposing, right? What would you do?"

"Wear it to my wedding and then put it away," said Serena. "That's the one thing I won't re-purpose, unless one of our daughters wants to wear it someday."

"That's a good plan," said Greer. She saw no reason to be anything but agreeable and friendly. She and Serena would be living in the same city for the next year.

But she had to admit, she was happy when the Two Love Lane girls came up and hugged her.

"You never told us about your Perfect Wedding scrapbooks and Pinterest page!" said Miss Thing.

"Yeah, sorry," said Greer, blushing.

"I've seen you cutting paper in your office," said Macy with a laugh, "and you always put the scissors down when I come in. I remember asking you once what you were doing, and you fobbed me off."

Greer kept blushing. "Yep, that was me working on a scrapbook. I don't know why I didn't tell you about it. I thought you might tease me, I guess."

"Why would we?" asked Ella. "You're right—what's wrong with doing some advance wedding preparation? And putting yourself in the right mind-set for love to come your way? I can't wait to see what kind of gowns and cakes you like."

"Thanks," said Greer. "I like flipping through the scrapbooks. It's funny how my tastes have changed as I get older. I don't know if it's me or the times."

"Maybe both," said Miss Thing.

"While you were talking onstage," Macy said, "three college girls standing next to me said they had wedding Pinterest pages that they keep private and share only with each other."

"And only one of them had a boyfriend," said Ella.

"I had no idea," Serena said, "that so many single women keep notes on their dream weddings."

Jill walked up. "I know, right? My good friend Sheila has an entire paper file filled with clippings of her favorite gowns, cakes, and flowers. She's been keeping it for years."

"A woman's wedding day is her chance to play princess," said Macy. "Or queen for the day."

"The fairy tale never quite leaves us," Greer added, "and it takes many forms."

"My friend Janie just had a Goth wedding," Jill said. "She wore black and a spiked dog collar, and they left on the coolest Harley I've ever seen."

"And I just went to my niece's wedding in Fort Lauderdale," said Miss Thing. "They got married in the pool. She wore a white bikini and a veil. And a dolphin brought over the rings."

"Good Lord," said Greer. "I'm downright dull compared to those ladies."

The light chatter kept on for a few minutes. Everyone laughed. But the truth was, Greer was nervous about the contest. She could tell Serena was, too.

* * *

An hour, a big glass of champagne, and lots of dancing later, it was time to find out who'd finaled. Those five finalists would then have to compete to win *Royal Bliss*.

The most exciting finalist so far was the bride with a partner serving in Afghanistan. She walked up with his stand-in, but she was able to FaceTime her fiancé, who was so excited for her. When Serena's name was called, Greer wasn't surprised. No one was. Serena laughed and cried little tears and ran up on the stage. Wesley clapped madly for her. She was number four of the five finalists. Kiki ran over to her and held the microphone under her chin.

"I'm thrilled beyond belief," said Serena. "This is a dream come true."

And the audience went *Awwww*, all together as one. Serena was clearly their favorite.

"She's so freakin' adorable," Macy said. "And confident, too, the way she kissed Wesley when they got introduced. People were impressed."

"She *is* bubbly," said Ella. "So much so I have a hard time envisioning her in the operating room."

"Me, too," said Greer. "But then again, I have a hard time imagining Wesley there, too."

"How about them in the bedroom?" asked Macy.

"I've already wondered," said Greer.

They started laughing.

"Stop," they said at the same time.

They were not mean girls. And they knew when they were approaching Mean Girl Land.

"It's time," Ella held Greer's hand.

"You did great, no matter what," said Miss Thing, who'd come up behind her.

It seemed right that they were the ones who would surround her. Ford, Jill, and Wesley were nearby, and part of Greer wished Ford could be right by her side, but that wouldn't have been appropriate. It wasn't like they were together. She'd known him two days.

So why did it feel as if she'd known him forever?

At the podium, Henny cleared her throat. Pierre sat on the left side of the stage, his arms crossed over his double-breasted suit. He looked very serious and very cross. But he'd looked like that since the beginning of the night. Only Kiki could soften his features, and at the moment, she was busy preening in front of a small mirror compact, oblivious to the fact that she was onstage in front of a large audience. But then she put her compact in her bra and held her microphone at the ready again.

"Okay," Greer said under her breath. "Let's get going."

She couldn't help noticing Ford's face. His gaze was riveted on the stage, on Henny at the podium. It was as if he genuinely cared, as if he were really worried about Greer getting into this contest. That warmed her heart.

"And the fifth finalist is . . ." Henny began.

Greer's breath became shallow. She really did want *Royal Bliss*, so badly.

She closed her eyes, but she didn't see the dress in her mind, she saw her disappointed parents. She wanted to do something to make them proud of her again. *Something*.

"Are you okay?" whispered Ella.

"No," she said, her eyes stinging with tears.

Ella held her hand tighter. "Have faith."

"The last future bride to final. . . ."—Henny looked over at Pierre, stony-faced in his chair, then back at the audience—"is . . . Greer Jones," she said in firm tones.

Greer couldn't believe it.

"Go on up," Macy said, laughing in her ear. "You're a finalist!"

There was a guy from Channel Five's local news with his camera focused on Greer.

"If this doesn't spur some interesting conversations around Charleston, I don't know what will," said Miss Thing.

"Unbelievable," said Ella. "Your story touched a lot of women, obviously."

So Greer went, accompanied by a lot of cheering. Onstage, her arm wrapped behind Serena's back, she grinned and waved at the crowd. But inside, she realized that if she wanted to show her parents she could have a decent life without Wesley in it, this wasn't the way to go about it, being a partnerless future bride.

Her parents were old-fashioned. They wouldn't get how brave she was. At all.

CHAPTER THIRTEEN

When Greer went onstage to join the other four finalists, she was visibly in shock. Ford noticed how pale she went as soon as her name was called. Her smile was too bright. Her eyes were wary. And he wasn't sure why. This is what she wanted.

It was true that Pierre appeared to be sulking, and maybe that accounted for her uptight reaction. He wasn't a guy you wanted to anger if you could possible avoid it.

Kiki held the mike under Greer's face, and all she said was, "Wow. Thank you all so much."

Henny stepped into the awkward moment and congratulated everyone, then reminded the audience and the finalists how the rest of the contest would play out: there would be three challenges that week. Whoever had the most points at the end of the third challenge would win the gown.

"The winners will participate in the first challenge tonight," she said. "They'll play a short version of the *Newlywed Game* with their partners."

Everyone cheered, but Ford's heart sank. No way could Greer participate. The military bride, Lisa, was able to connect with her faraway soldier on FaceTime, so she could play.

"The next challenge will be a wedding cake bake-off fund-raiser the brides will host for a great charity," said Henny. "The public will sample five distinct wedding cake recipes chosen by the brides and baked by one of five local wedding cake vendors. They'll vote on their favorite based on taste and presentation. The winning bride gets a bundle of points. However, more points may be accrued if their soul mates can determine which cake belongs to their future bride. If they're right, their votes are doubled."

Greer couldn't do that one, either! Luckily Lisa would be allowed to use her father as a stand-in for her partner.

"The third challenge," Henny said, "takes place at a luxurious beach house on the Isle of Palms, where the future brides and their One-and-Onlys will be treated to a weekend of fun, parts of which will be telecast. The public will vote via text or online ballot that will be tallied and the results reported on the Lowcountry Live morning show on Channel Four. FaceTime will be allowed to include our military bride's true love in the weekend assessment."

It was obvious Greer wouldn't be able to compete. At all. She just stood there, looking sad. And quiet.

"A lot of good it does being a finalist," Macy said to Ford. "She can't compete without a partner."

Pierre did look amazingly happy now. In fact, he was outright chortling. No one chortled. Only bad guys in films.

So Ford made a decision. He walked up onstage in his borrowed white dinner jacket, got on one knee, pulled off his gold signet ring, and in front of the entire room, asked Greer, resplendent in her sequined gown, to marry him.

CHAPTER FOURTEEN

Ford couldn't believe he'd done it. But he had.

Why the hell not? he'd told himself as he walked up the steps. What did he have to lose? The entire crowd shifted and actually began shouting when he got on one knee. And when he took his ring off his hand, there were several loud, feminine shrieks from the audience.

He didn't have time to look anywhere but at Greer. Her mouth hung open. She was gorgeous even when gobsmacked. Maybe more beautiful than she'd ever appeared before because there was nothing guarded about her expression. She had no time to react.

Kiki, Pierre's diva, must have recognized the moment's incredible viral marketing potential and came running over with the mike in her hand. She crouched and stuck it under his chin. Her feathery shrug made him want to sneeze, but he managed to stave it off.

And then it was done. The words, "Greer, will you marry me?" hung in the air.

The entire ballroom went silent.

Would she play along? Having a groom would certainly help her chances to win that dress. He wasn't sure what she'd do. It was what he liked best about her.

She swallowed. "I want to say yes," she said, "but I have to be honest with everyone. We only just met. *Yesterday*."

Bloody hell. The audience went crazy—of course. That was a move Ford never expected. He thought she'd say yes or no, but either way, he'd anticipated walking away with the audience believing his proposal had been *real*.

Dear God. She was too honest for her own good.

"I really like you, Ford, and I want a chance to win *Royal Bliss*, but—" Her brow puckered as she obviously searched for the right words.

What was she, one of those American Girl Scouts? They called them Girl Guides in England; Anne had been one. Honesty required at all times.

"But you have no chance to win the challenges without a partner," he said, easily adjusting to the new parameters. "Why don't we get to know each other this week while the whole town watches? I'm in this, Greer. I'm open to going wherever this adventure takes us. Please let me be your partner in your quest to win *Royal Bliss*." He put his right palm over his heart.

Oh, God. What had come over him? He hated dating reality shows and all that fake crap. But he couldn't let her walk off the stage without giving everything he had to help her win that gown. Greer's eyes widened.

Yes, I'm putting on! Play along, will you? he tried to tell her without speaking.

The crowd went ballistic.

Romance fever, love sickness, whatever you wanted to call it. Charleston had it.

Greer was so damned calm as she thought it over. He

could almost see the cogs in her brain turning as she stared into his eyes. He looked right back, and for a brief moment in which he had utter clarity, it wasn't fun and games anymore. This had nothing to do with rescuing her from a cruel emcee named Pierre and an amused audience, and everything to do with rescuing himself.

Say yes, he thought desperately. *Say yes. Dear God, please.*

And not because he would be embarrassed if she said no. Not because he was worried she'd lose the contest if she said no. He wanted her to say yes because she fit like a glove in his arms and she made him laugh, and he didn't even know her but he felt like he'd known her forever somehow. It had come at the auction, that feeling, when he watched her, mesmerized, as she stood with her finger trembling in the air and bid on that dress.

And then he pushed the crazed, insane feeling of wanting to be with her forever aside. He was a panicked, soon-to-be father who was afraid to handle his issues alone. That was all. And this outrageous scenario was an excellent distraction from that, not to mention a way to keep her happy enough to continue posing for him.

Yes, those self-serving, perfectly understandable reasons were why he'd strode up the stairs and knelt before her on the stage.

"Okay, you can be my partner," she said, loud and clear, with no hesitation.

The roar was deafening. At this point, it was a fairly drunken roar. He pushed his signet ring on her left ring finger—it was much too large. And then he stood, took her in his arms, and kissed her.

People stomped their feet. They hooted and hollered. Whistles bounced off the rafters. He had no idea how, but from some corner a boat horn sounded.

"Oh, my God!" he heard someone yell from near the stage and recognized the voice of Jill, Greer's friend.

The kiss went on and on. Her waist felt so good. So did the curve of her shoulders beneath the cold, hard-edged sequins. And her mouth . . .

He couldn't get enough. He forgot all about the yelling. Where he was, silence reigned, a soft, cushiony silence where everything was calm and good and right.

And then it was over. The noise spilled in, like bad music when you open the door to a dive bar.

Greer smiled up at him. He smiled down at her and thought, *What have I done?*

"What have we done?" Greer whispered without moving her mouth. She'd make a great ventriloquist.

"Go with it," he murmured.

"Good God Almighty!" Pierre hissed from the podium into the microphone. "Ladies and gentlemen, this was not a staged event. I'm in as much shock as you are." He shook his head. "It looks like we got ourselves a solid five-way contest," he concluded in a ragged whisper.

The whooping reached a new crescendo. Ford didn't like having all this time to think about what he'd done. But he held tight to Greer's hand, which was sweating.

"Sorry," she said. "This feels kind of surreal, and my palms sweat when I'm nervous."

"There are a lot of things I don't know about you," he said quietly.

"Likewise," she murmured.

Thankfully, Henny stepped forward, put two fingers to her mouth, and blew a piercing whistle. So much for sophistication! She was able to regain control of the audience, so that was all that mattered. "This has been quite an evening," she said. "And we're not done yet."

It was time for *The Newlywed Game*!

* * *

The seats were being quickly rearranged on the stage. When Greer went to sit down, she had to walk by Pierre.

"You think you're the cat's meow with your temporary engagement," he said. "Let me tell you something. You don't mess with Pierre Simons."

"We just gave your contest some extra pizzazz, and you loved it!" she said.

"I can do some serious damage to your business," he replied.

"You need to see a counselor. Did you have a mean mother or father?"

"My mother wasn't a nice person. My father ignored me."

"Boo hoo. Move on. Meanwhile, I'm calling your bluff. If you wanted to bring down Two Love Lane, you'd have tried before now."

"I had no time. Now I do. I've got Kiki. She does all my dirty work. I'm heading to Scotland for a month to go salmon fishing—"

"Do you really think I care you're going salmon fishing? What else are you doing? Touring a whiskey distillery? Buying a kilt?"

"Kiki will be here watching your every move," he went on, as if she hadn't spoken. "So you'd better find ways to be steamrolled by the other contestants on your own, or she'll make sure it happens for you."

"You're awful," Greer said. "I'm recording this conversation, and if Kiki and I were ever in a mud wrestling fight, I would take her in the first thirty seconds."

"Baloney," he said as she pushed past him and sat down.

He was right. She was full of baloney. She wasn't recording the conversation, and she didn't like mud. She'd mince around and try to avoid tangling with Kiki. But she could threaten. She could also be the bigger person, ignore Pierre, stay in the contest, and hope to win fair and square. Another option would be to walk away from the contest entirely, but for two reasons she wouldn't: one, *Royal Bliss* was still as beautiful as ever, and she wanted it, especially now that she was "really–not really" engaged until she and Ford decided otherwise. And two, she wasn't sure if Pierre was lying. Maybe he really *was* going to mess with Two Love Lane if she won.

A frisson of fear ran through her. A brat like Pierre might not be worthy of her attention, but she would be required to expend energy on him anyway because she had no idea how unpredictable and destructive he might turn out to be. She reassured herself that if she needed to battle him, the man had no idea what a force she was when she teamed up with Macy, Ella, and Miss Thing.

So with all that on her mind, she was pretty much in a daze when Henny asked her three questions about Ford during La Di Da Bridal's version of *The Newlywed Game*: (1) Name his favorite TV show, (2) where did you two first make love, and (3) what is his most irritating habit?

Greer guessed: (1) *Game of Thrones*, (2) we haven't made love yet, and (3) he, um, snores.

Everyone went *Oooooo* at the second answer.

"What do you expect?" Greer said to the audience. "We only met yesterday, remember?"

At that, a lot of random pieces of advice were yelled out by the audience as to where they should first do the nasty. The most popular one was on the beach.

The correct answers Ford provided were: (1) *Breaking Bad*, (2) we haven't yet, but I'd love to do it on the beach, and (3) I'm a sore loser when I play chess.

Everyone shouted all kinds of support about the beach answer, the most prevalent being, "Wear suntan lotion on your butt!" and a couple of women even yelled, "I'll do you on the beach, Ford!"

"What good was getting engaged?" Greer whispered in his ear. "We're still losing."

"We got one right—we haven't had sex yet," he said while the catcalls continued.

"Okay," she said, "but couldn't you like *Game of Thrones* like everyone else? And so many guys snore. Plus, you're telling everyone about a *beach* fantasy? There's sand."

"I don't snore, we'd be on a blanket on the beach, and I've never seen *Game of Thrones*," he said. "Count me among the few nerds who haven't. I'm an *Office* fan, the American version. I still can't believe Steve Carell never won an Emmy. The guy's brilliant."

"I wish you'd told me all this before now," she said. "Not that we've had *time*." She felt bad whining when he'd been so nice to agree to play the games with her.

"Well, if we ever play again, you'll know," he said.

"We'll never play again." It made her sad somehow. "This is our one chance. My favorite color is red, and my favorite food is sausage pizza," is all she could whisper in his ear because it was time for the bride next to her to guess things about her partner, and Kiki came up waving her microphone.

Serena only got two out of three questions right for Wesley. She felt his most irritating habit was whistling. Wesley thought it was his tendency to catalog his cereals in Tupperware. Greer felt guilty and slightly pervy wanting to know where they'd first made love: it was in Wesley's office. She couldn't believe he'd been that daring! Or Serena! Serena giggled hard and turned bright red when she answered that one. And Wesley's favorite TV show was, surprise, surprise, *Game of Thrones*.

In the end, it turned out that Greer and Ford tied for last place. Lisa came in first with her partner answering on FaceTime. Serena and Wesley came in second.

"No points for us," said Greer as she and Ford walked down the steps of the stage into the crowd again. "Do you think we can still win?"

"Sure," he said. "We'll get in a groove soon enough."

Her heart swelled. "Thanks for trying to help."

"I told you I'd have your back," he said. "You're posing for me, and I'm helping out here."

A small part of her was disappointed he didn't say he wanted to propose marriage to her because she made him feel so happy, he wanted to spend the rest of his life with her. But the bigger, logical part of her was thinking that she knew nothing about him. For all she knew, he could be a serial killer on the loose. She doubted that. But she'd better stay on guard.

They ran into their posse. What would they think about the engagement? It was obviously *not real*. But for some reason, Greer still felt giddy. It was understood by the world that she and Ford were together. She'd accepted his proposal, and she was wearing his ring, after all. They'd also kissed in front of a huge crowd and discussed the fact that they hadn't had sex—yet—the presumption being that they would soon, and probably on the beach.

Except for the beach part, the idea of sleeping with him made her swoon . . . she was ready. She was so beyond ready!

She drifted a few feet away—he was caught up talking to Wesley and Serena—into the cocoon of her friends.

"You look perfect together," Miss Thing whispered in her ear.

"Thanks," Greer whispered back, "but he's just helping me stay in the contest, of course."

Miss Thing pulled back and gave her a stern look. "Honey, no man marches up on the stage like that and proposes—out of the blue—without feeling something in his heart. My only question is what do *you* feel in *your* heart?"

"It's too soon to tell," said Greer. "And he's only here in the United States a short while."

"I knew with my guy the very first time I laid eyes on him," said Miss Thing. "Keep doing crazy things, sweetie. You're getting so good at it!"

Greer was swept up by all her other friends, too.

"Oh, my God," Jill said again. "Go consummate this fake engagement right now, sistah. I just wish I had your new bedroom ready." She gave Greer a giant wink.

Greer tried to look excited. "I can't wait for the new bedroom," she lied.

"You're so in charge," Ella said, looking her up and down. "Getting engaged without looking at algorithms and statistics? Or even knowing your man? Where's that Greer?"

Greer gave her a nervous smile. "Still here. As practical as ever. I think."

Ella laughed. "And a lot less predictable. I like that."

She passed her off to Macy, who was with Deacon now. They were holding hands. Deacon hugged her first. "Don't worry. I'm keeping an eye on this Ford guy for you. I'm going to sidle my way over there to meet him now. He may be a short-term relationship, but he'd better take it seriously."

She laughed. "Thank you, Deacon."

Then Macy was on her. She held both her hands. "Something is *happening*," she told Greer. "I don't care that this is a fake relationship. It felt so real to everyone in the audience, including me. Do you feel like a rock rolling down a steep hill? You just keep going faster and faster? And the landscape keeps changing, and you can't slow down?"

Greer nodded. "Exactly like that."

Macy looked thoughtful for a moment. "Do you want to stop? Or keep rolling?"

"Keep rolling," said Greer.

Macy sucked in a breath. "I'm getting goose bumps." She looked down at her arm.

Greer looked at her arm, too. "So am I."

"I'll be right here if you ever need to talk." Macy's tone was solemn. "Day or night."

Greer almost got tears in her eyes. "I'll remember that."

And then Ford arrived back at her side, and they said good-bye to her friends and entered the rest of the crowd, where random people congratulated them over and over. One inebriated woman told Greer she was a phony and selfish and should be disqualified for trying to be a partnerless bride and then having a fake groom, but Ford quietly blocked her with his body and they moved on, his hand on her back.

"Trolls suck," he said.

"They do." She felt so protected.

"Think you can come over tonight to pose?" he asked. "It's only ten."

"I can stay until midnight," she said. "I have a new client coming in tomorrow at nine."

"I can get you back before you turn into a pumpkin."

"Okay." She paused. "I have no idea if Scotland Yard might be conducting a manhunt for you right now. I know nothing about you, really."

They were still pushing through the crowd. "Tell you what," he said. "You want to talk to my mother?"

"Sure," she said.

"Fine." He pulled out his phone.

She saw the word *Mum*.

Awww.

She put her ear next to his. She liked how that felt. The part of his head behind his temple was so warm and his hair really soft. He smelled good, too, like that bay rum cologne and virile man.

"Hello, Mum?" His voice was bright.

Greer heard a loud English voice. "Darling, how are you?

"Great, Mum. I've got an American friend here named Greer—I'm going to paint her portrait for the Manchester art show. Would love for you to chat with her."

"Of course, darling. Put her on."

He handed the phone to Greer. "H-Hello?" Greer felt so nervous talking to a stranger across the ocean. She turned a little bit away from Ford.

"Hello, Greer. This is Ford's mother speaking. I'd like to reassure you he's a dear boy who's all about his art. I'm sure if he's painting you, you're a lovely woman."

"Um, thank you."

"When he was eight years old, he cut all the pink roses off our neighbor's prize rose bush, put them in a vase, painted them as a gorgeous still life, brought me the painting as a gift, and threw the roses in the rubbish bin. That's how sweet he is—and dedicated to his art."

Greer couldn't help laughing.

"What?" Ford asked. "What's she saying?"

"Thank you, Mrs. Smith," Greer said. "I feel as if I know him better now."

"You're welcome, Greer, and do be gentle with him.

Don't tell him I said this, but he's much more sensitive than he lets on."

"Okay," Greer said.

"Now tell him I can't talk. I just took the corgis out, and I'm gasping for tea." And she hung up.

"So?" Ford asked.

"She just took the corgis out, and she's gasping for tea, so she can't talk. She sounds like the Queen. Her Majesty likes corgis, too, and probably gasps for tea."

He grinned. "All English people do. Even on sweltering afternoons."

"What's sweltering?"

"High seventies Fahrenheit."

"Hah."

"My mum is much more approachable than the Queen," he said.

"She was." Greer grinned, thinking of him throwing out the roses and keeping the painting. "I liked her. Is your father as nice?"

"He's an absolute bear but a somewhat tamed one, thanks to Mum," he said. They were finally outside. "She knows enough to let him roar occasionally, knock over tables, and dive into rubbish bins. Metaphorically, of course. He's never raised his voice, and his manners are excellent."

"Your family sounds interesting. Who else is there?"

"My sister Anne. She's a writer, mother, and wife."

"What kind of writer?"

"Historical romances."

"Really?"

"She does very well for herself. She hits the *New York Times* list regularly. Her pen name is Anne Roth."

"I've heard of her!" Greer laughed. "How fun."

"You'd like her. She's very opinionated."

"I'm sure I would."

"She's also my manager."

"Wow, she wears a lot of hats."

"She's extremely competent, and we're very close." They were at the curb. "I've also got a brother. Rupert. He's five years older."

"What does he do?"

"He's in between jobs right now. He's brilliant, and he's funny. But he hasn't found his niche yet." He paused. "The truth is, he's an alcoholic who won't get help. He might have other substance abuse issues going on as well. We're not sure. He makes it very difficult for us to help him. He turns us away."

"Oh. I'm so sorry."

"Yeah, me, too. It's sad."

She held his hand. "I like how you love. It's not easy, but you do it anyway."

"It's not all hearts and flowers, is it?"

She shook her head.

"Are you feeling good about going for a quick sketch session?" He seemed to want to change the subject.

"Sure." She shivered just a little. It wasn't cold in the least. Nerves had struck again.

The cab came a few minutes later, and they were on their way to the studio.

Ford held her hand and looked steadily at her. "Nothing to fear," he said.

"All right," she said back, and broke her gaze away. She focused on the buildings sweeping past, but she couldn't help wondering who he was trying to convince.

There *was* something to fear. She saw it in his eyes. The question was, what was he afraid of?

CHAPTER FIFTEEN

At the studio in the old cigar factory, Ford poured two glasses of champagne and tried very hard not to think about his brother. Rupert was always in the back of his mind. He lived in fear of getting a phone call from home that something had happened to him. He'd try, instead, to concentrate on the fact that Greer, a woman he was extremely attracted to, was with him and willing to sit for a portrait he knew would be exquisite.

From the moment they'd entered the building, he'd sensed her shyness mixed with excitement and was touched by it.

He handed her a flute of champagne. "Cheers," he said.

They touched glass rims, and she took a sip. "Mmmm," she said, shimmering and curvy in her evening gown.

A beat of comfortable silence passed.

"How into this are you?" he asked her.

Her eyes widened. "What do you mean?"

"This portrait sitting can take a variety of forms. I want to work with you however I can get you. So I'll present you the options, and we will go with what suits you best."

"All right," she said.

"We can do this with you fully clothed, half-clothed, or nude," he said simply.

She froze. "Oh."

He chuckled. "No need to be anxious. We'll go where you want to go."

"But you're the artist."

"Who'd have an empty canvas without you. Your feelings matter."

She released a breath. "Which option do you prefer?"

He shook his head. "I'd rather not choose. I'd like to follow your whim."

She thought for a few seconds. "Would one of those three choices help you more than the others . . . at that show in Manchester?"

"Kind of you to ask," he said. "Yes, actually. Nude portraits always cause a bit more buzz, I think."

She bit her lip. "I told Miss Thing I'm going to be more bold." She looked up at him from beneath fringed lashes. "How many women get to be painted nude? In the prime of their lives?"

"Not many, I should think," he said.

"Then let's do it." She drained her glass. "Another, please." She held it out.

He refilled it. "Nude it is, then."

She laughed. "Oh, my goodness," she whispered, and looked at him over the rim, her eyes soft with worry.

"There's nothing to fear," he assured her.

She shot him a teasing smile. "I'm only doing this because I spoke to your mother. I know you're a real artist."

"Of course I am." He certainly wasn't going to subject her to having to strip in front of him. So he gave her instructions for disrobing behind the screen in the corner where he kept a stack of canvases and a couple of black robes hanging on a coatrack. "You can hang your dress there," he said. "I'll set up in the meantime. Take your time."

In short order, she appeared in front of him again in the smaller black silk robe. The ivory chaise lounge with its plump silk pillows and a small table where he'd placed her champagne awaited her.

"Ready to begin?" he asked.

She nodded and slowly slipped off the robe. She tossed it on the table and stood before him in all her naked glory. The light was artificial, casting shadows beneath her chin, below her breasts, and a thin sliver at the top of her thigh. Her glass of champagne, with its bubbles rising steadily to the surface, was a suitable complement to her elegance, her stillness.

"You're beautiful," he said in his professional artist's voice. "I'm honored to have you pose for me."

"Thank you." She shot him a slightly scared smile, backed up a step—he noted she was obviously self-conscious about exposing her backside to him—and sat on the chaise lounge. She kept her knees together and folded her hands in her lap.

"Right," he said. "Lean back in any position you choose, then make a quarter-turn toward me. I want to spend a few minutes doing a full-body sketch, but whenever you want to warm up or cover up for any reason, grab the robe."

"Will do," she said in a quiet voice. She did what he asked, turning slightly toward him.

Her beauty took his breath away. "Excellent," he said, maintaining his positive, almost professorial manner, and began to sketch. She kept her eyes on his easel. He saw curiosity there. Her left arm was draped over her belly, his signet ring on her middle finger.

"You've got the ring on," he said. He felt a jolt of shock seeing it there. And then a ridiculous sort of pride. What a splendid woman to be wearing it!

"I figure I should get used to it for a little while," she said, her tone teasing. Her right hand propped up her jaw. "Even fake engagements have certain protocols to follow."

They were creating this crazy story together. He supposed it was quite hilarious. A sort of meaningless caper. If he had to do anything silly with anyone, he was glad it was with her.

But he focused again on the work. He had to work fast. He was afraid she'd disappear, like a beam of light covered by a cloud.

She laughed.

"What's so funny?" he asked.

"How intense you look," she said. "Sorry—it's actually not funny. I laugh sometimes when I'm nervous."

"That's fine." He grinned. "I do tend to get carried away."

"Should I not interrupt you by speaking?"

"Oh, no," he said. "I chat all the time when I sketch and paint."

"I'm assuming you didn't paint Serena in the nude."

"No. Her mother commissioned the portrait. She was barely out of school."

"Did you get to know her well through conversations while you worked?"

"I think so. I understand her."

"Can you explain? Or is that a private thing? You mentioned at The Rooftop that she had a rough childhood."

"A whole ten years have gone by since I painted her, and she's never told me I can't talk about her history. She does herself, every once in a while, and doesn't seem bothered." He made a quick stroke of the charcoal pencil. The sketch was promising. "She had a very unhappy home life," he told Greer. "Her late father was an alcoholic, and they had to pretend he wasn't. Simple as that. The entire family covered for him until he died in his fifties of pancreatic cancer."

"How sad. When was that?"

"When she was in boarding school in London. It was why her parents sent her. They didn't want her to see him decline."

"But what if she wanted to *be* with him during his last days."

"I know."

Greer sighed. "Wow. That helps me understand why she's so relentlessly cheerful. She probably had to keep up appearances, pretend nothing was wrong."

"I think so. And she knows I relate. She's met Rupert and my parents. They came over one day when she was sitting for me. After they left, I told her we always kept a stiff upper lip about Rupert's issues. But it's difficult sometimes."

"I can imagine." Greer looked contemplatively at him. "There's nothing difficult going on in Wesley's family, as far as I know. They're all-American. Two parents, three boys. Wesley is the oldest. Everyone has done well for themselves. No one has been left behind. It's a wholesome story. The only thing that went wrong for them is when I turned down Wesley's proposal."

"I wonder what sort of ripples occurred in their household after that happened?" Ford asked.

"I wonder, too," said Greer. "But I've never really

asked. It's something I've lost the privilege to know. And I'm okay with that. The ripples in my own home were enough to deal with."

"Understood." She wriggled a little, and immediately, he grew rock hard. He was glad the easel protected her from seeing him aroused. He wished it hadn't happened, but nature would have its way, no matter how much he willed himself to be immune to her sensual charms while he worked. He'd simply have to work through it.

But he couldn't find it in himself to speak. He would focus on sketching. He'd already finished the first. He was now on the second—same pose but a more energetic pencil stroke.

She was quiet, too. The vent overhead ticked comfortably, and the air came on. The cigar factory building was vast and empty at that hour, save for his little studio. Outside the night sky over Charleston was inky black, the stars obscured because of lights glowing from homes crowding the crisscrossed streets of the peninsula.

But if he looked out toward the harbor and the vast Atlantic beyond that, he could see the stars, perfect little points of light. The sky was nature's canvas.

His own measly works . . . Would they ever amount to anything beyond clumsy attempts at human expression? He was good, he knew. He had expertise with oils. But his work wasn't memorable. There was something he couldn't break through. Some veil. Was it merely that he'd reached the pinnacle of his ability? And he was pounding on a door that was forever shut to him?

Or should he keep trying to open it?

It was a frustrating question.

It was eleven forty. She'd been so helpful, and now her eyes drooped. She was probably very tired after the night she'd had.

He put his charcoal pencil down. "Time to call it quits," he said.

Her eyes widened slightly. "Already?"

"Said the sleepyhead." He opened a drawer and tossed the pencil inside. "Come, let me get you home."

She smiled and sat up. "It's funny. I feel entirely comfortable now. And I'm not sleepy. Only relaxed."

Relaxed.

He had to suppress the spike of lust that rose in him when she said that. She was like a sleek cat there on his chaise lounge, warm and vital. He came over to the small table, picked up the black silk robe, and tried to hand it to her. "I'm very glad," he said.

She stood in front of him and purposefully gave it back. "Seems a little silly, now that you've seen me." Her voice was soft. "It's only a few steps to the screen."

"Fine," he said, amused, turned on. "If you're comfortable, go right ahead."

She walked away from him, a barefoot goddess. The curve of her bottom made him jet a breath too loud.

She looked back at him over her shoulder, her gaze like a banked fire.

Whoa, he thought. "You're beautiful," he said.

"Thank you." She smiled.

And that was when he stopped being a painter who commanded his studio and was only a man again, one who'd fallen under the spell of an extremely sexy woman.

CHAPTER SIXTEEN

Greer saw that Ford couldn't break his gaze away, and she was glad. She'd been nervous when she'd first disrobed. But as they'd talked, she'd grown more and more comfortable reclining on the chaise lounge with its plump silk pillows and letting Ford's gaze roam over her. She'd admired the planes of his face, taken in the thoughtful way he'd gazed at her—as if she were something mystical and marvelous to behold—and everything changed.

She became a woman on a mission: she wanted to seduce the English painter.

In the Dewberry ballroom he'd had her back under trying circumstances. He'd saved her chance to win *Royal Bliss*. And at the studio, hot as he'd looked in his white tuxedo jacket and the black bow tie, which he'd untied and carelessly draped around his neck, he'd been nothing but sensitive and kind.

Watching him paint, she couldn't help but sense beneath his cool composure the hot, masculine tension in him that he'd generously unleashed to the world when he'd kissed her on the stage as if he were her man.

Hers.

"Greer—"

"Yes?"

Everything in her rejoiced when he took the two steps that separated them and cupped his hand over her bottom. She turned slightly to face him, leaned into him, and closed her eyes while he caressed her.

Bliss.

"I want you," he said, his voice sounding the worse for wear.

She smiled into his shoulder. "I want you, too."

He continued caressing her.

"You were a good egg tonight at the Dewberry."

He chuckled. "I was, wasn't I?"

"What if this . . . what we're doing now—"

"This?" he asked, and kissed her neck.

"Yes," she whispered, and let him knead her bottom and kiss her deeply, thoroughly, her bare belly pressed up against his tuxedo. She pulled back for air, and knew she was about to wreak havoc with her own plan to sleep with him, but that was how she was—it was her nature to be honest, to get everything out on the table. "We're getting to be real friends now. What if this complicates things, and we stop helping each other? You need this portrait for your career. I need that gown—for less obvious reasons, I suppose. But they feel real to me."

He brushed a thumb over her lip, back and forth. "What's wrong with complicated? When it feels so good? Give me that over simple and sex-deprived any day."

She laughed. "You have a point."

"You're like a lush flower," he said in her ear. "A peony, I'd say. Blush pink at the moment. And so delicately beautiful."

He kissed her again, his hand caressing her nipple. She gave a tiny moan and wrapped her arms around his waist.

She lifted her thigh ever so slightly and pressed up between his legs. It was his turn to groan. She loved the sound.

"We don't have much time," she said.

"Midnight." He picked her up and set her on the edge of the counter under the transom window, opened it to let in a great warm gust off the harbor. "You'll be in bed by then."

"The fresh air feels so good," she said.

He kissed her. She wrapped her legs around his waist. He moved to her breasts, lavished them with kisses, and reached behind to break the grip she had on his waist with her ankles. He spread her legs open, kissed her belly, moved to her thighs. And then he nuzzled her center with confident attention until he pulled her bottom close to the edge and began a more intense yet playful game, teasing her until she scooted even farther forward of her own accord so as not to break contact. Her spine arched over his head and she moaned, almost oblivious with pleasure. But she remembered to at least run her fingers through his hair. He used his fingers then, deep inside her, and she let herself go.

Wave after wave took her. He stayed with her. And when she was done, she literally fell back on the counter, dazed and weak. "So much better than crème brulée," she gasped.

He laughed. "I hope so."

She laughed, too, and curled into a fetal position. "That was exquisite work."

"It was entirely my pleasure."

"I could go to sleep right here, right now."

"Good."

He was petting her hair. She shut her eyes and let him. She reveled in the attention. What had she done to deserve it? She didn't know. And she didn't care. Some things you shouldn't have to earn.

The best things in life were free, she saw with a new clarity.

She forced herself to sit up. "Hey," she said. "Let's not forget about you."

"Let's forget about me," he said back, his eyes teasing and warm. "You're exhausted. Let me get you home. And we can take up where we left off next time."

She yawned. "Are you always this nice?"

"No," he said, with a wink. "So enjoy this enlightened, thoughtful version of me while you can. Plenty of times I make my own sort of demands."

His message was unmistakably sexy.

"Oh," she said, and kissed him. "I look forward to that."

True to his word, he had her back to her apartment by eleven fifty. She was in bed with the lights out at midnight.

CHAPTER SEVENTEEN

The next evening, Greer sat down at La Di Da, where *Royal Bliss* was back in the front window, feeling more relaxed than she had in years. It had to have been her sexual shenanigans with Ford. An utterly delicious torpor had overcome her and stayed with her all night and the next day at work. She'd had such a hard time focusing at Two Love Lane, she'd had to drink an extra cup of coffee. She also took a lot of breaks from the phone and computer to walk out to the front porch and stand with her face in the sunshine, breathing the sea air. But everything she did reminded her of the night before at the studio, when she'd sat beneath the transom window and let Ford have his way with her. It made her weak in the knees remembering. Each time she did, a bolt of desire shot to her lower abdomen.

Could anyone tell? It was a little embarrassing. Even at lunch with Miss Thing and a mutual friend, she couldn't stop daydreaming about Ford. She'd had to cross her legs, but then she'd uncrossed them—nothing was working! She could hardly wait to see him again that night for a few more sketches . . . and whatever else would come afterward.

But meanwhile, she had to win the wedding cake bake-off. She had no points from the first challenge. So she had to go big or go home.

Chatting with all the brides the day after they'd been chosen as finalists was fun. There wasn't a mean one in the bunch. And she didn't feel at all guilty about being in the contest.

Henny disappeared in the back room to take a few phone calls and said she'd return in a jiffy. "Get to know each other," she said.

Fine, they said. They would. Each one of them looked around a little warily.

"Hi," said Greer, realizing she could be in the hot seat, and sure enough, someone immediately pounced.

"Do you think you two will actually stay together?" asked one bride, who was a yoga instructor. Her name was Carol.

"I don't know," Greer said. "I mean, it was pretty crazy. I was already in the contest, but having a partner helps, and hey . . . if he's willing to be my partner, I'll take it."

"That's not very romantic," another bride said. She was Toni, a cashier at Target.

Greer recognized her because Target was her favorite store. She was there way too much buying random kitchen gadgets, cute tops, sandals, books, and chocolate. "I'm not going to lie," she said, "and pretend to be in love with him. Do you think I should? I just met him."

"No," Toni said. "I like you, and I appreciate your honesty, but I don't think it's fair or right that you're in the contest. You're not in love, and you aren't getting married, and you don't have a real soul mate."

"Wait," said the military bride, Lisa. "She does, too, at least a potential one. I heard him ask her to marry him. No guy does that without meaning it at some level."

"How could he mean it?" Toni asked. "They met the day before. She admits she doesn't love him."

"You ever hear of arranged marriages?" Lisa asked. "Sometimes they work. And my own best friend got married on her first date. Seriously. In Vegas."

"Did they stay together?" Serena asked.

"No," Lisa said, her cheeks pink. "But they lasted six months!" she added. "That's pretty darned good."

Greer wanted to be patient. "Someday I'd like to get married," she said for the umpteenth time. "Why shouldn't I look for my dress *now*? Especially one that will bring true love into my life? Weddings don't—"

"Just happen by themselves," Toni and Serena finished for her at the same time.

"They don't," said Greer, feeling exhausted. And small. And confused.

Serena shrugged and smiled. "Greer, you have a point. Marriage was on my mind for years, way before I met Wesley."

"Thanks for telling me that, Serena." Greer honestly appreciated it. She also hoped no one would find out Serena's groom was Greer's old boyfriend, which would make things even more awkward around the other contestants.

Carol smiled. "This is a special group of women. I feel it. And even though Greer is in a slightly different boat from the rest of us, I can't fault her. She's been honest the whole way through this contest. She hasn't broken any rules, and a lot of women start planning their weddings before they even have someone to marry. I say let's all just enjoy the experience together."

"I want to do that," Toni said wistfully. "But I still wish you'd drop out, Greer, because everybody likes your story. They want to see if you two fall in love. So they're going to vote for you, and *I* want that dress." Her voice cracked just a little.

"I wish we all could win *Royal Bliss*," Greer said. "Honestly."

"I have high hopes for you and your new man, Greer," said Lisa. "When he put his hand over his heart, it made me cry."

"It was sweet," Greer said. "I was very touched."

"Sorry, Greer, but we all know he was totally faking it," Toni said.

"There's such a thing as faking it 'til you make it," Carol said. "I've done it myself."

"That's what I mean about shopping for my gown *now*," said Greer. "I want to fake it until I make it."

"I think you make a lot of sense," said Carol.

"I kind of do, too," said Serena.

"Me, three," said Lisa.

"Thanks so much." Greer was grateful for their support.

Toni sighed. "I guess your 'fake it until you make it' idea is okay, but I'm still not happy. But don't mind me. If you'd been one of my best friends doing this, I'd be all for it, probably."

"Thanks for giving me a chance," said Greer.

There was a comfortable silence. At least they were getting along.

And then she got an idea. "If I win," she said, "cross my heart, every one of you is welcome to wear *Royal Bliss* on your wedding day. As long as you return it to me in my size so I can wear it, too, when I get married."

"Like *The Sisterhood of the Traveling Pants*?" Lisa asked.

"Exactly," said Greer.

The rest of them started laughing.

"What's so funny?" she asked.

"Would you ever share *Royal Bliss?*" Toni asked the other women. "Think about the history associated with it! It's one-of-a-kind."

"A treasure," Serena agreed. "No way. I'd never share it, except with my future daughter."

"Same with me," said Toni.

"I wouldn't share it, either," added Carol. "Sorry. Plus, what if you spilled red wine on it?"

"Um, dry clean it?" Greer said.

"As if!" Serena said. "It would never come out."

"Okay," Greer said meekly.

"Your idea won't work for me," said Lisa, "but thank you for the offer. I'm so tiny, there's no way we could alter it down for me without cutting out some fabric, so I couldn't get it back to you in your size."

Which admittedly, was way bigger than Lisa's size.

"All right," Greer said. "But if I win, the offer still stands, and I'm sorry you can't take me up on it," she told Lisa.

Henny reappeared. "Is everything all right?"

"Fine," said Greer.

"We were just discussing," Serena said, "the best way to make sure the mothers of the couple getting married complement each other's look at the wedding."

Henny's face brightened. "That's always an interesting topic!"

The other women nodded but didn't elaborate. For some reason, no one seemed to want Henny in on their new closer dynamic.

But she figured out it was happening. "Ladies, I'm glad to see y'all bonding," she said. "I heard you stop talking about something when I came over again. Good for you. Brides need to support each other. You'll be competing, but that shouldn't stop you from looking out for each other."

"Right on," murmured Lisa.

Henny sat down in the circle and smiled. "All righty," she said, "it's time to get the bake-off rolling."

Everyone clapped.

"Let me explain the voting first," Henny said. "The people who come to the event get two ballots apiece. They can split their votes, or give you both. We want them to feel some power and extend the fun for them as they walk around the ballroom at Hibernian Hall, looking at your displays and trying to make up their minds."

"Suits me," said Toni, the Target bride.

"The number one thing you need to know," Henny said, "is to be as creative as possible. Your goal is to get people to vote for you. It's actually more about you and your overall display than the cake alone. So make a statement and pull in those votes, however you feel you can within your budget. There are no rules, really, limiting your creativity. Understood?"

They all said yes.

Henny smiled at all of them. "Okay, now I'm going to have you pick a number out of a hat."

Greer got the number five, and it turned out that meant she got last pick of the five local vendors who would be baking the cakes. They'd bake two identical ones. One would be for display, and the other would be for the public to consume. The cakes had to be the right size to feed one hundred guests.

Greer got the doughnut store, and felt her heart sink. Yes, everyone loved doughnuts, but hadn't that wedding cake trend passed? She'd cut out several pictures of different versions of the tiered, ringed creations several years earlier—and now the new trends were much more, well, cake-oriented. Real cake, the kind that had crumbs, and icing.

Beaded cakes were in. They were probably the hottest new look. But so were cakes inspired by geology that featured marble, geodes, and precious metals. Tropical cakes were trending, as were floral-and-fruit ones. Lace cakes and cakes covered by ruffles were all the rage as well.

The other ladies were excited about choosing from their vendors' selections. They pored over the photos included in their vendor's file, oohing and aahing, and generally had a ball selecting their cakes.

But what could Greer do? Her file held photo samples of doughnut-themed tiered cakes. They were almost identical to each other. Sure, the icing varied, but that was it.

How to make this wedding cake special? How to make everyone turn to her doughnut cake and say, "I'm voting for *this* one"?

She had no idea. She tried to logic it out even further, and all she could come up with is that everyone loved doughnuts, and her cake would cost less than the other cakes. They were each given five hundred dollars in their budget, which was to be used for the cake and to decorate their cake table however they wanted to reflect their wedding theme and personality.

What could she do to make people vote for her cake?

She thought about it while walking back home to the Baker House. And when she got there, she saw Jill's car parked out front. Jill had come into Two Love Lane that morning to pick up the keys to Greer's apartment.

"Tonight," she'd said, "when you come home, everything will be in place. Your bedroom will be transformed."

Now Greer stood in her living room. "You move fast," she called toward her bedroom.

Jill came out, a big grin on her face. "Hi. Hope you had a good day."

"Great. How about you? How's Fern?"

"My day's been good, "Jill said, "and you'll be happy to know Fern's staying in your room. I couldn't move her. She's like a queen, all dignified on your new bureau, with those beautiful fern fronds cascading around her."

"See?" Greer was excited. "She's like a person."

"I've never met a plant like a person," said Jill with a laugh. "She's my first. And she looks amazing in her new surroundings."

Some of Greer's nerves departed her. Maybe this room transformation would work out, after all.

"As for moving fast," Jill said, "I've been renting a storage room for a year and filling it with special finds I'd purchase every month with money I scraped together after I paid my bills. I'm glad I can finally use my inventory."

"I am, too," Greer said. She decided then and there that if her room was awful, she would simply tell Jill she couldn't keep it that way and help her move the new furniture back to her storage room and get her old stuff back.

"Ready to see it?" Jill asked.

"Sure." Greer's stomach had butterflies. "But I hate to take some of your inventory, especially because you're not letting me pay for any of this. You're losing money."

"I'm *investing* money in my business," Jill corrected her. "You're my guinea pig. Doing this free is the least I can do. And I have a re-buy program. If you ever get sick of this theme—or it outlives its usefulness—I'll buy the furniture back pro-rated by the number of months you kept it."

"I love how confident you're sounding," said Greer. "Good for you."

Jill held out her hand. "Trust me, Miss Jones. Now take my hand and close your eyes."

Greer felt a stirring of excitement. Or dread. She wasn't sure which. She did as Jill asked, following her across her hardwood floors, felt herself pass over the threshold into her bedroom, and waited for more orders.

"Okay," said Jill. "Before you open your eyes, do you remember what I said about once you commit to making your living space your loving space, you'll start noticing changes across the board?"

"Yes."

"I can see a change in you already. You're not wearing one of your executive-looking pantsuits. You're in an A-line skirt. With flowers on it! What happened?"

"I forgot to go to the dry cleaners, is all," said Greer.

"Why?"

Greer thought about last night and couldn't help smiling. "I had other things to do."

Jill laughed. "The way you said that, I know exactly what those other things were! It's already working. Remember that when you open your eyes. It's already working and no way do you want to stop the momentum, no matter how shocked you are by what you see."

"Okaaay," said Greer.

"Now open your eyes!"

Greer did. She did a full three-hundred-and-sixty-degree turn. Her bedroom was now a . . . a boudoir. Or a bordello. A very pink one. It definitely wasn't a regular bedroom anymore.

Jill smiled broadly. "Welcome home to 'The Working Diva Without a Man' theme, guaranteed to bring a man into your life faster than you ever would otherwise. Go lie down on your new bed."

Which was covered in a leopard print coverlet and about eight toss pillows in various shades of pink. A big black velvet portrait of Elvis in a gilded gold frame hung above it. And opposite the bed was the Elvis-decoupaged bureau. Fern sat on top of it, her pot wrapped in a giant pink velvet bow.

"My goodness," said Greer, lying down on her bed. "This is . . . everything I expected. And more." On the ceiling above her head was a picture of the entire *Baywatch* crew in their red bathing suits.

"Do you know how valuable that Elvis picture is?" Jill said. "It's a collectible. I'm not even going to tell you; you'd get nervous. And that *Baywatch* poster is giving you California vibes. We all need some of that. What do you think of the mattress?"

Greer had sunk into it. "It's very fluffy," she said. She wasn't used to fluffy. It was kind of fun.

"I almost gave you a water bed instead."

Greer sat up. She definitely felt perkier. Who wouldn't? "I didn't know they still made those."

"Oh, yes." Jill sat on the bed next to her. "So do you feel the energy?"

Greer bit her thumb. "I think I do. Actually"—she looked around the room, at the pink ottoman studded with fake diamonds, the fringed lamp, the faux white sheepskin rug in front of her small fireplace, and the big, inviting pink armchair—"I know I do."

Somehow, this bedroom was making Greer feel a little more loosey-goosey. But that was neither here nor there when she had a bake-off to worry about, and she had only the next day to get ready.

When Jill left, she ran to the arts and craft store on Calhoun Street and picked up some supplies. Ford called while she was there.

"Still coming over?" he asked.

"Yes. See you there at eight."

She ran home and worked on her bake-off stuff, then finished up a Perfect Wedding album—her nineteenth one. She filled eight pages with pictures of flower arrangements. Then she rode her red Vespa to the cigar factory. She waited on the elevator, and when it opened, Ford was standing there.

She almost jumped.

"I saw you coming on your Vespa," he said and tugged her into the elevator.

She laughed.

"Need any help with this bake-off?" he asked.

"I'm not sure," she said. "I'll let you—"

He pulled her in before she could finish.

It was a very slow ride to the studio. The elevator kept stopping between floors.

CHAPTER EIGHTEEN

The evening started out totally wrong, and Ford knew it was all his fault. What was he doing pressing all the floor buttons and making out with Greer in the elevator? He needed to have a productive evening of *painting*, not one in which he spent all his time either imagining making love to her or initiating foreplay.

But she was so delicious.

And so right for you, a forbidden, ridiculous voice in his head said.

He managed to pull himself together when they got to the studio and he saw a missed call on his phone from Anne. He knew what that was about. She was checking up on him. She'd ask questions: How far along was he with the sketches for the portrait? Would he make it in time for the showing? He'd need to figure in the stretch it took to ship the canvas over the ocean, too, and get it to the site as well.

And then worse, he saw a text from Teddy: *Feeling good, considering I'm eating for three.*

* * *

Dear God, it was nearly impossible to imagine Teddy pregnant. She had a big heart beneath her tough exterior, but she simply wasn't interested in revealing it very often, even to him. She found it a show of weakness. Even so, he'd been her biggest fan. Along with her stubborn reticence came a fierce independence he'd found refreshing. And when she did show her softer side, she'd been irresistible—at least to the old Ford.

New Ford—post-wedding disaster—recognized that he'd fallen for her out of sheer ego on his part. She was gorgeous, chased after by many men, and he was the privileged one she'd decided to open up to. They made a beautiful couple. The English tabloids thought so, as well as their friends.

But never again would he get involved with someone because he felt flattered by all the attention. The stupidity of it, the shallowness. . . .

He was embarrassed to have been reeled in so easily. But the hard lesson he'd learned had brought him to a new place. He was more humble now. Looking back, he saw that in a way he'd been as careless with women's hearts as Teddy had been with his. He'd never wanted to love anyone. Not really. He'd only wanted to play when he wasn't busy painting, with people who mattered little to him.

No more. When he wasn't painting these days, he wanted to think. To count off his blessings each day. To be with people who loved him for who he was—a painter on a lifelong journey—and whom he loved back.

Now that Teddy was pregnant, he had to wonder if she'd need to open up more. The babies would require demonstrations of love, wouldn't they? Could she manage to be emotionally available to them?

"What is it?" Greer asked, her arms around his waist from behind.

He shook his head. "Teddy. She's texting me about her appetite."

"Oh," said Greer, and dropped her arms.

He sighed. "She's eating for three, but she feels pretty good."

"I'm glad. It would be much worse on you if she were having complications."

"Yes," he said, striving to sound upbeat.

They both knew it was time to get to work. She undressed behind the screen, walked to the chaise lounge in her black robe, as he'd instructed her to the first day, and dropped the robe.

He swallowed, but his throat was dry. Her face was serene when she sat—like a princess, he thought. She swung up her legs and leaned back on the cushion.

Her strength, her sensuality, her beauty hit him hard. Could he get everything he saw in her in the portrait? He would do his best, but . . .

He didn't think he'd be able to.

A feeling of failure assailed him. Sometimes his talent felt like a bucket of water with a hole in the bottom, carried in the desert. Such buckets were useless, weren't they? They didn't do what they were supposed to. You knew at the beginning, too, that there were no lasting alternatives—fingers in the hole would have to come out at some point—and yet who in their right mind would put down that bucket of water in the glare and heat of the sun?

Was it worse prolonging the time to the inevitable thirst and dehydration? Or better to get the suffering over with sooner?

He was desperate. He wasn't in charge . . . the bucket was. *The damned bucket with a hole in it ran his life.* And that fact ate at him. It made him furious.

"You okay?" Greer asked.

"No," he said. "Not really."

She sat up a little higher. "*Oh.* I'm sorry."

"It has nothing to do with you." He couldn't help that his voice was clipped. "It's me, feeling sorry for myself."

"Can you tell me more?"

And so he did. He told her about the bucket. About the hole. About how he wasn't able to achieve his vision completely—on any project he did—and it made him crazy.

She stared at the wall for a moment, then looked back at him. "Throw the bucket away," she said.

"But that's just as bad. In fact, it means I've given up." He jabbed at the painting with his brush.

"No, it doesn't."

"How so?" He stopped painting. He didn't feel like hearing anyone else's well-meaning attempt to comfort him. He was ready to pounce on whatever she said and be bitter. He'd have to try very hard not to do so. It would be rude of him, and she didn't deserve rudeness.

"Well," she said, one of her hands resting lightly on her breast, "you throw away the bucket and cut into a cactus for water. They're like sponges inside. Slake your thirst there."

"Right," he said. Accompanied by a very short laugh.

She waved a hand at him. "Pooh on you. You're not willing to listen, are you?"

"Yes, I am," he said, feeling stubborn. "But I don't feel like dealing in metaphors anymore. You're suggesting that I come at this from a whole new angle, but that's much easier said than done. Finding a cactus in the desert is *easy* to do in a made-up story. Finding one in my life is much harder."

"But not impossible," she said.

"Thank you for caring," he said, "but it's time to move on."

"I have one more suggestion, and then I'll shut up about it."

"*You* don't need to shut up about it," he said. "*I* do. Examining your talent level is one of those unsolvable things that all artists grapple with, I suppose, and I should just get on with it—with my painting." And he did. He added a few brushstrokes. And he felt fine about them.

Fine.

It was such a lackluster word.

"So go ahead, tell me your suggestion," he said, realizing he'd been talking too much to let her.

"Okay," she said. "Drink, and drink, and drink *before* you go into the desert. Drink from life. Then you won't need the bucket *or* the cactus. The magic is already inside you. It's a part of you. Not something you have to carry around or look for. That's your problem. You're trying too hard to *find* it."

He had to smile. She was onto something. He most definitely tended to try too hard, and she was the first person who had ever come close to understanding him. Anne, even though she was a fellow artist, had never related to his frustration with himself. Her creative muse was always at her beck and call. He'd never once heard her doubt that the universe was supporting her, and she could write reams and reams of stories that pleased her no end with little to no suffering for her art involved.

"Thank you," he said to Greer. "You've made a good point."

She sent him a pert smile. "You're welcome."

She had intuition coupled with a well-grounded intelligence, a compelling combination that spoke to him. He wanted a companion like that, he realized then. Someone he could express his doubts to. Someone he could bounce ideas off. Someone he could respect and learn from.

He hadn't realized how much of a student of life he still was . . . until meeting Greer. He'd thought he'd known it all, hadn't he? And then Teddy's betrayal had happened, and here he was, raw and new. Starting over, really.

But it felt okay to do so with Greer. She was a comfort, a *friend*.

They kept working, and he felt more at peace. If he simply forged ahead and didn't think too hard about it, his painting was definitely good. It was painstaking work, but it would be something worthwhile if he simply stopped thinking so hard and painted, one stroke at a time.

And then for no reason at all—nothing had changed; a loud jet had flown overhead, a phone rang down the corridor—something shifted. It became easier. He was in a moment of flow, one of those inexplicable times when everything was in sync: his brain, his heart, his brush.

He had to run with it, try not to breathe and ruin the spell. Greer watched him without saying anything. Could she tell something was different? Better? She didn't let on if so.

Look. Paint. Look again, this time at the curve of her cheek. Next time the tapering of her nose. Paint. Dab. *Create*.

It was the rhythm of the artist in flow, as natural, it felt, as breathing, as the tide going in and out, the moon rising and falling, or making love to Greer the night before beneath the transom. When he was in it, he didn't know why he wasn't *always* there.

Because it felt so right.

In fact, he finally caught the pose he wanted to use in the portrait. It was a great feeling. As he was painting the outline of it, he could feel that it was the one. Adrenaline surged. His breathing became shallow but even.

There was something different about her . . . was it tied into the fact that they'd fooled around the night before? Or had some good conversations? She was more at ease with him now. She was also more alluring than ever, and lively. Wittier than ever. Warmer than ever. All the good things that showed up in body language and facial expression were there in her.

The most interesting thing was, the closer he got to the essence of her, the more there was to know about her.

So it was severely frustrating when about ten minutes into that marvelous state of inspired productivity, he received a call from Gus. Their dishwasher had overflowed while everyone was out of the apartment. The kitchen and living room in the flat were filled with water. Luckily, the dishwasher had ended its cycle. But the damage was done.

Hopefully, the water hadn't leaked through the ceiling. So far they hadn't heard from the downstairs neighbor, which was a good sign.

He'd gone from flow to *overflow*. The irony wasn't lost upon him.

Greer got it, too.

"It's too bad we have to leave," she said. "You were different these last few minutes. I can't explain, but I felt lighter on the couch. As if you and I were connected by something else. We were along for the ride, but we weren't in charge. It was relaxing and exciting all at once."

He paused in putting away his paints. She'd floored him with her acute awareness. He didn't know what to say, other than, "I was making progress. Yes."

Which sounded lame. But he didn't want to think too hard about how much he was beginning to like her. Actually, it went beyond *like* to something deeper. He *craved* her. Craved being with her. And that scared him.

But luckily, he had other things to think about. Greer dressed quickly, and they left the studio together. She took his bike; he rode her Vespa. He got there first, of course.

When she arrived, she stayed long enough to help get every towel in the house out and soak up what they could. And she found them the name of a water damage company. Then she left at his behest. There was literally nothing she could do, and there was no place to sit. He had to stay there and wait for the water damage company to show. He told Gus he could go out. He didn't mind. He was in a fantastic mood, despite the dishwasher issue.

Things had gone well at the studio that night.

But when Greer left his apartment, some of his excitement about the portrait left him. Cleaning up the water with her, he'd had to grab towels from his bathroom, and on the way, he'd seen the box in his room with Teddy's teddy in it. He'd been gripped once more with a sense that he didn't run his life. It ran him.

He felt trapped.

But it was his own fault. He couldn't blame his ex-fiancée for the fact that he might soon be a dad. He'd taken that chance every time he'd slept with her. It was a sobering thought, that because he'd been willing to gamble, he might have a huge responsibility—two, in fact—for the next eighteen years, and really, for the rest of his life. Because one didn't stop being a father, no matter how old the child. He knew that from watching his dad, who was still very worried about Rupert, and Rupert was thirty-five.

He waited until the next morning to tell Anne about Teddy. It was time. The floor in the kitchen was still damp. They had a giant fan blowing on it, thanks to the water restoration company. Drake and Gus woke up early to go sailing, and he made them eggs and toast to send them off.

"What's this?" Drake said, looking at his egg.

"It's an *egg*," said Ford.

"In the *shell*," Gus muttered.

Ford had gone to Williams-Sonoma on King Street and of course had picked up a box of egg cups, a few plates, glasses, and some silverware as soon as he'd moved in.

"You two plonkers need to learn to eat an egg properly." Ford sliced off the top of each egg, put a pat of butter on their tops, a little sprinkle of salt and pepper, and handed the boys a spoon. "Now eat." He threw a few pieces of toast like Frisbees in their general direction. They caught them and kept chewing. Apparently, the soft-boiled eggs were to their liking. "Dip the toast in the yolk, and then go about your day knowing you've been well fed."

"Ta," Gus said sarcastically.

Ford whipped him with a dishcloth on the ear.

"Ow." Gus grabbed his earlobe.

Drake laughed, then took a gulp from his mug and spit it out. "What *is* this shit? It isn't coffee!"

"Strong black tea, boys," said Ford. "Strong black tea. Nothing better for a hangover."

It was Gus's turn to laugh. "I dig tea," he said, and took a gentle sip from his. "Damn, my head hurts."

Ah, if only their little girlfriends could see them now.

"I'll make gentlemen out of you two yet," Ford said, right as Drake grabbed Gus's free arm and twisted it backward. Gus put his tea down and screamed bloody murder, which was Ford's cue to escape.

He went outside and called Anne on his mobile. Told her about Teddy.

"Good God," said Anne. "I'll go visit her. Tell me what you want me to say."

"I have no idea," he admitted.

"This is frightening," Anne said, "considering how ill she used you. Yet exciting, too, to think that my baby brother could be a father soon—to twins, no less."

"Exciting for you, maybe," he said. "Terrifying for me."

"Look," said Anne. "The terrifying part is only that if you're the father, you won't know the particulars of your arrangement with her for a good while. You'll be in limbo, while your baby is crying, pooping, laughing, and growing in Teddy's house. Darling, it's incumbent upon you to prepare as if they are indeed yours. You'll want to be fully involved if they are, from the get-go. Contact the family barrister immediately and let her know what's going on."

"I don't want Mum and Dad to know. They've already got Rupert to worry about."

Anne sighed. "Give them credit, will you? This is hardly terrible news. You'll not only survive but you'll thrive being a dad, and they'll love being grandparents. And if it turns out you're not the father, you'll at least have had the comfort of their support until you know. Because they *will* support you, no matter what."

"Right," he said.

There was a long pause. He felt very emotional. And alone. "Bollocks," he said. It was all he could get out. It was a plea of sorts, he knew, one he could indulge in with his only sister.

She gave a little hiccup of a cry. "Oh, my sweet brother, I know. Life has thrown you a giant curveball. And you're feeling alone. But you're not. You've got us."

"I know. And I'm grateful."

"We both knew someday you'd be a father with Teddy as your wife. So . . . she's not going to be. That's fine. And here you are, perhaps reaching fatherhood just a little bit sooner than we thought you would. But it's all right. It's better than all right. It's bloody marvelous if you really look at it."

"My life feels on hold until I know."

"You have to keep living."

"But I can't make any decisions. Not until I know."

"Why should anything change? You can be a father from whatever position in life you choose. You don't stop being you just because you might have made a baby. Or two. Your needs matter, as well. Were you contemplating any big decisions when you got this news?"

He sighed. "No. But I met someone. I like her."

"Oh." Anne didn't say anything more.

"It's not like that. We're not even in a relationship. I mean, we *are*—an arranged one. . . ."

"What in God's name?" Anne exclaimed.

He told her about their temporary engagement that all of Charleston knew about and supported.

"So it's that girl . . . the same one you stalked because she's perfect?"

"Yes."

"She'll pose for you if you act as her fiancé?"

"Right. Although she didn't ask me to go that far. I volunteered when I realized she would never win a wedding gown without a partner."

"You asked her to marry you? Onstage?"

"Uh, yes. I did."

"Good of you," is all Anne said.

"You're being awfully calm about this. It makes me nervous."

"Oh, don't be nervous," Anne said. "I simply know that if I press, or become excited that you say you really like someone, you might not tell me as much as you are. And I love hearing every juicy detail, especially something as dramatic as a public proposal! I'm a romance writer, darling. We love stories like this, although in my historicals the baron would have outright married her, consummated the marriage—maybe gotten her pregnant—then disappeared on the Continent for years, fighting Napoleon, while she languished at the castle back home." She gave a short laugh. "Of course, I don't want to know *everything* in your story."

"And I won't tell you *everything*," he said.

"Are you making progress with the portrait?"

"Somewhat. But she's awfully busy."

"You'll do it," Anne said. "Not only will you finish it, but it will be your best work yet."

"Always rooting for me, aren't you? Do me a favor. Let's not pretend I'm really good—yet."

"Way to think. I love you for the artist you can be."

"Thank you for misquoting *Jerry Maguire* so well."

"Shut up, little brother."

"I feel better now. We're fighting."

They were both laughing when he hung up. He always felt much better after talking to Anne. He could and he would get the portrait done, and he wouldn't agitate over whether it was his best work or not. He was coming to the conclusion that analyzing himself and his art didn't get him any closer to becoming better.

In that spirit, he ran five miles, came home and did his daily hundred push-ups, and ate his own soft-boiled egg in an egg cup. Two, as a matter of fact, with dry toast and a mug of tea. His spirit felt revived from the tea alone. His parents had instilled in him that he was of strong constitution and character, and that fact consoled him. He damned well would keep calm and carry on.

Greer called him about ten A.M. to ask about the water damage and if all was well.

"We're drying out," he said. "Thanks for lending assistance. And your Vespa."

"My pleasure," she said. "I'm getting a little behind on the preparation for the bake-off. Any chance you could come help? The girls are taking over for me at the office today so I can tackle this."

"Of course."

"Meet me at Macy's garden shed." She gave him directions.

When he got there, he laughed. She wore a pair of cut-off denim shorts, a man's V-neck white T-shirt, and Reeboks that looked as if they'd seen better days. She already had pink paint on her nose, and she was holding an electric screwdriver.

"You look like a pin-up girl on a hardware calendar," he said. "A very competent one, of course."

"I'm an ace with tools," she said. "Watch out."

She explained to him what she was up to.

"You got all this just this morning?" he said, looking around the shed at her supplies.

"Sure." She shrugged.

"But you don't have a car. How'd you get them here?"

"A friend took me in his pickup truck." She sifted through a toolbox, looking for something. "Pete."

Pete, Ford thought, and couldn't believe he felt slightly

jealous. But no way would he ask about him. He had no right, no claim on her.

"What a glorious day," he said instead. "I can see the edge of the harbor from here. It's shockingly blue."

They took a minute to look at it together, and then they got to work. They had a great time. A fat cat named Oscar came and joined them, and a while later, two kids from next door, who were suitably impressed.

"We're getting our mommy to take us to your cake party tonight," said the older one. She must have been five.

"I'm coming, too," croaked the younger one, like a frog. He couldn't have been more than three.

"Good," said Greer. She crouched down and hugged them both. "I'll see you there."

An hour after the kids left, things got a little hot and heavy when they took a break for lunch in Macy's kitchen. Greer wasn't hungry.

"Too much adrenaline," she said.

He got her against the kitchen counter, and they kissed until the only option was either getting completely naked and risking Macy walking in or going back to work.

They went back to work. They had four hours to go before the bake-off.

The rest of the afternoon flew by. Not once did they talk about Teddy and Ford's possible looming job as parent. And Greer didn't talk about anything deep, either. They kept it low-key, and he liked that. He *needed* that.

"You're coming with me," Greer was saying. "Absolutely no one can leave Charleston without walking across the Ravenel Bridge. And then afterward, we'll go to the gospel brunch at Hall's Chophouse. My treat."

He grinned. It felt so good to be able to relax with someone. Really relax. He didn't even remember the last time he'd felt this good being with someone. He wanted to tell her, but he didn't know how. And it probably wasn't a great idea.

"Sounds good," he said, "but you'll have to let me return the favor in London. We'll ride the Eye, then walk across Westminster Bridge and go to afternoon tea at the Library Lounge. Great views of Parliament."

She looked at him for a second, and he saw a glint of sadness, or regret, or something. Whatever it was, it stole a bit of the spark from her. "Okay," she said in a politely cheerful voice, but things felt less upbeat after that.

It couldn't be that she was wishing he'd stay in Charleston.

But why couldn't it? He was wishing the same thing. He wasn't one to beat around the bush. He put down his paintbrush, went over to her, and took her gently by the upper shoulders. "I don't want to go back to London," he said. "You're a lot of fun. It's been too long since I've had this much fun."

A smile formed on her lips immediately. "I was thinking the same thing."

He kissed her until she dropped her wet paintbrush on her sneaker.

Things got better again.

They had an hour to go and were on a last-minute run to a discount store that had everything in the world in it that you might need for your home: HomeGoods. Greer was buying some things for the bake-off table. "You're sure the doughnut shop is holding up their end of the deal?" he asked her.

"Yes, they are," she said. "They're fantastic. And super-excited." She tossed him a wry look. "Don't be disappointed if we don't win. This is a real long shot. But even if we don't, I had fun, and I'm proud of us for giving it our all. You and me. And Oscar. He oversaw every-thing."

"I couldn't agree more," Ford said, and grinned at the memory of Oscar's tail tirelessly waving while the cat watched them work in the shed.

"If I can get at least second place at the bake-off and then knock the next competition out of the park, I can still win the whole shebang," she said.

"I have full faith you will," he said.

"We have one huge advantage in the bake-off."

"What?"

"Out of all the blindfolded partners in the taste test, you're more likely to know which sample cake is mine," she said. "Especially as I made sure we didn't get cake doughnuts. We got the original light, airy, classic ones."

"I never thought of that." He liked how strategically she was approaching this challenge. "At least we have that going for us. We also have your charm. Don't forget that."

"And your pecs," she said, looking at him over some reading glasses she'd donned to read price tags. "They might bring in some votes."

"You American girls are cheeky," he said.

"And you love it," she said back, and kissed him.

He loved everything about *her*. When she turned back to her shopping, he realized how close he was coming to another disaster.

CHAPTER NINETEEN

Arriving at the bake-off almost felt anti-climactic to Ford after the great day he'd had with Greer. The event was being held at Hibernian Hall, a beautiful old dancing room that had held many prestigious events in Charleston.

The first thing they did, aside from experience mild panic because the doughnut people hadn't arrived yet and Greer's table was empty, was go greet all the brides and their true loves.

"That's a truly beautiful display," Greer said to Wesley and Serena.

"It's on its way," Serena said back, and tweaked a bunch of flowers she'd put on the table.

"Just wanted to say hi," Greer said. "*We* still have tons to do."

"Oh, wow," Serena said, eyeing her flowers still.

"Good luck," said Ford.

"Catch you later." Wesley grinned.

Serena waved the tips of her fingers and smiled in their general direction.

"They were perfectly friendly," Greer said low as they

walked away. "But not as friendly as they were before the contest."

"She's nervous," Ford said. "That's all. And focused on what she has to do."

"You're right," Greer said.

They were back at their table. Ford bent over, grabbed one side of the peg wall they'd borrowed from her friend Pete—who'd built it for a school carnival years before—and which they'd painted pink that morning. Greer took the other side. Together they hoisted it onto the table. It rested on an A-shaped frame that kept it secure and standing. The front side with the pegs was perpendicular to the table and made an eye-catching—if currently empty—display.

"This is going to be really cool." She was speaking to Ford even as she was eyeing her pink wooden backdrop.

He was next to her now, his arms crossed over his chest, his eye also on the display. And then he took a sideways step so he could be closer to her. "May I, madam?" He held his arm out.

"Sure," she said.

He curved his arm around her waist and pulled her closer. "I've enjoyed this day. And don't worry, the doughnut people will come."

"If they don't, we'll look pretty silly." She laughed. "Thanks for being part of why I'm happy right now." She looked him right in the eye.

"*That* was kind of you." Deep inside he let a glow of contentment push down any misgivings he had about opening up too much. Holding her felt exactly right. "And I'd like to say, in the words of Gus and Drake, 'Right back atcha, dude.'"

"I mean it." She turned slightly, stood on her tiptoes, and kissed his cheek.

"Thanks." That was more than sweet to him. That was a validation he sorely needed. When Teddy left him, he wondered if he was able to make *anyone* happy. He turned Greer in his arms just a little bit. "Hey, we're in a fake engagement. How about a public display of affection? It's what we're supposed to do, right?"

"It can't hurt."

He kissed her full on the mouth. Then they pulled apart. He liked her. A lot.

Her brows shot up, and her eyes were a little wary. "Are you faking it until you make it right now? Because if so, you're really good at it. I'm feeling all warm and fuzzy."

He contemplated telling her the truth, that he was getting a massive crush on her. But at the last second he changed his mind. "I'm absolutely playing the wedding game," he said. "Am I doing it well?" He strove for a happy-go-lucky grin.

"Too well." Her face lit up. "The doughnut people are here!" she said, and rushed to the top of the stairs to greet them.

"Right," he murmured as he watched her go. "The doughnut people are here." Let her think he was simply pretending. That he thought of her as nothing more than a new and great friend. It was best that way.

CHAPTER TWENTY

"Okay, so let me describe it," Greer was saying on the phone to Ella, who was down with a stomach bug and couldn't come to the bake-off. Ella refused to use a smartphone. She was on a flip phone kick. She wanted to go back to a simpler time, probably because her other Sicilian grandmother had come to live with the family. Ella's latest *nonna* refused to watch TV or listen to any singer on the radio who became famous after Frank Sinatra. And the newest *nonna* hated Alexa, the talking streaming device. She thought Alexa was possessed.

So Greer couldn't send Ella a smartphone camera photo of her cake display.

"Tell me every detail about the table," said Ella. "I'll pass everything on to Miss Thing."

Miss Thing was cooking supper for their elderly accountant so she could get free tax advice on her winnings from *The Price Is Right*. She'd invited Pete from Roastbusters to join them because he'd made a special drink in her honor when she came back from Hollywood: *The Price Is Right* cappuccino, made with California almond syrup and a dollar-bill sign drizzled on top of the froth in caramel. When someone ordered it, Pete would say the person's name, then, "Come on down!"

Miss Thing had ordered it every day since being back. So had Greer, as a matter of fact.

"Well," Greer began, "there's a big sign I painted on wooden planks Pete nailed together for me. It says A HOLE LOTTA LOVE. You know, *hole*, *H-O-L-E*. Because our wedding cake theme is doughnuts."

Ella laughed.

"It looks very cute and vintage," said Greer.

"You're so artistic," Ella said.

"Thanks, and then we have this pegboard I borrowed from Pete and painted bright pink this morning."

"It's already dry?"

"Oh, yeah. Hours ago. And on every peg—which we wrapped in parchment paper—we hung doughnuts. All different kinds."

"Oh, my God, I love it," said Ella.

"And then we have small glass bottles I converted into vases and they're sitting on top of the pegboard. They're filled with white, blue, and pink hydrangeas Macy's little neighbors picked for me today from their mother's garden, with her permission. And next to the vases is the word DOUGHNUTS written in metal marquee letters that light up. I got that at HomeGoods this afternoon."

"What a find!" Ella said.

"I know. I was so excited! The A HOLE LOTTA LOVE sign is on the left-hand side of the front of the table. On the right side is the actual doughnut wedding cake."

"You have that *and* the doughnuts on the pegs?"

"The doughnuts on the pegs are for the public. They can take one home with them in a little paper bag that says, 'Glazed and Delicious from the Mr. and Mrs.' and at the bottom of the bag it says, 'Greer and Ford.'"

"How'd you get that printed up so fast?"

"I called in a favor to our printing company." Greer saw Pierre's henchwoman Kiki out of the corner of her eye, and cringed inside. She'd looked her up on Facebook and Google and found out the woman basically had nothing to lose by hitching her wagon to Pierre's.

Kiki was waving her arms around and yelling at Henny.

"I have to go very soon," Greer said fast to Ella. "We have three minutes until the door opens. But let me quickly tell you about the doughnut wedding cake. Have you heard about the Golden Doughnut?"

"No."

"*Forbes* wrote about it. A single doughnut covered in a gold icing with little shavings of twenty-four-carat gold on top. You can get it for a hundred dollars in New York."

"Are you kidding?"

"No. So I asked my local doughnut vendor to make me a gorgeous tower of pink-frosted doughnuts, with beautiful tone-on-tone pink nonpareils sprinkled on them, and I surrounded them with more flowers from Macy's neighbor's garden, so they look very pretty, like we're at a backyard reception. But at the very top of the pink tower, out of reach of prying hands but easily visible, the vendor is putting her own version of the Golden Doughnut. It's really going to stand out. She's making true metallic gold icing that has a hint of champagne in it, and I actually think she's putting gold flake on top. One of the members of the public will win it. But they can't be eligible to take it home unless they vote for me. I checked with Henny, and she said that's fine. It shows initiative. She said no one is stopping the other brides from doing something creative to win votes. She told us that at the beginning, too."

"You're so smart to listen so well! Do you have a sign that says, 'Win the Golden Doughnut?'"

"I actually have a shirt on that says that. I made one for Ford, too. It's a tight white T-shirt, and it shows off his pecs."

"Smart."

"And Macy's little neighbors are carrying baskets filled with slips of paper they're handing out that say, 'Win the Golden Doughnut.'"

"Adorable."

"Of course, *they* want to win it." Greer chuckled. "I'm going to have to get the vendor to make them one later. There's a table with copies of all five cakes that the public can taste test samples from, but I intentionally told the doughnut people *not* to make a Golden Doughnut for that cake. It has to be one-of-a-kind."

"Smart. How will you find out exactly who voted for you so you can choose a winner?"

"Easy. They have to put their ballots in a box on my table. So when they do, I'll have them sign a little notebook with their name and phone number. That way I can keep track and text whoever wins. They don't even have to stay to the end. I'll deliver the doughnut if they have to leave, even if they live fifty miles away."

"Wow. That's dedication."

"It's all I can think of to do."

"You were too hard on the doughnut idea," Ella said. "Everyone loves doughnuts. A lot of gorgeous wedding cakes are just for show. You slice into them, and they're *meh*."

"I've had cakes like those, but these vendors are amazing, Ella."

"I'm sure they are. But believe in your Golden Doughnut!"

"I will."

"What do the other displays look like?"

"Very pretty. All of the cakes are stunning. Wesley and Serena's is probably the prettiest and coolest. It's a beaded cake. But only two other finalists are giving away little wedding favors, and neither giveaway has a *wow* factor. At one table with a gorgeous lace cake there are mints made in little wrappers with the bride and her groom's names on them. And at a table with a tropical-themed cake, they have beer cozies printed with the couple's names and wedding date on them."

"And you have your doughnut wall and a chance to win the Golden Doughnut."

"Right. Wesley and Serena have a collection of beautiful photos of themselves doing different things, in gorgeous frames. That's it. But the overall feel to their table is very classic and romantic, more than any of the others."

"You're going for the vintage, homestyle look," said Ella.

"Yes. We're dealing with doughnuts, after all."

"Honey, you played this right. I don't see how you can lose. Even if the other wedding cakes are prettier."

Greer started feeling hopeful. "I tried really, really hard to make the best of what I'm working with."

"And I think it will pay off," said Ella. "Have any of the other brides said anything to you about your display? And your Golden Doughnut shirt?"

"No, but they're looking nervous. Serena seems a little angry."

"Well, she can take her anger and stuff it. Ford proposed to you, fair and square, and you had no idea it was coming. And before that, you were willing to present yourself as a partnerless bride, and the audience loved it enough to vote you into the finals. You've done nothing wrong. So where's Ford now?"

"He's heading my way. He went outside and up and

down the line of people waiting to get in. He introduced himself and showed off his shirt."

Ella laughed. "He's adorable."

"He *is* pretty cute."

"Seen him naked yet?" Ella asked.

"Hey, now," said Greer.

"Tell me when you do. Oops, my latest *nonna* might have heard me say that. She just hit her cane hard on the floor. She pretends to be deaf but only when it suits her. Gotta go."

Greer said good-bye and hung up right as Kiki opened the doors to the ballroom and the public poured in. The crowd was composed mainly of younger women, but there were some families, too, with small children, and older couples who simply loved love and wanted to check out how other people celebrated weddings.

Greer's table was besieged immediately.

And the crowd didn't stop. She got so many entries to win the Golden Doughnut, her ballot box was stuffed to the top. She had to keep pushing votes down. And everyone thanked her over and over for the doughnut wall. They loved it! Little kids beamed when they got to hold their bag with a doughnut of their choice tucked inside. Young women thought the doughnut wall would be a great addition to their wedding receptions, especially when Greer mentioned it would be nice with a coffee bar nearby. She showed them a sign she'd seen on Pinterest that said, WE GO TOGETHER LIKE COFFEE AND DONUTS.

And everyone laughed at the A HOLE LOTTA LOVE sign.

She hardly got to see Ford. He was busy meeting people at the other end of the table, and then, of course, they had to take him away for the blindfolded taste test. Two of the five future spouses guessed their bride's cake accurately: Wesley and Ford. The other three didn't, and those brides weren't very happy because now Serena and Greer's votes would be doubled.

Greer made eye contact with Serena when both their guys guessed right. Greer clapped, and she grinned at Serena. Serena smiled back but didn't show her teeth, a telltale sign of a woman not pleased.

Whatever. Greer could only do Greer, and Serena could act however she wanted. And sure, tensions were running high, and a little pique was to be expected when a person was desperate for a dress and someone else wanted the exact same one.

In fact, the other four brides, having seen the success of the Golden Doughnut giveaway, quickly came up with their own. Toni got her friend to bring in a hundred-dollar Target gift card. Carol gave away three months' worth of yoga lessons at her studio. Lisa offered to bake twelve dozen homemade granola bars, good for freezing, and Serena took off her watch and put it on the table.

"She's kidding, right?" Macy said when she saw that. She'd arrived late because she'd had to attend a board meeting at Deacon's nonprofit, the Sustainability Project. "It's a Rolex."

"I don't think she's kidding." Greer sighed.

"Maybe it's a fake," said Macy.

"I doubt it." Greer folded her arms and watched her ballot box stay just the way it was. Not a single new vote came in after the Rolex got put out. In fact, two people came over and said they knew just where their ballots were at the top of Greer's box, and they wanted to take them back. Of course, she let them, and they brought them straight over to Serena's table and stuffed them in her ballot box.

The votes would be tallied by Henny and a representative from Channel Four a half hour before the event ended.

"Please tell me Kiki isn't involved in the ballot counting," Greer asked Henny, when Henny came over to check on her.

La Di Da's manager rolled her eyes. "No, thank goodness. But she told me to tell you she's here to help you in any way."

"You mean all the future brides, right?"

"No," Henny said, eyeing Greer over her spectacles. "Just you."

Greer wished she had on *her* reading glasses so she could eye Henny right back. "I don't like what you're implying, Henny. Kiki and I aren't in cahoots, I'll have you know."

"Sorry." Henny looked mildly abashed. "I just don't understand her interest in you in particular."

"Pierre wants Kiki to intimidate me out of the competition. Her offering to help me is something you might hear a goon say in *The Godfather* to someone who's about to get axed."

"Oh, dear." Henny fingered her pearls. "Pierre would do that?"

"Henny. Please. You know him as well as I do. Of course, he would. He doesn't like me being in the contest. We have a history, you see. We could never find him a match at Two Love Lane."

Henny gave her a tentative smile. "I feel for you." She paused. "He's not easy to get along with. Thank you for being honest with me and for bringing such interest and enthusiasm to this competition. You certainly know how to shake things up."

"You're welcome," Greer said.

At the end of the evening, she gave away the Golden Doughnut to a Mr. Percival Remount of Folly Beach.

"I'll never eat it," he said, and then changed his mind and took a bite out of it right then and there, which made Greer love him.

She also lost the bake-off to Serena.

Right after Henny made the announcement, someone started playing *Queen's Greatest Hits* over speakers hidden in the walls somewhere.

At their table Serena and Wesley hugged each other hard, but while they were hugging, Serena peeked at Greer over Wesley's shoulder.

Greer waved.

Serena squeezed her eyes shut and kept hugging Wesley.

"I hope it was worth losing a Rolex," Greer yelled to Ford over the music.

"At least we got second place," Ford yelled back. "You told me you had to get that to have a chance to win."

"Right," said Greer, and tugged on his hand, then kissed him with almost everything in her—she held something back—but it was still way better than hugging like Serena and Wesley. And everyone watched.

"Hurrah!" her two favorite little kids yelled, the ones who'd visited her at Macy's garden shed. Their mommy tried hard to cover their eyes.

Greer took note and stopped immediately. Ford would understand.

"Let's dance!" she said. "Another One Bites the Dust" was playing. The little kids danced with her, and so did some teens and grownups. Ford walked away to give a party favor bag of doughnuts to an old lady in a wheelchair.

Macy came running over and started dancing next to Greer. "You're not at all like yourself. Ever since we got back from *The Price Is Right*. You're making out.

Dancing. Smiling way more than usual. Did you have any vodka before you got here?"

"No," said Greer. "I'm just having fun. I hope you are, too."

"It was wonderful," said Macy. "But aren't you worried about not winning the gown?"

"I—" Greer shut her mouth and opened it again. "Of course, I am." But then she smiled. She couldn't help it. She was thinking about Ford in his "Win the Golden Doughnut" shirt. He looked so hot! She hoped he'd wear it always, just to remember today. And if they didn't get to sleep together soon, she was going to die of frustration.

"Greer." Macy snapped her fingers in front of her face. "Greer!"

"*What?*"

"Are you in love?"

Greer blinked. She felt a little faint, actually. She'd forgotten to eat that day, highly unusual for her. She'd had no appetite because she'd had butterflies in her stomach. She'd been sure it was about the contest. Her heart had raced. All day she'd felt weird feelings of exhilaration followed by some anxiety, and then exhilaration again. And then anxiety.

She wanted to win *Royal Bliss* so badly!

But maybe all that craziness had been about Ford, the way he'd smiled at her when the two little kids came over to the shed. And the way he'd petted Oscar. And kissed her in the kitchen. And walked away from her to give that old lady a party favor bag of doughnuts just now. What would it be like if he flew back to England and she never saw him again?

"I think I need a doughnut," is all she said to Macy, and then fainted right on top of her.

CHAPTER TWENTY-ONE

It was the morning after the bake-off. The night before Greer's friends Macy and Deacon had insisted on taking her home after she'd fainted. Ford had volunteered and was quite disappointed when he'd been told to stand down—in a friendly manner by Deacon.

"I get that her long-term friends want to claim the privilege of attending to her," Ford had said, "but *I* want to take her home."

"Nope," Deacon said. "But thanks for the offer."

"I *like* her," Ford said.

"And she may like you," Deacon replied easily. "But you're in limbo, as far as I'm concerned."

"Limbo?"

"A bachelor with no personal commitments beyond family, and even there you probably shy away from getting too involved. Limbo looks a lot like freedom, right? But it sucks. I remember being there myself." And he took off to get his truck and pull it around the front of Hibernian Hall to pick up Greer and Macy.

Ford had gone home and had one scotch too many trying to forget what Deacon had said about limbo. He'd been right—limbo *did* suck. Gus and Drake had come home from the pubs on Upper King Street three sheets to the wind themselves and had urged him to go find Deacon and beat him up. But Ford dubbed them "young fools" and "daft buggers," and they called him an "ancient relic" and "stupid Brit." All three of them accepted their insults, no problem, because Ford discovered some expensive cigars he thought he'd already smoked but hadn't. They were in the top drawer in the kitchen, where he'd gone to look for a corkscrew. The cigars had rolled behind the silverware.

So they adjourned to the porch to smoke their bounty then went to their rooms to sleep the evening off.

Now it was one P.M. the next day, and Ford slunk into Roastbusters to order a coffee before he dropped by Two Love Lane to pick up Greer. They were heading to his studio, and he wanted to take the very last edge off his hangover. He couldn't help remembering that the last time he'd brought her to the studio, he'd found his sweet spot—flow, some artists called it—where the painting had come easily. And he wanted to get there again.

Don't try so hard, he reminded himself.

That had been Greer's advice, and he intended to take it.

A happy guy at Roastbusters handed him his cup of coffee. "So you're the guy who proposed to Charleston's favorite partnerless bride?"

"One and the same," said Ford. "Thanks for not writing anything on my cup, by the way."

"Roastbusters doesn't do that. I call people over. I say, 'The sweetie with the mocha frap.' Or 'the future judge who got the black coffee.' And they always know who got what, and we never mess up."

"From now on, feel free to address me as the artist who has to go home too soon," Ford said.

"And I'm Pete," the guy said. They shook hands. "Those lovely young ladies at Two Love Lane are like my daughters. Except Miss Thing. She's a hot tamale, isn't she?"

"She certainly is," Ford said, intrigued that Miss Thing had inspired such a compliment from the barista. Did he have a crush on her? Did Miss Thing know it?

He'd mention it to Greer later. Maybe her matchmaking algorithms could sort it all out.

Pete's forehead scrunched up. "You know what? Greer's smart. One of the smartest people I know. She wouldn't get into something over her head. So I'm gonna trust her on this one."

"I think you should," said Ford.

Pete shrugged. "It's you who might be in over *your* head. You seem like a nice guy. I've seen you in here a few times. You say your *pleases* and your *thank yous*. You don't try to pick up the college girls."

"Uh, thanks. I guess. For watching out for your college-aged customers. But what do you mean I—"

"I mean if you have anything but the best intentions with Greer, she's going to smack you upside the head with them." Pete chuckled. "I don't know exactly what she's up to with this so-called engagement, but she must have her reasons. So stay on the straight and narrow."

"Good advice." Ford eyed the barista with some amusement. "I'm glad to have met you. She's mentioned your name several times . . . I was a little jealous. Now that we've chatted, I still am."

Pete grinned and winked. "I haven't run out of steam yet."

Greer had a lot of friends. That was the takeaway lesson along with Ford's coffee-to-go.

Two minutes and a narrow cobblestone alley later, he was at the wrought iron front gate at Two Love Lane. It squeaked when he opened it, which sent a wave of nostalgia through him. His grandmother's garden gate had done the same thing. The fountain with the cherub spouting water reminded him of every English garden he'd ever stolen naps in—quite a few. It was his favorite hobby from boyhood to the present day. The sound of the trickling water falling into a stone receptacle always sent him into a peaceful doze, but he ignored the lure of the tree and bench he passed—both excellent resting spots—and ascended the broad steps and knocked on the massive door. It opened so fast, someone must have been looking out a window and seen him coming. Or maybe there were hidden security cameras.

At any rate, Ford got the feeling that people in Charleston were worried about who he was and whether he could somehow hurt Greer.

"Well, well," said Miss Thing, her hand on her hip. She smiled, her red lipstick reminiscent of Hollywood glamour from the fifties. Her shiny gray dress was kind of boxy and almost to her knee—very chic in a matronly way, if that was possible. She'd put a round pearl brooch on the collar, which stood up and encircled her neck like a fortress wall. Her shoes were low-heeled leather with square toes.

Hot tamale? If he didn't know any better, he'd think she was dressed like his mother, the quintessential British matron. Or the Queen.

"Have you gotten the tour?" Miss Thing asked, and let him in.

He crossed the threshold and felt an indescribable sense of well-being. Maybe it was the smell of baking. Or the beautiful old staircase. He also enjoyed a view through two open French doors of an office with an antique desk and a chair covered in strawberry-colored silk.

"Not really," he said.

"I'm making cookies," Miss Thing said. "Do you like chocolate chip?"

"I love them," he said.

"Well, come see the kitchen. We'll have tea, too. The hot kind." She giggled. "Around here, when you say we'll have tea, everyone assumes you mean iced."

"I've never had iced tea, and I don't mind if I never do. But I'd love a good, hot cup of tea. Thank you. I'm here to pick up Greer. Did she tell you?"

"She sure did." Miss Thing walked him through the foyer and down a well-lit hall with a large rectangular glass window at the other end. Behind the huge oak outside, Ford saw a bit of blue sky. "But she got ambushed by a client a few minutes ago. Sometimes they get very emotional about their dating situation and come running in here for advice without making an appointment. I'm sure she'll be finished soon."

They walked into a kitchen that was very cheery. The cookies were on a cooling rack on the counter. "I'll just put on the kettle." She filled one from the tap and put it on the stove.

"You even have an Aga," he said. "I feel like I'm back home."

She laughed. "I'm an Anglophile myself. I love Her Majesty, Queen Elizabeth."

He thought it was cute how formally she said that. "Have you ever been to the U.K.?"

"No," she said. "But that's next on my bucket list. After

I see Buckingham Palace, I'd like to wear Wellies and stay in a cottage in the Cotswolds more than anything."

"I hope you do." He didn't tell her he had a lovely five-bedroom cottage in the Cotswolds he'd be happy to lend to her or invite her to when he was staying there. He preferred that everyone on this side of the Atlantic not know about his identity in England because having a title meant people treated you differently. Maybe someday he could tell Miss Thing. But he had no idea when that would be. "I hear you did very well getting your *Price Is Right* bucket list goal met. In fact, I'd like to not only congratulate you but to thank you for the drinks you provided Greer and her friends at The Rooftop. I was honored to be designated one of them. I saw you at the cocktail party the night we got, ah, engaged. But I never had a chance to thank you properly."

Miss Thing was busy getting two mugs ready while he spoke. "It was my pleasure," she said, and looked at him quite pointedly. "I understand Greer wants this wedding gown, and I have to admit I encouraged her to do something crazy. I hope she won't regret it."

Hmmm. What could he offer her for reassurance? "We've enjoyed getting to know each other well in a very short time. There's a mutual respect between us. Does that make you feel any better?"

"It does. Have you two discussed what happens when this fake engagement and the contest is over?"

"No. It's pretty self-evident, isn't it?"

"I suppose it is. You'll go your separate ways." The tea kettle started a soft whistle. Miss Thing let it get a little louder, then she poured the boiling water into the two mugs.

"I've known Greer only a short time," Ford said, "and I already think she knows how to take care of herself better than most. So I don't think you should worry about her."

"She's a very strong woman," Miss Thing agreed. "But of course I worry about her because I love her." She dunked a tea bag up and down in one of the mugs.

"She's very lucky," he said, "to have you as a friend."

Miss Thing stopped her dunking. "I like you, so I'm going to give you fair warning: You can't be around one of my girls for long and not fall head over heels. You might not be able to walk away."

She was just like Pete.

"I can take care of myself," Ford assured her. "Greer and I will always be friends. We'll both be fine."

But he could tell Miss Thing didn't believe him. Her mouth pursed when she brought tea and those delicious American chocolate chip cookies to the table. But they managed to talk nonstop about the Royal Family until Greer showed up in the kitchen.

Her cheeks were flushed. "Sorry I'm a little late."

"We've had a fine time," said Miss Thing. "Ford has kept me well entertained."

He stood. "Miss Thing has been delightful company."

"She always is," said Greer.

"You look good," he said. "Are you feeling better after last night?"

"Oh, yes, within a minute or two, I was fine. That's the first time in my life I've ever fainted. I got too caught up in the bake-off preparations."

"Nothing is more important than taking care of your health," said Miss Thing. "A doughnut would have done the trick. Now eat a cookie. It's good for the soul." She handed one to Greer.

Greer took a bite. "Oh, that's yummy!" She grinned.

"If anyone calls," she said to Miss Thing, "I'll be in the office again tomorrow morning."

"Where you off to?" Miss Thing asked.

"Posing for the portrait. Remember?" Greer took another bite of the cookie. "I'm taking half days all week, so we can get good daylight."

"Oh, of course. You haven't taken vacation since last year." Miss Thing's cheeks turned pink, so Ford guessed that Greer had told her she was posing nude.

"We're headed to my studio," he said, hoping Miss Thing would realize it was serious business. "If you'd ever like to come see it, I'd love to show you around."

"Oh!" She took a deep breath. "Well, I-I—"

"Just say the word," he said.

She seemed relieved he didn't push. "The truth is"—he waited for a polite let-down or even a mild rebuke—"I'd love to visit your studio."

"Fantastic," he said, and was about to suggest a block of days that would work for him.

"Tomorrow at noon," Miss Thing added in firm tones. "Greer doesn't have a mother in town. So I'm standing in. See you then."

He and Greer looked at each other, and he saw laughter dancing in her eyes.

"I look forward to it," he said to Miss Thing.

She waved a hand at him. "All righty, off you go." And to Greer she said, "You be good."

"Do I have to be?" Greer whispered to her as she hugged her good-bye.

Ford pretended not to hear.

"Oh, never mind." Miss Thing chuckled and kissed Greer's cheek.

* * *

And so Miss Thing stayed true to her word and visited the studio. Ford enjoyed every moment of her perusal of the space, and especially enjoyed her veiled comments about how she expected him to be a gentleman at all times and her not-so-subtle probings about his family, which he deflected by producing a beautiful small cake he'd purchased at Saffron for them to share with more hot cups of tea.

For the entire work week, he was gratified that Greer spent every afternoon at the studio. Each day at one P.M. he'd stop at Roastbusters first to say hello to Pete and get a coffee. And then he'd head to Two Love Lane to pick up his favorite portrait poser. He'd be sure to say hello to Miss Thing, Ella, and Macy if they were there. He was always amused at how they'd hover the way mothers and best friends did. It was as if he and Greer were going on a date instead of to work. While she tied up loose ends in her office, the women would crowd around him, ask questions, feed him, or give him tea, and then they'd shoo the two of them out the door with many exhortations to have fun.

Out in the open air, it was as if he and Greer had broken out of a very pleasant jail and were finally free. They'd laugh. And occasionally, walking to the studio, they'd hold hands—very briefly, though. It was always when they were on King Street, between Wentworth and George, in the vicinity of the College of Charleston. Almost on cue, a student who'd seen them onstage would call out, "Hey, you two! In love yet?" or something teasing like that. So they'd grab hands and shout back, "We're working on it!" Or "What do you think?" and maybe even give each other a peck on the lips.

It was all in fun.

At the studio, Greer was a great model, very patient. She didn't complain when she'd come to the easel during a break and look at what he'd accomplished, only to see that he'd done very little obvious work. He'd gotten the pose he wanted on canvas, but it was filling it in, capturing it the exact way he envisioned it in his head, that frustrated him now. But this stumbling through the dark was always part of the process—at least his.

The other habit they'd fallen into, besides walking to work, was a much more intimate one.

But she held back. "I don't feel right," she said. She was talking about sleeping together. "No matter how protected you are or I am, you're in an awkward position. What if you *are* a dad? This is a stressful time for you. I'd rather not take any chances with my heart, and you don't need a new relationship, either. Not that we're truly headed in that direction. But it's smart to stay vigilant."

"Right," he'd say. "We're having fun. And we're good friends."

"Yes," she'd say, "and I want to keep it that way."

"Agreed."

Every day when his lust peaked and he longed to bed her, she'd find another way to satisfy his cravings. And he, hers. There was a forbidden aspect to it, too. He'd put the DO NOT DISTURB sign on the door to keep socializers on the corridor away while Greer was posing nude. But it came in handy, too, when they explored each other's bodies and brought each other to exquisite pleasure, which was somehow made even more enjoyable because it was mingled with frustration. Each time they made the conscious decision to thwart a true coupling, their desire to actually go there deepened.

He couldn't deny, however, that a small part of him was actually relieved they weren't having sex. Greer was right. Their relationship could go only so far this way. They both knew that and accepted it.

He'd been a bachelor a long time, and he'd had a lot of fun, but it was time to admit to himself that sex was more than sex. He knew as well as any thinking adult that certain intimate acts sometimes carried with them expectations that others didn't. Avoiding a full-fledged sexual relationship meant avoiding bigger questions.

So creative, no-strings-attached sensual play was the order of the day. Sometimes it took place on the sofa. Or the countertop. Sometimes she was on her knees. Or he was.

Every evening, after they were finished working and frolicking, they'd stop somewhere cozy like Butcher and Bee, or The Ordinary, have a good bottle of wine between them, and something simple like oysters or a cheese plate, and then he'd take her home. He'd never actually been upstairs to her apartment. She'd kiss him and run. She had work to catch up on, always. Sometimes he'd go back to his studio to work himself.

And no matter how much fun they were having, always in the back of his mind, he wondered about Teddy. Was he a father? Or not?

So Greer was right. He was in no place to get in deep with anyone. And he liked her more and more every time she showed that sort of understanding.

He'd go to bed thinking about her. And he'd wake up thinking about her. Somehow it made his limbo—the torturous waiting for news from Teddy that would go on for many more months—easier to bear.

CHAPTER TWENTY-TWO

All week long, while the "Working Diva Without a Man" theme was outperforming Greer's expectations in a huge way—even though she hadn't yet had an actual man in her bedroom—she meant to call Jill and tell her how well things were going.

But she didn't have to. Jill came into the office. She shut the door and burst into tears.

"Why are you crying?" Greer put away her latest Perfect Wedding album—she'd been cutting out pictures of possible bridesmaid gifts—and gave Jill some tissues. Then she sat next to her, holding her hand. "It's okay," she said. "Whatever happened, we'll get through this."

"It's shocking, Greer. It's my own personal love story. And until now I haven't told a soul about it. Not even Ella."

"Are you sure? Ella loves you."

"Yes. You'll see why in a minute. Prepare yourself."

"I'm ready," Greer said. It was impossible to shock her. She'd heard many different love stories as a matchmaker: crazy ones, sad ones, thrilling ones, and beautiful ones.

"Today I got an invitation," Jill said, her voice trembling. "It's to a tech conference in Manhattan."

"I got that, too!" Greer said. "I get everything in the office related to tech. Was it a black rectangle with bold white writing?"

"Yes," said Jill. "But this isn't merely *any* tech conference. And I think it was sent to me on purpose."

Greer winced. "Are you sure? I mean, that company sends advertisements to pretty much everyone."

"Yeah, they're really big. But I'm sure. It was intentional. I don't buy their products. I'm an Apple girl, through and through."

"Oh, okay." Greer didn't want to say that she thought Jill was being a little . . . weird. "So why do you think it was intentional?"

Jill sighed. "There's a guy who's going to be at this conference I used to date. None of my family or friends ever knew I loved him very much."

Okay. It *was* something shocking . . . but not so shocking. Occasionally, people had secret romances. "What happened?" Greer asked.

"He was really sweet," Jill whispered. "But one day we were together, and then the next we weren't."

"Why?"

"He proposed," Jill said. "It was a really nice place, too, and I felt so special. But I said no."

"That's okay," Greer assured her. "You can't say yes to every proposal, right?" She thought back to her and Wesley.

"Exactly." Jill tossed her a sad smile. "You need to wait for the right one."

"So why are you letting this one get you down?"

Jill shrugged. "Maybe because he's . . ." And she named a business tycoon known all over the world.

Someone who'd been selected *Time*'s Person of the Year, whose net worth was so high, only a few people in the world surpassed him. He owned the company who'd sent the tech conference invitation. It was one of only five major companies that he owned. He'd diversified into films, airlines, and even space travel.

Greer had to sit still for a minute. "Jill, are you kidding? I mean, seriously. *Are you kidding?* Or are you talking about a man with the same name as the famous guy?"

Slowly, Jill shook her head. "One night he visited our family restaurant in the Bronx, and that was that. We fell in love instantly. It was fate, I think. He usually didn't stop in the Bronx. Manhattan was more his style. He'd had a flat tire on his limo, and while it was getting fixed, he came in for some minestrone. I told him he could use some fattening up and brought him carbonara instead. Have you ever noticed how skinny he is when you see him online or on TV?"

"Yeah. Um, I've noticed."

"And he liked that I spoke to him so frankly and ignored his order, and we just hit it off." She smiled. "Carbonara brings out the lover in people, you know? I always made him carbonara after that, when I'd visit him at his penthouses."

"As in plural?" Greer asked, trying hard to remain calm.

"Yes, um, he has them all over the world. I went to Hong Kong, Dubai, Sydney, Florence, and some other places. My favorite was this adorable castle he has in Scotland . . ." she trailed off. "I know this is hard to believe."

"It-it's wild." Greer swallowed. "But I do believe you."

It was the craziest love story she'd heard yet.

Jill wiped at a tear. "So I mean I would have *loved* to accept his proposal. It was at that castle in Scotland. He'd hired a bunch of pipers to play under my window. And then he came in with dozens of white roses, my favorite flower, and . . . and. . . ." She flung her arms out dismissively. "It's too hard to talk about. Let's just say I decided I wasn't in love as much as I should be."

"You can't force yourself to love someone, even if he *is* a billionaire," said Greer, and she believed that with all her heart. "So it's okay. Don't beat yourself up. You're after *true* love, Jill."

"But it *is* true love," Jill said. "I was lying to myself. I love him with everything in me. The thing is, I was scared. I didn't want to leave my family forever and travel the world. I need to see Momma and my *nonnas* and my sisters at least a couple times a week to be happy. And with him, I couldn't do that. He wanted me with him always. But when I told him why I couldn't marry him, he said, 'Okay, so we'll fly you back to New York each week. I'll do anything it takes to make you happy.'"

"Oh, my God. He sounds *great*." Greer was on the edge of her seat. "Would he have flown you on a private plane? With your own flight attendant bringing you anything you want?"

"Yes. Her name is Esme, and she makes his favorite pound cake, so she keeps the plane pantry stocked with it. And it's always filled with tons of the best champagne, but—"

"But what?"

Jill shook her head. "I'm afraid to fly."

"Oh, Jill."

"To get to his penthouses, I had to be knocked completely out and attended by a physician in case I woke up and started freaking out," Jill said. "After a while, I said that wasn't something I wanted to do anymore. He offered to put me on one of his yachts and take me around the world that way, but I'm a modern girl, Greer. Yachts take too long. I don't care *how* many hot tubs they have on them."

There was a long silence.

"I'm afraid of flying, too, but . . . can't you get therapy for that?" Greer was shrieking inside when she said that, but outside, she was calm. Very calm.

"Have *you* gotten therapy for it?" Jill was showing a little bit of pique.

That was good! She was still emotionally engaged with this guy, obviously.

Greer shook her head. "No, I haven't."

"You see what I mean," Jill said, crossing her arms.

Greer put up her palms. "Okay, I get it. But let's slow down. Here's the important question: if you could see your family every week, would you want to marry this guy?"

"Of course! I *love* him!" And then Jill burst into tears. Big, convulsive sobs.

"Oh, honey." Greer hugged her. She had hope. She had real hope . . . and as exciting as it was that this guy was a powerful gazillionaire, what she had hope about was the fact that Jill was honestly in love and there was only One Little Thing separating her from her happily ever after—

Flying on a plane!

Dear God, Greer said to herself, she was going to have to conquer her own fear, too, because no matter what— she was going to get Jill past hers, if it was the last thing she ever did.

"The Mancini family doesn't separate," Jill moaned. "After Papa died, we all moved down here to be with Ella. It's how we are, and I love that about us. I will never marry a man whose lifestyle doesn't allow me to be with them, no matter how much I love him!"

"We're going to get you over your plane phobia," Greer said.

Jill rolled her eyes. "Right."

"Won't you even try?"

"He hired the best plane phobia person in the world to help me, and it didn't work."

Yikes. Greer didn't know the right way to get someone over her flight phobia. How could she do any better than the world's leading expert? "I have this procedure," Greer told Jill. "What if we tried it together?"

"On a real plane?" Jill's forehead started sweating.

"It would have to be a real plane," Greer said, and took Jill by the shoulders. "What if we can make it work?"

Jill stared at her, slightly wild-eyed. "It won't," she whispered. "And he won't move here to Charleston. He's—he's too busy."

"Understandably," said Greer. "I saw him a few days ago on TV with Mark Zuckerberg at some business summit in Washington."

"Yeah," said Jill, "and today he's in Russia, visiting their president there."

"Oh, my God. I didn't see that in the papers this morning."

Jill shrugged. "A lot of times, he manages to sneak away from the media. He's got security teams galore."

"Then how'd you know where he is? Are you still in touch?"

"Not really," Jill said. "Harry tells me what he's up to. He's his favorite bodyguard. We text sometimes."

"Okay. So you keep up with him through his bodyguard. That's it?"

"No. Occasionally, I get presents."

"Presents?"

"With no note," Jill said. "He's terrible at writing notes. He's embarrassed about his handwriting. He's a leftie, and it looks like chicken scratch—"

"But you're sure these presents are from him."

"Yes."

"Why?"

"Because they're fancy necklaces and bracelets. And fresh flowers, too. I keep those because they'll only die if I return them. But Tiffany takes the jewelry right back. I always send it back. Diamonds and emeralds aren't appropriate, not unless I'm his real girlfriend."

Greer had to tell herself to breathe. She had no idea what to do or say. "This is . . . *weird.* I-I-I still can't wrap my head around it." She ran a hand through her hair. "You haven't been dating anyone else?"

Jill shook her head. "No other guy appeals. I love him, Greer. I really do. So I've been lying to my family and I've pretended to date every once in a while. I go to Barnes and Noble and read. Or the craft store and look at yarn. Whenever Momma asks if I'll bring a guy I've been seeing to dinner, I conveniently make up a story about how we broke up."

Greer slapped the top of her desk. "How long have you loved this guy?"

"Three long years," Jill said. "It's been rough."

"How did you disappear to his penthouses all over the world without your family and friends wondering where you were going?"

Jill sat up higher. "Before we moved down here, I was living with a couple of girlfriends in Kingsbridge Heights, and I used to tell everyone I was working out-of-town jobs as a hand model." She held up her hands. "I have beautiful hands, right? So everyone believed it."

"You do have beautiful hands." Greer felt as if she were living in an alternative universe. "And . . . he still hasn't given up on you?"

Jill winced. "I think he has. I haven't gotten flowers or jewelry in three months. I was sure he'd finally gotten the message. Until today, when I got that invitation."

"But Jill"—Greer got up and pulled the oversized tech flyer out of her inbox—"I got it, too. And probably tens of thousands of people did."

"It's a sign," Jill said, her mouth stubborn. The Mancinis were a superstitious lot. "Whether he sent it to me on purpose or not, it's important. I have to do something about it. I've never gotten any mail from this company. And look what it says."

Greer turned the invitation over: "You have to love your wi-fi provider," she read out loud.

"No," said Jill. "The other thing."

Greer searched her flyer. "Um, it gives me details about the conference. The dates, the place, and all that stuff. It says he's the main speaker. He's giving the keynote."

"Exactly," said Jill. "I have to go there. I feel it in my Mancini bones. I got this flyer at the exact moment I was thinking about him, which is all the time, of course. But still. I can't hide anymore. It's time to put this romance behind me once and for all. It's too painful—" Her eyes brimmed with tears again.

"Don't jump ahead of yourself just yet. Do you know if he's dating someone?"

Jill's fact turned red. "I shouldn't know, but Harry tells me. And he hasn't been dating."

"Well, that's good."

"We love each other," Jill said. "He used to like hearing what I bought at the grocery store. He can't go there anymore. He gets mobbed."

"That's sad."

"He's lonely, Greer. Everyone treats him with kid gloves because of who he is, or they try to get something from him, and he's sick of that."

Greer had no choice but to try to get these two together. "And not even Ella knows about him?"

"Nope." Jill's expression drooped. "It's been so hard not to confide in anyone. I haven't because I'm too afraid it will leak. And then he'd think I was after him only because he's famous and rich."

Greer sank back into the chair cushions. "I'm honored you told me. I just need to catch my breath, okay?"

"Okay, I can go outside and text Harry and see how they're doing in Russia—"

"No! Not yet." Greer steepled her fingers. "We're going to tackle this. You're my client. I'm your advisor. We make a great team."

"You can try," said Jill, and blew her nose on another tissue. "But there are too many obstacles. The fact that I can't fly, and my mother's disapproval. . . ."

Greer's mind boggled. "Why would she disapprove? He's *amazing*. And he loves you, obviously."

Jill sighed. "If my mother ever knew I actually traipsed around the world and stayed with a man she's never met, a man I gave my virginity to . . . you don't know the Mancini family."

Greer hated to see the sadness on her sweet face. "I know you're facing certain expectations from your family—we all do," she said, "but give them some credit. They love you." Greer handed her another tissue.

Jill let out a shaky breath. "Thanks for reminding me."

They hugged for a long minute, and then Greer's phone rang.

"Get it," Jill said. "I'll work on cleaning myself up."

"Okay." So Greer took a quick call about an upcoming banquet one of her clients was attending with a woman she had set him up with. The problem was that an old flame of his would be there, someone who'd burned him badly. "Living well is the best revenge," Greer told him. "Let her see you happy and handsome and perfectly okay without her in your life. You're successful and kind and you can hold your head high."

He seemed to welcome hearing that.

"I have one caution, though," she said. "Do *not* use your date to show off to the old flame. We don't want your current romantic interest to feel used in any way. And your old girlfriend will see right through it and believe you care about what she thinks more than you do."

"Right," he said.

When she hung up, she thought, *Whew, being a matchmaker is never dull.* That guy was a U.S. senator from the Northeast. He'd seen their algorithm segment on the *Today* show and gotten in touch. His old girlfriend was a national news reporter at one of the major television networks. His current romantic interest was a local Charleston woman who'd moved to DC to take a job at a big nonprofit—an old friend of Macy's they'd set him up with. The two of them loved sailing and horses, and they both wanted to change the world.

So far, so good.

But Greer knew things could change on a dime. Kind of like what would inevitably happen with her and Ford. They couldn't continue this way forever. Soon the portrait would be finished. And so would the contest. The thought of things changing made her sad. He'd be going back to England soon.

After the phone call, she told Jill, "We're talking about your old boyfriend today, but we definitely don't want you to lose steam with Erospace Designs."

"Absolutely not," said Jill. "I want to succeed on my own."

They came up with a plan to meet again soon and discuss not only the boyfriend, but also Greer's bedroom and how things were going there.

"Good, I hope?" Jill asked.

"Not bad," said Greer. "I mean, no one's been up there yet. Besides me. And you. And the guys who moved the furniture in."

"So?" said Jill. "Don't worry. It'll happen. Your Erospace-designed bedroom won't let you down. I promise."

It was good to see an extra bounce in her friend's step when she left the room. But Greer's smile faded fast. Things were getting complicated with Ford. She liked him too much. She thought about him all the time, the same way Jill thought about her business tycoon, and she counted down the minutes until she saw him again.

She tried to act like her own mother and told herself the right guy might walk into her life and she wouldn't even know because she was too distracted with Ford!

The Ford fling must cease, she decided. No more nookie after portrait posing. Nothing. Not even a kiss. He'd understand.

No more fling, she texted to him. *Must keep eye out for real partner. Sorry.*

Fine, Ford wrote back.

Her heart actually hurt when he texted that.

This weekend, he wrote, *just friends. No fooling around. But lots of portrait posing.*

Good plan, she texted back, her eyes burning, and promptly switched off her phone before she could change her mind or burst into tears.

CHAPTER TWENTY-THREE

Greer had exactly twenty-four hours to prepare for La Di Da's final challenge, the big weekend at the Isle of Palms for the finalists in the contest and their One-and-Onlys. So the five future brides got together for a fun dinner at Magnolias on East Bay Street the night before. They chatted for almost two hours. They were becoming fast friends, and Greer was glad, although Toni tended to see the cup as half empty and still wasn't completely on board about Greer's participation.

Serena was winning so far—they all knew that—and was in a wonderful mood.

Everyone was happy Lisa was bringing a stand-in for her groom in Afghanistan. She'd decided on her father, who was from Johns Island and had never stayed at the beach, even though he lived a few minutes' drive away. He planned on making the group his prize Frogmore Stew, a Lowcountry specialty, one night. Henny was kind enough to give him his own suite, too, and as he was a disabled veteran, they put him on the first floor, facing the beach.

They'd just gotten to dessert when Carol put down her spoon. "I've loved hanging out with y'all, but throughout this dinner, I have to admit, I've felt very uncomfortable."

There was a beat of silence.

"You did?" Greer asked, feeling concern. "I'm so sorry."

"Me, too." Lisa swallowed a bite of carrot cake. "I couldn't tell."

"I couldn't, either," said Toni, putting her spoon down by her chocolate mousse.

"What's wrong?" Serena asked softly.

She and Greer exchanged a worried glance over their cappuccinos.

Carol hesitated, then whispered, "I want to stay single." It was hard to hear her with all the background noise in the restaurant, but her sad expression said it all.

Greer was genuinely surprised. Her new friend had looked so happy with her partner. "Wow," she said. "That's big news."

"It is," Carol said. "I was thinking about breaking up with my fiancée already, but now I know for sure, after sitting here and seeing all of you look so in love."

The women started talking at once, trying to comfort her.

"Are you sure?" everyone asked in one way or another.

"Yes," she said with shiny eyes, although no tears fell. "And I don't want to continue in the contest."

"But you can stay in as a partnerless bride," Lisa reminded her.

"It would be tacky coming off a split-up, though," Toni said.

"That's for her to decide," Greer said. Toni obviously wanted one less person in the competition.

"If you did stay in, you'd stand no chance," said Lisa, "with the way the rules discriminate against partnerless brides."

"Oh, my God, partnerless brides really *are* becoming a thing," Serena murmured to Greer, who actually felt a little bit proud she'd coined the phrase.

They talked about Carol's dilemma a few more minutes, and then she smiled. "I feel much better, actually, making my decision. I'm sticking to it. Please don't feel bad for me."

Lisa put her hand over hers and squeezed.

"You said we *all* look in love," Toni said to Carol. "But we know Greer isn't."

She was always bringing that point up.

Greer sat up straighter. "Carol was only speaking in general terms." She turned to Carol. "You had a lot on your mind that you wanted to share."

"I meant what I said," Carol said. "All of you, including Greer, look and act in love. And I was thinking, 'one of these people is not like the others.' It wasn't Greer. It was *me*."

"But . . ." Greer could hardly speak. "But I'm not in love. Not yet. I don't know when it will happen . . . or even *if*."

Carol chuckled. "You could have fooled me. Look at her, everyone! Look at the sparkle in her eye! And the way she's"—she got a little choked up—"she's *happy*. It's so obvious." She sighed. "And I'm not. Not like you four, at any rate."

So everyone started looking at Greer.

Greer widened her eyes. "Hey, I was happy before this contest, okay?" But she knew something was slowly changing in her, and it had everything to do with getting closer to Ford.

"You're right," said Toni to Greer. "You're not any different than you were at the beginning. I don't care how awesome you and your convenient groom looked together at the bake-off, especially when you were making out."

Serena eyes Greer speculatively. "You *do* have a crush on Ford. Who wouldn't?"

"Yes, well"—Greer scratched the side of her nose—"he's cute, I'll give him that."

"He's way more than cute," Serena said. "He's got it all. Looks, smarts, talent, and . . . and. . . ." She stopped talking. A blush spread across her cheeks.

"Wesley's such a nice guy," Greer reminded Serena.

"Of course, he is," Serena agreed, and raised her finger to attract the waiter. "Sometimes, though, I wonder if I'm just inventing this love between us. Out of desperation or something. And I can't help comparing him. . . ." She shook her head. "Forgive me, ladies. I'm so sorry I have to go now. I have a little more packing to do."

The other women looked at each other.

"Serena," Lisa said, "Are you sure you don't want to talk about it?"

Serena smiled. "I'm fine. *We're* fine."

"It's natural to have doubts sometimes," Carol said. "You wouldn't be human if you didn't. It's when those questions keep torturing you that you know you need to step back."

Toni and Lisa agreed.

Greer did, too, even though her circumstances were different. She couldn't say she and Ford were a couple. They had a fake engagement, and everyone knew. She couldn't say they were in love, either. But wasn't every relationship a constant walk of trust? The stress of always keeping your heart open could sometimes get to a person.

Even if she'd wanted to take Serena aside to reassure her, she couldn't. They gathered around Carol to say a special good-bye. She wouldn't be coming to the beach.

"Wish me luck, ladies," she said. "This isn't going to be easy. But I know it's the right thing to do."

Wesley arrived then and watched the women share a big group hug and a promise to get together sometime in the future for lunch, when Carol was ready. When the final good-bye was made, he and Serena walked rapidly away. Serena was holding tight to his hand.

Greer took off in the opposite direction to walk home—alone—to the Baker House. Walking by herself in Charleston had always been such a pleasant experience for her. But that night, she felt lonely, for the first time since she could remember. She immediately wondered what Ford was up to, especially as she'd begged off posing for the portrait so she could go to dinner with the other contestants. This weekend at the beach, they could make up the time, she'd told him.

She decided to call Ella. Now that Macy was married, she was less inclined to call her out of the blue. It had been a year, but Macy and Deacon were still in the honeymoon phase, and no telling what they were getting up to at ten P.M.

"How are things progressing with the portrait?" Ella asked.

"He's getting antsier, less happy about it instead of more," Greer said. "I have no idea if that's typical of artists, and when I tried to ask him, he gave me a vague answer."

"Artists." Ella sighed. "They're so complicated."

"They sure are." Greer stepped from the curb to cross the street to Colonial Lake.

"So how's the sex?" Ella asked.

Greer laughed. "You've got a one-track mind."

"Of course. I still can't believe you guys haven't gone all the way. But I get it, what with him being so wrapped up in his ex and her pregnancy."

"It's just better for me this way," said Greer. "Last time I was at the studio, we went up to the roof after he finished working. The stars were out, he brought up a blanket, and we had some wine. We talked a lot about the portrait."

"And?"

"And then we had our best sex-capade yet."

"Lucky!"

Greer laughed. "It was so awesome to be outside, right there in the city with no one the wiser." She remembered the cool sea breeze on their skin. Any laughter, sighs, and moans they'd made blended into the nighttime sounds coming from the streets below.

"You might be the queen of algorithms at work and a math whiz," said Ella, "and you might act like a surrogate mother to your clients, putting their needs before your own, as we are wont to do at Two Love Lane, but gosh, Greer, you deserve this *so much*."

"Thanks." It was true—being with Ford made her realize she needed to be kinder to herself. She thought of the way he observed her from behind his easel, with non-judgmental, appreciative eyes, and when he held her close and lavished tender, passionate kisses all over her body.

"I think you like him," said Ella. "I mean, really, *really* like him."

"I do," said Greer. "And it makes no sense at all." She paused a beat. "I mean, we don't fit the algorithms." She and Ella had checked that past weekend, using every bit of information they had to get a decent compatability reading.

"What have I always said?" Ella asked. "Love knows no logic. Number crunching doesn't always predict who falls in love, and it can't explain *why*."

"I'm not in love," said Greer.

"Oh, yeah?" Ella chuckled.

"Hey," said Greer. "Are you laughing at me?"

"No." Ella's tone was airy. "I just like seeing you out of your comfort zone."

"I'm *fine*," Greer said, but her friend had already hung up.

Greer's new bedroom had definitely taken her out of her comfort zone, with its pink and diamond accents and its Elvis pics. She threw her purse on her pink armchair. "What's going on with me?" she asked Fern. Greer couldn't hide anything from Fern. She sure looked beautiful in her big pink bow.

You love him, Fern said without speaking, without moving a single leaf.

"You, too?" Greer scowled at her favorite housemate, then crawled into her much softer bed and looked up at the ceiling, at the silly *Baywatch* poster Jill had put there. She admitted to herself that she'd gone past the crush phase with Ford. On the roof of the old cigar factory, fooling around like a carefree chick in her young twenties instead of the thirty-year-old businesswoman she was now, she'd never felt happier.

But if she was so happy, why were hot tears falling steadily from her eyes into her ears? And why were sobs choking her throat? Ford was only here temporarily, and he might be a father. He had never told her he loved her, had never acted like they had anything particularly special beyond friendship and a mutual physical chemistry.

Where was the soul-mate stuff? Had they ever genuinely connected that way?

The honest answer was yes, twice, but both times had been fleeting. They'd connected at the auction when he'd left, and she'd never forget how he'd nodded to her, and she'd acknowledged him—as if the souls of two strangers were saying hello. It happened again when he'd proposed to her onstage. She'd seen something in his eyes that moved her, that made her feel it was just the two of them, and the world was far away.

But apart from those two occasions, they'd never examined what was between them. They'd only focused on their own agendas—which was smart. It was also practical and showed a lot of maturity.

"To hell with maturity." She sat up on her elbow and wiped her tears with her arm. "If this is love," she told Fern, "I'm miserable. I want to fall out of it as fast as I can."

Fern's leaves drooped. She was indifferent, maybe even amused, the same way Ella had been.

"Love's supposed to be great," said Greer, and pulled a pillow over her head.

But she couldn't hide, even in her sleep. She dreamed she and Ford were making out in the pink armchair. They had the best sex she'd ever had, and when she woke up the next morning to get ready for the last challenge of the La Di Da contest, she wondered if he'd stick to their promise not to touch each other at the beach.

He could try, but she was one "Working Diva Without a Man" who wasn't going to keep her hands off him anymore. The walls were coming down. She'd rather have mindless, fabulous sex with Ford than worry about shielding her heart from him. That was boring.

After seeing Carol break up and Serena express mild doubts about Wesley, and then Jill being mixed up about her boyfriend, Greer realized everything in the love game was risky. It was useless to protect herself.

Life was short.

And Ford was hot—too hot for his own good.

CHAPTER TWENTY-FOUR

Ford packed up his easel, his canvas, his paints, brushes, and solvent and headed to Greer's house in Drake's SUV to pick her up. It was time to go to the Isle of Palms for the La Di Da beach weekend. He was so used to not being invited up to her apartment that he was shocked when she told him through the intercom that she needed him to come up.

"You parked in a good place?" she asked.

"Yes. I got lucky." Parking in Charleston was difficult. And he wasn't used to driving with the steering wheel on the left, nor did people in the U.K. have the massive cars Americans drove. It had taken him a few minutes to parallel park between a Beemer and a Honda Accord. By the time he was done, he was sweating.

The buzzer sounded and he opened the door, went up the elevator, and knocked on 3-A. No one came. He knocked again.

"Just a minute," she called from inside.

Thirty long seconds later, she opened the door. She wore a pretty floral robe that skimmed her thighs. "Come on in," she said.

"Sure." He walked in, and she shut the door behind him.

"Hey," she said, and when he turned around again, she was completely naked.

She was gorgeous and sexy, and he wanted her like he'd wanted no other woman. "You look incredibly hot," he said, and pulled her close. Her hour-glass figure was made to be adored.

She shook her head and smiled. "Let's go see my room."

"Wait," he said, and kissed her first, a long, slow kiss that he didn't want to break.

She didn't, either, judging by the way she clung to his neck. But when he slid a hand down to her rear and pulled her against his erection, she pushed her hands on his chest. "Wait," she said, sounding a little breathless. "Let's go see my room."

He was happy to follow, but he wasn't going to make this easy for her. "I thought we weren't supposed to fool around. You texted me. You told me to forget it. You said you had to look for the real thing. Love with a capital *L*."

"I never mentioned love," she flung over her shoulder.

"You might as well have," he said. "You said you needed to find a real partner."

"Okay, so I did," she said.

But before he could answer, he was assailed with pink. Leopard spots. Diamonds galore. *Baywatch*.

Elvis!

"This is . . ." He looked around. Even the fern wore a huge pink bow. "Colorful. Uh, spirited."

"Welcome to my loving space," she said with a shy smile.

Her loving space? The polite Englishman in him came to the fore. "It's enchanting. In its own way."

"This used to be my living space," she explained. "But now it's my loving space, thanks to my friend Jill at Erospace Designs. Eros. Get it? The god of love."

"Oh, that's clever. I was thinking aerospace, as in NASA."

"It's a play on words." She gulped. "I'm her guinea pig client. She removed all my bedroom furniture and redecorated this way, claiming that my sex life would take off. And I have to say, even though I was highly skeptical, it did. That very same night she put in the furniture, I kissed you at The Rooftop."

"And that was some kiss. Do you think this"—he spread his arm wide—"is responsible for our incredibly good chemistry?"

She laughed. "Who knows? It's fun, at any rate." She took his hand. "I want you in my bed, Ford. No more stopping."

He picked her up right then and there and tossed her on the bed. She gave a cry of delight as he pulled off his shoes and trousers.

"Spread your legs, cupcake," he said.

"Cupcake? I can't believe you called me that," she said with a laugh, and bounced in place. Then she did as she was told.

He reveled in the view as he unbuttoned his shirt. "We had our reasons for holding back." He bent, pulled his wallet out of his trousers on the floor, and removed a condom. "But I can't think of any right now," he said, pulling the latex sheath on. "I can't think of anything but you and how perfect you look on your leopard-spotted bed. I'd *love* to make love to you." He crawled on top of her, and she shuddered a little in his arms.

They already knew each other's bodies so well, knew exactly how to bring each other to the ultimate pleasure.

"No foreplay," she murmured in his ear. "I'm ready."

He teased her with his fingers, and she whimpered. "Yes, you are," he murmured. He couldn't hide that he was, too. He bent low and lathed her nipple with his tongue.

She groaned. "I'm tired of being mature."

He smiled into her warm, woman-scented flesh. "It's a burden sometimes."

"I don't care anymore," she murmured, and ran her hand down his side, then cupped him with warm, eager fingers.

Exquisite torture.

"About what?" he managed to say.

"About protecting my heart." She wrapped her hand around his erection. "It's not really living, and I want to live."

"Good God, so do I," he said, gritting his teeth.

"I want you inside me." She was beginning to sound more herself. Sure, not strained, the way she had been when he'd first arrived. "I want to be filled with you."

"You're beautiful," he said, his voice like gravel.

The clock ticked behind them.

He looked down at her, and her eyes were smiling.

"*This*," he said, and entered her, plunging deep.

She closed her eyes, turned her head to the side. "Ford," she whispered. "*Ford*."

He began a slow stroke, in and out. There was something different about making love to her properly. He felt even more protective of her. He also liked her that much more. Something locked into place that had never locked into place before.

It was right, in a way it had never been.

She caressed his back, gripped him tighter with her thighs. "Let's not think about the future. Or our current challenges."

"I dare you to name them," he said.

She laughed. "The portrait."

He suckled her left breast, clasped her right buttock with his hand, stroked in and out.

"Winning my dress," she said with a sigh.

He kissed her silent, his tongue colliding with hers. "I think I like pink and diamonds," he murmured.

"And Elvis posters?" she said.

"No," he said with a grin. "We can do without those." And then he moved faster. And faster.

She rode along with him and finally arched her back and let herself go. When she did, he followed immediately after, a swell of sensual shock-and-awe rocking him, rocking her.

When it finally left them still, he rolled off her. "That was good. Extremely good."

"I agree," she said, and chuckled. "Credit the room."

"No," he said. "I credit *you*." He smiled and kissed her.

They did it all over again, slower this time, with her on top. He marveled at her athleticism, her supple movements, her grace. He absorbed her fierceness when she came and brought him to that place of no thinking, only hovering on a plain of utter sensual abandon.

And he wondered how he could ever leave her and go back to England.

Greer sat up on her new, softer mattress. How could they ever leave her bedroom and go to the beach? The last thing she wanted was to have a TV camera in her face, producers of the contest hovering, and to participate in a competition.

All she wanted to do was be with Ford. In their own little cocoon.

"Gah," she said, picking up on an expression of his,

and rolled out of bed. "We have to be at the Isle of Palms in an hour. We're cutting it awfully close. We have fifteen minutes here, and then we have to skedaddle."

She ran to her bathroom, shut the door, and came out a minute later with her hands full of bottles and toothpaste. "It's free," she said, indicating the bathroom. "I'll be packing."

"And dressing," he reminded her on his way there, and kissed her one more time, their naked bodies pressed hard against each other.

She noticed that he instantly became aroused again, but he backed away and a minute later came out of the bathroom with his hair slicked back from his forehead. He pulled on his boxers and trousers. "This is going to be a tough weekend if we don't get much alone time."

"We'll make it happen," she said, slipping on her bra and panties.

He didn't seem able to look away. Yes, he'd seen her plenty of times now, naked, but she felt today's romp between the sheets had done something to rev up their chemistry even higher.

"God," he said, and shook his head.

She paused. "What are you thinking about?"

"The painting. It doesn't come close to capturing you. The essence of you. You're so much bigger a presence than what I've managed to paint. You're like a constellation of stars, your own sign. And I painted a sparkle of sunlight on the water."

She shook her head. "I loved what I saw last I looked at the portrait. Remember, none of us know what you had planned in your head. We see what *we* see." She paused. "To be honest, I don't care what the artist intended. I'm selfish. Once I'm standing before a painting, it belongs to *me*. I interpret it the way I want to."

"I like that," he said.

And he did seem happier. He was helping her pull some clothes out of the closet when he saw a couple of her Perfect Wedding albums stacked on the hat shelf. He read the binder. "Perfect Wedding number ten," and "Perfect Wedding number eleven."

"Oh," she said. "I threw those two in there because there are a few things I wanted to look at before I talk to one of my clients about her upcoming wedding. The rest are on a shelf in the living room."

"These are your wedding scrapbooks?"

"Yes." She pulled one down. "I've been doing them since I was a kid. It was difficult then to get a hold of wedding magazines. I used to have a connection at the Waterloo drugstore. She was a friend of my mother's. She'd save me old copies of *Brides* and any magazine that might have wedding articles in it."

He flipped through it, his face unreadable.

"What do you think?" she said. "You're the first person I've ever shown one to."

He handed it back to her. "I think it's a girl thing. The whole fairy tale notion."

She shrugged and put it back on the closet shelf. "Maybe it is."

He examined her face, as if he were pondering something.

She began to feel self-conscious. "What is it?"

"I just want to know why," he said, "a perfect wedding is so important to you."

"You said it yourself. Women like fairy tales. Maybe it's because when we were little, we pretended to be princesses."

"Did you do that? Pretend to be a princess?"

"Sure." She shrugged.

"What was it like at your house?"

She felt slightly stressed at such an all-encompassing question. "It was . . . nice. My parents are both very down-to-earth people. Our house was calm and well-run. But we were always prepared for Mother Nature to throw a wrench in our best-laid plans. Some years were extra hard. Dairy farming isn't easy. We had to go with the flow. Mom used to say we had to be brave and face reality head-on."

"They didn't mind having a daughter with such an active imagination?"

"No." Her eyes began to sting. "They thought it was silly of me, but they seemed to understand."

"What is it?" He came over and wrapped his arms around her waist. "What's wrong?"

She shook her head. "Nothing."

"It can't be nothing."

She closed her eyes. One tear fell out of her left one.

"Hey," he said in a soothing voice.

She opened her eyes. "I don't know why I'm crying."

"It's okay," he said in a gentle tone. "We don't have to talk about it."

His look of concern made her feel worse, so she pulled herself together. "No, it's all right," she said, and braced herself. "It's hard to face, but the truth is, I'm not sure my parents ever loved each other. And growing up always wondering in bed at night, or at the dinner table, when they'd be completely courteous with each other, I used to sit there wracking my brain trying to figure out if we were . . . normal."

He sat on the bed and pulled her onto his lap. "No family is normal."

"I know."

He squeezed her tight. "But when you're a little girl,

you want to see your parents show affection to each other. They didn't do that?"

She shook her head. "But they were always respectful. And kind to each other."

"You just didn't see any passion there?"

"Never." She sighed.

"Did they laugh together?"

Her mouth tilted up on one side. "They used to be amused by *me*. So yes, they'd laugh together at things I did. But they never had inside jokes or teased each other. At least not that I saw."

"So they shared a peaceful sort of relationship?"

She sighed. "Yes, I think it was, so I can't say they were or are unhappy. They had an arranged marriage, in a way. Two farming families wanted to unite, and they were brought up believing they were meant to be together. I know that sounds old-fashioned, but these old Scandinavian families still cling to tradition."

"I understand perfectly," he said. "I think every culture tries to preserve power that way, by uniting the children. It happens in England. It happens in Charleston. It happens everywhere."

She gave a little laugh. "So I think that's where my obsession with a Perfect Wedding started. I wanted a romantic relationship for my parents." She gave a little cry that came from somewhere deep inside, an old, old place as worn and faded as one of her mother's quilts. "I've never said that out loud before."

He hugged her close. "I'm glad you did."

She sighed and allowed herself to be held another minute. "Ready to go?" she asked eventually, grateful to him for his patience.

"Sure," he said. "We'll perk up at the beach. You'll see."

She wasn't ready to go. But it had to be done.

They raced downstairs with her bags instead of taking the ancient elevator, which could be slow, and managed to get them in the SUV without smashing the portrait, which he'd wrapped lightly in paper and stowed in the back. The easel was folded and ready to go. They got in, put on their seatbelts, then looked at each other.

"We're off," he said. "Good luck this weekend trying to win *Royal Bliss*."

"Thank you for trying to help me," she said back. She felt lighter, having shared such heavy stuff with him. "And I hope we'll have plenty of time for the portrait."

"My deadline's coming up fast," he said, as they crossed the Ravenel Bridge. "Much faster than I anticipated. Being in Charleston has been really great. It's helped me get through an otherwise awkward phase—the recently dumped one."

"Although you dumped *her*, right?"

"The way anyone would when you find out the other person has betrayed you, so technically, yes."

"Still. You're the one who walked. Good for you."

"I certainly didn't chase her and try to fix things."

"Some people would have. But you believe in yourself too much to go back to a person who didn't value you."

He shot her an amused glance. "You're kind to remind me how lucky I was to escape."

She laughed. "I'm only telling you because you need to be the same way when you paint. Cast off the doubt in your head. Walk out on the distrustful thoughts throwing shadows on your work. Flip the bird at cynicism and skepticism. They don't deserve your company."

"Hmmm," he said. "You might have something there. I tend to pull up a chair and give them my full attention. I even offer them drinks. My best scotch."

They chuckled together.

"I'm serious," she said.

He nodded. "I know." His tone was serious, too. "And I appreciate it."

"Speaking of which, any word from your ex?"

"No," he said. "And I consider that good news."

The quieter mood in the car was a far cry from their impetuous adventure they'd had in her bedroom but was still just as intimate. She refused to go back to protecting herself. She wanted to stay here, in this place of risk, of uncertainty, because that was where Ford was most himself. She craved being with him that way. In bed, when he'd filled her, she was with that man she'd seen at the end of the auction, and onstage. He was a man who saw her, really saw her, in a way that no one else ever had. He'd brought out the adventurer in her, too, the vulnerable woman who wanted to be free of worry but who knew she could fight for what she wanted if she had to.

He'd brought out the woman she'd made it her business to hide.

He reached across the seat and took her hand. "When we get there, things will be crazy, I'm sure."

She looked out her window at the harbor below, almost bursting with happiness that they were holding hands. "I'm sure they will. But I still think I can do it. I can win the gown. Serena's definitely ahead, but I'm not so far behind I couldn't overtake her."

"Do you think the other three have a chance?"

"It's only two now," she said, and explained about Carol dropping out.

"That's sad for her, but good news for the rest of the contestants."

"Carol says she's happy, so I'm going to believe her. As for the other two, I honestly think they'll have to work very hard to win. But what do I know?" She tried not to think about Kiki and Pierre, but she simply had to. "I have to watch out for Kiki."

"Why?"

"Pierre wants me to lose."

"He told you that outright?"

"Yes. He cares more about petty revenge than this new bridal department. We were never able to find him a match at Two Love Lane. If I don't lose, he's threatened to bring it down. Those are his words. He told me on-stage the night I became a finalist."

"I'd like to see him try." The irritation on Ford's face made her happy. He looked over at her. "You never told me any of this."

She shrugged. "It's hard to take a fool like him seriously. Then again, foolish people are dangerous, especially when they have money and power—and mindless minions like Kiki."

"You're wise to stay cautious around both of them," Ford said. "Is there a chance they'll try to fix the contest?"

"I wouldn't put it past him," she said. "Henny has a good head on her shoulders. I think she won't let him get away with it if he tries."

But if she wanted a solid chance to win *Royal Bliss*, Greer couldn't rely on Henny. She had to rely on herself. And Ford, of course. She still believed there was a chance to take home the dress of her dreams, the dress that would really make her Perfect Wedding perfect.

"I'm starting to feel competitive," she said when they pulled into the driveway of a gorgeous beach house.

"Good," he said, "because we're here, and there's the truck from Channel Four, and I see balloons hung all around the railing of an upstairs porch, and this, I can tell, is going to be an utter circus all weekend. You'll need to be on your best game."

A camera man came trotting over, his camera on his shoulder.

"Let's start right now." She leaned over and kissed Ford.

CHAPTER TWENTY-FIVE

Greer woke up on Saturday morning at the beach house feeling cozy and happy. She didn't even mind the soreness between her legs. She knew a very good way to get past that. She leaned over and kissed Ford's shoulder.

He groaned, turned over, and hugged her close. He was hard against her stomach, but he kept his eyes closed.

"I could get used to waking up at the beach," she said, and left off the part about how she could get used to waking up with him.

He smiled and kept his eyes closed.

"Okay," she said, "a few more minutes of snoozing."

"Mmmhmmm," he said.

"Then we have to get going," she whispered.

She rolled out of bed and went into the bathroom and called Macy. She knew she'd be awake at seven A.M. Marriage hadn't changed the fact that Macy was an early riser. She liked to tend her garden before the heat of the day. Every Saturday Deacon went to the gym at six thirty A.M. and then came home, and they made a big breakfast together.

"Tell me everything," Macy said.

"At six last night, we had an introductory dinner catered by Co," Greer said.

"I love Co."

"It's fantastic. The curry shrimp was my favorite. And then there was a welcome speech by Henny, the manager at La Di Da."

"She seems nice."

"She is. Thank goodness for her because after her speech we had a rules overview by Kiki, who's sulky and cold. She reminded us that La Di Da's reputation is on the line, and we'd better be grateful contestants who show a lot of energy and enthusiasm during the media coverage."

"She's the Stepford Wives microphone girl from the finalists' cocktail party?"

"Exactly. After that, we had individual and couples' interviews with the news station. We did really well, I think."

"When will those be broadcast?" Macy asked.

"Today at noon."

"I'll record it. I can't wait! Did you two seem like a real bride and groom?" She sounded so hopeful.

Greer laughed. "I think so. Even though everyone knows we're not actually together. Things are going . . . well."

"*Well?*" Macy squeaked.

"I think so."

"You sound like you've had amazing sex recently. Did you?"

Greer sighed. "I did. In my crazy pink bedroom. And here at the beach."

Macy actually dropped the phone. There was a big clattering noise. "I'm sorry—it fell. Oh, God, I'm so excited!"

"Don't get too excited. I mean, we're having fun, that's for sure. But I don't see this going anywhere."

"I said the same thing about Deacon."

"Yes, but Ford lives in England. And he might be a father soon. Remember?"

"Yes, I remember. So?"

"*So?*"

"Nothing is impossible with true love."

"No one's said a word about true love!"

"And I'm not pushing you. Only reminding you that love changes everything. And I mean, *everything*. Now tell me what else happened last night."

"Okay. At nine o'clock, we played volleyball in the pool, which was lots of fun. I hit Wesley in the head with the ball by accident, and it bounced off and hit Serena in the head. I swear I didn't mean to do that. They were pretty toasted by that point, so they didn't care."

They both laughed.

"And then at ten, we dried off and had a late dessert outside on the porch. It was extra dark. Just a few lanterns were lit low. And it's because we were listening to a short lecture given by a local turtle expert. She said we need to turn off the lights on the front beach so the turtles feel comfortable coming up on the sand to lay their eggs."

"Oh, yeah," said Macy. "Lights out. I've heard of that."

"I had heard that before, too, but it was exciting to actually be there and know that maybe a tortoise was crawling up the beach at that very moment. This morning, we're going to look for some nests at seven thirty."

"That's coming up. How fun!"

"Yes. I need to go in a minute."

"Okay, but anything else?"

"Nothing, really, except that at one point during the

turtle lecture, I thought Ford was playing footsie with me, but then I realized it couldn't be him because it wasn't coming from that side. He was on my left. So I pulled my feet in."

"Who was it?"

"Well, the person sitting across from me was Wesley. But it couldn't be him, either, for obvious reasons. Or if it was, he must have thought it was Serena's foot. She was sitting on my right."

"So you chalked it up to the darkness and the drink and a case of mistaken foot identity?" She could hear the grin in Macy's voice.

"Exactly. Everyone was getting along extremely well. We had an especially good time with Serena and Wesley. Wesley was very funny, funnier than usual. And Serena was more affectionate with him than I've ever seen her. Maybe it was because she was playing for the cameras to win the contest. But I hope it was genuine."

"I hope so, too."

"I'm glad you're giving her the benefit of the doubt," said Macy. "We could all use that."

They said their good-byes, and Greer brushed her hair and her teeth. She wouldn't take a shower until after their turtle expedition.

When she walked quietly back out to the bedroom, she thought about how she and Ford had finally retreated to their rooms at eleven thirty the night before. All the fun of the evening had paled in comparison to the moment he took her face in both hands and kissed her senseless, then pulled down her bikini bottoms and kissed her between her legs while her top was still on and he was crouched in his Hawaiian board shorts.

He'd looked up at one point. "I've been wanting to do this all night."

But she couldn't speak at that moment.

He went back to work and seconds later, her knees buckled and he had her on the plush carpet. He rolled over her and out of nowhere produced a condom and they had a quick, down-and-dirty coupling that left them both gasping for air.

After that, they slept like babies all night.

The morning sun made diagonal lines on the floor through the blinds. She walked through them, her calves striped with light, and got close to the bed. Ford was lying on his side. He opened an eye. "Thank God you're not clothed," he said.

She wasn't. "I always sleep in the nude."

He rolled on his back. "I never would have guessed that. You're so tailored and together by day."

"I am, but there's a time and a place for everything, right?"

"Right. Come on over here."

She did. "We only have ten minutes before we have to be in the kitchen."

He smiled sleepily. "We can do a lot in ten minutes. Want to try?"

And they did. They arrived only three minutes late, and everyone could tell exactly what they'd been up to, but weren't they supposed to be lovey-dovey?

The entire weekend was a dream come true, as far as Greer was concerned. She was happy, really happy, and about ninety-nine percent of that was Ford. She posed for him twice in their room. And each time he threw down his paintbrush and grumbled that he couldn't do anything until he'd made love to her, which he did, quite thoroughly, once on the bed and the other time in the shower.

Early Sunday afternoon, Greer took a peek at the painting. It was almost finished. "It's been a great weekend," she said, "and I love that you were able to get in some painting time."

"I think it's good," he said. "But I want it to be better."

"What could make it better?"

"I don't know. It feels like whatever it is, is only a little bit beyond my reach."

She kissed his cheek. "Well, I love it. You made me look beautiful."

"That was easy. You *are*."

But they had to stop talking and get ready. They were supposed to attend an afternoon barbecue, mixing with local residents and the media. It was their third and last public affair. The first had been on Saturday at noon, after the turtle nest hunt. They'd had lunch at the Windjammer, the best beach bar in the South. They got involved in a real volleyball game there and had a blast. And then Saturday night, they attended the grand opening of a bar in downtown Charleston as the special VIP guests. People actually lined a red carpet and threw confetti at them. There were shouts about who their favorites were, and plenty of people yelled, "Hey, Greer and Ford! How's the engagement going?"

Miss Thing had been at the top of the line, leaning over the velvet rope, more excited than anyone there. So just for her, Greer had kissed Ford in an old-school Hollywood way, with her foot in the air and her arms wrapped around his neck. The hooting and hollering had been deafening, but she'd loved every minute of that kiss.

"You were born to be cherished," Ford told her in her ear.

"That was nice of you to say," she whispered back.

It was as if no one else was there.

"I mean it," he murmured.

And they kissed again, this time quietly and fervently. She felt it in him, his sincerity. And in that moment, she knew beyond a shadow of a doubt: she loved him. She was head over heels in love with Ford Smith. When he pulled back, she couldn't speak.

"You okay?" he asked her.

She nodded, and over his shoulder she saw Miss Thing dabbing at her eyes with her white cotton glove. She was crying. And Greer knew why. Miss Thing had guessed! She knew Greer was in love.

There was nothing to be done about it, was there? She'd enjoy it while she could.

So on Sunday afternoon at the barbecue, she laughed. She chatted. She interacted with many friendly people who'd come out to see the La Di Da couples and give them advice and support. She also bonded even further with her fellow brides. Lisa was having an especially hard time.

"I enjoy having my father here," Lisa said, when she and Greer were going through the buffet line together, putting cornbread, cole slaw, and pork barbecue on their plates. "But I miss Buck." Buck was her fiancé.

"It must be so hard," Greer commiserated.

Ford was at the other end of the line chatting with a bunch of women who'd met him at the bake-off. Together she and he had decided on the way over to sit at different tables and woo double the votes, but then at the last minute, Greer saw Lisa and changed her mind. She wanted to have some girl time with her. She could visit with the voting public after lunch.

Lisa nodded. "It *is* hard, but we'll make it through. Only seventy-two days until he gets home."

Greer was moved by her friend's devotion. And for the first time, she felt a terrible pang of worry that maybe she shouldn't try to win the gown. Because if she did, she couldn't share it with Lisa. Lisa had already said there was no way she could wear it without cutting it down drastically, which would make it impossible for Greer to wear it when she got married because she would never be a size zero.

"Buck's enjoying seeing you in this contest, isn't he?" she asked Lisa when they sat down at a picnic table.

Lisa chuckled. "He loves it, and everyone he works with does, too. He's taking some ribbing because we've FaceTimed and it's been on TV, and he feels like a star in a way. So do I. No matter what happens"—she broke a piece of cornbread in half—"I've had a ton of fun. Haven't you?"

Greer smiled. "I have. I really have. Although"—she looked over at Kiki, who wore a bored expression in the buffet line—"I could do without Kiki's warnings about how we have to act."

"Yeah, they're definitely not just pep talks." Lisa took a sip of sweet tea. "She's doing her best to remind us the contest is a marketing ploy, not just a chance for us to enjoy ourselves."

"Speak of the devil," said Greer.

Kiki came over with a plate that held a small pile of shredded pork and nothing else. "You ladies need to mingle. Hurry up and finish, why don't you?"

"We wouldn't want to skip dessert," said Lisa. "It's banana pudding. And this was the only table with room to sit down. Congratulations on hosting such a successful event."

Kiki lowered her finely plucked brows.

Greer was impressed with Lisa's diplomacy. She stood. "I'll get us both some banana pudding, Lisa." Lisa gave her a thumbs-up, then turned to talk to a couple who were proceeding to sit down at their table. Greer looked at Kiki. "How about you? I can carry three bowls."

"Not interested," said Kiki.

"Um, okay," said Greer, and started to move away, but Kiki turned and touched her arm.

"Don't forget what Pierre told you," she murmured.

"I haven't," Greer said back in a low tone. "But I intend to try my darnedest to win this thing fair and square. You'd better watch it, Kiki. How do you know I'm not recording you?"

"Who cares? I've said nothing wrong. Pierre told you to give the contest your all, that's all. He asked me to relay that message to all the contestants." Kiki's gimlet gaze was annoying, to say the least.

"Isn't that kind of him?" Greer said. "And how generous of you to help him the way you do. Where is it you're from, Kiki?"

"Los Angeles."

"By way of west Texas, right? And I heard a two-bit strip joint loomed large in your professional background." Kiki opened her mouth to speak, but Greer cut her off. "Hey, I don't hold that against you. In fact, it makes me wonder why a gal who knows what it's like to struggle would hang out with a man like Pierre. He's good at taking women's money, but he's not a nice person. Aren't you afraid he'll drag you down?"

Kiki lofted one brow. "How is everything at Two Love Lane?"

Greer narrowed her eyes at her. "Peachy," she said, and took off.

Ugh. The sisterhood angle hadn't worked. Maybe banana pudding would help her feel better.

When she got back to the table with two heaping helpings of the fluffy, scrumptious Southern concoction,

Kiki had disappeared. Lisa and the couple were surrounding an iPhone and chatting to Lisa's husband in Afghanistan. Lisa turned the phone toward Greer, and she waved. "Hello, there, Buck!"

"Lisa tells me you're all having fun," he said. There was a green Army jacket hanging on a wall behind him.

"We sure are," Greer said. "Wish you could be here."

"Me, too." Buck's earnest face was so cute.

"Only seventy-two days," she told him, a lump forming in her throat.

"Seventy-one now," he said with a laugh, and looked at his watch. "It just turned midnight here."

Lisa was blooming with happiness all through that call. It was such a sweet thing to witness. So when Greer ran into Ford a few minutes later at the La Di Da Bridal hoedown, featuring a team of country dancers—the girls dressed in short bridal gowns and veils, and the guys in jeans and black coattail jackets and bowties, with no shirts—she clapped, hooted, and hollered along with everyone else.

But her heart was back there with Lisa and Buck.

"I can't let Lisa and Buck's story change my mind," she said in Ford's ear. "I mean, I'd love to lend her the gown if I win, but it won't work. She's already said so."

"They're a very nice couple," he said, his eyes still on the dancers, a carefree grin making him so handsome, she wanted to kiss him.

"Is it wrong to want something so much?" she asked him. Was she talking about him or the gown? It was hard to tell. She wanted both of them. Desperately.

He looked at her for a few silent seconds. "It's human nature," he said. "You can't escape wanting. It takes you places, so it's not a bad thing, usually. You've enjoyed yourself in this contest, haven't you?"

"Yes. So much!"

"Chasing something changes you sometimes."

"I can see that," she said.

"But not always for the good. It's a risk you take."

"What do *you* do about wanting something badly?"

"Try not to get consumed by it. Try to outwit it. Stay balanced. But I've not had much luck."

And then the floor opened to the crowd, and he dragged her onto it. She liked how honest he was, and it felt good holding hands with him. He had such a firm, warm grip. Together they did their share of *do-si-do*-ing, and once they even met Kiki across the floor with her dance partner. Kiki had settled down enough that Greer felt semi-relaxed again.

When the female dancers all switched partners, she found herself for a few seconds with Wesley. She smiled at him. They'd come a long way. And she was happy for him.

"I'm getting cold feet, Greer," he said, looking right into her eyes. "It's not like it was when we were together. Maybe I still have feelings for you."

And then she was swung off to the next man, and the next—a blur of figures and colors, the noise of the fiddle piercing and shrill—until she found herself back with Ford.

"I gotta go," she whispered, and ran off the floor.

CHAPTER TWENTY-SIX

It was Sunday night, and the results of the contest were in. Kiki told everyone they'd be announced from the beach house in half an hour. The huge public response was quite the triumph for Pierre. Too bad he was still in Scotland. According to the TV station manager, they'd been inundated with votes. People were able to text their selections to a special number sponsored by the TV station. They could also go online to the station's Web site and vote that way. And that was it. No votes could be placed at La Di Da's Web site. It wasn't set up properly to accommodate the process, and as far as Greer was concerned, that was a good thing. It meant it was much more likely that the contest wasn't fixed. And the fact that the mayor of Charleston was involved in oversight added to her comfort levels. Everyone knew he was a person of integrity.

But Pierre was a wily man. And who knew what he was capable of?

Even so, the contest results were hardly on her mind at the moment. She'd felt numb ever since the square dance. She didn't know what to do. Should she talk to

Serena? Should she talk to Wesley? Should she tell Ford what had happened?

Or should she just shut up and hope that Wesley had been drunk . . . or in a temporary panic when he'd confessed his worries to her? If so, surely by now, he regretted it. He really should apologize to her for making her feel uncomfortable, but in a way, she hoped he never came near her again. She could live without the apology. She just wanted him and Serena to be happy.

And she'd been worried that it was Serena who might be getting cold feet! Wesley had seemed devoted to her. Greer would never forget the day of the auction seeing them walk toward her on the corner of Calhoun and Meeting, hand in hand, and how excited he'd been to tell Greer they were getting married.

"Shut the front door!" Miss Thing exclaimed when Greer snuck off into the dunes and called her three besties for a group chat. "He did this during a *square dance*? What is this, *Oklahoma*? Did he take you on a ride in his surrey with the fringe on top next?"

"*Miss Thing*!" Macy exclaimed. "This is serious business."

None of them had been able to go to the barbecue event. Miss Thing had still been working on her taxes for her *Price Is Right* winnings with their elderly accountant—the one who acted in love with her. Once more she'd asked Pete from Roastbusters to come to dinner, too, as a buffer. Macy and Deacon had had a special dinner to attend with his Aunt Fran and her devoted beau, Colonel Block. Ella's niece had had a piano recital. No Mancini ever missed a piano recital.

But Greer welcomed Miss Thing's sass. Maybe she was worrying overmuch. "We were together less than ten seconds," she said. "And then I left the dance floor."

"I can't say I'm surprised he hasn't gotten over you," said Macy. "You're a real catch."

Greer moaned. "You're sweet, but that's the last thing I want to hear."

"When I saw them together onstage the night you guys became finalists," Ella said, "and they kissed like the world was ending, I got the feeling from Wesley that it really *was*."

There was a beat of silence.

"I-I never noticed that," Greer said.

"I didn't either," said Miss Thing.

"He seemed uncomfortable to me," Ella insisted. "Like he was putting on a show. Your kiss with Ford seemed so much more real in comparison."

That warmed Greer's heart.

"Now that I think about it," Miss Thing said, "when they walked up the red carpet at that super-fun grand opening, Serena was all smiles, and Wesley was like an undertaker—even though they were heading into a bar, and drinks were on the house."

Greer chuckled. "Miss Thing, you always manage to make me smile. But the truth is, every time I see them, they look totally into each other."

"Maybe he's been trying to make it work with Serena," Macy said, "and most of the time he can manage it. But apparently, not all the time, and some of us are nosy enough—or shall I say, intuitive enough—to notice."

"It's why y'all are matchmakers and I'm your biggest cheerleader," said Miss Thing.

"Well, what should I do?" asked Greer.

Nobody said anything over the line for a few seconds. The breeze was blowing strong off the water, and she stood to face it, knowing full well by the time she returned to the house, her hair would be a mess. They were going on TV in half an hour, and Kiki had told them to clean up and look good.

"Take it minute by minute," Miss Thing suggested. "Sweetie, you aren't responsible for Wesley's behavior. I wouldn't go to battle stations just yet."

"I think that's excellent advice," said Ella. "This could potentially be very damaging for their relationship. And maybe he regrets saying it."

"I agree," said Macy. "Let it go for now. But if he corners you again, Greer, you'll have to do something about it."

"Yes, I will." Greer blew out a big breath. "Let's hope this whole thing just goes away. But I feel much better having talked to you."

"We miss you," Ella said.

Greer got tears in her eyes. "I miss you, too. Things will go back to normal starting this week. It'll be nice to have the contest behind me."

"Everything's fine at the office," said Macy, "so don't worry. You're keeping up with what you have to."

Greer thought of Jill. Had Ella's little sister been thinking about what she'd said? That she ought to go after her man, come hell or high water? After this weekend, they were going to sit together and make some real decisions about what to do. But Jill needed to figure out a plan soon, before the tech conference happened.

"That's right," said Miss Thing. "Right now, Greer, you just enjoy being with your young fella. He makes me wish I were your age again. I hope you're getting lots of nookie. Isn't that how English people say it?"

"They do," Greer said. "I'm having a bunch of fun. My heart's getting involved, but I'd rather not run and hide."

"That's right," said Macy. "Whatever happens, you will still be our strong, loveable friend and sister of the heart. You'll always have Two Love Lane to come home to."

"What Macy said," said Ella. "*Arrivederci.*"

"*Ciao, bellas.*" Greer blew them all a kiss through the phone.

Walking back to the house, she mused on how it was so hard not to tell Ella, Macy, and Miss Thing that she loved Ford outright. She just wasn't ready. If she did, they'd ask her what kind of future she saw with him, and she didn't want to go there.

She also wished she could tell them about Jill's romantic dilemma. Especially because Greer had a lot of hope for a good outcome, but it would be tricky getting there. But who knew? Maybe with Greer's help Jill would find the courage to get on a plane and track down her business mogul, tell him she loved him, and have the happily ever after she deserved.

"There you are!" Henny said when she walked in.

Greer felt the tension before she even looked around. Kiki was prowling the kitchen, going back and forth with her phone to her ear. Maybe she was talking to Pierre. In the living room one of the two cameramen had set up his equipment and was fiddling with the blinds at one of the windows. He looked displeased about the lighting and asked Henny to adjust the slats while he looked through the camera lens, which was pointed at the fireplace. Greer caught a glimpse of the other cameraman outside, grabbing a last-minute smoke, his eyes narrowed in the sun.

The TV station manager, in a gray suit and combed-back hair, was in the adjoining hallway consulting with the anchorman and anchorwoman hosting the announcement "party." Pretty in pink, the anchorwoman held a sheaf of papers in her hand. Her fellow anchor wore a double-breasted navy suit. The three of them looked sharp and were studying those papers with serious expressions, occasionally whispering to each other.

Toni sat on one corner of the sofa, her legs crossed, the top one kicking back and forth like a pendulum. Her fiancé sprawled with his arm behind her, a seemingly casual pose but for the deep furrow on his brow.

Lisa sat next to him, clinging to her phone. Presumably, Buck would be able to get on FaceTime during the announcement, but one never knew with the military's schedule. Lisa's father, who'd made them all a delicious pot of Frogmore Stew for dinner Saturday night, was on her other side, his mouth in a taut line. He twisted his U.S. Marines ball cap in his gnarled fingers.

Serena and Wesley stood at the piano, holding hands. Her face and neck had blotches of pink on it Greer had never seen before. Wesley was preoccupied with studying the painting over the fireplace mantel, but his free hand was gripped in a fist dangling at his side. They were together but seemed apart. Maybe Greer only felt that way because of what Wesley had confessed to her that afternoon.

Ford was the only one who looked relatively relaxed. He held a drink in his hand. Only lemonade. The contest rules prohibited their drinking anything stronger. He looked fresh and masculine in nicely creased khakis— his new favorite style of trousers; he called them his Charleston pants—and a starched blue button-down. Loafers and no socks completed the look. He winked at her. "Have a nice walk?"

"Yes, I did," she said. "We still have another five minutes, right?"

"Yes, but—" Henny grabbed her pearls. "But this is the big moment!"

Greer felt abashed. "Sorry I worried you. I'm so

excited to find out the outcome." But inside, she wasn't as worried about the contest results nearly as much as she was about Wesley and Serena. It wasn't her business—but it was. Wesley had involved her. And she liked Serena. She hated to see her hurt.

Kiki came from the kitchen. "All right, it's time," she said, never a barrel of laughs, which could be why she and Toni seemed to hit if off well.

The anchors stood in front of the fireplace. Ford walked over to Greer and took her hand. At his touch, a feeling of utter happiness ricocheted through her.

"I like your Charleston look," she said with a grin.

He grinned back. "Drake and Gus took me under their wing. We went to Dumas and Ben Silver. It took them a long time to convince me not to wear socks with my loafers."

She chuckled, and for the first time, felt a clutch of nerves.

"You look wonderful yourself," he said, "a real beach girl."

"Thanks." She'd worn her favorite sundress for the occasion. She'd had it since before she'd broken up with Wesley. She'd bought it in her mid-twenties on a visit to Charleston for an alumni event at the College of Charleston and taken it back with her to Boston, where she spent one summer working at MIT, crunching numbers with a bunch of nerdy but fantastic teammates. They'd all been kicking ass in the math world. It was simple cotton, a pretty but now faded floral print, and it reminded her that she didn't need to impress anyone as long as she was happy with herself.

The announcement party went on for an excruciating but exciting fifteen minutes, the two anchors traveling between the couples, the roaming cameraman following them and panning from couple to couple, sometimes focusing on only one face at a time, depending on who was being asked a question.

Did you enjoy yourself?

Why do you deserve to win Royal Bliss?

What does it mean to you if you win?

If you lose, how will that change your wedding plans?

They asked Greer and Ford, *How did this temporary engagement go? Could it turn into something real? Any sparks this week? Or will you go back to being a partner-less future bride, Miss Jones?*

"We did what we said we would," said Greer. "We worked together as partners to try to win the gown. It's been tons of fun." *Oh, God*, she was thinking. She was the worst liar. This thing with Ford had most definitely turned into something real.

"Yes, but could you two possibly fall in love?" asked the female anchor.

"We're all for love," said Ford. "Who isn't?"

Both anchors looked bemused by that answer. Greer wished she could be anywhere else but there. She was head over heels in love! No doubt about it. And it was painful to have to put on an act.

"It's been quite the adventure," Ford said. "I don't regret asking her to marry me in the least."

"Even though the plan is to move on after the contest?" the male anchor asked.

"Yes, wouldn't that sting?" the female anchor asked. "After all, you volunteered to be her partner so she could have a chance at winning."

Ford shrugged. "And she agreed to my out-of-the-blue proposal. Because of her, I've met some really great people in the contest and in Charleston. A world-class city, that's for sure. Yet everyone acts like my next-door neighbor. I feel I could ask anyone here for a cup of sugar, and they'd say yes. And throw in a chess pie with it, to boot."

"Diplomatic answer, sir," said the female anchor, her mouth curved up in a pleased smile.

It most certainly was. Greer loved his sense of humor, his ability to be flexible. She loved *him*.

The two anchors finally retreated to the fireplace. The cameraman with the stationary camera was already at work, beaming their faces to the local public watching on their television sets and online.

Ford held Greer's hand tighter. "It's the moment of truth."

"Yes," she whispered, every cell in her body on high alert. She still wanted *Royal Bliss*. She wanted it very much. But even more, she wanted to tell Ford she loved him.

CHAPTER TWENTY-SEVEN

The real moment of truth Greer longed for was to tell Ford she loved him—and she would do it that very night. She'd wait until they'd packed everything up and left the beach. And then in her apartment kitchen, she'd make him some pasta carbonara, the way Jill had for her true love, and she'd confess her feelings.

She hoped he loved her, too.

She wouldn't think about the future. All that mattered was now.

"There's something I want to tell you," he murmured in her ear. "Later tonight." And then he squeezed her hand.

She smiled. "Me, too."

And then they stood quietly waiting.

The cameraman with the stationary camera kept it poised on the two anchors beneath the painting over the mantel. And finally, finally, the anchors got to the crux of the matter . . . who had won the La Di Da Bridal contest? Who would get to wear the exquisite gown *Royal Bliss* at her wedding and keep it forever?

It would be something the winner could hold and

touch, to remember her Perfect Wedding and the history associated with it! The fabulous royal story it came with, and the ones the winner would attach to it herself. . . .

"The public has voted, the race was extremely tight, but they've chosen a winner," the male anchor said.

Greer held her breath.

"And that winner is"—the female anchor smiled broadly—"Serena McClellan!"

Serena gasped. Toni did, too. Lisa smiled and gripped her father's hand. Greer felt a slow release of tension. She'd be okay. At least she knew that.

"Dr. McClellan, you've won *Royal Bliss!*" the female anchor said in a loud, clear voice.

With a happy cry, Serena turned to Wesley, who embraced her.

And Greer felt nothing. That is, she felt okay. She wasn't torn up about it. It was odd. She'd thought she simply *had* to have that gown to be happy. . . .

Pierre would be ecstatic Greer had lost. So would Kiki. Ah, well, let them enjoy their petty revenge, Greer thought. She'd gotten a lot from entering this contest: new friends, a wonderful weekend with Ford. A sense that she could do anything she put her mind to doing, as she had in the bake-off. She smiled at the memory of the pink pegboard. Pierre would never be able to take those memories from her.

Wesley unfortunately made eye contact with Greer. For a split second, she froze. He did, too. But she clapped. She clapped and smiled, and she did her best to not only appear to be a good sport but to genuinely feel happy for Serena.

But how to do that when Serena's fiancé had been so disloyal that very day?

Serena accepted a lovely trophy of a woman clad in a

bridal gown from Henny and thanked the TV audience. Wesley stood beside her, his arm around her waist. "Thank you," she said to her fellow future brides, her eyes wet with tears. "I got so much more from this contest than this beautiful gown. I made new friends."

Exactly what Greer felt. And Lisa, too. It had been an amazing experience.

It wasn't Greer's fault, what Wesley had done. It wasn't. But she felt terrible, nonetheless. She felt guilty. Now she realized that the other night he'd been playing footsie with her on purpose. Maybe he thought she'd liked it! She hadn't said a word because she'd believed it had been an accident.

She should have spoken up sooner. Naïve, that was what she was. Naïve, and silly to have entered this contest, to have given up time at work for a gown. To have daydreamed about a gown—and not about what a wedding was truly about, the beginning of a day-to-day life of a couple who must always keep each other a top priority, who needed to communicate when things were going off the rails, as apparently they had with Wesley and Serena.

But did Serena know?

Greer clapped. And kept clapping. Ford did, too.

"It's okay," he told her.

"No, it's not," she said. She was worried about Wesley and Serena. And burdened by her unwitting part in the matter. She'd tell Ford later, and she'd ask him if she had in any way appeared to encourage Wesley that weekend.

And then the cameras were turned off.

The clapping stopped but not the talking. People were congratulating the couple.

"Excuse me," said Kiki. "Excuse me, please." She

strode rudely through the crowd, blocking Lisa and Toni as they made their way over to speak with Serena. Greer didn't move. She knew she had to go over there, too. She was trying to find the courage.

"Could you come with me and distract Wesley, please?" she asked Ford. "I-I want to congratulate Serena without him there. She's right—we women did become friends."

"Sure," Ford said, and eyed her in a way that made her realize he knew something was up.

She'd told him as much when she'd denied that everything was okay. But she couldn't explain, not right then. Later, she would.

They began to walk—but not hand-in-hand. She was too agitated for that.

"Everyone," Kiki said, now at Serena's side, "please be still a moment." She raised her palms.

The room quieted. No one moved. Serena was still smiling, but she appeared overwhelmed. Greer wasn't surprised when Serena put her head on Wesley's shoulder.

Kiki glanced at Serena coldly—which Greer found shocking; something in her knew something was terribly wrong. She braced herself.

Kiki lifted her chin. "It has come to my attention in the last five minutes that we have had some unethical behavior in the contest. But to interrupt the broadcast would have caused a great deal of dissatisfaction among the viewing public. And truthfully, there is nothing we can do. The winner stands as is, unless she forfeits her status. But . . ."

Serena lifted her head from Wesley's shoulder, her mouth agape. "Why would I ever forfeit my status?"

Lisa's brows were raised in puzzlement. Even world-weary Toni was wide-eyed.

Greer looked at Ford. What could be the matter? He gave her a light shrug, as always, reading her mind. They'd have to wait to find out.

Kiki looked at Greer. "The people who ran the contest didn't know that Dr. Donovan"—Wesley's new moniker—"was your former boyfriend, Miss Jones."

Lisa and Toni swung their gazes to Greer. Lisa's eyes registered hurt. Toni's jaw jutted out, and her eyes narrowed.

"That doesn't matter," Greer said instantly. "He's not anymore, and he hasn't been for four years. He's with Serena, who knows all about our former history. And I'm happy for them both."

"That's a gracious statement." Kiki tossed her hair. "But it's come to our attention that today at the hoedown Mr. Donovan expressed his devotion to *you*, Miss Jones, not to his own future bride."

Greer blinked. How had they known that? Unless someone had overheard. But it had only been a matter of seconds. How?

"Are you denying it, Miss Jones?" Kiki said. "Why would you? When you're the one who told me yourself via text?" She held up her cell phone. "I have the message right here."

"I couldn't have," Greer cried. "I haven't been using my cell phone. You said you just received the message in the last five minutes."

"You sent it about an hour ago," Kiki said, "when you were outside. I only just now *saw* it. I was too busy preparing for the announcement party to check my texts."

Greer was flummoxed. "Show me that message."

Kiki held out her phone. The text read: *I never told you this, but Wesley and I dated for many years. He came on to me at the hoedown. He said he's getting cold feet and wonders if we should be back together. Someone needs to tell Serena.*

Greer couldn't believe what she was reading. "I never sent this!"

"Show me!" said Serena. "I want to see!"

She looked down at Kiki's phone, and her face turned beet red. "Wesley?"

"What?" he said desperately.

Kiki grabbed her phone back. "Incidentally, you came in second place, Miss Jones," she said. "You and Serena were neck-and-neck."

But Greer didn't care. She didn't care at all. "What's going on here? How did that text get on your phone?"

"Greer?" Serena asked her in an urgent voice. "Is it true? What did Wesley say exactly?"

She shook her head. "I can't remember. But he never said he didn't love you, Serena. He does."

Serena looked at Wesley next. "What did you say to Greer?"

He winced. "Nothing. I mean, I said something very stupid. And I regretted it immediately and was going to tell her later what a mistake it was. I got caught up in the moment, and to be honest, I was panicked about getting married. I got cold feet. But I love you, Serena. I don't love her."

Serena's lower lip trembled. *"What did you tell her?"*

"Serena, it was a mistake," Greer said quietly.

Wesley gripped Serena's hands, but she yanked them away. "I told her I wondered if I should try to win her back," he said, "but I don't want to! I was being a fool!"

Serena burst into tears. Then looked at Greer. "And you felt the need to share this with Kiki? Not with me?

You want the dress *that much*? You were trying to sabotage me and Wesley? Because guess what, it worked." She strode over to Greer and shoved the trophy at her. "I want nothing to do with this contest, or this gown, or any of you! I'm *through*!"

And she stormed out the door to the back porch.

Wesley ran right after her. "Serena!" he called. "*Serena!*"

She ignored him.

Greer watched in stunned silence as they disappeared down the stairs.

With trembling hands she put the trophy on the piano and looked back at Ford. "I didn't do this," she said. "I never told Kiki anything. I'm not someone who would ever sabotage another person, no matter how provoked I was."

But his expression was grim.

A horrible feeling coursed through her, part shock, part anger. "You don't believe me, do you?"

"Of course, I believe you," he said. "But as you say, you were put in a very difficult position, very unfair to you, and I wouldn't blame you if you wanted to call Wesley out. What he did was wrong."

"I agree, but I *didn't* call him out." She glared at him. "I told *no one*."

"Then explain those texts," Toni said. "You said yourself how much you wanted the dress. From the very beginning, you said you wanted it. You wanted it so much you entered the contest as a partnerless bride."

Greer remembered telling Ford how much she wanted the gown that very day at the hoedown.

"But that doesn't mean—" She looked wildly around. Everyone was staring at her. "How can I explain—?" She blew out a breath. "I keep my phone locked. But I went to MIT. I know high-level hackers. Someone messed with Kiki's phone. It's within the realm of possibility."

"But when I hear hooves, I think horses, not zebras," said Toni's boyfriend. "The most likely explanation is that *you* sent that text."

"I didn't," she insisted. "Besides, why are you so focused on me? As soon as Wesley spoke, I got away from him. I was hoping he was caught up by a sense of misplaced nostalgia, or panic. I *want* him and Serena to be happy. He said so himself tonight that he regretted what he said."

"That may be, but why did you never tell us about you and Wesley?" Lisa asked, sounding on the verge of tears.

"I didn't think it was important," Greer said. "I wanted to move on. So did he."

Lisa shook her head. "Still, it feels wrong somehow."

"I'm sorry," said Greer. "People break up. It's nothing to be ashamed of."

"Then why did you hide it?" Toni asked. "I thought we were your friends."

"You are, but it was because of reactions like this, and the general sense of awkwardness I wanted to spare Serena," said Greer. "The only thing that went wrong was when Wesley spoke out of turn to me, and he's apologized to Serena. He really owes me an apology, too, but I'm fine without one. I only want those two to patch up their differences. I want Serena to wear *Royal Bliss* at her wedding."

She looked around. "Someone else caused this problem. Not me." She pulled out her phone, went to her text messages, and held it up. "Look. There's nothing here to Kiki—" And then she stopped, horrified. There was a text to Kiki. With trembling fingers, she opened it and saw the damning words:

I never told you this, but Wesley and I dated for many years. He came on to me at the hoedown. He said he's getting cold feet and wonders if we should be back together. Someone needs to tell Serena.

Her jaw worked. "I have no idea how this got on my phone," she said. "Or who sent it." She tossed her phone on top of the piano. "Someone is setting me up, and they're very sophisticated."

Everyone was completely silent.

"I want to find Kiki." Greer picked her phone up off the piano and swallowed the lump in her throat. "I know she's at the bottom of this, she and Pierre. They both wanted me to lose and told me so. I don't know what good it did them to make Serena so unhappy. But for some reason, they wanted her gone. They did this. They're master manipulators."

No one believed her, she could tell. It *did* sound ridiculous. And no one was willing to help her. Ford looked at her as if he pitied her.

"Lisa," she said. "Toni. I don't want the gown enough to do this. I really don't. And now I don't want it at all. Someone must have overheard Wesley today at the hoedown. Maybe one of the hired dancers. We were standing right next to a pair of them."

But neither Lisa nor Toni said a word. Lisa's father looked at her disapprovingly, and so did Toni's boyfriend. The camera people silently packed up, stealing occasional glances at the drama. The anchor people and the TV station manager had moved to the kitchen.

Greer had to find Kiki. She stormed into the kitchen, gripping her phone tightly. "Where are you, Kiki? You've set me up, and you know it!"

But no one was there. She came back out to the living room, her legs and arms shaking, her breathing shallow.

Ford held his arm out. "Come on," he said, his voice soothing and warm. "Let's go to the room and pack up."

She stared at him. She wasn't a baby. She didn't need to be led to her room like a naughty child only to leave in disgrace a few minutes later. She ignored him and walked past him, past all of them, up the stairs to the suite she'd shared with him so happily on the second floor, and started packing.

The portrait stood on its easel. She refused to look at it. How she ever could have thought Ford was seeing her, the real Greer, the one who wanted to be vulnerable and yet not be afraid? She didn't think it was possible until she met him. And now, she realized it wasn't. She'd put herself out there and been hurt, and she was afraid. What else could go wrong?

A lot!

Love didn't change anything, after all, contrary to what Macy had told her.

She'd take a cab home. But she wanted to be gone quickly, before Ford came up and started treating her as if she were a rabidly ambitious contestant with no integrity.

She got out her phone, so repugnant to her now— someone had gotten into her account and had done something absolutely awful with it!—and made the call. There. In five minutes, the cab would be waiting outside. She could pack in five minutes.

Then she saw another text, this time from Pierre: *Congratulations, Miss Jones. You won the La Di Da Bridal contest. Dr. McClellan has officially forfeited the contest. Royal Bliss is yours.*

She jabbed at her phone's keypad, adrenaline coursing through her, making spelling mistakes right and left so egregious that autocorrect couldn't correct them properly. But her message was readable: *Why did you do this? You wantd me to lose! Why did you chinge your mine? I don want Royal Bliss anymore. Give it to somone else!*

But she never got an answer.

CHAPTER TWENTY-EIGHT

An hour later Ford rang the buzzer at Baker House. But Greer wasn't answering. Maybe she wasn't at home, but he suspected she was. What a bloody awful afternoon it had been. He knew she'd been hurt. He hadn't meant to hurt her, too. He believed her—she would never intentionally sabotage the contest. And maybe some expert hacker had placed those texts on her phone and on Kiki's . . . but he had to admit to himself, he had felt some doubt at the beach house.

As Toni's boyfriend had said, the most likely explanation was that Greer did it—maybe in a moment of utter panic. Perhaps she didn't even remember!

It killed Ford to doubt her even for a second, but after what he'd been through with Teddy, he was unwilling to give all his trust to a single person, except for his sister, Anne. He'd never seen Teddy's betrayal coming, or that of his good friend, the groomsman. He'd done his best at the beach to be supportive of Greer and at the same time, protect himself.

And he was here now, wasn't he?

Reaching out.

His phone buzzed, and he looked down. A message from Greer. He held his breath and opened it. *Go away*, the text said.

His heart hurt to read that. He sighed. *Come on*, he texted back. *I believed you. I still do.*

Not a hundred percent, she said. *I saw it in your eyes. Please leave. You don't need me to pose anymore.*

Someone walked in with a bag of groceries, and he followed behind. *Coming up*, he wrote.

I won't answer the door, she wrote back.

I'll keep knocking, he texted. *I'm not having this conversation via text.*

When he got out of the elevator, her door was open. He pushed it and walked in, shutting it behind him.

She was sitting on her sofa, her arms crossed, her legs crossed, too. "Say what you have to say, please," she said, "and then go."

He refused to stand and look down at her, so he sat next to her on the sofa. She scooted away from him.

"I know you're upset," he said. "You're right. I held back at the beach. I tried to be supportive, but a small part of me was afraid to back you all the way."

A tear fell down one of her cheeks. "I already know this."

"But I needed to explain *why*," he said. "You know about Teddy. You know I was recently betrayed. I'm very careful now."

"I get that," she said. "But it still hurts." Her face was pale.

He tried to put his hand on her knee, but she moved even farther into her corner of the sofa. "I want us to be friends," he said. "We're amazing friends. I'd be devastated if we weren't. I messed up today, okay? I should have been more vocal supporting you. But it's easy to say that now. Then, it was a very tense situation, and we were all in shock."

"I'm not interested," she said, and finally looked at him. "I was going to tell you tonight that I love you. I *love* you, Ford."

He didn't know what to say.

"And I don't care what risks are carried with loving you," she said. "Remember by the piano you said you had something to tell me, too?"

"Yes." He felt like a brute. A heartless brute.

"What was it?"

His heart sank. "That we were essentially done with the portrait and we should go celebrate."

"Whoopee," she said slowly, sadly.

He looked down at her hand, resting on the cushion. His signet ring was gone.

"I already dropped it off at your house," she told him, "with Gus."

He stood. "I'm sorry," he said. "I got here as fast as I could. I didn't even stop at my house. It took me a few extra minutes to pack up the portrait and then I got stuck behind an accident on the Isle of Palms connector."

"That's what you're sorry about?" she asked, and looked him right in the eye.

"No," he said. "You know what I'm sorry about."

She stood, too, her arms still crossed beneath her breasts. "Tell me what you're really sorry about then."

He took a second to remember her face before he said the damning words. "I can't love you back."

"You can't?" she asked. "Or you won't? There's a big difference."

"It doesn't matter," he said. "Either way, I have to go."

She didn't say a word, just looked steadily at him, her

expression unreadable now. He felt impelled by her silence to say more. "I can't *stay*." His voice cracked a little. "I'm not even the person you think I am. You wondered when we first met if I required an art patron. No, I don't. I do quite well financially. My real name is Stanford Elliott Wentworth Smythe, Eighth Baron Wickshire."

She gave her head the very slightest shake. And still, she said nothing.

His heart—it was breaking in two. He backed toward the door. "Good-bye, Greer. Thanks for everything."

"Shut the door on your way out," is all she said, and there was nothing there . . . nothing he could take away with him. No sense of their connection, of all they'd experienced together. She was a stranger. Even more a stranger than she'd been on the first day they'd met, when she'd been a warm, and funny, and impassioned stranger who hadn't felt like one.

He shut the door with utmost care, and when he heard the latch settle into place, a great loneliness nested deep inside him, too, like a gaunt hound settling before an empty hearth on a chill winter day.

But he was safe again, and that mattered more.

He walked back to the flat, only blocks away, with his phone buzzing in his pocket, over and over. He ignored it. He knew in his heart it wasn't Greer. It was someone else, probably Anne. Or maybe even Wesley.

He couldn't help an audible grunt. So much for that friendship. What a wanker Wesley was, hurting both Serena and Greer with his wishy-washy confession to Greer that he immediately regretted.

Ford didn't feel up to answering.

But when he opened his flat door and saw Gus practicing "Black Dog" by Led Zeppelin on his electric guitar, he remembered how much he and Anne had loved listening to Zeppelin together as teenagers, and he took out the phone. Sure enough, she'd tried to reach him several times.

He was a selfish bastard. It finally occurred to him that perhaps something could be terribly wrong at home. His gut roiled at the thought one of his parents could be ill—or Rupert, or even Anne's kids, or her husband Edward—and Anne had been unable to reach him.

He called her immediately.

"Darling," she said.

He heard the panic in her voice, and his stomach dropped. "I'm sorry. I was away from my phone. What's wrong?"

"Everything is stable at the moment, but Teddy is in hospital. Complications from the twins. She's been asking for you."

"Bloody hell," he said.

"I know. I've been with her the past twelve hours. Didn't want to call you. But the doctors have said she might be in here for—hold on to your hat—*months*. Her parents are here at the moment, but she seems a bit inconsolable. Is there any chance—?"

"I'll look up flights right now. I'll get out either tonight or tomorrow morning."

"Oh, thank God." He heard Anne sigh. "You know I don't mind being here for her, especially if these are your babies we're talking about. But I do have so many irons in the fire."

"Of course. I was already planning my return."

"Already?"

"I'm done here," he said, "as of today."

"Oh." There was a pause. "That doesn't sound good."

"Professionally, I'm all right. Not ecstatic about the painting, but fairly pleased with it. It won't take me out of the game but it won't advance me, either."

"Stop saying things like that."

"I know what I know," he said. At least when it came to his art. He knew nothing about love.

"All right," Anne said. "I'll grant that you do."

"I'll put finishing touches on it at home. But personally, everything is more in shambles than ever."

"I'll be here waiting with your favorite supper. Lamb and Yorkshire pud, is it not?"

"Yes, although if I ate thistles right now, I wouldn't notice."

"We can talk. But only after the children give you massive hugs. And Edward pours you a whiskey."

"Sounds lovely," he said. "Does Teddy want to talk?"

"She's sleeping. But I'll be sure to let her know you're on your way."

"I should see her by tomorrow night."

"I must confess I look forward to having you on this side of the Atlantic again," Anne said.

"Thanks." Her concern and affection touched him, but when he hung up, all he felt was gloom. He was going back to a frightening situation with Teddy. He hated the idea that her health or the babies' might be in danger. And he had to acknowledge to himself that the responsibility for being at Teddy's bedside was not welcome. He'd take it on as his duty. And he'd fulfill it without whining. But to get through it properly, he must admit it was going to be rough going. Perhaps his life wouldn't be his own for a good while.

Then again, it was no better than what he deserved, and his commitment to Teddy and her needs was what karma had put in his lap. He obviously needed to grapple with situations larger than his own personal miseries to right his ship, which was floundering.

Saying such an abrupt good-bye to Gus and Drake—without any chance of a drunken farewell party—was much more difficult than he'd expected. They'd become like younger brothers. He gave them his British mobile number and said they were welcome any time to visit. He also said he understood they had limited means as students, and he'd like to foot the bill for their plane tickets. All they needed to do was tell him when they were coming.

"Bro," Gus said, "we can't ask you to pay for our tickets."

"Yeah," said Drake. "Dude, you're a struggling artist."

"I'm also a baron," he told them, "with sixteen hundred acres of prime farmland and a manor house I'll inherit someday. I've currently got three homes in England with loads—pardon, I mean *lots*—of room. So lads, I'm quite able to purchase your tickets and put you up."

"What the *fuck*?" Gus said, his mouth agape. "There's a video game I like called *The Flying Baron*. Don't you have to be a German pilot to be a baron?"

Ford chuckled. "No, I'm English. And I don't have a pilot's license. But I'm still a baron."

"Duuuuude," Gus said. "That's so sick."

"Quite boring, most of the time," Ford said, "which is why I never brought it up. But as I'm leaving, I'm more inclined to share. So circle some dates on the calendar, and come over. Either together or separately, but I hope it's together. I'll miss you two brats taking the mickey out of each other."

They shared a group hug but quickly dispersed because bros didn't do that longer than a few seconds. As he made a phone call to his landlord to explain his sudden departure, as he bought his plane ticket online, and then packed his bags, Ford felt genuinely sorry about leaving Charleston. He'd made friends here. He loved the city. It had soothed him, uplifted him. And he was leaving behind the best woman he'd ever known, apart from his mother and Anne.

So why leave Greer? a voice inside chided him, an absolutely silly voice that didn't take into account reality. *His* reality was Teddy. At least for now and perhaps for a good while to come. And his priority was also breaking out as an artist, not for the wealth or fame but because he wanted to touch people—before he was old and grizzled. He wanted success now, in his prime, when he could enjoy it. The portrait of Greer, he knew as he carefully prepared it for transport in the cargo space of a jumbo jet, was not going to be the work of art by which he achieved his dream, but he would defend it, always, because of its subject.

By the next evening, he was in London. Teddy's situation was, indeed, serious. She'd be hospitalized for at least the next two months and not able to leave her bed. She was clingy and emotional, completely understandable in her circumstance. During the first week, Ford did his best to calm her, to support her. Her parents, who remained in London to be with her every day, made hints that a possible reconciliation between the former engaged couple might be in the works, which Teddy did nothing to deny.

His parents were quite somber about the whole situation, as he expected they'd be. They didn't want him going back to Teddy, whether there were children involved or not. His family stayed away from the hospital, including Anne. Rupert hadn't even bothered to get in touch when Ford came back and had neglected to return his texts or phone calls.

One busy day he took time out to visit the outskirts of London to see his brother. His flat was a mess. Rupert's eyes were bloodshot. They sat at the kitchen table, strewn with old newspapers and beer cans.

"Got nothing to tell you," Rupert had said. "Nothing." And he'd stared at Ford as if he didn't know him.

"I've just come back from America, Roo. It's lovely there."

Rupert lifted one shoulder and dropped it.

"Mum and Dad are well," said Ford. "Anne, Edward, and the kids, too. Everyone sends their love."

Still Rupert said nothing.

"Are you hungry?" Ford suspected he was. He was far too thin. "Can I buy you a curry?"

"I can buy my own curries," Rupert said.

There was a protracted silence.

"So," Ford said, "have you read any good books lately? I'm on a Dick Francis bender. Third time around, but I never tire of him."

Rupert sighed. "I told you, I got nothing for you."

"I don't need anything," Ford said, trying to stay calm. Part of him was angry. Another was terrified. "I'm on your side, Roo. We're brothers. Is there anything I can do for you? Would you like to go back to the center?" The treatment center. The one Rupert had been to twice. "If you don't like that one, I can find you another."

Rupert stood then on shaky legs. "Get out," he said.

Ford complied, but at the door, Rupert asked for money.

"All out," Ford had said, and walked down the steps with a string of epithets following him.

Things hadn't changed there.

At any rate, it was understood that he'd handle the Teddy crisis on his own now that he was back. Teddy wasn't a family member. No one even knew if Ford was the father. Anne had fulfilled any obligation his loved ones had to Teddy, which was exactly none.

He'd finally journeyed home to Surrey after that first trying week at the hospital. He'd unpacked, set up the portrait, and was looking at it—simply looking at it—not able to decide if it was the portrait itself that made him sad because it was not all it could be, or the absence of Greer in his life that made his heart ache. He decided it was both.

Not a word had passed between him and Greer since he'd come home. And he had no one, really, to call in Charleston to check up on her. Wesley and Serena were no longer an option. He supposed he could contact her work colleagues—Macy, Ella, and Miss Thing—but it seemed too early for such an effort. They might hang up on him. He wasn't sure if they'd ever be willing to speak to him again, and quite frankly, he knew he had no right to ask for any attention from them.

One person that came to mind—and it was a long shot—was Henny, at the La Di Da shop. Surely she'd be able to tell him something of what had happened to Greer after the contest. He picked up the phone. It was only four P.M. Eastern Standard Time. Henny was likely still at the store.

"Well, hello," she said, when she picked up. "How are you, Mr. Smith?"

They exchanged a few pleasantries. He'd got used to how slowly conversations began in Charleston. Once underway, however, they picked up speed at an alarming rate.

"I'm back in London," he said. "Just wondering how the contest turned out."

"You're not still engaged to Miss Jones," Henny said. It wasn't a question.

"No, I'm not. It was a temporary thing. We were clear about that." He'd offer no excuses. The whole world knew it had been an impetuous decision. He and Greer hadn't hidden a thing from anyone.

"I know," Henny said, "but you two were such a cute couple."

"Um, thank you," he said. "Henny, let's get beyond polite chitchat, shall we? Are you alone? Because I want honest answers, please, not platitudes."

"Well, I . . ."—she fumbled with the phone—"let me take this outside." There was some silence, followed by, "Girls? I'm calling my granddaughter. I'll be outside a few minutes."

He heard some vague answers and the rattle of a door and perhaps the whiz of a car going by on the street.

"All set?" he asked.

"Sure," she said. "What would you like to know?"

"What happened to Greer's phone? And Kiki's?"

"I honestly have no idea," Henny said. "I'm troubled by it, too. Greer was so convincing when she said she hadn't written that text."

"Yes, she was. Why would Kiki and Pierre have wanted Serena to lose? Greer thinks that was their design."

"All I can think is that they wanted Greer to win, and so they knocked Serena out."

"But my impression from Greer is that they wanted her to *lose*. They came right out and told her so."

"I hate to sound like a nosy body," said Henny, "but I heard Kiki talking to Pierre in the back room at the store. He's returned from Scotland, you know. And they were saying that Greer's story would bring in the most people to the new bridal department. Pierre said he liked her partnerless bride angle. And then of course everyone loved you. In fact, they put out a press release the day after the contest saying Serena had dropped out for professional reasons and that the new winner is Greer."

"How did the public react?"

"We've had people calling us off the hook asking when the bridal department is opening, and nine out of ten of them ask about Greer, too, and whether or not you two officially got together. They don't even seem to remember Serena, and she was the original winner. There must have been enthusiasm for her at some point. It's uncanny how no one asks about her."

"Props to Serena—she's lovely—but I wonder if Pierre rigged the contest originally so Serena would win, and then he changed his mind. Maybe she never had the votes, after all."

"I-I don't know," said Henny, "but I'm sick of his shenanigans and Kiki's. I'm only hanging on so I can retire with full benefits. I've got one more year. I feel like I'm between a rock and a hard place."

"I'm sorry about that," Ford said. "Truly. Pierre's not pleasant. Nor is Kiki."

"No, they're not. I see my role as buffer between them and the public."

"You do a fine job," Ford said. "Did Pierre actually give the gown to Greer? And is she taking on a public role as the winner of the contest?"

"We did deliver the gown to Greer, and she turned it down. She said she wanted no part of the contest and would be happy for another finalist to have it. What she doesn't know is that Pierre was under no obligation to find a third winner. The rules specified only a first-runner up was eligible to move into the winning position. So he has the dress in his possession. I have no idea why he hasn't put it back on the floor to sell. Meanwhile, Greer hasn't totally backed away from her experience. I've heard that she and her colleagues at Two Love Lane are doing their best to get Wesley and Serena back together. At least to talk. Wesley's still here, and he's working at the medical university, but Serena turned down her job and took a new one in San Francisco."

"That sounds like a permanent rift to me. So how do they propose to get them back together?"

"I have no idea," Henny said. "But Two Love Lane has clients across the country. I presume they have some strategy."

"I wish them luck," he said. "Speaking of strategy, I've got a proposition for you. Entirely ethical, too. It's about how to make your final year more endurable at La Di Da."

"Oh?" Henny sounded quite interested.

"Didn't you say you grew up with Pierre?" he asked her.

"I did."

"Well, I've noticed something about him, something maybe we could work with. . . ."

When he hung up with her fifteen minutes later, Ford was pleased they were both on the same page. But he couldn't shake how awful he felt for Greer. No wonder she didn't want the wedding gown. The whole story was sad.

What was to become of *Royal Bliss*? He'd never know. But at least he knew that Greer had returned it, and he was proud of her. He was also sorry he'd been such a lackluster fake groom. He hadn't rushed to support her in her time of need. No, he hadn't. He'd thought about himself. She might as well have been a partnerless bride for all the aid he never gave her.

He looked again at the portrait. And he felt as if he'd

fallen down a tunnel, like Alice. Time seemed to stop, and in a very weird way, he saw the portrait for the first time. At initial glance, the painting was of Greer. But the actual person on the canvas was him. He recognized himself in every paint stroke. He'd been constructing a story about himself. It was fear-based, destructive.

As much as he'd pored over Greer as she'd posed for him, he'd stood in the way of really seeing her.

The painting was all about him. All of his paintings were, and he supposed that was natural. Everything he saw was filtered through his perceptions, but there was a way to transcend that. He'd seen it on canvases painted by great artists. It was what set them apart, he realized.

But his paintings . . . his were about holding back.

No, his portraits said over and over. *No, no, no.*

He had to sit down. And so he did, on the edge of an armchair. He swallowed once or twice. He breathed. He even coughed, wondering if he'd come back to the reality that had propped him up for years.

But no, he still saw the real painting. It was glaring to him, in fact, what the problem was. His eyes stung, and even through the blur, he saw the problem: *He didn't believe he deserved the freedom to get outside of himself.* He didn't want it—not when Rupert couldn't function with freedom. Not when his parents were always bogged down with worry, too.

He rang Anne. "I'm supposed to go see Teddy tomorrow, as always. Could you possibly fill in for me? The doctors all say the babies are doing beautifully. It's only a matter of Teddy resting now. I think . . . I *know* I have to start Greer's portrait over."

"But you only have eight days until it must be in Manchester."

"I'm aware of that."

"Wretched man."

"Wiser man. Man who can see. Finally. And I don't know why. A lot of things, I suppose."

Anne gave a little cry of delight. "Go," she said. "Don't stop. I'll take care of Teddy the rest of the week. If there's even a hint of concern about the babies, I'll call you immediately."

"Thank you. Her parents will think I'm selfish," he said. "Teddy might throw a temper tantrum."

"No, Teddy won't. This scare has matured her. She understands you're a real artist, darling. She appreciates your devotion to her in hospital, and I know she'll say you deserve some time off to work on this project."

"Thanks, Anne. Truly. I love you."

"You're welcome. And I love you, too."

He stood. He pulled another canvas out of the closet in the corridor, where he kept spares. And as if under a magic spell, he painted Greer as she really was. The truth of her shone like the sun. It was Greer. Fearless Greer.

Painting her, he was the man who loved Rupert in all his imperfections, who would never turn his back on him. He was the man who accepted that he couldn't fix his brother.

And he was the man who loved Greer and would never turn his back on her, either. He would stop saying no to love. He would embrace who and what he had and not destroy it only because the world had too much sadness in it. He wouldn't let the sadness win. He would see— truly see—and not just what he wished he could see.

He'd hold the world in his hand and he would find something there of truth and beauty. He would find love shining from it, like flecks of gold in a pan of river silt.

CHAPTER TWENTY-NINE

"Greer!" Jill came up behind her on East Bay Street and nearly scared her out of her skin.

"What?" Greer had literally just finished throwing away her last Perfect Wedding albums.

"Sorry, didn't mean to sneak up on you like that."

"It's okay." Greer had already been feeling a little flustered, so she couldn't blame Jill for her being on edge. The morning after Ford left town, she'd gotten rid of the Perfect Wedding albums at home, but she'd purposely ignored her newest ones, which she kept at work. Now, two weeks later, she was ready to purge her life for good of anything remotely associated with Perfect Weddings, so she walked up to Roastbusters and slid the bound books, ones she'd labored over with such love, into Pete's trashcan.

She was done with fantasies of happily-ever-afters for herself for good. Instead, she'd continue laboring over them for other people. Their love stories—and the spirit of the house at Two Love Lane, which was infused with laughter and love—would keep her from being an utter cynic.

They started walking down the cobblestone alley to the house that had stood there over two hundred years.

"I was just coming to see you," Jill said.

"Good. You've been avoiding me. I've been trying to get you to talk about this tech conference and whether you should go."

"I know," said Jill. "But I can't think about that. I have business problems."

They walked through the wrought iron gate, the one with the entwined hearts and secretly embedded lovers' initials, then continued up the steps of Two Love Lane and sat on the new porch swing. They swung back and forth, and the rhythm, Greer hoped, was as soothing to Jill as it was to her.

"Tell me what's going on," said Greer.

Jill shrugged. "I quit Erospace."

"You can't do that!"

"I have to," Jill said dully. "I can't find enough clients."

"You have to keep trying," Greer insisted. "Maybe you should switch up your marketing practices."

"I've tried." Jill wiped away a tear.

"Starting up a business is hard," Greer reminded her. "Have you thought about getting some partners instead of doing this by yourself?"

"No," Jill whispered.

"Well, let's talk about that. You need a support network. And I'm your biggest fan."

"You are?"

"Apart from your family. What do they think of your issues with Erospace?"

"I'm afraid to tell them," said Jill. "They know I've put all my savings into it. And the *nonnas* aren't even sure they approve of what I do. They *tsk* a lot when I talk about it. So I quit talking about it." She sighed. "I'm usually such a fighter. But I find I'm giving up so easily. It's not the Mancini way."

"It's not," said Greer, "and I think I know why Erospace is losing steam. Let's go into my office. I have some news for you." She'd spent the past two weeks seriously distracting herself from missing Ford by immersing herself in her job.

"I'm not sure I want news," Jill said meekly when they got to her desk.

Greer turned to her. "You can't keep hiding from your old boyfriend," she said. "How's Harry?"

Jill brightened. "Oh, he's great. He went on a golf trip to Myrtle Beach, and—"

"I know you like him," Greer interrupted, "but you shouldn't be texting your boyfriend's old bodyguard. He's not the person you really need to talk to. Don't you want resolution? I promise you—you'll have way more energy to tackle your Erospace issues if you can iron out other areas of your life, including the romantic side."

She should know. She was in a rut romantically herself. So she was focusing every bit of determination she had to make sure she was more successful than ever at Two Love Lane. No way was she going to fall apart on all fronts.

Jill hesitated, then nodded. "You're right."

Greer pulled up a file on Jill's business baron. "He's in New York this entire week at the conference. Let's get on a plane, rent a hotel room. I'll take you all the way to the door of where he's staying or lecturing, and then you're going to march in and say your piece."

"But . . . what's my piece?" Jill asked, her face pale.

Greer shrugged. "I don't know. But it will come to you on the plane ride. That's your metric, Jill. Maybe you've been using your flying phobia as an excuse not to face whether you want to commit to this guy."

"That's not fair. It's a real phobia."

"And if your love for him is real, it will come to a head, and you will choose one over the other."

Jill made a face. "I thought love advisors would be soft, gentle people."

"Nope," said Greer. "Not always."

"What about your own love life?" Jill asked, a bit of accusation in her tone. "Twice I've tried to chat with you about it, at Harris Teeter by the produce section—but you ran away—and at Roastbusters, where you managed to change the subject. I asked Ella, too, and she told me you're freezing everyone out."

"Right now, we're focusing on *you*," said Greer, feeling prim and defensive. "And you can tell your sister my door at work is open at all times if she'd like to chat."

"Except for the times you've had it locked the past two weeks, which she said you've done every day, pretending you're too busy to talk." Jill grinned fondly. "Hey, I'm just giving you a taste of your own medicine."

Greer released the tension in her shoulders and shot Jill an apologetic smile. "You're right. Maybe we can help each other. You're unlike any client I've ever had, and I'm learning a lot from you."

"You're the best." Jill gave her a hug. "I'd love to help you, too."

"All right, then. I'm going to buy our plane tickets, courtesy of Two Love Lane, and you need to clear your schedule for the next two days. We're headed to New York."

Jill shook her head. "That's so nice of you. I'm not exactly rolling in dough lately."

"It's fine. We have a slush fund for special emergencies. Someday, you will, too, at Erospace Designs."

"Thank you for believing in me." Jill smiled, but it quickly faded. "I'm *so* scared."

"I know," Greer said. "I'll be with you on the plane. Before we go, we'll practice my technique for making it through each flight without totally losing it, okay?"

Jill nodded and gulped. "I'm more scared of seeing him than going on the plane."

"I'll be with you almost every step of the way. But one thing I've learned as a matchmaker is, the last step is up to you and your man. I can only take you so far. We've been trying hard here to get Wesley and Serena back together, but at some point, only they can help themselves. Wesley thinks he's jinxed. And Serena, well, she's not interested in being with a guy who got such cold feet that he came on to his ex-girlfriend."

"I can't blame her," said Jill.

"Nor can I," said Greer. "But everyone is flawed. Every couple has problems. You just have to decide—the both of you—whether the love between you is strong enough to weather the storms."

"I don't want to be a quitter before I even *try*," Jill said, sounding extremely doubtful. "In love or in business."

"Come here." Greer took her to the window and pointed out at the small glimpse of East Bay Street they had from Two Love Lane's cobblestoned alley. "Look," she said. "There's a possible Erospace client in one of those mansions."

"I hope so." A faint, sad smile curved Jill's lips.

"By flying to New York—not driving," Greer said, "you'll be taking your romantic destiny into your own hands. We'll think about Erospace when you get back."

Greer let the curtain fall back in place.

"I feel more hope about Erospace already," Jill said. "I-I can't believe I told you I might quit."

Greer could see in the way she held herself straighter that Jill was serious. She walked her to the front door, they hugged tightly, she reminded Jill to pack, and she came back to her desk feeling hopeful for her friend.

Meanwhile, every day she had to face the truth that she'd tried to take her destiny into her own hands, and it hadn't worked out. She'd told Ford she loved him, but he'd left her. It was a hard place to be. *So* hard.

But is it truly over? a voice inside her said.

What she needed to do was talk to her parents and find out how to face a reality that didn't include true love. But how to go about it? How to admit to them that she knew something was wrong between them? Every day of her childhood she'd wondered what was missing in their home. . . .

She sat for a minute, sighed, closed her eyes. And remembered she had Charleston to support her. This city. It had given her so much. Her best friends. It had given her beauty. It had taught her that strength can come, can rise up amid the broken, the frightened, and the forgotten. Charleston had shown her that love can and does conquer all.

She could do this.

She picked up her phone. Dialed. "Mom?" she said, and started to cry.

CHAPTER THIRTY

Ford had never felt this way before. *Free.* He woke up at night wondering if the feeling would go away, but then something inside him that was calm and big asserted itself and the petty fear withdrew. He saw Rupert again, and this time his brother was more responsive to him. Perhaps it was because Ford told him he hated his addictions, but loved him and would forever. They'd even gone out to lunch, and Rupert had hugged him when he'd left. He didn't ask for money, either.

Ford also told Teddy, who was doing well in hospital, enjoying visits from a myriad friends now that she was settled in, that he'd support her as a friend, no matter what. He said there was no way they'd be getting back together and for her to inform her parents of that fact. He told her that his attorney was drawing up papers for joint custody of whichever child was his—if either was—and that he was prepared to be a father but not her husband or lover, ever again.

"I like this new Ford," she said quietly. "You're brighter somehow, as if something has been lifted and you can see your way. If either one or both of these children are yours, I'll be proud to tell them you're their dad."

It was the nicest day they'd had in years, that day. He realized they could co-parent well, if they had to. And some of the pressure of that concern was lessened.

The portrait Ford had swiftly painted of Greer looked nothing like the one he'd painted in Charleston. The new one, he'd been told by Anne and the gallery owner in Manchester, was brilliant.

"It will headline the show," the Manchester gallery owner said. "And it will wind up at the Tate Modern. Mark my words."

"Bloody genius," Anne had said.

The odd thing was that Ford knew it was, too, and felt no sense of ego about it. He didn't even feel *responsible* for it. He'd merely been the instrument by which the portrait came into being. No longer were his brushstrokes carefully constructed to tell the story he wanted to tell. Now they reflected truth, and truth only. Greer's portrait was a blur of color coming together with a powerful energy that revealed her essence, which he couldn't even put into words. All he knew was that he loved her.

He couldn't wait for her to see the new painting—it wasn't going to the Manchester show, after all, much to Anne's surprise and the gallery owner's chagrin. He was taking it to Charleston. He'd cleared a way back to Greer, back to a place he'd come to love, and it hadn't been easy. But it had been vastly rewarding. More than ever, he was glad for his siblings. They had a chance for a new closeness that he hadn't realized he'd been craving. That morning he and Anne had gone together to pick up Rupert and take him out for a coffee. Rupert smelled of stale beer, but he was sober, or very nearly so. Ford explained to him why he was going back to the United States. Anne already knew.

"You're not telling her you're coming?" Rupert had asked him.

"No. I'm afraid she'll think of reasons not to see me. All valid. I want to be there when they occur to her so I can state my piece."

"What if she shows you the door?"

"It's a risk I have to take," Ford said. "The payoff if she agrees to give me another chance is greater than any fear I have that I'll fail." He noticed Rupert was genuinely listening. And when they dropped him off at his flat, he leaned in the car window and said, "Best of luck," the way a brother should, and reached in to shake Ford's hand.

When they drove away, Anne had tears in her eyes. Ford did, too. He reached across the seat and took her hand.

"We'll have to keep this up," he said.

"What if you aren't here to do that?" Anne said. "What if you stay in America?" She blew her nose on a tissue from her bag. "Sorry I'm so weepy."

He gripped the wheel. "We'll find a way," he said. "Planes exist for a reason. I'm financially solvent. I could fly here every month and stay for a week." He laughed. "You're being awfully optimistic about my chances to win Greer back."

She gave a shuddery laugh. "Oh, I know you. You'll win her over. And not by being a phony. You're a genuinely good guy, and don't forget it."

When his plane took off from Gatwick, he felt ready to take on the challenge and joy of loving someone. But would Greer accept him? That was the question.

CHAPTER THIRTY-ONE

Greer was at Jill's apartment on Society Street helping her decide what to wear when she saw her business mogul ex-lover in New York.

"This one or this one?" Jill held up a black polka-dotted dress and a red floral A-line skirt and peasant blouse.

"I think you should wear whatever makes you feel most confident," said Greer.

Jill stared long and hard at her closet. "Then it'll be this." She pulled out a pair of soft cotton trousers with a wide black-and-white pinstripe. She paired them with a fitted gray tank top, black lace-up sandals, a wide-brim black felt hat, an oversized gray handbag, and super-chic sunglasses.

"This is my late grandfather's hat," she said. "He wore it in Sicily. It'll give me courage."

"You'll look amazing in that." And it was true. Greer was getting so excited. "Let's go over my rules for getting through a flight without losing it. It works for me every time."

Jill sat next to her on the bed. "Okay," she said tentatively.

Greer had just finished advising her, and they were rolling Jill's two bags out of the apartment, when a red Corvette with a dent on the side pulled up at the curb.

"That's Aunt Rosaria's car!" Jill said, shutting her apartment door behind her. They kept rolling. "I wonder why she's here? She's usually at work."

"It's lunchtime. Maybe she left for a little while and has come by to say hello." Greer searched down the street for their cab, which should arrive any second.

"I don't know," Jill murmured. "She's never done this."

"Do you want to go back inside?"

Jill shook her head. "Let's see what she says first." And then she gasped.

Greer's heart started racing. "What?"

But before Jill could answer, Aunt Rosaria walked up the sidewalk to them.

"Jilly?" Aunt Rosaria said. "You make bedrooms for sex. It's not what your *nonnas* expected you to do, a good girl like you."

"I know, Aunt Rosaria," Jill said.

"We hear you are losing money," Aunt Rosaria said.

"How?" Jill's face paled. "I've never told a soul I was. Except for Greer."

Aunt Rosaria waved at Greer. "We have our ways." Greer didn't say a word. "Okay, you left your checkbook on the kitchen table, and your *nonnas* grabbed it and looked."

"They did?"

Uh-oh! Greer glanced at Jill, who was pale. Her hands gripped the handle of her luggage tight.

"Yes, they did," Aunt Rosaria said, "and they have

decided they want to be your *silent partners*. I want to be one, too."

Jill bit her lip. Her face was scarlet. "I couldn't ask that of them or you, Aunt Rosaria."

Aunt Rosaria nodded so vigorously that Greer thought she'd shake her head off. "Yes, you can."

"No," said Jill. "It's so sweet of you all. But I need partners who believe in my mission."

Aunt Rosaria drew herself up tall. "We do. Jilly, you must make my living space my *loving* space. I ask you with no shame. Woman to woman."

"Oh." Jill gave a short, surprised laugh, her cheeks flushed. "You mean for you and Uncle Phillip?"

"Yes, Jilly," Aunt Rosaria said, leveling a look at her niece, who dropped her eyes to the pavement.

"It would be my great honor, Aunt Rosaria," Jill said quietly.

"Hmm." There was an agonized silence. Then Aunt Rosaria spoke. "I want my bedroom painted gold. With a beautiful canopy bed that has draping red velvet curtains."

"With gold tassels on the corners," Jill exclaimed, then started to cry.

Aunt Rosaria took her face in her palms. "We believe in you. Your *nonnas* like your spunk. They always knew you were an artist inside. As did we all." Her smile was tender. "Your late father's tremendously talented daughter has found her calling, and he would be very proud to see you embrace it."

Jill swiped away a tear, and then she flung her arms about her aunt's neck. "Thank you. And I'm so glad you and Uncle Phillip are still interested in romance."

Aunt Rosaria laughed. "Of course we are, snookums. And soon all our friends will be calling you, too. Wherever you going with that luggage, have fun! And remember you're a Mancini *and* a Romano. You tell yourself that whenever you need courage, *bella*."

"I will, Aunt Rosaria!" Jill called to her, and waved like a little kid.

When they finally got in the cab, happiness and relief were written all over Jill's face. "I don't have to hide anymore. I never did. I'm a Mancini and a Romano. I forgot how powerful that combination is."

"This is your time," Greer said, hugging her friend hard.

"I've got goose bumps," Jill said, holding out her arm.

Greer had them, too. "Hey, can I call your sister? Prep her a bit for what you're about to do? And then put you on the phone to finish up with her? Don't you want her to be rooting for you?"

Jill looked at the ceiling of the cab and bit her lip, then back at Greer. "Okay," she said. "She'll be shocked."

"And she'll also be proud," Greer said.

Jill wiped at her eye. "She will, won't she?"

"Can we also let Miss Thing and Macy in on it?"

Jill nodded.

Greer got the ball rolling, very diplomatically but also with faith that she'd be given the benefit of the doubt for keeping Jill's secret, and handed the phone off. By the time Jill had finished talking to Ella, she'd said, "Heck, tell Momma, too. And the *nonnas*. And the sisters. I want everyone's good vibes. Love you!"

On Interstate 26, right before the airport, Greer received a text from Ella: *Thank you for helping my sister*, was all it said, with three heart emojis. She couldn't help smiling to herself. All was well. Her colleagues—her best friends—were the best.

An hour and a half later, she and Jill were in their seats

in coach on a Delta flight to JFK. Jill had done beautifully with Greer's instructions. Greer had told her that every time she walked onto an airplane, she looked left into the cockpit and silently urged the pilot to fly them safely to their destination. And if the pilot wasn't there, she then had to look at the flight attendant and say, "Please tell the pilot I wish him or her a very pleasant trip." And if the flight attendant wasn't available, she had to stop at Row 2 in first class and say hello to whomever was sitting in the right aisle seat. Once, she told Jill, it had been Sylvester Stallone.

"It works, my method," she reminded Jill at the last minute when they were walking down the ramp to board the plane, and Jill started humming too loud, so loudly that her fellow passengers looked at her strangely. "I've never been in a plane crash. And you know seeing Sylvester Stallone in the second row that one time *proves* it's effective. He'd never let a plane go down. Everyone knows that."

"Right," said Jill, her lips white.

"Don't forget you're a Mancini and a Romano," Greer added.

That last bit seemed to do the trick way more than Greer's OCD crash-avoidance strategy. Jill cried only during take-off and when the wing flaps came up and the wheels came down right before landing at JFK Airport. By the time the wheels hit the ground, she was fine.

"I think I can do this," she said. "Usually, they have to knock me out."

"The more you do it, the better you get," Greer said. "And it helps, too, if you travel with someone who's scared to fly. Like I wasn't afraid even once, because I was worried you'd be."

Jill brightened. "Then that means I'll be fine a lot,"

she said. "My *nonnas* hate flying. I'll take them with me wherever I go. And when I teach them how to not be afraid, I'll bring Momma. She hates flying, too. I have a whole list of people I can take with me."

"And you can help them all get better," Greer said. "By the time you're finished with your list, you won't need anyone with you at all. You'll be awesome."

The rest of their day was filled with spa and beauty appointments in Manhattan. Jill had decided to go after her man the following morning and tell him she loved him. The day dawned bright and sunny, and after a small breakfast which Jill only picked at, Greer walked her nervous friend into the Jacob Javits Convention Center. She would leave her outside the room where a conference lecture was streaming live. Her business mogul was in there. He was sitting on a panel, so if Jill interrupted, at least the whole presentation wouldn't fall apart. He could excuse himself for a moment.

And if he got angry at Jill's interruption, that was Jill's answer: She wasn't really the woman he loved.

Jill put her hand to her mouth. "Oh! I hear him!"

Greer laid a hand on her arm. "Just speak from your heart."

Jill nodded. "You'll be watching on livestream?"

"Yes. I'll do it right from here. Give me a minute to get my laptop set up."

So Jill waited. She was practically quivering. Greer worked as fast as she could. Thirty seconds later, her screen was bright, and she was linked to the workshop inside.

"Oh, my gosh," said Jill, almost crying when she looked at the screen. "There he is! What a hunk!"

Greer smiled. He looked like a very brainy nerd to her in his jeans and with the pocket protector in his white button-down shirt and freshly parted, wet hair. But he was adorable in his own way. There was a soul mate for everyone. Jill's just also happened to be a billionaire.

"You look fabulous," Greer reminded her.

"I'm ready," Jill said, her voice firm again.

"Good luck," Greer said. "I'm proud of you."

"Thanks," the youngest Mancini sister said, and then with one last look over her shoulder at Greer, she opened the door to the room and was gone.

Another door opened at the same time in Charleston, South Carolina.

"Sorry," Miss Thing said at the fourteen-foot-high entryway of Two Love Lane. "She's in New York. She's with a client."

Ford had gone straight to Two Love Lane from the airport. "And she'll be back when?" He tried not to be agitated.

"Tomorrow night." Miss Thing smiled. "Come in and have some tea, hon. I have cookies, too. Almond poppy-seed thumbprint with raspberry jam."

"Thanks for the kind offer," he said, "but I've got to get to New York." He pulled out his phone to call a cab but hesitated. "I mean it," he added. "I appreciate your not slamming the door in my face."

The stylish if offbeat office manager came out on the porch, resplendent in another matronly high-end sheath dress, this one brown silk shot with gold thread. She had a demure matching feather fascinator perched on her curls. "We don't treat people that way at Two Love Lane," Miss Thing drawled. "Especially a potential soul mate for one of my girls."

He put his phone back in his pocket. "You think I might be Greer's soul mate?"

"I think there's a strong possibility." She shot him an affectionate smile. "The fact that you came back to win her speaks volumes. That's why you're here, isn't it?"

"Yes, actually," he said, "it is."

"Are you in a huge rush?" Miss Thing indicated the porch swing. "I wanted to tell you something that might help you."

"I'd love to hear it," he said.

They sat on the swing.

"Greer called her parents a couple days ago," his elegant companion said. "She told Macy, Ella, and me that she'd had a very eye-opening conversation with them. She asked them if they loved each other. She mentioned that she never got the feeling that they did when she was growing up."

"And?"

"Her mother said that she was right. Theirs was an arranged marriage. They had tremendous affection for each other that some would call love. But it had never been the romantic kind." Miss Thing made a sad face.

"Poor Greer, hearing this after all these years," he said.

His companion sighed. "Greer told us it was freeing, in a way. Her parents both assured her they were happy and would always stay together because they couldn't imagine life without each other."

"Ah." He wasn't sure what to say. If they were happy, who was he to judge?

"They also said that having Greer was the best thing in their lives they'd ever done, and they didn't want her to marry anyone she didn't love. They apologized for always pushing Wesley on her, and her mother in particular said she never should have chastised Greer for not marrying him, which she did not long ago, the morning of the auction."

They were swinging fairly high now. The longer she spoke, the more Miss Thing pushed her feet hard against the porch floor.

"I hope her mother's apology helped," he said.

"It did. But the kicker was that"—Miss Thing paused—"the kicker was that they'd both heard of her wedding gown contest. They hadn't called her because she hadn't called them about it, and they assumed—rightly—that she was worried they'd be worried."

The swing slowed down.

"How did they hear about it?" he asked.

"Through Wesley's parents. Anyway, they thought it ironic that she was technically engaged for a while to a man she didn't know. And they prayed it would end. They didn't want her falling into the same trap they did."

Ford sighed. "So they were happy when she told them it was over?"

Miss Thing looked at him for a few seconds. "She didn't say that. She told them she loved you desperately and wanted to be with you. And she asked them to come to Charleston to help her get through the heartache of your breakup that wasn't even really a breakup. Because, you know, your engagement wasn't really an engagement. It was a convenience. She said she only wished they were coming down for her *wedding*. With you as her *honest-to-goodness* groom. She didn't care about the gown anymore. All she wanted, she told them, was you."

"Good Lord." He sighed. "I really messed things up, didn't I?"

Miss Thing allowed him that small interjection but then continued her smooth narration of events. The swing stayed stationary. "So Mr. and Mrs. Jones are arranging for someone to take care of the dairy herd and will soon be on their way. They'll get here about the same time Greer does tomorrow night, and they'll ride home from the airport together."

Ford looked at the plank porch floor, then back up at his seatmate. "Thank you for telling me that."

Miss Thing's eyes shone with tears. "You're welcome." She held out her hand.

He lifted it and kissed it. "You're a true lady," he said.

She inclined her head and said, "And I believe you're a true gentleman."

"I'm going now," he said, and stood. "Back to New York. I only landed there five hours ago from Gatwick. Would you mind giving me Greer's hotel information?"

Miss Thing paused. "You know, I think it best you stay here. At the moment, she's fully engrossed in working with her client, and who knows how available she'll be? You may stay at my apartment—"

"That's all right, thanks. I can bunk with my old mates if I have to. They already know I'm here. But I really want to go to New York."

"All righty." Miss Thing smiled. "Not to say you'd be an unwelcome distraction there, *Lord Wickshire*"—she paused, knowing full well he'd be taken aback at her calling him by his title—"but I really do think so much could be done here. In Charleston." She lofted a brow. "Do you get my drift?"

He paused. "No. Sorry. All I can think to do here, while she's gone, is sock Pierre Simons in the jaw."

Miss Thing looked both ways, as if someone were listening. "I really should have been a matchmaker myself," she whispered. "Let me say it again: *There is much you could do to prep for Greer's homecoming.* Apart from socking Pierre in the jaw. In fact, you might enlist his help. He owns a women's clothing store. It might come in handy. It's where a certain gown—" And then she waggled her penciled-in brows.

He finally figured it out. "You're saying—" The more he thought about it, the more he loved the idea. "You're brilliant."

She nodded vigorously. "Yes, Lord Wickshire. I admit that sometimes I am. But time is of the essence. I'll do anything, and so will Macy and Ella, to help you."

He stood stunned for a second, and then he took off down the steps. "Thank you, Miss Thing," he called over his shoulder.

She blew a kiss at him. "You're welcome, darlin'!"

He got on the phone and called Anne right away.

CHAPTER THIRTY-TWO

Henny put down her pen, turned her inventory sheet over, and followed Pierre into the back room at La Di Da. "I have something to say," she told him, refusing to be cowed. She was older than he was, she'd known him since he was a boy, and their mothers had been best friends.

"And that is?" He was looking over her shoulder at the TV set in the corner. He could never get enough of *MacGyver* reruns.

"I've got one more year here," she said, "before I retire."

His face fell, and for a moment, he looked like the sweet little boy she'd known, the one whose parents had ignored him. He was always over at her house, eating supper with *her* family, while his parents went from party to party. His face used to light up whenever her mother made mashed potatoes. "I hate that you're retiring soon," he said.

"Why?" she asked him point-blank.

He blinked his eyes. "Because . . . because you're very efficient."

She pushed harder. "Is that all?"

"You're excellent with the customers."

She inhaled a breath. "I'll ask one more time . . . why will you hate for me to retire?"

He rolled his eyes. "Well, we've known each other a long time."

"And do you have many friends you've known that long?"

He hesitated. "No. You know that. Why are you rubbing it in that no one likes me? Only the moneygrubbin' gold diggers like Kiki give me the time of day."

She let him stew for a minute.

"I have an idea how to change that," she said. "And instead of watching you connive and be nasty with Kiki in the next year, I'd like to work on this project instead. If I do, however, it will require you to stop being such a greedy little bastard."

"*Henny.*" His eyes narrowed. "You can't call me that."

"Just watch me," she said dryly. "You lose me as a friend and you really don't have anyone to deliver a eulogy at your funeral one day. Let's be real about this."

He sniffed. "Fine."

"So anyway," she said, "you know damned well you hijacked that contest and that Greer was the winner all along. You got Serena's hopes up and dashed them to get to Greer, which was vile of you. And then you made Greer look like the villain. You also knew Greer would be so miserable as a result, she'd never want *Royal Bliss*. But you had to see her have it actually in her possession first, didn't you? To make her feel even worse when she let it go. Meanwhile, you have her unique partnerless bride story and her dramatic onstage engagement to lure customers into *La Di Ba Bridal*. You got lucky that she had the courage to enter the contest, but I have to say the way you turned it around on her was brilliant."

"Thank you."

"But wicked. So wicked that you're going to lose me as a friend and employee unless you lighten up and listen to my idea."

"Fine," he snapped.

But she could tell he was genuinely rattled. His eye started twitching, just a little.

"All right." She exhaled. "I propose we sell the women's clothing store, including the bridal department. Plenty of people would snatch it up."

"*What?* That's stupid." He curled his upper lip and looked at his watch. "I'm getting bored, Henny."

"Too bad," she said. "You have to keep listening. You owe me that. How many pork chops did you eat at my house growing up? How many bowls of my mother's mashed potatoes did you devour?"

"Hmmph." He looked at the ceiling.

"The Simons family," she said patiently, "has never gone into men's wear, and I know why. You have extremely low self-worth. You and your father both pandered to your mother. She ruled the roost. Your mother's passed now. Forget trying to please her. Do something for the Simons men. It's been a hundred fifty years since y'all opened your apparel store. Isn't it time?"

"But I'm the last Simons man," he said, "and I will be unless"—he turned red and ugly—"unless I can get married and have children. But those gals at Two Love Lane—"

"It wasn't their fault they couldn't find you a soul mate," she said. "It was yours. You're selfish and shallow. Like your mother. And beneath your bluster, you're a wimp like your daddy. But it's not too late for you to become nicer. And braver."

"Huh," he said.

"Here's how. You need to step away from your parents' influence and do something for *you*. You'll be a happier person if you open a men's clothing shop. I know you, Pierre. I guarantee you'll love lingering over the bow tie table. You'll want to teach every man how to tie one properly."

"There's a trick to it!" he said. For a split second, his face lost its cynical lines. His eyes were no longer hard.

"And how about shoes? How many men have you longed to tell how to decide between brown tasseled loafers and white bucks with their seersucker suits?"

"Too many," he said. "It drives me up the wall when—" His phone rang.

"Ignore it," she said.

"It's Kiki." He took it and put the phone to his ear.

"Why do you keep her around?" Henny whispered. "She's as phony as you are. It's time to start associating yourself with people of character. Like me." She poked his chest with her finger. She hadn't done that since he was ten and he'd made fun of a little boy on their block for being poor. "Tell you what," she said. "You come to dinner tonight at my house. Charlie and I will be pleased to have you. I'll even make mashed potatoes."

But then he walked around her. "Return to the floor," he said dismissively, the phone still to his ear. "You always were too nosy for your own good, Henny."

Ford walked into La Di Da without a woman to accompany him. Yes, it felt strange. But he was glad to do it. It brought home even more to him the fact that he needed Greer by his side to be happy.

Henny was at the front desk, her face pinker than usual. When she looked up and saw him, she put her hand to her chest. "Mr. Smith. *Hello.* I assumed you were still in England."

"Last time I talked to you, I was," he said, and looked around. "I'm here to see Pierre."

She leaned toward him. "I'm sorry to say our plan didn't work. It was clever. It made sense. But he would have none of it. In fact, I only pitched the idea a half hour ago. He completely dismissed it."

"I'm sorry it didn't work," he said. "I wish it had. It would have made Greer happy to see him take his focus off using women to compensate for his extremely low self-esteem."

"Nicely put."

"I talked to my sister about him. She's the one who phrased it that way." He grinned. "And he *is* a damned good dresser."

"I agree on all points," said Henny. "It would be good for him."

"I'm actually here for another reason," he said. "I might need your help, please. Imminently. But I won't know until I talk to Pierre. Is he here?"

"He's down the street at the macaron shop, his favorite snack place."

"Great." He strode to the door. "Hang in there, Henny. We might succeed with him yet."

She gave him a thumbs-up. "I'm here to assist you in any way, Mr. Smith."

"Thanks." He hoped he'd be back in a few minutes. And then he could really get to work.

Greer was glued to her screen in a lobby at the Jacob Javits Convention Center in Manhattan.

"Um." Jill stood up. "Uhhhh. . . ."

Uh, oh, thought Greer. She sounded a little nervous. And she was wobbling, too. Maybe her heels were too high. When your knees turned to jelly, that could happen.

The panelists turned to face her. Jill's beloved did a doubletake. And then he half-rose from his chair.

"I'm Jill Mancini," she said, "and I'm here to speak to my favorite man in the world. Apart from my dear, departed father, that is. I hope you don't mind giving me the floor a moment."

The room was quiet.

Her techie billionaire sat back down, but Greer could tell he was on tenterhooks.

"You've all seen *Notting Hill*." Jill looked around the room and smiled.

Greer was happy she seemed to find her center.

"I'm kind of like Hugh Grant when he went to that press conference to declare his love for Julia Roberts," Jill said. "Except . . . I'm a woman. And the person I love is not a movie star. He likes computers, and airplanes, and movies. He even likes rockets, and he wants to use them to make the world a better place. Plus, whatever I'm saying isn't scripted. It's real."

The room stirred. Her man didn't take his eyes off her.

Greer was dabbing at her eyes with a tissue.

Jill said she loved her favorite guy and wanted to spend the rest of her life with him, and Greer broke into a little sob.

"I don't care how many scaredy-cat fliers I have to recruit to sit with me on a plane," Jill said with fervor. "I'll do it to be with you," she concluded, "because you mean that much to me."

No one understood the flying reference, but it didn't

matter. Jill's guy left the stage. He went down to the audience, walked past a row of people, and picked her up in his arms.

When he kissed her, she held onto the brim of her hat.

It was better than any movie. And about six hundred thousand people live-streaming the event saw the whole thing, including Macy, Ella, and Miss Thing.

CHAPTER THIRTY-THREE

Greer arrived at the Charleston airport without Jill. Jill had stayed behind in New York with her business mogul lover for a whirlwind weekend of crazy monkey sex (Jill's own words). Greer was so happy for her friend, and Ella, of course, was ecstatic—and in shock still, as was the entire Mancini family, except for one of the *nonnas*.

"I saw it in a dream," that *nonna* said.

And of course, all the superstitious Mancinis were on board with that. They believed in intuition, in curses, in spells, in special blessings, and in visions.

Anyway, Greer and the girls would have plenty to talk about when they reunited a couple days from now. She was taking two days off to spend with her parents. Two days was all the senior Joneses could afford to leave their dairy cows. But she was so excited they'd finally agreed to come visit Charleston. Her mother had seen it long ago, for one day, when she'd dropped Greer off at the College of Charleston her freshman year. Her father hadn't been able to leave the farm, so this would be a first time for him.

Greer really appreciated how hard it was for them to

break away from home, and even though very few people understood—some thought her parents heartless, in fact—farmers understood their family dilemma. She was proud to be from farming stock.

So it was a fantastic reunion when fifteen minutes after her flight, her parents arrived on theirs.

"I'm so excited you're here," she said as they all rolled their luggage out to the airport parking garage.

Her father chuckled. "For a young woman with a broken heart, you're awfully cheery."

"I'm glad she is," her mother defended her. "Maybe she's getting over this man, and we can enjoy our two days off together even more."

Greer pressed the button on the garage elevator. "His name is Ford," she said, "and I'm as broken-hearted as ever, but I'm so happy for my friend and client, Jill Mancini. Remember that name. You'll see it in the papers and online soon enough." And she explained why.

They were suitably impressed by both Greer's professional success in New York and Jill's bravery. "You have a good life," her father said from the backseat.

Her mother beamed at her from the passenger front seat.

"I do," said Greer. It felt so good for her parents to know that, to acknowledge that.

"And we're a good family," said her father, his hand on the back of her seat, and sounding as if he needed reassurance.

Greer's eyes burned at that. She and her mother exchanged glances. She could see her mother was moved, too.

"Yes, we are, Papa," she told her father. "We're a wonderful family. We love each other. You and Mom have both worked so hard to keep a roof over our heads. And you two brought me up to have a big heart. Thank you." She looked at him in the rearview mirror.

He sat back, a contented smile on his face.

Her mother reached over and squeezed her hand.

That moment was enough. If they had to turn around and go home right then, Greer would have had a shining memory of their visit to cling to.

"The days are getting long," her father said, when they arrived at Baker House. Greer was happy to have a spare bedroom. And then she remembered her own. How could she have forgotten it? All the pink! The diamonds! The Elvis pictures!

She was aghast. She was glad she always kept her bedroom door closed.

"I can't wait to see the whole apartment," her mother said. "I love the kitchen already." They'd parked their suitcases there for a moment to grab a glass of water. "Your decorating reminds me of mine."

"That's on purpose," said Greer. "You always made such a sunny home for us."

"Yes," said her father. "Give us the grand tour so we can see how else your mother has influenced you."

"Oh, but you have, too, Poppa." Greer could tell he was hoping she'd say so. "Look at how well-organized my books are. And every bit of furniture here has been painted by me, using techniques you taught me."

He was very pleased.

Greer could see no way out of showing them her room, especially when her mother saw the shut door. "What's in there, dear?"

"Oh," she said, "that's a bedroom. It's my roommate's bedroom. She's out of town for a couple days."

Her mother's mouth dropped open. "You never told us you had a roommate!"

"I just took one on," she said, "to save money."

"Smart," said her father. "What's her name? And where'd she go?"

"Ah, her name is Elena," Greer said. "And she went to Disney World. For her mother's birthday." She couldn't believe the lies she was telling. "I'll sleep in her room, and you can have mine."

"Let's see yours," they said, and walked past her closed bedroom door, thank goodness.

But her father didn't like the double bed in what was really her guest room. "Your mother and I prefer a king-sized," he said. "Is Elena's bed a king?"

"Oh, no," said Greer. "It's only a queen."

"Well, that's better than this one," he said, and rolled his luggage out the door.

Her mother immediately followed suit.

"I don't think you'll like it, Poppa!" Greer called after them. She couldn't get around her mother's luggage to beat both of them to the door. "Elena has interesting taste."

Her father flung the door open. And stood in shock. When her mother caught up with him, she stopped in her tracks, too.

"She really loves Elvis," Greer said, and tried to sound matter-of-fact about it.

"I can see that," her father said.

What would they do? Greer folded her hands in front of her. "There are towels in her bathroom," she said.

"Right." Her mother's voice was faint.

But they rolled their luggage in and unpacked. When they came out again, a few minutes later, it was as if nothing had happened. Greer fed them some appetizers, and then she took them to her favorite restaurant, where her mother and father split a piece of New York–style cheesecake for dessert. Greer, of course, had crème brulée.

It was the story of her life.

Ford cornered Pierre in the macaron shop. "He'll take exactly nothing," he said to the big-eared boy behind the counter, who was busy stacking pastel pink macarons into a cellophane bag.

"*Hey*," said Pierre.

Ford grabbed him by the arm. "You're coming with me."

Pierre stumbled alongside him as they crossed the street and entered a leafy park surrounded by a wrought iron fence.

"I'm Lord Wickshire, otherwise known as Stanford Elliott Wentworth Smythe, Eighth Baron Wickshire. You know me as Ford Smith."

"Uhh . . ."

"You're a very unpleasant guy who messed with several women's psyches during this contest you rigged. I know you did. I spoke to Kiki. She was easy enough to break down when I offered her a position at a clothing shop in Mayfair in London with a woman I know who's even more frightening than Kiki is. Her name is Rosemary Dunhill."

"The actress?"

"Yes, she owns clothing shops on the side." She was Teddy's mother, of course.

"I'm well aware."

"She said she'd get Kiki in line. She'd make a lady out of her if it was the last thing she does—a woman of integrity, polish, and grace, she told Kiki—and guess what? You didn't give Kiki enough credit. She jumped at the chance."

"Damn." Pierre's drawl became more pronounced. "I wondered why she didn't show up for work this morning."

"She's on a plane to London as we speak. So Kiki told me the name of the hacker in Scotland you hired to place that text on Greer's phone. And from there it's easy enough to put you behind bars."

"You—"

Ford grabbed him by the shirt front. "Shut up," he said. "I'm going to give you two choices. Pick one. You will get me *Royal Bliss* right now. Or you don't. And I call the police."

"I'll get *Royal Bliss*," Pierre whispered.

"We'll be borrowing it, but it might never find its way back to you. Greer will wear it, if she'll have me and if she cares to don it at our wedding. And then we'll be offering it to the other finalists. If Lisa marries last, we will cut it down permanently to fit her, and she will keep it henceforth."

"Okaaaay," said Pierre.

Ford released him. "I also expect you to provide bridesmaid dresses to some women I hope to be sending into the shop."

"Fine," Pierre said low.

"I've brought my own tux," Ford said, "but my groomsmen will need tuxes. I realize you don't carry them—foolishly. You're too stubborn to listen to Henny, the only friend you have and can trust. Your future happiness begins in your switching over to men's wear. But as you're too egotistical to accept good advice, you can at least arrange for said tuxes to be purchased at another men's store."

"Will do," Pierre whispered.

"Speak up," Ford said.

"*Will do*," Pierre said. "Not only will I help you, I will arrange the entire thing."

"Almost the entire thing," Ford qualified. "There are a few things only a bride's true love can do. But otherwise, I'll accept your offer. Make it much more lavish and romantic. Not a bit cynical or fake. I don't want to see any evidence of your hand in it, do you understand?"

"Yes."

"Good. Now go apologize to Henny and get started. The wedding will take place tomorrow at six o'clock at Two Love Lane, in the back garden. Seating for one hundred. Heavy hors d'oeuvres reception to follow across the street at the Carolina Yacht Club."

"Have you even proposed?"

"No. But I have the ring."

"Show me," Pierre said.

"No."

His face fell.

"But I'll allow you to attend the wedding if you commit to apologizing to every one of the five finalists before it begins. Save Greer's apology for the actual wedding site. I don't want you ruining my own surprise proposal. If I don't hear from the other four, however, before the wedding, you can't come."

"This will be the wedding of the year! I never miss important weddings."

"You will this one, if you don't apologize. I doubt you will. You're a foolish little man. You could be the next Beau Brummel, with your sartorial know-how, but instead you choose smallness of character and a silly fake whisper."

"I've stopped whispering," Pierre said. "And just

watch me become the next Beau Brummel." He stalked off, but then he began to run, and when he flung open the door to La Di Da, he wore the look of a determined man. "Wait!" he called to Ford at the door. "What kind of tuxes?"

"I'll be in white tie!" Ford called to him. "I'll let you decide for the rest of the lads." Three of whom were older than he was: his father, Greer's father, and Rupert.

Pierre gave him a thumbs-up and disappeared inside.

CHAPTER THIRTY-FOUR

The morning dawned bright. Ford woke up happy at his old flat. The boys still hadn't found a tenant for his room and probably never would, considering Ford had paid his portion of the lease until the end of the leasing period and also paid theirs off for the entire year. Oh, they'd been ecstatic about that, and really grateful, so he hadn't minded a bit when they told all their friends that having a rich English pilot friend rocked.

Today, he'd be getting engaged. He prayed so. And tonight, if the universe was on his side, he'd be getting married. Rupert, Anne, and his parents were on their way. Rupert promised to be on his best behavior, but if he wasn't, Ford refused to let his brother's choices affect him. He also asked his parents and Anne to avoid stressing about Rupert. He wanted them to enjoy his big day. He couldn't wait for them to meet Greer.

His newfound clarity had yet to abandon him. There was a chance Greer would think him arrogant or presumptuous to propose. She might send him on his way. If that happened, he would be wretched. He would put up a huge fight. But in the end, if she said no to his proposal, he would also be able to look back and say that he'd tried his very best. He'd walk around England a broken-hearted man who went for it, which was better than merely being broken-hearted, wasn't it?

He hadn't been able to connect with Greer's dad until that morning. He'd explained everything, and her father gave his permission for him to ask for her hand in marriage. Mr. Jones would make sure Greer was at the French crêpe place for lunch, which was right around the corner from the College of Charleston's Randolph Hall, where Ford had first met her at the auction. After lunch, Mr. Jones would get Greer to Randolph Hall's main gathering space, presumably on a rambling walk. Ford would be waiting there to propose.

Everyone else was at battle stations, preparing. The four other contest finalists, including Serena—who agreed to come if Wesley wasn't there—were bridesmaids. The ladies of Two Love Lane would share the role of maid of honor. They had called Greer's friends the night before, and a good many of them from Waterloo, college, and grad school were actually flying or driving in that day for the surprise event. And of course, many locals were invited as well. Ford had purchased a big block of rooms at the Omni Hotel on Market and East Bay for them to walk right into, gratis.

The moment of the proposal was at hand.

And Greer wasn't there.

He waited for forty-five minutes. The sapphire-and-diamond ring, which his mother had given him—a gift from her grandmother—was, of course, burning a veritable hole in his pocket. He texted Mr. Jones. But he got no answer. What to do?

He called Anne. "She's not coming," he said. "I have no idea where she is. Her father isn't answering his texts."

"Oh, dear," she said. "When's the wedding?"

"Four-and-a-half hours."

"And she doesn't know it's happening. Nor that you're in America and about to propose."

"No. She knows none of that."

Anne sighed. "Is there the slightest possibility that she does know—and she's trying to let you down easily? Maybe her mother spilled the beans."

He raked a hand through his hair. "Only a sister could offer such a horrible scenario so blithely and get away with it. I've already been left once at the altar. Can lightning strike twice?"

"I have no idea," said Anne. "Maybe we should Google that."

"Should I stay here much longer?" he asked.

"I don't think so," she said. "Give it another twenty minutes, and if they don't show, you'll go to Plan B."

"What's Plan B?"

"You'll have to figure that out in the next twenty minutes."

"Have you been drinking?"

"My little brother's getting married today. What do you think? The key lime margaritas at the hotel bar are divine."

He offered a few rich words of which his mother would disapprove.

"You know I'll be there if you need me," said Anne. "Stay calm. I believe in Greer."

"You haven't even met her," he said.

"But you love her. So I know I will, too."

Twenty minutes later, he left Randolph Hall, despondent. Panicked. Still no answer from Greer's father.

He was wandering lonely as a cloud—let him indulge

in Wordsworth on the most romantic and wretched day of his life!—down King Street when he got a call from an unknown number.

"Ford? This is Patricia. Greer's mother."

"Patricia?" He stood stock still. "Where are you? You didn't come to Randolph Hall. Is everything all right?"

"It's fine, dear, but—"

"But what?"

"We're in Columbia. Columbia, South Carolina. It's the state capital, about two hours out of Charleston."

"Yes, yes, I know."

"My husband's phone died. I left mine at the apartment by accident, so I had to borrow this one from a woman we just met in a diner. Greer is talking to the line cooks and telling them how good their fried chicken is. She has no idea what's going on, if that's any reassurance."

"That's good news," he said, as relief poured through him. "What happened?"

"It's a long story, and I don't have time to tell you. She's coming. She can't see me on this phone. We'll be back in Charleston by five. She thinks our flight departs at eight o'clock."

"The wedding's at six."

"Okay."

"I still haven't proposed, Patricia. I can't do that via text. Or a phone conversation. It wouldn't be right."

But there was a click. She'd hung up.

Greer's father had never seen a gorilla. He'd told her that morning over a French toast breakfast she'd whipped up. He'd wanted to see one his entire life, he'd said. Greer's mother had laughed and said, "That's cute." And she'd looked at Greer's father shyly, the way a girl with a crush looks at the guy she likes.

Greer had never seen that happen.

And so that adorable exchange between her parents about the gorilla stuck with her all through their boat tour to Fort Sumter. She wondered if sleeping in her very pink bedroom had had anything to do with it! Maybe it was merely getting away from the farm?

No, it had to have been the pink boudoir!

Or had she imagined their sweetness to each other?

They finished the Fort Sumter tour at about eleven thirty.

"Dad." She was so excited, she couldn't stand it. "We're going to Columbia today. Their zoo has gorillas. You're finally going to see one."

He was silent for a moment. And then he said, "Aw, no, honey. This is your day to show us the city you love."

"Dad," she said. "I'd be much happier showing you a real gorilla. I'm not taking no for an answer."

"Well, when would we be back, honey?" her mom asked. "I want to have dinner in Charleston before our flight leaves."

"We can make it back by five," Greer said. "We'll go to the zoo and have lunch. There's a place I read about in Columbia that has the best fried chicken in the world. It's only a two-hour trip up there."

"I don't know," her father said. "I think it's a bad idea."

"Why?" Greer asked him.

"Because," he said.

But he never articulated a good answer. It was so obvious he wanted to go!

"We're going," Greer told him. "Think of all the talking we can do on the way up. I promise I'll get us back by five."

And that was that. They had a wonderful day. Her dad's reaction to the gorillas was priceless. He was like a kid. And her mother enjoyed seeing him that way as much as Greer did. Her whole demeanor was lighter. Playful.

But by the time Greer drove them back to Charleston, she was hot, sweaty, and exhausted.

"I can't believe you have to leave in a few hours," she said.

"It's a bummer," said her father. "But we sure have loved being with you. I wish we lived closer."

That admission broke her heart. "I hope we can do this again soon," Greer said over the lump in her throat. "I miss you two so much."

They offered her soothing words, the kind sweet parents do, but Greer felt alone when they got out at Baker House. They'd go upstairs and pack. After that, they'd stow the luggage in her car and grab a quick dinner at the crêpe place, where they'd originally planned to eat lunch, and then they had to be at the airport by six thirty or so.

After she dropped them off in the terminal, she'd head back to her apartment. And she knew all she would do once she got there was water Fern, change the bed sheets, wash the towels, straighten the kitchen, and miss her parents and Ford.

He'd left a permanent ache in her heart.

The dread of her parents' departure kept building in Greer's chest. At the crêpe place, her father was very annoyed that his phone was dead again. Something had to have gone wrong with the battery.

"Or maybe it happened when you accidentally dropped it in the sink last night," said her mother.

"It barely got wet," he said. "But who knows?"

Greer's mother took out her phone. "Do you two mind if I make a call outside to the Ladies' Auxiliary at church? I have to miss a meeting tonight, and I forgot to tell them."

"Sure, Mom," Greer said.

A minute later her mom came back inside. She looked a little worried.

"Is everything okay?" Greer asked her.

"Yes," her mother said, but she didn't elaborate. Greer's father, too, seemed more somber. Of course, they were all worried about parting from each other.

They finished their crêpes nearly in silence.

Greer sighed. "We might as well head to the airport," she said.

"But it's only 5:30." Her father looked even more grim.

"It's actually 5:45," Greer's mother said. "That clock on the wall is wrong."

Greer laughed. "It's said 5:30 for as long as I can remember. Shall we?" She stood.

"No," said her mother. "No."

"But, Mom—"

At that moment Ford threw open the door and walked in. Greer almost fainted at the sight of him.

"Thank God I've found you!" he cried. He was in a long black tailcoat and wore a white bow tie against a crisply starched white shirt.

"Ford," she said, barely able to speak.

"It's been a great day," her mother said. "We had a marvelous time in Columbia. First, we saw the—"

"*Mom*," Greer said.

"It's perfectly all right," Ford said, and bowed before his mother. "Lovely to meet you, Mrs. Jones. You're absolutely lovely." He took her hand and kissed it, then he turned to her father and stuck out his hand. "Nice to meet you, as well," he said in that hail-fellow-well-met way men did.

"And you," said her father, pumping his hand.

"Wait," Greer said. "I haven't introduced anyone. And how did you know we were here, Ford? Why are you here? I thought you were in England!" She put a hand to her forehead. Was she dreaming? Was this really happening?

Ford was back in Charleston!

And he was dressed like a baron, a far cry from the man in the gray plaid blazer and boat shoes.

"No time for proper introductions, darling," Ford said. "The portrait," he called out, sounding like a baron.

The owner of the restaurant came striding over, the most stunning nude portrait Greer had ever seen in his hands.

"What—" she stammered. Her eyes immediately filled with tears.

"It's you," her mother whispered. "It's beautiful." She took her husband's hand.

"My goodness," Greer's father said gruffly. "You're a real artist," he said to Ford.

"Thank you," Ford said, then turned to Greer. "It *is* you. It's *really* you."

"I love it," Greer said, wiping tears away. "It's so different from the other—"

"Because the other was painted when I still couldn't see," said Ford. "When I got back to England, I realized that you mean more to me than anyone or anything in the world. I will never, ever put you anywhere but first in my life again."

He got on one knee and paused a beat.

Greer's hands were shaking. Her heart raced. She could barely breathe.

"Greer," her favorite Englishman said carefully, slowly, "I love you with all my heart. Will you do me the great honor of being my bride? Can you possibly have me when the future is so uncertain?"

She knew he was talking about the babies, about his possibly being a father.

Everyone in the restaurant stopped talking. Her mother had her hand to her mouth. She was smiling. Or crying. Maybe both. Greer's father looked well pleased. Had they known this was coming?

"Greer?" Ford looked up at her with those beloved blue eyes and she remembered the auction, how she'd almost tried to coerce him into bidding on *Royal Bliss* with her. "What do you say, my love?"

She sank onto his thigh, remembering the first time she'd met him—his thigh was her favorite place in the world to sit—and put her arm around his neck. "I say yes, Ford. I *will* marry you. I love you with all my heart, too. And I will love everything and everyone you'll bring into my life."

"My dear, dear Greer," he said, his voice cracking. He put the most splendiferous ring on her left ring finger. "You've made me the happiest of men."

They stared into each other's eyes a moment—dumbstruck, the both of them, by the power of love to connect and make whole—and she leaned in for a prolonged kiss of celebration.

But he merely gave her a peck and hoisted her to her feet. "We'll have to save the kiss for after the vows, darling." He paused. "How do you feel about getting married right this minute?"

Her mother looked at her phone. "In ten minutes, actually."

Greer was in a daze. "What's going on? How can that happen?"

Ford winced. "I know it's little notice. I was hoping to propose today at lunch, but you had a change in plans. No pressure, but a great deal of your friends and family, both local and out-of-state, and most of my family from England, are waiting, along with a minister, to witness our vows—if you're interested. We can always put them off. Take as long as you want to decide: months, years. I'll be waiting. I simply wanted you know that I would marry you yesterday if I could, and today, if I can."

Greer stared at her parents. "You knew?"

They both nodded, their eyes alight with love, concern, and hope.

"But I'm very glad I got to see those gorillas," her father said.

Greer laughed.

"Honey, only if you're ready," her mother added. "And we're not going home tonight. We're staying until tomorrow."

Greer gave a little sob and hugged her mother. Rather, she let herself be hugged. It was good to rest there a moment in her mother's arms, to think about what was really happening. This scenario was nothing like the Perfect Wedding she'd always imagined. She hadn't been consulted on the food or flowers or the venue.

She could say no, if she wanted to. She had that option.

But she realized then, as her mother held her, how little all those trappings she'd so focused on in her scrapbooks meant in the big scheme of things. What mattered was the who and the why—not the what.

And just like that, the four other finalists in the contest came running through the restaurant doors with *Royal Bliss*. All of them wore gold-colored dresses. Once again, she was in shock—to see them, and to see *Royal Bliss*. Lisa also carried a tux, which she handed to Greer's father, and a beautiful pink dress, which she gave to Greer's mother.

"What do you say, Greer?" Serena asked her. "Should we try to restore good memories to *Royal Bliss*? The rest of us have made a vow to wear it to our own weddings. Even Lisa. Pierre suggested if she goes before any of us and has to size it down, she can at least cut out the special beaded bodice when she's through, and we can sew it into a new gown. Those beads are what we're all after, anyway."

"Pierre?" Greer couldn't believe they'd been talking to him.

"Ford has tamed him," Toni said. "Long story. But a good one."

Greer took a deep breath. "You all are wonderful to be here. Serena, you came from so far!"

"I did," she said, "because I think you and Ford are so good together. I had to be here." She kissed Greer's cheek. "I'm even going to have lunch with Wesley tomorrow."

"Oh, I'm so glad!" Greer said, and clung to her hand.

But Ford intervened. "Sorry, ladies, but time is passing. Greer, should we delay the nuptials? Or would you like to wear *Royal Bliss* and get married in the garden at Two Love Lane, in, oh, about six minutes?"

Greer's phone kept ringing. It was Macy. "I have to get this," she said, her voice trembling.

"Are you coming?" Macy asked.

"Yes," Greer said, her eyes filled with tears. "You're at Two Love Lane?"

"Yes, and you wouldn't believe how gorgeous the back garden looks. I can't wait for you to see it." She paused. "She's coming!" she called out to someone. There was a round of cheering.

Greer giggled. She actually giggled. Just like Macy had when she was first in love.

It was all so surreal.

"I've got something borrowed for you," Macy said. "My pearls that I wore to my own wedding, a gift from my mother. Ella's got something blue—a garter from Jill's collection of sexy stuff. By the way, Jill's here, too, with her new man."

"Really?"

"Yes, and Miss Thing has something old she and Pete decided on together—his late wife's wedding veil. It's stunning."

"Oh," Greer said, choking up.

"I know," said Macy. "Pete's so crazy about you. And very proud to offer the veil. Your engagement ring is something new. It's gorgeous, isn't it? Poor Ford. He's been looking for you all day so he could put it on your finger. We love him, Greer."

"I do, too," said Greer, overwhelmed but so happy. "Let me get my gown on first. I'll be right there."

"Get out, everybody," the restaurant owner told the other customers. "Your food is on the house. No way is a bride dressing in my cramped little bathroom. She'll dress out here where she has space for this gorgeous dress to shine."

So that was what Greer did. She donned *Royal Bliss* in the crêpe restaurant. But Ford had to leave first.

He wasn't permitted to see her in it before the wedding.

"I'll see you there," he said at the door. And then he strode back in, his coattails fluttering, and kissed her properly. "My love," he added, and left her to be adorned as a bride.

Don't miss the next book

Second Chance at Two Love Lane

Coming soon!